COUNTRY PLOT

Recent Titles by Cynthia Harrod-Eagles from Severn House

THE COLONEL'S DAUGHTER
A CORNISH AFFAIR
COUNTRY PLOT
DANGEROUS LOVE
DIVIDED LOVE
EVEN CHANCE
HARTE'S DESIRE
THE HORSEMASTERS
JULIA
LAST RUN
THE LONGEST DANCE
NOBODY'S FOOL
ON WINGS OF LOVE
PLAY FOR LOVE
A RAINBOW SUMMER
REAL LIFE (*Short Stories*)

The Bill Slider Mysteries

GAME OVER
FELL PURPOSE
BODY LINE
KILL MY DARLING

COUNTRY PLOT

Cynthia Harrod-Eagles

severn
House

This first world edition published 2012
in Great Britain and in the USA by
SEVERN HOUSE PUBLISHERS LTD of
9–15 High Street, Sutton, Surrey, England, SM1 1DF.
Trade paperback edition first published
in Great Britain and the USA 2012 by
SEVERN HOUSE PUBLISHERS LTD.

British Library Cataloguing in Publication Data

Harrod-Eagles, Cynthia.
  Country plot.
  1. Romantic suspense novels.
  I. Title
  823.9'2-dc23

ISBN-13: 978-0-7278-8146-5 (cased)
ISBN-13: 978-1-84751-416-5 (trade paper)

All Severn House titles are printed on acid-free paper.

Severn House Publishers support the Forest Stewardship Council [FSC], the
leading international forest certification organisation. All our titles that are printed
on Greenpeace-approved FSC-certified paper carry the FSC logo.

Typeset by Palimpsest Book Production Ltd.,
Falkirk, Stirlingshire, Scotland.
Printed and bound in Great Britain by
MPG Books Ltd., Bodmin, Cornwall.

One

On the day Jenna came to think of as Lousy Monday, everything went wrong from the start. She somehow slept through the alarm. When she did wake and saw the time, she flung herself from the bed with a curse – not the most propitious way to greet a new day.

Rushing to get dressed, she stuck her thumb through her tights, and then couldn't get the new packet open and was forced to rip at it with her teeth. She found a spot on the suit she wanted to wear, and the skirt of the other one had lost the waistband button. She wished she was one of those orderly people who did repairs as soon as they were needed, and never put clothes away with missing buttons or trailing hems. *Maybe next life*, she thought, struggling with a large safety pin.

Of course, it meant she'd have to keep the jacket on all day. The firm expected a degree of sartorial elegance from employees, and a safety pin would be very much frowned on. She imagined it appearing in her annual assessment as Lack of Attention to Detail and Poor Forward Planning.

And while she hopped, lurched and fumed about the bedroom, dropped her lipstick, poked herself in the eye with the mascara wand, somehow managed to hit herself painfully on the forehead with the hairbrush in her frantic raking of her mane, Patrick slept serenely through it all. He remained curled deliciously in their big bed with its smart navy-blue sheets, dark curly head cradled on his arm and what looked like a smug smile on his lips, because he was working from home that day and didn't need to get up.

To be fair, he always looked as though he was smiling when he was asleep. Normally Jenna found it endearing, but today she had an urgent and breakfastless need to feel resentful about something. She toyed with the idea of waking him up to ask him to do the dry-cleaning run (he wouldn't have hesitated to do the same to her) but in the end ran out of time even for that. She grabbed her bag and keys and headed out into the big wide, and made do with slamming the front door behind her hard enough to make the door frame tremble. *Sleep through that, muchacho!*

She felt a sense of relief on arriving at work, because she loved her job as a features editor at *TopMet* magazine, and there were some interesting projects coming up. But when she opened her email, she saw there was one from Ken Elvaston, deputy head of HR. Everybody had been talking about the cutbacks for weeks now. Other departments had already shed jobs, and there was no reason to expect editorial would escape. The email requested her to go and see him at ten fifteen. *He seeks to intimidate me with the use of the quarter hour*, she thought. On another day, she might have daydreamed that he was going to tell her she was in line for a promotion and a big bonus, but things like that didn't happen on Lousy Monday.

Looking up, she saw Julie, the department creep, watching her, until she caught her eye and looked away hastily. Was it paranoia, or did Julie already know? Julie always knew everything, and the neat, precise, prissy little madam was not the sort ever to be 'let go', as they called it nowadays, curse her immaculately-suited bod and unnaturally tidy work station! Jenna felt a sudden urge to go over there and tip her cooling Starbucks over Julie's shiny black hair, but she decided she couldn't spare it. It looked as though she was going to need all the caffeine she could main-line to get her up to the eighth floor where HR had their bunker.

And of course it turned out just as she'd dreaded. Ken Elvaston, who'd had nine-tenths of his personality surgically removed to fit him for the job, told her in a dreary monotone that the company was letting her go, while simultaneously managing to look down her blouse in a way that made her skin crawl. He enumerated her statutory rights, handed her a 'severance pack' as he ghoulishly called it, and told her she had thirty minutes to clear her desk. Why the hurry, she wondered as she found herself at the lifts again. What did they think she was going to do? Set fire to the place?

Back in the department most people were avoiding her gaze like anything, and she didn't keep much in her desk anyway, so it didn't take long to put her few possessions into a plastic carrier, say goodbye to a couple of embarrassed colleagues who said,

'You'll soon find something else,' and, 'I'm probably next,' and shake the dust of the place from her shoes for ever.

All the same, though she tried to be flip, she found herself rather shaky as she walked back to the tube. It was horrible to be dumped, and in the present economic climate it wasn't exactly going to be a cinch getting another job. She thought of phoning Patrick to tell him she was on her way home, but she felt close to tears and didn't immediately want to talk about it. She needed the journey home to take some deep breaths and get her emotions in order. Lousy old Lousy Monday! She looked at the other people waiting on the platform and wondered what they were doing there. Why weren't they at work? She resented their air of leisurely calm, as if being in transit at this hour of the day was perfectly normal. When the train came rattling in, she didn't even like the novelty of being able to sit down. She had been part of that frazzled, strap-hanging, long-suffering band of sardines who travelled to work and back during the rush hour. Now suddenly she'd had her membership cancelled. She didn't like it. She felt lonely and left out.

She had got the tears under control by the time she came up out of the tube and walked through the streets to the flat, but she still wanted comforting, and looked forward to bathing in Patrick's understanding and sympathy (and he'd better not make any jokes or she'd clonk him with her carrier bag, which contained her work mug and so would make a satisfying impact). She was surprised, as she came in through the front door – calling out: 'It's me!' so that he didn't think it was a burglar – not to find him at work on the computer or at his slope, which were both in the second bedroom that had been converted into an office for him. He wasn't in the living room, either, where he sometimes went if it was just reading he was doing. So much for working at home, she thought. The house seemed unnaturally quiet. Had he gone out? Popped down to the corner shop for something? Surely the idle hound wasn't still in bed?

'Patrick?' she called. No answer. She looked at her watch. It was a quarter to twelve. No, even he wouldn't lie in until this time. But as she went down the passage to the main bedroom, she saw the door was shut, which made her tighten her lips, because they always left it open during the day to air the room.

She opened it urgently, and yes, there he was, in bed, asleep. Well, she could do something about that, at least.

'Do you know what time it is?' she demanded loudly.

He stirred and murmured.

'Wake up, you ratbag. It's a working day. You're not supposed to be enjoying yourself.'

And then, as he started to sit up, rubbing his eyes and scratching his head sleepily, she noticed two things. One was visual: there was an extremely expensive-looking lady's watch on the bedside cabinet on her side of the bed, and she knew it wasn't hers because she had never owned an extremely expensive lady's watch, though she had always aspired to being an extremely expensive lady one day.

The other thing was aural. From behind the closed door of the en-suite bathroom there came a very small sound, such as might be made by a mouse bumping into the cork-topped stool in the corner, which was slightly uneven on its legs and rocked if you touched it. She knew that sound intimately. But they didn't have mice, not in their new-build second-floor luxury two-bed apartment on the border between Fulham and Chelsea.

A feeling of tremendous heat flooded her face and brain, a sense of shock that made her mouth dry. Patrick was still making a show of waking up, but Jenna's now eagle eye had spotted a long, blonde hair in the dent on the navy-blue pillow on her side of the bed, and Jenna's hair was tawny, verging on red – oh yes it was! Her heart seemed to have contracted and gone very hard, like a muscle in spasm, and she felt as if she was trembling all over, but her mind was still working fast. She stepped round the bed and picked up the watch (it looked like Cartier, and if so, those things round the edge weren't cubic zirconas!) and cried, 'Darling, is this for me? It's gorgeous! But why didn't you give it to me last night, then I could have worn it to work. What's the occasion? It isn't my birthday.'

She slipped it on to her wrist, noting out of the corner of her eye with satisfaction that Patrick had thrown a shocked blank, unable to think what to say. She came round the bed to his side, planted a smacking kiss on his brow, and said, 'You're so sweet. I'm just going to pop into the bathroom, and then I'm going to jump into bed and thank you properly.'

He didn't manage to dredge up a word, but as she headed for the bathroom door he did jerk out a hand and make a gurgling noise which she assumed was his attempt to stop her. Too late. With her heart pounding she opened the bathroom door. Despite knowing what she was going to see, it was still a jolt to find a strange woman in there, clad in bra and pants, sitting on the cork-topped stool (*gotcha! I know every sound this flat makes!*) trying to put on her tights. The woman (about her age, slim, blonde, horribly attractive) stared at her with a kind of sick, shocked look that provided just a touch of balm to Jenna's bruised soul. Like Patrick she had nothing to say. She looked as if she might cry.

Jenna gave her what was meant to be a controlled, social smile – but which on reflection probably came out as a terrifying grimace – and said, 'I think you're in the wrong flat,' and stalked out again.

Patrick was struggling into his underpants. 'Jenna, wait,' he said as she passed him. 'We must talk.'

She looked at him scornfully, hoping her trembling didn't show. 'What on earth for?' she said. She grabbed her overnight case from the top of the wardrobe and quickly packed a few things, without the slightest awareness of what things they were, since appearing to be calm and unconcerned was taking all her mental effort.

'What are you doing?' Patrick cried.

'That doesn't even deserve an answer,' Jenna said, slamming the lid down and zipping it so fast she zipped the side of one of her nails into it. 'I'll come back for the rest of my things later.'

And she left without another word, hearing Patrick behind her calling, 'Jenna, wait! Where are you going? Let's talk. Let me explain,' and other similarly useless things. She felt immensely proud of herself for the way she had handled the situation. She floated head-high down the stairs, almost elated, imagining how small and ashamed they must be feeling now. It wasn't until she got out into the street that the brief euphoria wore off and she started to feel sick.

Jenna had met Patrick at a book launch at Holland House four years ago. The book was a 'celebrity title' by one of the Young Royals about various palaces and stately homes in England, so there was a motley array of interests at the party, quaffing the champagne and scarfing the canapés. There was plenty of press there, plus PR bods, minor-royal hangers-on, and all the usual liggers from the world of publishing. Elements from the National Trust and the private families who owned the houses mentioned in the book could be identified by the high polish on their shoes and the uncomfortably warm tweeds they were wearing – it was the end of April, and obviously it was much colder in the country than in town. There was a Simon Schama element of TV gurus and celebrity experts, and the glamour brigade of famous female historians, poshed up to the nines and trailing clouds of Guerlain and Elizabeth Arden strong enough to fell a miner's canary.

Jenna mingled with the crowds, enjoying herself by identifying the famous and placing the non-famous in their categories. She noticed Patrick because she could not quite be sure which slot to drop him into. He was beautifully dressed and had an expensive haircut, was elegant and superior enough to be one of the Young Royals set; but he was standing alone, ostentatiously not mixing, which was emphatically *not* YR behaviour. He was regarding the scene with a sort of lofty amusement that both interested and annoyed her. She drifted past him to the buffet table for a look, and then drifted back again for another, and on her second pass he noticed her and smiled. Thousand-watt teeth, she thought. He *must* be a YR. Or a movie star.

'Hi,' she said. 'Good bash, don't you think?' She remembered he hadn't been joining in, and added, 'As these things go.'

'What on earth is that on your plate?' he responded, looking with arch horror at a round, yellowish thing she had picked up.

She scrutinized it. 'I think it's a chicken tikka vol-au-vent.'

'Please tell me you're joking. Who would eat such a thing? Who would even think anyone *else* would eat such a thing?'

'A lot of the canapés are Indian,' Jenna said. 'They've got miniature pakoras and bite-sized samosas as well.'

'Good Lord! What's going on? A Glories of the Empire theme, to go with the book?'

'You don't go to a lot of these things, do you?' she said kindly. 'Caterers like Indian snacks because they taste of something definite, and go on tasting the same for a long time.' She looked at her plate. 'I wouldn't have put chicken tikka in a vol-au-vent, though. It doesn't quite work, visually.'

He peered too. 'It looks as though someone very, very tiny has been sick in there,' he said solemnly. 'It's a leprechaun's vomitorium.'

She laughed. 'Thank you for that thought. Now I definitely won't eat it. What are you doing here, anyway? I've been trying to work you out. If you don't know about Indian canapés, you're not one of the usual launchistas.'

'Who do you think I am?' he asked, amused.

He seemed to want her to be outrageous, so she obliged. 'Your suit is expensive enough for you to be an agent, but you're not networking, so it can't be that. Hmm. Posh, but not sociable. Estate manager for one of the statelys?' she hazarded.

'Thank you for the "posh",' he said. 'I'm an architect. Since the author doesn't actually know the first thing about architecture, the book had to be checked for gaffes, and have the correct vocabulary inserted. You know, replacing "those twiddly bits on the bridgy things" to "the pinnacles on the flying buttresses", and so on. My firm was chosen because the senior partner is on the Sandringham guest list, and I got the job because I'm the most junior associate. It's a perfectly dreadful, meretricious book. But slightly less meretricious since I did my part in it.'

'Wow,' Jenna said. 'When you answer a question, it stays answered.'

'And,' he added, 'I'm perfectly sociable, in the right circumstances.'

She grinned. 'Well, you're talking to me. How bad can that be?'

'So what are you doing here?' he asked. 'I can't place you, either. Something in the publishing world, I imagine.'

'I'm a researcher in the features department on *TopMet*,' Jenna said, and seeing him throw another blank she added: 'It's a magazine. We're doing a feature on lesser-known statelys next month, so we were on the guest list in the hope that we'll give the book a mention. I got to come because the goody bags will be book-related, and no one else was keen. It's the cosmetics and fashion launches they all want. I'm here with the features director.' She looked around. 'She loves these do's, whatever the subject. Where the crowd is thickest, there you'll find her.'

'I'm quite happy where I am, thank you,' he said, and Jenna felt a warm blush coming up through her neck because he looked at her as he said it, and it was just enough to suggest he was interested.

Oddly enough, she hadn't fancied him that first time she met him. He was good-looking all right, and his presentation was perfect, but she preferred fair types, and his very dark, almost swarthy looks didn't appeal to her. But when later, as the party was breaking up, he had asked her on a date, she had said yes without hesitation because, my God, a man who actually asked you out was rare enough these days, and she hadn't been on a proper date since breaking up with Jamie five – no, six! – months ago. There'd been dinner parties with married friends where you're supposed to get on with the one unattached man invited 'for' you, and group outings with other singles to pubs and clubs where you're supposed to pick up strangers. A couple of disastrous experiments, leading from those episodes, which she tried not to think about, convinced her that if a man was unattached there was usually a reason. So to be asked – straight out, like that – by a more than presentable man if she would have dinner with him, just the two of them, in a proper restaurant, was not something to be turned down.

She didn't sleep with him on the first date, but that was because he was being a gentleman: by the end of the evening she was fancying him like mad. He was different. She liked his serious-ness, and his certainty about himself and where his career was going. All the other men she knew were racked with self-doubt: it was nice not to spend the evening listening to self-pitying moans. They slept together after the next date and were practi-cally living together after six weeks. Six months – almost to the day: had he timed it? – he asked her to move in with him.

Everyone told her how lucky she was, and she knew it was true. It was hard enough to get a boyfriend at all these days, let alone one who would commit himself to living together, and had nothing obvious wrong with him – indeed was intelligent and ambitious and successful. It was not long before he had been made a partner; at about the same time, she'd got promoted to features editor, and they moved to the better flat. Nice flat, nice job, nice man. And the next stage was that Patrick would ask her to marry him, and with a bit of luck (and if necessary a bit of hinting) it would happen before she was thirty, everyone's goal in life. Lucky, lucky Jenna! Her friends told her she had it all.

Until Lousy Monday struck.

Like many a broken-hearted person she headed for the river – in her case, not to throw herself in, but because there was always something comforting about moving water. She walked from Albert Bridge along the embankment for hours – all the way to Lambeth Bridge, in fact, where she discovered that her feet were sore and she was tired and starving hungry. She left the river and found a sandwich bar in Horseferry Road where she sat on a high stool at the window bar and wolfed a chicken salad sandwich and a cup of coffee. Then, since her car – her beloved purple Mini Cooper called Florence – was still parked outside the flat (she really hadn't been thinking straight, had she?) she got a taxi back there.

In the blankness of her misery, during her embankment walk, she had heard her mobile ringing in her handbag several times, but hadn't answered it. In the cab she took it out and looked at missed calls. Yes, Patrick had been calling her. There were three messages in her voicemail box and two texts. She deleted them without listening to or reading them, and turned the phone off.

At the flat she paid the taxi off, and then felt a sickness of misery and loathing come over her. She did not want ever to come here again. She wished she could get all her stuff out now, and have it over with. She looked up and saw there was no light on in the living room. Of course, he might be in his office – you couldn't see that window from here. She hesitated a moment, and then rang the bell on the street door. There was no reply, even to a second and third ring, so she decided to chance it, let herself in and went upstairs.

Everything was quiet. He was out. The bed was made – it looked so innocent – and lying on it was a note in his strong, dark, tidy hand:

> *Jenna, where are you? Why aren't you answering your phone? I've gone out looking for you, but I'll be back, so if you're reading this, don't leave. We must talk. Ring me on my mobile and I'll come straight back, but <u>don't leave</u>. It's not what you think. P.*

In a panic now, afraid he would come back any moment, she packed her clothes and belongings into whatever suitcases and bags came to hand. It was fortunate that she didn't have a lot; and some things she was perfectly willing to abandon in her haste to get away. It struck her as she darted round how much of what was in the flat was his, or chosen by him. His taste. His place. Now she examined her belongings, it was as if she had been camping out here.

The phone rang once, making her jump, but he had put the answering machine on. She thought she heard his voice, and kept away from it, terrified that he was leaving a message for her. She left his note where it was on the bed. Even in her shocked and panicky state, she observed that he did not speak of love. No 'I love you'. Not even 'Jenna darling' and 'Love, P'. Just an order not to leave until she had his permission. *Not what you think?* Well, let's see – naked blonde hiding in bathroom, having left her watch beside the bed, bloke pretending to be asleep: hard to figure that one out, wasn't it?

Oh Patrick! Was it all a sham, the whole four years? Her heart was sore and the last thing she wanted was to let him talk, to hear him try to explain the obvious away. She was afraid she might believe him – and afraid she would not.

Two

With Florence stuffed with her belongings, Jenna fled home, which in her case was the one she had grown up in, a large, shabby three-storey house in Muswell Hill. Her father, a palaeontologist, was dead, and her mother, who was trying to grow old disgracefully, now lived permanently abroad with a lover, an ex-Guards major turned watercolour painter. They moved nomadically from Spain to Portugal to Italy to Greece in search of landscapes and a particular quality of light. There was no real reason Ma and the Major shouldn't get married, but they seemed to enjoy a sort of frisson from living in sin, and since they weren't doing anyone any harm, the family didn't mention the 'm' word.

They were all quite proud of her, really, for her enterprise, and were glad she was happy. Her lover, whom they all called simply 'The Major', seemed a nice man, Jenna thought. She just wished he'd dump the moustache.

The family home was occupied by her brother Oliver, his wife Sybil, and their three children, Allegra, Inez and Tertius. Jenna could never be quite sure whether the children's names were a joke – perfectly possible given Oliver's puckish nature – or a serious attempt to set them aside from the norm. The children bore them with dignity. Actually, as they went to private schools, they probably didn't know anyone with normal names anyway, and would have stood out far more by being called Mary, Elizabeth and John.

The numbness of shock, reinforced by the weariness from her long walk, was wearing off by the time she got to Muswell Hill, and she was only just able to park the car safely and stagger to the front door before collapsing into tears and abject misery. Sybil was a good person to collapse towards: she was brisk and efficient and quite unflappable, but very kind. Oliver was away – he was a civil engineer and worked on enormous international projects. At present, Sybil said, he was working on a dam in northern India, and would be back at the weekend. 'So you just take your time, poor thing, and cry all you want,' Sybil concluded. Jenna loved her brother but was glad not to have to face him yet. Discovering your man in bed with another woman was like an embarrassing illness, and she wasn't prepared to expose its anatomy to another member of the male sex yet.

Sybil had all the right ideas about how to handle a jilted woman. Jenna spent the next few days on the sofa watching self-indulgent movies, reading comforting favourite books (*I Capture the Castle*, *A Company of Swans*, *Persuasion*), and being brought delicious food by Sybil, not to mention tubs of Ben and Jerry's, chocolate biscuits and fresh boxes of Kleenex. When the children came home from school, Sybil told them that Aunty Jenna wasn't well, and hooshed them off to play in the garden or another room. Jenna adored them, but couldn't have coped with them just now. They reminded her too much of what she had hoped to have with Patrick and now never would.

From time to time in her busy schedule Sybil would come and sit with her so that Jenna could pour out her misery.

'I loved my job,' she wailed, 'and I've lost that as well as Patrick. I haven't even got anywhere to live now.' Patrick owned the flat in Fulham. Jenna had rented before, so she'd had nothing to sell when she moved in with him. It hadn't seemed a risky move at the time. How naive she had been! What was that poem? *I thought that love would last for ever. I was wrong.*

'I loved that flat. Now I've got nothing. Nothing to show for four years of my life. I'm nearly th–thirty. I'll never find another b–boyfriend . . .'

Wisely, Sybil did not attempt to refute any of this, merely listened, nodded sympathetically, and made another cup of hot chocolate.

By the third day, Jenna was up to telephoning various friends to explain where she was and why. They were all shocked and sympathetic, perhaps the more so because they were worried for themselves. *You and Patrick were so settled, such a good couple, so good together. If it happens to you, what hope is there for us?*

They condemned Patrick roundly. 'He's a rat – a pig – he's scum. He's not worthy of you. You're too good for him.'

To which Jenna's sad reply was, 'But if I can't even keep a man who's not good enough for me, what hope is there?'

They all assured her that she *would* find someone else, that her life was *not* over, that she *wasn't* doomed to eternal spinsterhood. 'You'll find someone much better. I never really liked Patrick, anyway. I always thought there was something not quite right about him.'

Why didn't you mention it before, then, Jenna thought. Not that it mattered. In a break-up, it's a woman's nature to assume it was because *she* wasn't good enough for *him.* And in any case, her friends had spent the last four years telling her he was perfect and she was so–o–o lucky. On the whole, she preferred Sybil's approach – to listen, say nothing, and apply chocolate cake in industrial quantities. For pin money, Sybil baked cakes and tarts for a very upscale farmer's market, so the house was often full of delicious smells, and dangerously well supplied with goodies. It was a wonder the children weren't fat as geese, but they seemed to have inherited good genes, and were whippet-thin despite having a mother who baked like an angel. Jenna wasn't quite so lucky, but felt she was off the leash for this week at least. Sybil's offerings seemed to soothe the places other comfort couldn't reach.

By the time the weekend arrived, when the children were off school and Oliver came home, she was over the floods stage, was sitting up and taking notice, and was able to play with the former and welcome the latter.

On Saturday morning the children were agog to talk to her.

'Did you have a cold?' Allegra asked. 'Your nose is still a bit red and you've got *huge* bags under your eyes. Everybody in our class had a cold last term except me. It wasn't fair. I didn't get to stay home *once*. Are you going to put some make-up on for when Daddy comes home? Mummy always does. I expect it would make you look a bit better,' she concluded kindly, 'and p'raps not quite so old. Can I look in your make-up bag? Sorcha Ravenscroft came to school in nail varnish last week but they made her take it off with smelly stuff. Do you like nail varnish? Do you think I'm old enough to have my ears pierced? Mummy says not.' Allegra was ten, and longing to be twenty-seven. Jenna could have told her that age was not all it was cracked up to be.

Inez, who was seven, had less complicated needs, and just wanted Jenna to play Tummy Ache and Greedy Gorilla with her. Tertius, who was nearly six, wanted to show her his entire collection of Carz, and then stage races and horrific crashes on the floor at her feet, which he really didn't need her to pay attention to. Sybil flew round doing housewifely things, and looked in from time to time to say she was grateful to Jenna for keeping the children occupied. Then as the moment approached for Oliver's return, she went upstairs to make herself glamorous.

Jenna was still in tracksuit bottom and sloppy T-shirt – her widow's weeds – but the general excitement of the house at the wanderer's return finally filtered through to her vanity, and at the last moment she dashed upstairs too, changed, whacked on some slap, and raked the knots out of her hair. She stared a moment at her image in the mirror, and felt her lip tremble and tears threaten from the back of her nose. She looked pale and haggard and Allegra hadn't been wrong about those bags. But what did it matter now? No one was ever going to love her again.

Since the first day, Patrick hadn't phoned once. She'd had her mobile turned off, but there was nothing on voicemail; and though she hadn't told him where she was going, he could have guessed, surely, and rung her on Oliver's landline. Well, he didn't love her any more, that was clear – not that she didn't know that already, after finding him in bed with another woman (and who *was* she, anyway? None of her friends had had any clue). She was homeless, jobless and manless, putting on make-up for her *brother!* How sad was that? But then she gave herself a brisk shake – *none of that, now!* – told herself not to spoil Oliver's return, and went down for the hugfest.

Oliver was shiny-eyed with tiredness and the long flight, not to mention the punishing work schedule and the horrible climate. He had been away three weeks this time. He hugged Jenna briefly but hard, and whispered, 'Poor old monkey-face,' into her ear. Sybil had told him the story during their daily telephone talks. He had to give his immediate undivided attention to his excited children, sit with them while they had supper, and then put them to bed, and then he wanted a long bath while Sybil prepared the grown-ups' meal; so it was not until he came down, clean, damp-haired, freshly-shaved and smelling of Radox, and was wandering round the kitchen with a bottle of Burgundy in his hand looking for the corkscrew, that he was able to address his sister's woes.

Jenna looked at him admiringly, thinking how handsome he was: tall and strong, with a slightly darker version of her own red hair – auburn, where hers was red-gold – and really blue eyes, instead of the greenish-blue hers were. They both took after their mother in colouring, while the rest of the family were dark like their father. It had always made her feel closer to him when they were children. When she had been mocked at school for being a redhead (*Ginger, you're barmy!*) he had made her see it as being different in a good way – special. He had been her hero: there was nothing, she had felt, that Oliver couldn't do. When she was about fourteen she had been so in love with him she thought she would die if he ever went away and got married; but he did go away, of course – to university first, which had eased the parting somewhat. He'd been going away ever since; but he always came back. And when he did marry, it was to Sybil, who was as unlike Jenna as could be, and whom she was glad to be able to feel was worthy of him. So that was all right.

Oliver found the corkscrew where Tertius had left it under the kitchen table – he'd been using it as an alien robot in one of his savage games – drew the cork and poured them all large glasses. 'First today,' he said. 'God, that journey gets longer every time I do it. Why doesn't anyone ever want a dam built in St Albans or Enfield?'

'Next time, maybe,' Sybil said, prodding the potatoes.

'The first thing I want to say to you,' Oliver went on, sitting at the kitchen table across from Jenna, 'is that you're not home-less. You can stay here as long as you want. It's as much your home as mine, after all.'

'Hardly,' Jenna said.

'It's true. We all grew up here, and Ma didn't give it to me or anything. I just live here by default, because no one else wanted to.'

'But she's bound to leave it to you in the end, because you *do* live here. Isn't she?'

He grinned. 'I hope to God she does. Imagine moving this lot out at a moment's notice! But I don't even know if she's made a will.'

'Michael would know,' Sybil said. Michael was not only the eldest sibling, but a solicitor. 'And if she hasn't,' she went on in her practical way, 'he ought to make her. If she died intestate the state would get most of it, since she's not married to the Major.'

'Where are they, anyway?' Jenna asked. Their mother commu-nicated more with Oliver than anyone else. In every large family there's always one sibling who is the correspondent, who keeps it all together.

'On a yacht, belonging to a friend of the Major's. It's been lent to them for some unspecified time. They're sailing up and down the south coast of Crete. But the Major's apparently got an exhibition coming up in September in Cannes, so they'll have to be back at Juan-les-Pins by then. You could do worse than think about angling for an invitation, Jenna. The Cap d'Antibes in September? How bad could that be?'

'It'd work for me,' Sybil remarked.

Jenna shuddered. 'No, thank you. I've no desire to see my mother disporting herself among the Eden Roc set. Why can't she live in a bungalow in Worthing and knit things, like anyone else's mother?'

Oliver laughed. 'Oh, come on! Which would you rather, if you were her? Cocktails at the Hotel du Cap, or a Thermos of tea in a beach hut in Bexhill? Even at the price of living with the Major . . .'

'But he's sweet,' Sybil protested. 'I like him.'

'Well, I'm not likely to have the choice,' Jenna said, feeling herself choke up. 'I'm going to end up all alone in a council flat with seven cats. I'll die and nobody will know, and the cats will eat me.'

'Oh, that's absurd,' Sybil said.

'It certainly is,' Oliver said vigorously. 'You'd never qualify for a council flat.'

Jenna couldn't help laughing, though it ended up as a snort forcing its way through the lurking tears. 'Beast,' she said.

Oliver refilled her glass. 'Seriously now, tell me what happened. Every detail.'

So she told him. He was wonderful to tell, because he really did want every detail, and he sympathized with her completely. By the time she had talked herself out, they had consumed Sybil's salmon with ginger and coriander, crushed potatoes and baby pak choi, and were finishing off the second bottle of Meursault before tackling her magnificently boozy tiramisu, Oliver's favourite pud.

'He's a stinker,' Oliver said in judgement. 'He doesn't deserve you.'

'Definitely not. He's a rat,' Sybil agreed.

'A louse,' Oliver improved. 'You shouldn't have got yourself mixed up with an architect, you know. You can never trust them. You should have picked a nice engineer instead. *Roads and bridges, docks and piers, that's the stuff for engineers. Wine and women, drugs and sex, that's the stuff for architects.*'

Jenna had heard that rhyme before, many times, but it still amused her. 'Yes, but where am I going to find a nice engineer?' she objected. 'You're married. Anyway, you're my brother and, to quote Sir Thomas Beecham, you should try everything once, except country dancing and incest.'

'I don't think I'm the only one. I'm sure I could set you up with someone if I put my mind to it.'

'I don't want to be set up, thank you,' Jenna said. 'I've had it with this whole relationship thing. I'm so off men, you wouldn't believe. How do you become a lesbian?'

'Two members have to put you up,' Oliver said. 'And there's a frightful initiation ceremony. I found out about it by accident and I'm sworn not to divulge. It involves biceps tattoos and Melissa Etheridge CDs. I can't say more.' He looked at her seriously. 'You wouldn't like it.'

Jenna laughed, but she cried a bit at the same time. 'Oh, Oliver, what am I going to *do*?'

'Oh, darling, everything will sort itself out in the long run. It's the short term we have to think about – what you're to do with yourself while you get over it. I'll bend the mighty brain and come up with something. I'm home for ten days so we've got plenty of time to talk everything through. For now, let's just enjoy pud, and then have coffee and lots of Marc in the drawing room. And some music. I'm so ready to listen to something that doesn't involve sitars and finger bells!'

Sybil brought the tiramisu to the table. 'You ought to take a holiday,' she advised.

'No money,' Jenna said. 'And with no job, I can't afford to put it on the credit card. I'm homeless, jobless, loveless, penniless and hopeless. Damn Patrick!'

Oliver reached across and laid his hand briefly over hers. 'We'll sort it out,' he promised.

He was such a comfort. And Jenna could see how the tiredness was catching up with him, and could not be so selfish as to keep him talking about her problems now, so she let herself be comforted, and reached for another subject.

'How's everyone else?' she asked. 'How's Rock?'

Oliver was the third child of the Freemont family. Michael was the eldest and Jenna the youngest, and Oliver came between two other sisters, Rachel and Harriet. When he was about ten, and precocious, he had announced to their parents one day that it was like being between a rock and a hard place, and the parents had thought it rather clever. For a time everyone had tried calling Rachel and Harriet Rock and Hardplace. Hardplace was too unlike a name and didn't suit Harriet anyway, so it lapsed. But Rock had stuck, and Rock Freemont was such a brilliant name for being famous with that Rachel had gone to Los Angeles as soon as she was able, to be famous properly in the best place for it. She had blagged her way into an agency in a menial capacity, and worked herself up, until she was now, at thirty-six, one of the big-name agents in Hollywood and earning shedloads of money. She had married a producer, Greg Scarpaccio, and they lived in a vast house in Beverley Hills that Oliver always referred to as Cliché Towers. Though she didn't communicate much with the rest of the family, she kept in touch with Oliver by email. He said it was from a residual sense of gratitude to him for having given her the fantastic name.

'She's in storming form, as always. Greg's producing the new Julia Roberts movie, and Rock's got a terrific part in it for one of her newcomers, one of those gets-you-noticed roles. Oh, and she and Greg are having another dog.'

'Another? They've got three already.'

'From what I gather, she was toying with the idea of adopting an African baby, like Madonna, and Greg talked her out of it. So she's having a dog instead. A designer dog, of course.'

'A Labradoodle?' Jenna said. 'I hear they're all the rage.'

Oliver looked impish. 'No, this one's a cross between a bulldog and a shih-tzu.'

Jenna worked it out, and then punched him on the arm. 'You're making it up.'

'I bet if I bred them I'd find a market for them in California. Actually, I think she's getting a schnoodle, which is a cross between a schnauzer and a poodle, and actually quite a sensible mutt, despite the silly name.'

'Just don't talk about dogs in front of the children,' Sybil said. 'They've always wanted one, and that's the last thing I need to complicate my life. It's a shame you can't go and have a holiday with Rock and Greg, Jenna. That would take you out of yourself.'

'It might put me in someone else,' Jenna said. 'I don't need any more fantasy and illusion in my life. I couldn't afford the fare, anyway. How's Harriet?'

Oliver and Sybil exchanged a quick glance, before Oliver said, 'She's having another baby. Due in October.'

'Oh, good for her,' Jenna said, but her voice wobbled a bit in spite of her determination. Harriet's little Martha was nearly two, and adorable. She had a nice financier husband and house in Greenwich and soon would have two children. Her timetable was impeccable: living with Richard at twenty-six, married at twenty-eight, had Martha at twenty-nine, and baby number two due at thirty-one. And here was Jenna, twenty-seven and nothing to show for it.

Sybil read her thoughts and sought to distract her. 'We saw Michael a few weeks ago,' she said. 'All of us went over for Sunday lunch.'

Michael, thirty-eight, was a corporate lawyer at a big company's headquarters in Swindon, and lived in an almost unbearably exquisite village in the Cotswolds. With his extremely beautiful wife. And their four children. *Oh hell, I'm such a failure*, Jenna thought.

Sybil was still reading her thoughts. 'He's getting an enormous bald patch,' she offered comfortingly. 'He's starting to look like a monk.'

Oliver burst out laughing, and Jenna couldn't help joining in. 'Oh dear, if I'm reduced to Schadenfreude, there really is no help for me,' she said, wiping her eyes.

'Never mind, monkey-face,' Oliver said. 'All will be well. One day, anyway. Let's go and listen to some Brahms.'

'I don't know what I'd do without you,' Jenna said. 'Family is a wonderful thing.'

Three

On Sunday morning her best friend, Izzy, rang her to say she had found out who the Other Woman was.

'Serious beavering combined with a spot of good luck,' Izzy admitted. 'This friend of mine, Dot, who works for Designers Guild, knows someone who knows something about a big job being done by Patrick's firm in Onslow Square—'

'Yes, I know. Penthouse suite. No expense spared. Patrick's working on it.'

'That's right,' said Izzy. 'Apparently the interior design's being done by Sotterton's – Dot said they'd hoped to get it at DG, which was why she took an interest. Anyway, this friend of hers, Beryl, works for Sotterton's, and she says the designer who's actually doing the penthouse is someone called Charlotte Anstruther. Sloaney-type, ex-public school. Tall, blonde, fairly eye-worthy, apparently. Beryl says she's on site an awful lot, more often than you'd think necessary, so suspected there must be a man at the bottom of it, and fair enough one day this bloke came to the shop to pick this Charlotte up for lunch. Said they needed to talk about the Onslow Square job, but Beryl said there was a lot more than that going on. They were obviously pretty friendly, and Charlotte took his arm and they were heads-together and laughing before they'd even got out of the shop. Charlotte apparently told Beryl the bloke was the architect in charge, and the description fits Patrick, so I reckon that's who it must be.'

'It makes sense,' Jenna said sadly.

'That's what I thought,' Izzy said sympathetically. 'Two people spending a lot of time together, alone in a half-built roof extension. Working late – you said Patrick'd been working late a lot recently. Standing close together, heads bent over the same set of plans. Fingers touching accidentally—'

'You don't need to go on.'

'He says, "We've got things to discuss – can't do it here with all the dust and building rubbish around – how about lunch?" One thing leads to another—'

'I said you needn't go on. I get the picture,' Jenna said. 'It was always going to be a worry, when he works on such exalted properties. Posh clients – rich, idle women, most of them – not to mention top-end designers, mostly female, who have to be super-glamorous to get the jobs in the first place. And Patrick's so gorgeous. And the domestic settings they meet in are so convenient.'

'Oh Jen, I'm sorry.'

'I just always thought *he* wouldn't be tempted – or that if he was tempted, he wouldn't fall because we were happy together. But she's much more his type than I am, obviously. They're a better match.' She sighed. 'I don't really know what he saw in me to begin with.'

'Now don't start that. Any man would be lucky to get you. You're gorgeous, bright, funny—'

'—and nobody wants me. How's Toby?' she changed the subject. Izzy was going out with a married man – if 'going out' was the right way to describe the relationship, which seemed to involve always being in, sitting alone at home by the telephone night after night and weekend after weekend.

'Oh, he's fine,' Izzy said. 'He thinks he might be able to come over this afternoon,' she added proudly. 'His wife's going to see her mother, and if she takes the kid with her, he'll be able to get away for a couple of hours.'

'So you're going to stay in all day on the off chance that he'll come over for a bonk, and then leave you to spend the night alone while he goes back to his nice cosy home?'

'He comes over whenever he can,' Izzy protested feebly. 'It isn't easy for him.'

'It seems bloody easy to me. He has it both ways and you have nothing. He never takes you out anywhere. You can't go on holiday together, or spend Christmas together—'

'Oh, I know, I know! I hate it!' Izzy wailed. 'I want a proper life. I want to sleep with him and go shopping with him and spend weekends with him and all that bourgeois happy shit.'

'Iz, you *know* he's never going to leave his wife. He uses you. You should dump him,' Jenna said gently.

'I can't! I'd have no one! I'd be alone!'

'But you'll never find anyone as long as you're involved with him.'

'I've invested two whole years on him – I can't throw all that away now. I'm twenty-nine. It's all right for you, you've got Patrick—' She stopped abruptly. 'Sorry, Jen,' she said more quietly. 'I was forgetting who's supposed to be comforting who.'

'We're in the same boat now,' Jenna said.

'A leaky bloody rowing-boat with no oars,' Izzy said glumly. 'What a life! What's wrong with us? What's wrong with *them*?'

'I don't know,' Jenna said. 'I miss him so much, Izzy. But I hate him too. How could he do that to me?'

'One consolation, if he cheated on you, he'll cheat on her just the same. You're better off without him.'

'Wise words, Izzy my friend. Now apply them to yourself.'

'Oh God, you're right!' Izzy said. 'Even if Toby left Jennifer and married me, I'd be wondering all the time if he was going to do the same thing again.'

'Chances are he would. Once they've tasted blood . . .'

'Oh don't. That's it!' Izzy said decisively. 'I'm going to give him up. Definitely. I'm going to tell him to sling his hook, and take my chances out there. It's the only way. Let one good thing come out of this conversation, anyway.'

'Good for you,' Jenna said. But she knew that Izzy wouldn't stick to it. She'd given up Toby at least six times before, and always took him back when he said he couldn't live without her, and swore he'd tell his wife about her at 'the first opportunity'. Only that opportunity never materialized. There was always some excuse. Well, one thing was for sure – Jenna was not going to play second fiddle to Charlotte in Patrick's life. She had the horrible object lesson of Izzy before her. 'You're an inspiration to us all,' she told her friend.

'Hang on, I haven't done it yet,' Izzy said.

Jenna didn't say, 'That's exactly what I mean.'

It was fortunate that she had the conversation with Izzy first and was feeling braced, because almost as soon as she put the receiver down, the phone rang again, and without thinking she picked it up. It was Patrick.

'Jenna, thank heavens! Why didn't you call me?'

'Hello, Patrick.' The sound of his voice was making her insides do acrobatics, and she couldn't manage any more than that.

'I've been worried sick about you. You just went off without telling me where you were going.'

'You should have guessed I'd be here. Where else could I go, after all?'

'I shouldn't *have* to guess,' he said crossly. 'You've no idea how worried I've been.'

'Not worried enough to make you phone here before now.'

'I've been very busy,' he said, giving himself away. 'I have a job, you know. *One* of us has to earn enough to pay the bills.'

'You know about me losing my job, then?'

'I tried to ring you at work,' he said. 'That obnoxious female, Julie, said you'd been let go.'

And even that didn't make you ring me here, Jenna thought.
'I'm sorry,' he added into the silence she left.

'Well, it hardly matters in the scheme of things, does it?' she said.

'Oh come on, Jenna, let's not make a big song and dance over this,' he said impatiently. 'I made a mistake, I'm sorry. Now let's be civilized about it. Come home, and let's talk about it.'

'There's nothing to talk about,' she said stonily.

'Look, I know you're angry, but do try to keep a sense of proportion—'

'A sense of proportion?' she said, amazed. 'I find you in bed with another woman, and *I'm* supposed to make the adjustment?'

'All right, I know it was unpleasant for you, finding out like that, but let's put that behind us. It's not as if I planned it. It was just something that happened. An aberration.'

'Not good enough,' Jenna said. 'You don't find yourself in bed with someone in a split second, like getting knocked down on a crossing. It takes time to get your clothes off, if nothing else. You could have stopped at any point, but you didn't.'

'But it didn't *mean* anything! I swear to you, Charlotte doesn't mean anything to me.'

'Unfortunately, while you were in bed with her, neither did I,' Jenna said. 'I wanted to say to you, "How *could* you?" But I can see only too clearly how you could. I'm sorry, Patrick. Even if I wanted to come back, I could never trust you again. And I don't think I do want to.'

'I think you do,' Patrick said angrily. 'You just want me to beg you. I thought our relationship was a bit more grown up than that. Besides, I have nothing to beg for. I've been damned good for you, and you know it. You had nothing when I met you. I'm sorry you lost your job, but it's a blessing in disguise really, because I know of a really good opening for you, a much better job, something you'll enjoy, something with real prospects. You don't want to throw all that away for the sake of a silly tiff. Come home, and we'll talk it through in a civilized manner, like two adults. That's my last offer. It's not as if you have that many options, is it? You can't want to sleep on your brother's sofa for ever.'

'If I'd been thinking of coming back, you'd have just talked me out of it,' Jenna said. 'Do you *hear* yourself? You don't even think you've done anything wrong, do you? It was only getting caught you regret.' She tired of it, suddenly. 'I'm going to put the phone down now. Goodbye, Patrick. Don't call again, because I won't talk to you.'

'Wait! Don't hang up!' he called urgently. 'I've got something important to say.'

'What?' she asked wearily.

'You'll change your mind about coming back,' he said. 'But I advise you not to take too long about it.'

'Is that all?' she said. 'You cheated on me, and now you're threatening me?'

'No! That wasn't it. What I wanted to say was – Charlotte wants her watch back.'

'What watch?' Jenna said, amazed at his cheek.

'The one you took. I don't say "stole", because I know you were upset, but—'

'If you are referring to the present you gave me, which you left on *my* bedside cabinet for me—' Jenna began.

He interrupted, sounding nervous. 'Now, don't mess around, Jenna. I mean it. That's a very expensive watch!'

'I can tell. Your generosity touches me greatly. And I wouldn't dream of parting with it. It's the nicest thing you've ever given me. It will always remind me of you.'

'You can't keep it! Charlotte's furious!'

'You'll have to buy her another one, then, won't you?' Jenna said with deep satisfaction, and put the phone down. She looked at her watch fondly. Serve him right, the cheapskate! Anyway, it was a small enough price to pay for four years of Jenna's precious life.

The family rallied round, each in their own way. Harriet phoned first.

'Oh Jenna, I'm so sorry! And after four years! We all thought you were settled down for good. But you'll find someone else, I know you will. You're so smart and modern and everything, I bet they'll be queuing up for you as soon as they know you're free. But you and Patrick seemed so good together. Richard and I have only been waiting for you to announce you were getting married. And you'd have had such lovely babies! I know you've always wanted a family.'

'But what about your good news?' Jenna said. 'Congratulations. Olly says you're in pig again.'

That was all it took. 'Yes, and we're so excited. A little brother or sister for Martha! We've talked about whether we want to know the sex beforehand, and we've decided it's more exciting if we don't, especially for Martha – though whether we'll be able to stick by it I don't know. They do rather pressure you when they do the scan, and it's hard to resist. And everyone offers you their second-hand things for the baby and of course it's awkward if you don't know – not that it matters for things like buggies, and I suppose it doesn't *really* matter if you dress a girl in blue things and vice versa, but when people offer you a choice of pink or blue it seems silly not to know. It's due in October, did Olly tell you? Which is nice because we ought to have got settled down in time for Christmas. It's going to be such a wonderful Christmas, with a new baby, and Martha will be old enough to really get the most out of it. She was too young last Christmas, though I'll never forget the expression on her face when we first turned on the Christmas tree lights. It made me want to cry. And the new baby will make it seem all the more special – it will help her understand the baby Jesus stories so much better. I'm sure she's going to be perfect with it, whichever it is, boy or girl, because she's got such a lovely little personality, and she's very gentle with her dolls. She was asking if she could have a little brother or sister just a couple of months ago, but we didn't tell her then because we wanted to be absolutely sure before we did. It would be terrible to disappoint her. We'll be telling her next weekend and making a little occasion out of it. I want her always to remember the day she first found out. It's so wonderful that it happened so easily, because we'd always planned to have them two or three years apart, only when you've been on the pill you don't know how long it will take your system to get straight again, but I must have fallen practically the moment we started trying. Richard's been so sweet. He's so supportive. I must tell you what he did when I told him . . .'

Jenna was genuinely pleased for Harriet, and didn't really want to talk about her horrible situation, so she listened happily and made the right remarks and thought about being an aunt again, and tried not to wonder if that's all she would ever be.

Michael was gravely sympathetic and then briskly professional. 'Have you thought about making a claim against him?'

'What do you mean, a claim?'

'Well, four years is a long time, and from what Oliver says you're coming out of it with nothing at all to show for it. I know the flat belongs to him, but don't forget, all that time you were making a contribution. These days, the fact that you weren't married doesn't make as much difference as it used to. There's a definite presumption of shared assets, and your contribution to the household budget gives you an equity in the total estate.'

'You mean palimony?' Jenna said.

She could almost hear him wince over the wires. 'We don't use that expression. But you need to think very carefully about your situation, Jenna. You've lost your job, and now through no fault of your own you've lost your home, too. Patrick is well able to afford to buy you out, and that's what he ought to do, morally as well as legally. It wasn't all one-way traffic, you know. He benefited from your contribution just as much as vice versa, and you ought to be getting the facts together and the papers served before you've been apart for too long. Now, I can't act for you myself because it's not really my province, but I can put you in touch with a really good man who understands this kind of case and will get you the best possible settlement. And before you ask, you needn't worry about legal costs, because Patrick is clearly the one at fault and he'll have to pay your expenses as well as his own. But I'll put up anything that needs to be found ahead of the judgement, don't worry, because I know how you're fixed. Now, let me tell you how we should approach it . . .'

To Jenna's surprise, Rock emailed her, via Oliver:

Jen, always thought Patrick too glam to be true. Wouldn't be surprised if he was closet gay. Better off without him. But bad luck about the job! Rotten for you, esp in recession. You should come out here – recession beginning to bite but still opportunities, and LA hooked on English accents etc which would give you the edge. Your CV good for mag work here – double the salary! Or you

could think about getting into my line. Your looks and personality
wd be a big hit and I've got contacts ;-) Think about it. Get the
career right and the men will follow – and if they don't, you've
got the career!

Even her mother telephoned, from a cellphone somewhere off
Corfu.

'Darling, I'm so sorry! What a blow. We quite thought you
were settled. And that nice boy – such a looker, so charming,
and a partner in the firm and everything! Frankly, I always
wondered how you'd managed it! Not that you're not a lovely
girl, of course, darling, but you *are* a bit scatty and careless. I'll
never forget that time you were dancing about with your skirt
whirling up and you had a hole in your knickers.'

'Mummy, I was ten at the time.'

'Were you? It seems like yesterday. But anyway, darling, I really
am sorry, I promise you. You must be so miserable. My heart
bleeds for you. And Clifford sends his condolences.'

It always caught Jenna out when her mother called the Major
Clifford. She always wondered for a split second who the hell
Clifford was. 'That's nice of him.'

'He *is* nice. We both think you ought to have a holiday before
you try to get another job – do you good to get away for a bit.
Clifford suggested you came out to us for a week or so, but the
weather isn't very nice out here at the moment, and frankly,
darling, this boat is such a wretched little teacup, there's hardly
room to swing a cat. *Just* about tolerable for two, as long as they're
two small ones and they don't mind standing close together, but
with three you'd have to take numbers just to turn round.'

'It's all right, Mummy, I wouldn't dream of intruding on you.'

Her mother's voice warmed with relief. 'Darling! It wouldn't
be an intrusion! We'd *love* to have you! But you just wouldn't be
comfortable in this horrid old tub, and at a time like this you
need to be comfortable most of all. It wouldn't be a holiday
otherwise, would it? And we both think you really *ought* to take
a holiday. Get you out of yourself.'

'I haven't got any money for a holiday,' Jenna said.

'You ought to go and stay with Michael and Camilla. The
Cotswolds are lovely at this time of year. And they have central

heating that *works*, unlike that wretched Muswell Hill barn. There's that charming room that Clifford and I stayed in at Michael's last year, with the en-suite bathroom and dressing room. You'd be comfortable there.'

'That was *their* room, Mummy – Michael and Camilla's. I don't think they'd give it up for me.'

'Wouldn't they? Well, perhaps not. In that case, you'd better not go to them. You might have to share with one of their ghastly children. I know they're my own grandchildren, but I can't help thinking they take too much after Camilla's side. I knew her father, you know, and he was an absolute pudding. Darling, I must ring off – this is costing a fortune. I'll give some more thought to where you might go for a holiday, and ring again if I think of something. Clifford sends his love. Bye, darling. Be good.'

Family! Jenna thought fondly as she replaced the receiver. You can't beat it when there's a spot of rallying round to be done.

Four

'I still think you ought to have a holiday,' Sybil said, presiding over Sunday night supper. 'You look really peaky.'

'Peaky!' Oliver snorted. 'That's the sort of word only mothers can use with credibility.'

'I am a mother,' Sybil pointed out. 'You saw to that.'

'What I *need*,' Jenna said, 'is to get a new job.'

'Not until you've had a break. You've suffered a shock, and you need to get away,' Sybil said. 'Also I'd like to be able to say, when Patrick phones again, that you're not living here.'

'You can *say* it,' Oliver mentioned.

'I'm no good at lying. If she weren't here I could sound convincing.'

'I don't have any money,' Jenna said.

'She needs a job,' Oliver said, 'and it may not be easy in the current climate.'

'Well, then,' said Sybil, ever practical, 'we must find her a job that *feels* like a holiday.'

Jenna liked the sound of that. 'What sort of thing would that be?'

'Oh, I don't know. Tour rep, or tourist guide maybe.'

'But those would be long-term jobs.'

'OK, tour rep would be, but I'm sure a lot of the smaller tourist attractions must take on temporary staff for the summer.'

'A lot of those places we went to down in Cornwall last year certainly would,' Oliver agreed. 'The lesser-known gardens and miniature trains and petting zoos and so on.'

'Or equestrian centres,' Sybil said. 'You ride and you're good with horses.'

'I doubt they'd take on short-term staff,' Oliver said.

'I wouldn't want to commit myself to a long term,' Jenna said. 'I need to get back into my career.'

'What about house-sitting, then?' Oliver said. 'That can be as short-term as you like.'

'Doesn't pay very much,' Sybil said.

'It's not supposed to,' Oliver argued. 'It's supposed to be a holiday.' He saw Jenna was looking tired, and knew she could not bear long arguments yet. 'You just relax and leave it to us,' he said. 'We'll think of something between us.'

'Between us?' she queried.

'The family. I'll talk to everyone and we'll brainstorm. We'll come up with the perfect thing for you. You just rest and read and don't even think about it until I bring you the solution on a plate.'

Jenna remembered her recent conversations with the family and thought Oliver's confidence might be misplaced. But he was the master manipulator. Perhaps he would get better results. And she liked the idea of 'the job that felt like a holiday'. She really did want to get away, she discovered. She didn't want accidentally to catch another of Patrick's phone calls. She didn't want to open the front door and find him outside. She was afraid of what he might say and what her reaction might be. Leaving had been done on the strength of the moment, but she didn't feel strong any more.

Over the next few days, as she got over the weak and weepy stage, she found her feelings about him veering about alarmingly. She still hated him for what he had done, and she was heartsore and grieving, but she missed him so much that her longing for him was sometimes almost stronger than the hate. The thought that he was just down the road and accessible was scary.

He had asked her to come back. Part of her wanted so much to go back. She wanted to sleep beside him, instead of in Oliver's spare room. She wanted to breakfast with him and go home to him after work, share all the familiar small conversations and actions of accustomed lovers, the bread-and-butter of relationships. And he had said he knew of an opening for her, a really good job that she would enjoy. She might have her life back, her good, lucky life that everyone had envied! All she had to do was to dismiss what he had done from her mind.

And was it so bad, after all? He said it was a mistake. People made mistakes. Wasn't the grown-up, the civilized thing to do to forget it, to put the past behind her? Nobody was perfect, after all. We all needed understanding. Turn the other cheek. To forgive was divine. Let bygones be bygones. There were plenty of clichés to choose from. He had asked her to come back, that was the important thing.

And if she delayed too long, he might change his mind. That insidious thought made her shiver. What if she missed her chance? He might meet someone else at any moment and her window of opportunity would slam shut. She'd never get another man as good as him. Let's face it, she was heading for thirty, and good men were thin on the ground. She ought to grab what she could, and think herself lucky.

She had almost got to the telephone on the stream of this thinking when she managed to stop herself. Craven, craven! He had betrayed her, deceived her, and had not even really felt he had done wrong. He had barely apologized. He had suggested she was being unreasonable in objecting. Had she really forgotten all that, just because she was scared no one else would ever fancy her?

Whoever else she might live with in her life, she would have to live with herself. 'And I don't want to live with a pathetic, cringing coward like you,' she addressed herself sternly in the mirror above the telephone table in the hall. She stuck her tongue out at herself, removed her hand from the receiver, grabbed a book, and went to sit out in the garden in the sunshine, because Sybil said she was office-pale and needed vitamin D.

If Olly didn't come up with anything, she decided, she would start looking for another job next week; and if she never had another man for the whole of the rest of her life, at least she would have her self-respect. A tiny voice in her mind told her that was a bleak prospect, not to say cold comfort, but she ignored it. The one thing she *wouldn't* do was go back to Patrick. That was definite.

Unless he begged her, the tiny voice added as a caveat, but she ignored it resolutely.

'I've done it,' Oliver said proudly, emerging from the house on a warm evening a few days later. 'I am brilliant, a genius, an unparalleled fixer. Feel free to worship me, oh mere mortals.'

Sybil and Jenna looked up from deckchairs where they were chatting and enjoying the last rays. The children (who should have been in bed) were playing at the other end of the garden, making the most of the oversight and effacing themselves in the shrubbery in the hope of extending it.

'Fixed what?' Sybil asked. 'I hope you mean that dripping tap in Jenna's bathroom?'

'Do I look like a plumber?' Oliver demanded scornfully. 'Did Churchill go to Yalta to unclog the sink? Did they discuss drainbusting techniques at Bretton Woods? Anyway, why don't you get Mr Thing in?' he descended abruptly from the heights of rhetoric.

'Because he has a call-out charge now,' Sybil said reasonably, 'so I was waiting for more than one thing to need attention. Thirty quid's too much when it's only a fifty-pee washer that needs changing. I'm sure you could do it, if you put your mind to it.'

'We're losing sight of the big picture here,' Oliver said, frustrated. 'We're not supposed to be talking domestica. I have news of great joy, news of great mirth. I've solved Jenna's problem.'

'You've found me a job?' she said, feeling a little curl of excitement in her stomach.

'A job that will feel just like a holiday,' Oliver said, taking the empty chair opposite the women. 'I spoke to Michael and Rock and then I rang Ma, and she's just rung back to say it's fixed.'

'Oh my God, I'm not going to have to be a chambermaid in

someone's villa?' Jenna said. 'She's offered me up at slave wages to someone she owes a favour to!'

'*No!*' said Oliver. 'Really, Jen, have a little faith.'

'In Ma? I can't think of any other reason she'd try to help me.'

'Have faith in me, I mean,' Oliver said. 'It's true she wasn't keen to stir herself, but when I hinted that unless we thought of something she'd be forced to invite you out for a long rest, she sprang into action.'

'Positively Machiavellian,' Sybil drawled. 'If this is going to be a long story, I need a drink. Oh goodness, those children! They ought to be in bed.'

'Give them five more minutes, while Olly tells us the plan,' said Jenna, 'and then I'll help you with them. I want to know my fate.'

'You'll love this,' Oliver promised. 'There's this old relative, a sort of cousin of Ma's, called Kitty Everest.' He pronounced the name Eave-wrist. 'It's spelled like Mount Everest, apparently, but it's pronounced like that. Anyway, she lives in this gorgeous old house in the country – like a stately home but in miniature – and she needs a live-in assistant, someone to do inventory and cataloguing work for her, and some secretarial. No special training necessary. Nothing a normal, literate, intelligent person can't handle. But she's a bit particular and doesn't want a complete stranger, so you'd fit the bill perfectly.'

Jenna looked doubtful. 'Live-in assistant to an old lady? I'm not going to end up helping her into the bath and seeing she takes her pills, am I?'

Oliver laughed. 'No, she's not old like that. She's only about Ma's age, perfectly fit and compos mentis. I probably shouldn't have called her old. I mean, sixty isn't old these days – look at the Major. Rock says Ma told her she was quite a tearaway in her youth. And Michael's met her, and he says she's nice – bright and funny.'

'Met her recently? I don't remember Ma talking about her.'

'He met her a couple of years ago. Something legal she went to him for, because of the family connection. I think that might have been when her husband died – did I mention she was a widow? He and Rock remembered her being around when they were little – they called her Aunty Kitty – but Ma sort of lost touch with her over the years. You know the way it goes. I mean, we never see any of our cousins, do we?'

'True. So how did Ma know this cousin wanted help?'

'It was Michael suggested it. He'd heard from a friend of a friend that Mrs Everest was thinking of selling some of the contents of Holtby House and needed someone to help with the inventory and so on. I rang Ma and put the fear of God into her. Ma rang Mrs E, Mrs E rang Michael, Michael rang me, I rang Ma again, Ma rang Mrs E again, and now all we've got to do is to confirm you're going, and when you'll arrive. It was as simple as that.'

'Wait, wait. You're going too fast. I need to think about it,' Jenna protested.

'What's to think about?' Oliver said. 'Look, it's live in, lovely house, gorgeous countryside, a little light clerical work and bags of time off to wander about the lanes and so on. You'll get your keep, plus pocket money, fifty a week, cash. OK, it's not a fortune, but frankly, there'll be nothing to spend it on so you can stick it straight in the bank. And Michael's got her to agree to a minimum of one month. So if you find there isn't much of a job there, you can spin it out and enjoy yourself. And if it turns out that she needs someone permanent, Michael says he'd be glad if you'd help her recruit your successor, because he doesn't want the old girl to get ripped off, or end up with some complete bastard living in her house.'

'He likes her, then?' Sybil said. 'He wouldn't be worried if he didn't think she was nice.'

'He says she's quite a character. He thinks Jenna would get on well with her. Come on now, Jen, what do you say? Isn't it the perfect solution? A real holiday in the country, with a little light work to keep you from getting bored.'

'And as long as no one tells me where Holtby is,' Sybil added happily, 'I'll be able to tell Patrick I've no idea where you are.'

Patrick! Jenna had forgotten about him for a blissful moment. Memories came crowding back in. She needed to get away. It was too easy to think about him here in London.

'In any case, even if you don't like it, it's only a month,' Oliver said. 'You can put up with that. But you'll probably have a whale of a time.'

'I'll do it,' Jenna said. 'Thanks, Oliver. Where is this place, anyway?'

'La la la,' Sybil said loudly, putting her hands over her ears. 'I can't hear you. I'm going to put the children to bed. Wait till I've gone to tell her.'

Jenna had mixed feelings about the countryside. When she was little, before her father died, they had had a country cottage for weekends and holidays in the depths of rural Buckinghamshire. She remembered wet weekends, when the cottage had a strange, mushroomy smell about it, and the bed sheets felt sticky with damp. The rain teemed down endlessly from a sky like the underside of a submarine – grey, dark and featureless. It dripped monotonously from gutters and branches and the eyelashes of morose cows in sodden fields. There was nothing to do, the sulky wood fire did little to mitigate the clammy cold, and even the cardboard of the indoor games went soft. Enforced walks were torture, for the mud stuck to your wellies in great joke clumps, weighing down your baby legs until you could hardly get along. You couldn't even sit down and throw a paddy because the grass was soaking and it was impossible to get dry again.

She remembered weekends for the tedium of packing to go down there – everyone had to help – and being crammed together in the car with bags of this and cardboard boxes of that, the biscuit tin never within reach, and the handle of Pa's precious frying-pan, swathed in newspaper, sticking into your back. And then there was the doom-filled moment on Sunday afternoon when Pa announced it was time to pack to come home, and you knew the weekend was over and it was school tomorrow.

But then there were the summer holidays, when cloudless days seem to stretch into a golden eternity, week upon glorious week. The meadow grass was waist high, patched with vivid wild flowers – poppies, moon daisies and cornflowers, scarlet, white, gold and blue – and the thick trees spread delicious cold shade under their skirts. Your hot skin smelled like biscuits, and you ran about barefoot in nothing but shorts and T-shirt day after day. There were ponies for riding and dogs for taking for walks. There was swimming in the cold-smelling river, and fishing for sticklebacks, standing calf deep in the little stream at the end of the field.

There was the church fête, with skittles and guess-the-weight-of-the-cake and a game where you rolled wooden balls down a slope into numbered holes, and stalls selling home-made sweets. The vicar who smelled of mothballs came round selling raffle tickets and Ma got into an argument with him, saying raffles were the same as gambling and therefore not Christian, and hurt his feelings. There was the village sports day, with egg-and-spoon and sack race and heart-bursting running, barefoot over the baked ground, with the smell of bruised grass and the delicious, maddening whiff of hot diesel from the fairground just warming up for later. And most of all there was the heavenly do-nothing of childhood summer afternoons, when the stunned heat lay over the land and you were content to lie on your back on the grass and chew a stem of rye, stare up at the deep, deep, endless blue and wait for teatime.

The strange thing was that in her memory both states, wet and dry, seemed to have been continuous, which was clearly impossible. The other permanency, of course, had been the presence of Pa, tall, balding, delicious smelling, his big hands always ready to whisk you up into the air and dangle you, shrieking with pleasure because you knew he wouldn't let you fall; telling you fascinating things about insects and plants; showing you how to do an archaeological dig in the compost heap; standing at the stove in the dark little kitchen, experimenting. He loved to cook, and at the cottage was his only opportunity. One year he had collected a whole basket of fungi in the woods and fields and fried them in butter, and no one would eat them, because Ma said he didn't know a mushroom from a toadstool and would poison them all. He had eaten them himself, and Jenna had been racked with torment because he looked so hurt and disappointed. Even now, years and years later, she wanted to go back and eat his 'fungus feast' with him and make it all right at last. When you were little you thought your parents would last for ever, like the sunny days; and when they were gone you remembered most of all the times you had missed a chance to make them happy.

She was old enough now to know that a month in the country would not be either perfectly wonderful or perfectly horrible, and that was good enough for her. She was looking forward to it, and her first sight of the village of Holtby was encouraging.

It seemed prosperous: near enough to the motorway to attract the well off, and far enough away not to hear it. It looked very pretty, with stone-built houses along the main street, a few interesting-looking shops, a snippet of village green with a row of handsome chestnuts and a stone horse-trough. She wound down her window and drove slowly, enjoying the afternoon air and the way the sunlight poured gold-green through the chestnut leaves. The horse-trough seemed to be full of water, which was unusual these days, and suggested a horsey local community. There was a handsome church and a nice-looking pub opposite it, The Crown and Cushion, with colourful hanging baskets and a sign saying 'Home Cooked Food' and 'Garden at Rear'.

The only problem was that she missed the turning for Holtby House on the first pass. Mrs Everest had sent her instructions but she somehow didn't see it and found herself trundling out of the village at the other end into open countryside, and had to look for a farm gate to turn round in. She spotted it on the second pass – a narrow lane just past the post office that hardly looked like a real road – but too late to turn into it, so she had to loop round the village green and make a third run. After that it was quite straightforward and in moments she was pulling into a stable yard through big stone gateposts which bore small notices, one of which said HOLTBY HOUSE and the other DELIVERIES ONLY. The coach houses had evidently been turned into garages at some point in the past, but the stables looked intact – though sadly empty – and one side of the square was a small stone cottage, behind which rose the blank wall of the main house, to which it seemed to be attached.

Jenna turned Florence and parked modestly at the side in front of one of the garages, and climbed out. The air was warm and still and smelled of grass, and somewhere nearby a blackbird was singing. She looked about her and felt a deep contentment stealing over her. She was glad to be here.

A small sound made her turn, and she saw a woman coming in through a gate in the wall beside the cottage, through which she could see a glimpse of sunny garden.

'There you are!' the woman called in a glad voice, as if she had been longing for Jenna to arrive. She was small and spare, dressed in jeans and garden clogs and a T-shirt, and had a Boris

Johnson-esque shock of unruly blonde hair. The overall impression was so youthful that Jenna said doubtfully, 'Mrs Everest?'

Only when she came close did it become apparent that the blonde hair was shot through with grey and silver and ash and the face was that of a woman of mature years. Even then it was remarkably smooth and unwrinkled, betrayed only by lines around the eyes and mouth; but she smiled with an energetic impishness, and her eyes were bright and intelligent. 'Bless you for pronouncing it right!' she said, putting out her hand. 'But you must call me Kitty if we're to live together. And I hope I can call you Jenna? What an interesting name, by the way.'

'I don't know what my mother was thinking of,' Jenna said smilingly, shaking the lean, firm paw. 'All the rest got perfectly plain, simple names. I think she'd run out of inspiration, or patience, or something, by the time I came along.'

'Five *is* a lot,' Kitty said gravely. 'For a human, anyway. Dogs manage things much better. But Jenna's a pretty name, and it must be nice to be different. There were six Katherines in my year at school. I'd lost touch with your mother before you were born, so you won't remember me. Harriet was just a babe in arms, and Oliver a toddler, but I knew Michael and Rachel. But why are we standing in the yard talking? You must need a drink after your journey. Was it difficult?'

'No, it was quite easy, except for missing the turning in the village.'

Kitty put a hand to her face. 'You know, I don't know why I told you to come in that way. I suppose because that's the way I always come in. You'd have found the front entrance much more easily. Never mind, you're here now. Let's grab your bags and take them in and dump them in the hall, and have a drink before anything else. I expect you're gasping for a gin and tonic.'

'I've been thinking about it ever since I left the motorway,' Jenna said.

Kitty grinned. 'I can see you're a girl after my own heart! I can't *tell* you how pleased I am you're here. I know we're going to get along famously.'

'I think so too,' Jenna said, and meant it. Anyone whose first thought for an arriving traveller was to get a gin and tonic down them was all right with her.

Five

They went through the gate in the wall and emerged on to a stone-flagged path that ran along the back of the house. Green spaces of lawn stretched away to a hedge and a distant vista of low, blue hills. On the left the lawn was bounded by a fringe of woodland and on the right by a stone wall, above which peeped the roofs of greenhouses. Of the house itself Jenna only gained a brief impression in that first moment: that it was oblong, built of pale grey stone, and had many windows – the tall rectangular sort, divided into small square panes, that said Georgian.

Kitty, toting two of Jenna's bags as if they weighed nothing, led the way through a door into a small stone-floored lobby, then turned right into a passage which led parallel to the back of the house and into what was obviously the entrance hall. There were black and white marble tiles on the floor and a graceful staircase of beautiful simplicity. Kitty put down the bags, beamed at Jenna and said, 'Just dump everything here, and let's have a drink before I show you your room.'

'Great idea,' Jenna said.

Kitty led the way through a sitting room, crowded with furniture, paintings, ceramics, silver, clocks, and a number of eclectic items Jenna would have liked to stop and examine – like a painted ostrich egg in a glass case and a stuffed owl on a bracket halfway up the wall. They passed it all, however, and emerged into a large conservatory built on to the back of the house. It could not have been more of a contrast – lofty, light, airy and spacious, with Italian tiles on the floor, a few pieces of comfortable modern furniture in bamboo and Sanderson print, and a couple of gigantic parlour-palms in glazed pots. Beyond, the green lawns spread to the distant hills, and the late sunlight slanted in at the door.

'Just the place for a sundowner,' Jenna said.

'Just what I always think,' Kitty agreed, seeming pleased. 'Now, you sit down. No, take that chair, it's more comfortable. Gin and tonic all right?'

'Perfect,' Jenna said, sinking down and stretching out. 'This is heaven.'

'Attagirl!' There was a glass-topped table furnished with decanters, glasses and ice bucket, and soon Kitty was making all the right clinking noises as she mixed G and Ts practically large enough to wash in.

In from the garden wandered two black dogs, tails wagging ingratiatingly, heads low and friendly. Both were mongrels, one mostly Labrador and the other something like Rottweiler crossed with Alsatian, to judge from its bushy tail. 'Ah, here are my boys. Are you all right with dogs? This is Watch, and that one's Barney.'

The dogs and the drink arrived at about the same time, and Jenna patted the former and then raised the latter in Kitty's direction. 'Well, cheers. It's nice to be here.'

'Down the hatch,' Kitty said. 'I'm thrilled to have you. It'll be so nice to have someone intelligent to talk to.'

'How do you know I'm intelligent?'

'Oh my dear, you can tell from the first glance at a person's face. So many people one meets nowadays are such cows.'

'Cows?' It seemed surprisingly condemnatory.

'Awfully nice, but not much going on upstairs,' Kitty elucidated.

Jenna got it. 'Well, I know what you mean. But aren't there lots of nice people in Holtby?'

'Nearly everyone's nice, and quite a few aren't cows. There are some ex-Londoners, moved down here in the migration of the nineties, a few commuter families, and quite a bit of county. One or two holiday homes, but we're lucky to have a lot of local people still living here, which is the heart of a village.'

'Have you lived here long?'

'Me personally? About thirty years now – how time flies! – but my husband's family has owned this house for a hundred and fifty years.'

'It's Georgian, isn't it?'

'Well spotted. About 1790, we think. The best period – not so austere as earlier Georgian, but still with the perfect proportions. By the time you get into Regency they can be somewhat blurred. I absolutely adore it,' she said with what sounded like a sad sigh. 'I still sometimes wake up and can't believe I'm living here. I grew up in an ordinary, respectable Edwardian house in an ordinary respectable Edwardian suburb. My parents used to take me to look at National Trust houses on Bank Holidays, and I used to think it would be the pinnacle of posh to live in a place with a two-line address – you know, like Holtby House, Holtby.'

Jenna said, 'I know exactly what you mean.'

'I'm sometimes afraid that was the real reason I married my poor Peter – the hope of living in this house one day. Of course, we had to wait until his father died. That's the gruesome part of family inheritance. And we had his mother living with us for ten years after that – but she was no trouble really, in a house this size. She had her own suite on the top floor.'

'How big is it?' Jenna asked.

'Three floors, nine bedrooms – four on the first floor and five on the second. It used to be eleven bedrooms, but Peter's father put in a guest bathroom on the top floor, and then after Agnes – Peter's mother – died, we sacrificed another on the first floor for two extra bathrooms. We did quite a lot of work then, including putting on this conservatory, which has been a godsend. Peter took a bit of persuading that it wouldn't spoil the look of the house, but once we had it he used it more than any other room. He loved the heat and lots of light. I think it reminded him of our years abroad – Africa and India mostly.'

The mention of India made Jenna think of something she had been wanting to know. 'I have to ask – I hope you don't mind – is your name anything to do with the mountain?'

'I don't mind – everyone asks that. Yes, it's the same family. Sir George Everest was Peter's great-great – I don't remember how many greats – grand-uncle. He was fiercely proud of the old man. Do you know about him?'

'No, nothing at all, I'm afraid.'

'He was a surveyor, and spent twenty-five years surveying the arc of the meridian that runs through Nepal. Tremendous work. He was knighted for it, and then the year before he died they named Peak XV, as it was known up till then, in his honour. It started out as Mont Eve-rist. How it got from that to Mount Ever-rest I've no idea.'

'It's a shame. I like the other better.'

'So do I. More elegant. Never mind. Now when people see

my name written down they think I'm from the double-glazing company. And so the world turns! I'll show you Sir George's portrait tomorrow. And the rest of the house, of course. But for now, it's to be an evening of relaxation. Have you finished your drink? Would you like to see your room? Perhaps you'd like a bath before dinner?'

'I hope you haven't gone to a lot of trouble making dinner for me,' Jenna said, heaving herself out of the downy embrace of the chair.

Kitty laughed. 'Bless you, I don't cook! Never have been able to. I could burn water. I have a wonderful help called Mrs Phillips who comes in by day and cooks for me, and also puts my washing in the washing machine and takes my ironing away. She's left everything ready for us.' She stood too. 'It's a funny thing that although she's worked for me for longer than I can remember, I can't call her anything but Mrs Phillips. I think she'd die of shock if I called her Brenda. And she calls me Mrs Everest – or, if I'm particularly in favour, "Mrs Everest, dear". That's another reason you have to call me Kitty. She'd get quite the wrong idea otherwise.'

She led the way upstairs, turned left at the first floor and opened the second door on the right. It was a beautiful room, large and lofty, with two tall windows to the front of the house, furnished with shining mahogany furniture and a washed-Chinese carpet on the polished boards of the floor. There were pale green curtains and counterpane, and a green vase full of white flowers on the dressing table. The windows were open a little and the most wonderful scent was drifting in. The front of the house, Jenna could see from where she stood, was covered with wisteria, and the trembling pale-purple blooms dripped heavenly perfume.

'It's lovely,' Jenna said appreciatively. 'Really lovely!'

'I'm glad you like it,' said Kitty. She opened a door in the right-hand wall. 'This is your bathroom.' It was grand: more mahogany, with white porcelain and brass fittings. There was a shower cabinet as well as a bath, and a luxurious number of blue and white towels.

'This is wonderful,' Jenna said.

'Well, Peter and I both felt very strongly about bathrooms. He wasn't at all country-gentry in that respect,' she added with a laugh. '*Real* county families, the top people, have dreadful chilly, draughty bathrooms with taps that drip, rust marks on the bath and never enough hot water. It's a badge of honour not to complain about it. They think there's something not quite *right* about comfort. They'd think this was awfully *nouveau riche*. I'm going to leave you now, my dear. Come downstairs whenever you're ready. Dinner can be at any time so there's no need for you to hurry.'

She went away, leaving Jenna to examine her new kingdom.

And what a kingdom! Everything had been thought of for her comfort – the flowers, plenty of hangers in the wardrobe, a box of tissues by the bed, hand cream on the dressing table. There was even a tin of biscuits on the mantelpiece among the china figurines, and a small pile of books left ready for bedtime reading: *Stalky & Co*, *Pride and Prejudice*, *The Nine Tailors*, *Brideshead Revisited* and *Carry On Jeeves*. Jenna smiled as she read the titles. Somehow she had no doubt that Kitty had chosen them herself.

She went to the window and pushed it up to lean out and drink in the perfumed air. *You've fallen on your feet here, girl*, she thought.

Jenna didn't think she had ever had such a good night's sleep. Waking from it was like swimming up from an immense depth of warm, dark water that had cradled her in unutterable comfort. She didn't even remember dreaming, and woke feeling luxuriously content.

She lay for a moment remembering the previous evening. The dinner of chicken casseroled with olives in a rich tomato sauce, followed by rhubarb pie, was delicious, and was accompanied by a glorious red burgundy and followed by coffee (Mrs Phillips left the coffee machine all ready to be switched on – 'Even I can do that,' Kitty said) and cognac. And they had talked and talked – she marvelled at what good company Kitty was, and how well they had got on together, considering the difference in their ages. But there was nothing old about Kitty, except the length of her memory and the richness of her vocabulary. Jenna had naturally asked her a lot of things about her past life (Peter had been a geographer and surveyor like his hero ancestor, and they had spent the early part of their married life mostly abroad), but they had also chatted about music, wine, current events, animals, holidays and other such neutral topics.

And when they were settled with their cognacs, Kitty had asked her in the most natural way what had brought her here, and Jenna had found herself telling about Lousy Monday quite freely, almost as she would have told it to Izzy. Kitty's sympathy was so natural and comforting that she went off to bed (early – 'This country air really knocks me out!') feeling as though a thorn had been drawn, and fell asleep as soon as her head touched the pillow.

Sunshine was trying to get in through the green curtains, so Jenna jumped up and went to open them. Below, the gravelled drive ran from the turnaround in front of the house down to the left and out of sight to the main gate. In the middle of the front lawn before her was a magnificent cedar tree, spreading its noble black platforms to the sun like something in a Merchant Ivory film. Birds were chirping and trilling madly from every direction, and suddenly Jenna felt she had to be out. Kitty had told her to sleep in and said they would breakfast at about nine, but she was wide awake now, though it was only seven, so she thought she'd go for a walk and explore the grounds a bit before she had her shower. She pulled on jeans and a loose-fitting sweatshirt, dragged a brush through her red-gold mane, and went downstairs.

The black-and-white hall was full of sunshine. The front door stood open – there was a small vestibule and half-glass doors between it and the hall – and she could see the two dogs lying down on the warm gravel outside. She stepped out into the birdsong-filled morning, and they jumped up and came to greet her, grinning and wagging their tails and even frisking a little, suggesting it might be nice to go off somewhere.

'My thought exactly, boys,' she said, and set off across the dewy grass with them romping about her foolishly. Barney raced ahead to the cedar tree and came back with a stick which he dropped at her feet beguilingly. She threw it for him. Watch made a token run, but stopped after a few lolloping steps to come back to her. He was an older dog than Barney, greying round the muzzle, and obviously thought stick-chasing was for the young and foolish. They proceeded in this way down to the belt of trees, which she discovered had been planted up as a very pretty woodland walk.

She ambled happily through this, noting there were bluebells just coming into flower, but started to feel a bit chilly and thought it was a waste of the sunshine, so she took a side path out before the end, and crossed the lawn to the boundary hedge down at the far end of the grounds, where there was the view to the distant hills.

The dogs by this time had left her and gone off on their own business, and she stood for a long time, enjoying the sunshine and the sweet air, and wondering what the name of the range of hills was. On the other side of the hedge there was evidently a track or footpath of some kind, because at one point she heard two people coming along it, talking quietly, though she couldn't see them because the hedge was six feet high and dense. But just as she became aware that she was hungry and thought it was about time to go back and get ready for breakfast, she heard hoof beats, and a moment later saw the ears of a horse and the top half of his rider coming along towards her.

Always interested in horses, she looked around for something to stand on for a better view, and spotted a tree stump a little further along. Balancing on it, she could just see over the hedge. The horse approaching was a very handsome black, groomed to swooning-point, walking collectedly on the bit. The rider was even more perfectly turned out, which struck her as odd at this time of day – who poshed up for the early morning hack? She was slim and looked as if she would be tall, wearing immaculate breeches and boots, tweed hacking jacket and black velvet crash-cap. Her corn-blonde hair was confined as if for the showground in a net, and her face was fully made-up, beautiful in a rather enamelled way. She looked hard as nails, like a professional showjumper: just by switching to a black jacket she could have gone straight into the ring at Hickstead or Olympia. One of the posh locals, Jenna thought: a County Tough. She was about to jump down, so as not to attract attention to herself, when the woman spotted her.

'Who are you? What are you doing there?' she demanded in ringing, authoritative tones. 'That's private land. Don't you know you're trespassing?' The horse passaged about a bit, upset by the sudden voice, and she checked it with a firm hand.

Jenna saw no reason to explain herself to a complete stranger;

but on the other hand, this *was* the countryside, and the woman was probably just looking out for her neighbour, which was the decent thing to do. So she stood where she was and said, 'I'm staying with Mrs Everest.'

The fact that she had pronounced the name correctly perhaps weighed with the horsewoman, for she frowned at Jenna with slightly less hostility; but she said suspiciously, 'I've never seen you before. And I didn't hear she had anyone staying with her.'

This Jenna thought was just rude; and besides, she had tired of the game. She said, 'Perhaps she doesn't tell you everything,' and jumped down and walked away.

'Stop!' the woman called after her; and when Jenna didn't, she said, 'I don't know what you're up to, but I shall check up on you, you know. And I have a photographic memory.'

Jenna gave her an insouciant wave of one hand without turning round, walking briskly towards the house and breakfast, heard the hoof beats resume, and thought no more about it.

Kitty was in the hall when she went back into the house, and said, 'Ah, there you are! Did you have a nice walk? Are you ready for breakfast?'

'Yes, it's lovely out. I'd just like a quick shower first, if you don't mind.'

'Of course. We'll eat on the terrace at the back – straight through the conservatory when you're ready. And do you like tea or coffee?'

'Tea, please.'

Ten minutes later, freshly washed and clad in a soft chambray shirt and stone-coloured cotton trousers, her feet in comfortable coral-coloured suede sandals, Jenna ran downstairs, through the crowded sitting-room and the airy conservatory and out on to the terrace, where one of the conservatory tables and two chairs had been set up facing the view, and the dogs had assembled already in a hopeful row. Kitty was in one of the chairs, and a pleasant-faced, comfortably-figured, grey-haired woman in an apron was putting things on to the table from a large tray.

'Ah, Jenna,' said Kitty, 'this is Mrs Phillips. Mrs Phillips, Jenna Freemont, whom I told you about. She's a cousin to some degree of removal, and she's kindly come to stay and help me sort things out.'

Mrs Phillips gave Jenna a careful look, as though memorizing her, and then smiled and put out a civil hand. 'Pleased to meet you,' she said in a local accent. 'Mrs Everest said you'd not been well lately, and I must say you do look a bit peaky. Never mind, you'll soon feel better, what with our good air and our good local produce. It's the minerals in the soil or something, so they say, but it's that healthy round here, nobody ever dies!'

'I like the sound of that,' Jenna said. 'And I certainly had the best night's sleep of my life last night.'

'Holtby air,' said Mrs Phillips and Kitty at the same moment, and they looked at each other and smiled.

'I'll get your breakfasts,' Mrs Phillips said, turning away. 'Have to see if we can't feed you up.'

Jenna sat, gazed at the view, and said to Kitty, 'It's hard to remember that I've come here to work, you've made me so comfortable. But we ought to talk about my duties. I mean, you've not invited me here to take a holiday, tempting as it seems.'

'Oh, no need to start today,' Kitty said, leaning back and half closing her eyes against the sun, like a large cat. 'You'll want to get your bearings and settle in.'

Jenna laughed. 'You mustn't encourage me to be lazier than I already am. At least tell me, what am I here to do? Michael said something about correspondence and – was it? – cataloguing?'

'I have some correspondence to clear up,' Kitty said, 'because I really can't get on with that wretched computer. Xander made me swap my dear old typewriter for it, and I wish I'd never listened to him. He said it would be easier because everything is stored inside it instead of on sheets of paper that can get lost, but I knew where I was with a typewriter and a filing cabinet.'

'Xander?' Jenna queried.

'Oh, sorry – my godson, Alexander Latham. He lives a few miles on the other side of Holtby. You'll meet him soon. He's the nearest thing I have to a son. I'm very fond of him. But I expect you'll be happy with the computer – I dare say it's all you ever use yourself?'

Jenna nodded.

'It will be useful for the other work as well. You see, the house is crammed with things, as I expect you've noticed – pictures, furniture, china, objets d'art – and there's a whole library of books. They all have to be listed and catalogued in detail. There'll be some research work to be done on the backgrounds in some cases, which I imagine you'll do on the Internet. I'm sure you're an expert on that.'

'I've done that sort of thing in my other jobs,' Jenna said. 'I'm sure it won't be a problem.'

'Good. And then I'll need a brief history of the house to be compiled – just a couple of pages. More Internet work for you, though I have papers and photographs and other documents you can call on. We can do that together – and I'd like some of the photographs incorporated in it, if that's possible. I have a scanner – it came as part of the package when I bought the computer.'

'That's fine. I'm sure I can do what you want,' Jenna said, and went on, hesitantly: 'May I ask what all this is for? Are you writing a book or something?'

'I wish that's all it was,' Kitty said. 'No, I'm afraid it's all going to have to be sold.'

Six

'Sold?' Jenna exclaimed. 'What a shame!'

'Yes, it is,' Kitty said. 'It's a collection that goes back through the generations, and every piece has its story. In a way, it's the story of the family itself. But you see, this house takes a great deal to maintain, and my income doesn't rise along with the costs. In simple terms, I can't afford to live here. I'm hoping by selling some of the contents to buy myself some time, so I won't have to sell the house. I'd like to be able to stay on here a few more years – ideally until I die, because it would break my heart to leave Holtby House. I love it so.' Her face was bleak, and Jenna was struck to the heart. Her own problems suddenly faded to triviality.

'I'm so sorry,' she said. 'How awful for you.'

'I want to do the right thing by the house,' Kitty said. 'There are repairs I've been putting off, and that's not fair on the fabric.

If there was one big thing like a Titian I could sell, I wouldn't hesitate or repine. It would be worth it to put everything right. But none of the bits and pieces, lovely though they are, is valuable enough to make any difference.'

'What about taking out a loan?' Jenna said, thinking hard.

'Loans have to be serviced. I'd just be adding to the costs, and my income wouldn't stand it.' Kitty pulled herself together briskly. 'Well, let's not talk about it now. How about my giving you a quick tour of the house after breakfast, so that you have some idea of the task ahead?'

She obviously didn't want to dwell on it, so Jenna followed her lead and changed the subject brightly. But the thought of the shadow hanging over this pleasant woman almost spoiled the delicious Full English that Mrs Phillips served up.

'You're spoiling me,' Jenna told her. 'If this keeps up I'll be as fat as a pig in no time.'

'We believe in breakfasts in this house,' Mrs Phillips said comfortably. 'Best time of day to eat. Fill the tank *before* you drive the car.'

'We don't go in for large lunches,' Kitty explained, 'so you'll find you'll burn it off by supper time.'

Kitty seemed really to have intended a 'quick tour of the house' but Jenna was so interested in everything that it took some time. On the ground floor were the drawing room and dining room, furnished and decorated like something from the National Trust, except they were stuffed with a great many more of what Kitty called 'the things' – china, glass, silver, clocks, curios and so on. There were lots of paintings, too: family portraits, which Kitty was very amusing about, landscapes and quite a lot of sailing boats. 'Peter's father was a keen sailor and he loved nautical pictures, so most of them were collected by him. Oh, look, here's Sir George Everest. I told you I'd show him to you. We keep him tucked away in this alcove because it really isn't a very good painting. It wasn't done from life, but from a photograph, some time after his death, which is probably why it looks so wooden.'

Sir George appeared to be a vigorous old gentleman with a huge beard and wild hair. Even Jenna, who had no expertise, could see that it wasn't a very good painting.

'Lovely frame, though,' Kitty said, touching it. 'Probably worth more than the picture. They were so terribly proud of him, you see, that they framed him with no expense spared. He used to hang in the hall in Peter's grandfather's time, but his father moved him in here so as not to frighten the visitors.'

Famous names popped up quite frequently. 'That's a sketch of Disraeli – he was a frequent house-guest. That pair of vases – ghastly aren't they? – were a gift from Prince Albert after the Great Exhibition. Sir Edward Everest was quite chummy with Albert and helped with the organization. Peter Scott did that painting of pheasants while he was staying here once. That cigarette box was a birthday present from Princess Margaret.'

Kitty's throwaway comments showed how used she was to living with history; yet Jenna felt that dispersing the collection would diminish it, and believed Kitty thought the same, though she would never make a fuss. She wasn't brought up that way.

In the dining room there was a long mahogany table round which Jenna counted twenty matching chairs, and there were more against the walls. 'It's George the Third,' Kitty said. 'Lovely piece, but impossibly large. The only people who buy these big tables now are corporations who want them for their boardrooms. And even then, most of them want new. It's been well used in its time. The Everests were always tremendous entertainers. Peter's father, between the wars and afterwards into the fifties, was always having house parties; and his grandfather was one of the Prince of Wales's set – he used to visit quite often. There are presents from him all over the house. He always made a point of leaving something.' She laid a loving hand on the end of the table. 'I feel I let it down rather. Haven't had a dinner party in years. It does reduce to quite a manageable size if you take the leaves out, but then you've the problem of what to do with them. And if you leave them out too long, the colour of the wood changes and they don't match any more. So I leave it be. I don't eat in here alone, of course.'

Beyond those two rooms was the library – 'Unusual to have it on the ground floor, but the first owner was an eccentric' – and the passage ended in a small, panelled door. 'That goes through into the cottage,' Kitty explained. 'Peter's grandfather had such huge shooting parties, he used to use the cottage as extra guest accommodation. But Bill Bennett lives there now, so it's locked. We both have a key in case of emergencies. You'll meet him later – he gardens for me in exchange for living in the cottage rent-free.'

On the other side of the passage were the kitchen and its attached sculleries, larders and storerooms, and the back lobby through which they had entered, which housed the stairs down into the cellars. The kitchen had been fitted out with modern units and slate work-surfaces, and there was a gas stove as well as an Aga, but there was also a massive old wooden dresser and an old-fashioned scrubbed wooden table in the middle of the stone-flagged floor. It was all spotless, and a rinsed-out dishcloth hung neatly over the edge of the porcelain sink. Mrs Phillips had finished and gone. Jenna would have liked to investigate the complex of rooms and cupboards beyond it, but they didn't linger there. Kitty obviously had no attachment to kitchen regions.

The other two rooms on the ground floor were at the back. Of the sitting room Kitty said, 'This was the kitchen of the original house, but only until around 1820. I more or less live in here now. There's a gate-leg table I use to eat on in the winter, and in the summer I'm in the conservatory most of the time, when I'm not outdoors.'

The other room, which had floor-to-ceiling panelled cupboards built into the walls, was empty except for a large round table in the centre.

'We call this the housekeeper's room,' Kitty said, opening a door on the far side and revealing a staircase. 'You see, the backstairs come down here. The Everest who had the kitchen built was a bachelor until late in life, and his housekeeper had this room as her sitting room. The maids used to sit round that table and do their sewing in the evening, while she read to them from the Bible. Compulsory virtue. Fierce old thing, she was. There's a watercolour showing the scene upstairs – I'll show you when we get there.'

Jenna asked what was in the cupboards.

'Oh, just household china,' Kitty said. 'Dinners for twenty-plus take a lot of crockery. Shall we go upstairs?'

'Oh please,' Jenna said, 'can we go up the backstairs? I always wanted to live in a house with two staircases.'

Kitty laughed. 'It *is* rather thrilling. I always wished I'd lived here as a child. Peter said he and his brothers used to race round and round, up the backstairs and down the main stairs, until someone caught them and gave them a clump on the ear. And they used to slide down the backstairs on a tray when they could get away with it. Boys have all the fun.'

On the first floor there had been three bedrooms along the front of the house and three along the back. The middle one on the front had been turned into the two en-suite bathrooms for Jenna's room and that occupied by Kitty. On the back, the middle bedroom had been turned into a bathroom, a cavernous place with a bath big enough to drown in.

To one side of it was what Kitty introduced as Lady Mary's Bedroom. 'You have to give rooms names in a house like this, just as points of reference,' she said. 'But in fact there was a Lady Mary and she did sleep here. That's her portrait over there.'

The portrait showed a pale face and dark ringlets and what looked like muslin draped about the shoulders, with a background of parkland and trees. The room was furnished with the only four-poster in the house. A damask-upholstered chaise longue stood at the foot of the bed, and there was a Regency dressing-table with a delicate silver and crystal set, and a fine writing-bureau and chair in one corner, but the room was cluttered with more modern furniture and personal items.

'It's a pretty room,' Kitty said. 'Peter's grandmother had it, and a lot of the things are hers, but the nicer bits date from Lady Mary's day. The bed is earlier, of course, but we believe she did sleep in it. She was a niece of the Duke of Wellington, and married Sir Ralph Everest in about 1820. She came to a tragic end, poor thing, and her ghost is supposed to haunt the house. You don't mind ghosts, I hope?'

'I've never seen one,' Jenna said. 'Do you believe in them?'

'I've never seen Lady Mary,' Kitty said, quite matter-of-factly, as if she were discussing birdwatching, 'but I have seen the Weeping Child. She haunts the top floor — she never comes down here, so don't worry about her. She won't pop up in your bedroom. I don't know who she is, but practically every old house that's haunted at all has a weeping child. Children must have lived really quite dreadful lives in the old days for so many of them to come back.'

Jenna wasn't sure if she was being roasted, so she said nothing, only exclaimed instead over the massed blue-and-white china displayed on a series of stepped shelves over the fireplace.

'Lady Mary collected it, and Peter's grandmother added to it. It always looks nice, I think, when there's a lot of it all together.'

'It's gorgeous,' Jenna said. 'It's a shame more people can't see it.' A germ of an idea came to her, but slipped away before she could get hold of it.

The other bedrooms were minimally furnished with modern pieces, but they all had pictures and objets d'art relegated from the main rooms over the years. Jenna could have pored over them for hours, but Kitty didn't want to linger. The sun was shining and she seemed to feel it was her duty to get Jenna out into it.

But on the top floor, Jenna couldn't help exclaiming over a series of six handsome, glazed-fronted cabinets lining the wall of the corridor, because they were filled with undistinguished-looking, even quite ugly, lumps of rock that struck a chord with her.

'Oh, golly, look!' she said. 'Geological specimens! It makes me feel at home. My father had a collection just like this, only not so large. He was a palaeontologist.'

'Yes, I remember,' Kitty said. 'He was an academic when I knew him, but didn't he work for an oil company later?'

'That's right,' Jenna said. 'He was with BP. He had to study rocks to see where it was worthwhile drilling for oil – mostly in places like Mongolia and Kazakhstan. I think that's why Ma's so dedicated to the Mediterranean centres of civilization. She once went on one of Daddy's trips and never got over the shock.' She looked at the rocks fondly. 'She hated Daddy's specimens, but he did his best to get us interested in his subject. On wet Sundays when we were kids he tried to make us learn the periods off by heart – you know, Cambrian, Devonian, Cretaceous and the rest.'

'And did he succeed?'

'Not at all.' Jenna laughed. 'And we still thought they were just ugly old rocks. Who collected these?'

'Oh, one of the ancestors, in mid-Victorian times. Collections were all the rage at the time. There's a huge one of butterflies, all in glass cases, in one of the bedrooms – rather more decorative. And Peter's great-grandfather collected stuffed birds.'

'I did wonder,' said Jenna, who had noticed an unusual number of them in different rooms.

'I'm rather fond of them, but they upset some people. There's everything in this house, if you care to look for it. Well, I won't drag you round the other bedrooms. Shall we go out while the sun is still shining and look at the gardens? That's my real passion. I hate housework – you couldn't force a duster into my hand without a gun to my head – but I don't mind how long I toil in the garden and grub about in the soil. Somehow that never seems like work.'

'I saw the woodland garden yesterday – was that your idea?'

'Yes, pretty, isn't it? Nice on hot summer days, if any. How far did you go? Did you see the walled gardens?'

'No, I didn't get that far.'

'Oh *good*,' said Kitty with endearing enthusiasm. 'Then I can be the one to show them to you.'

Watch joined them as they left the house, and padded along with them companionably. 'Are you put off yet?' Kitty asked. 'Now you've seen how much there is to do?'

'Not at all,' Jenna said. 'I'm looking forward to it. I love poking about in antique shops, and this'll be like the most glorious antique hunt of my life. And for once no one will be hurrying me.'

'Who hurried you before?' Kitty asked.

'Oh, Patrick hated old things. If ever I so much as glanced at an antique shop in passing he'd go spare. He said the English worship of old things was mawkish and stifled innovation. He thought all old buildings should be torn down and all antiques should be burned to make way for the modern.'

'He sounds rather a challenging character,' Kitty said carefully.

Jenna looked rueful. 'And I was determined not to think of him.'

Just at that moment they stepped through the doorway into the walled garden, and Patrick was obliterated from her thoughts. It was impossible not to be impressed. It was planted with neat beds of growing vegetables, divided by gravel paths and edged with marigolds and herbs over which early butterflies flitted. On the far side was the impressive row of Victorian greenhouses, with their curly cast iron ridge decorations and pinnacles, and the other walls were covered with espaliered fruit trees.

A man in blue French railwayman's overalls was hoeing one of the beds, and looked up as they came in. Watch trotted towards him, wagging his whole back end in greeting, and the man put down his hoe on the path, patted the dog, and then straightened up, waiting with a smile for them to come to him.

He was about Kitty's age, Jenna thought, a well-built man of middle height, with a good head of hair, brown threaded with silver, and a weather-tanned face that had got so used to being handsome all its life that it was handsome still, and always would be. His eyes were blue and humorous, his smile was boyish and attractive. This, Jenna thought, must be the Bill Bennett who lived in the cottage through the door to which they both had a key. Her fertile imagination at once concocted a romance where one or other slipped through it at night to conduct a gentlemanly – but no less passionate for that – affair. The way they smiled at each other made her feel she had got it right, and she was happy for them, especially Kitty, to whom she had already grown attached. Why shouldn't they have romance? But why didn't they marry? Maybe like her mother they enjoyed the thrill of the clandestine.

Kitty did the introduction. 'This is Bill Bennett,' she said. 'Bill, this is Jenna Freemont.'

Bill inspected his hand, wiped it on his trousers, and offered it. It was warm and dry and hard as a plank. 'Delighted to meet you,' he said in an educated voice. 'How do you like Holtby House so far?'

'I love it. And the gardens are wonderful. Do you do all this?'

'The vegetables, yes,' he said. 'Kitty and I have this wonderful arrangement. I mow the grass and attend to the hedges for her, and in return she not only lets me live in the cottage for nothing, but allows me to take care of the kitchen garden for her.'

'Which is a tremendous amount of work,' Kitty chipped in, 'as you can see.'

'Not to me,' Bill said. 'This part is my hobby. I always wanted an allotment when I retired, and this is wealth beyond my wildest dreams.'

'He grows all the vegetables and fruit I can possibly eat,' Kitty said.

'And she lets me eat all I want and give the rest away to anyone I like,' Bill said. They were smiling, and outdoing each other in gratitude. 'After a lifetime toiling away in an office for the Ministry of Defence, here I am in my very own secret garden, in a state of permanent bliss, and she doesn't even let me pay her rent!'

'It's obviously a very good arrangement all round,' Jenna said, thinking how well they were suited.

Kitty's next words killed the dream. 'He hasn't even mentioned that his wife does all my cleaning for me.'

Emma Woodhouse, caught again, Jenna chided herself. Oh well!

'For which you pay her,' Bill was saying to Kitty sternly.

'But you know she does far more than I pay her for. Honestly,' she added to Jenna, 'these two completely spoil me. Bill's always on hand, not only for gardening but if there's a fuse or a dripping tap or I think someone's prowling round the grounds, and Fatty dusts and polishes and scrubs my floors as if she actually enjoys it.'

'She does,' Bill asserted. 'The two things in life Fatty loves are cleaning and cooking. She couldn't be happier.'

Jenna hardly knew how to ask what she wanted to. 'Um—?'

Bill grinned, knowing what was on her mind. 'It's short for Fatima.'

'She's Turkish,' Kitty said. 'Bill's first wife died tragically young—'

'—and after years as a widower I scandalized everyone by turning up with a wife who's not only twenty years younger than me, but a *foreigner* to boot.'

Kitty smiled. 'There *were* one or two comments at church after morning service.'

'I'll bet there were. I heard some near-unprintable ones down at The Crown,' Bill agreed. '*Exotic* was the politest. In fact, that wasn't far wrong. When I first met Fatty she was an exotic dancer at a club in Portsmouth.'

'He doesn't mean *stripping*,' Kitty explained. 'She was a belly dancer. It's very skilled when it's done right. Takes years of training.'

'It was love at first sight,' Bill said. 'I must be one of the few men in Britain today who actually *did* say to his future wife, "Let me take you away from all this."'

Kitty smiled at him fondly, and said, 'Well, we won't keep you from your work. I just want to show Jenna my flower garden.'

'Do. It's a work of art,' he told Jenna.

They left him, and Kitty led the way through another gateway at the far side and into a second walled garden of the same size and proportions as the first; but in this the beds were planted with such a glorious array of flowers and shrubs that there was no earth to be seen. On the walls climbed roses and clematis, just coming into bloom; everything else was a tapestry, beautifully designed to make the most of different heights, shapes and colours. Jenna felt she could never have enough of gazing.

'You do all this?' she exclaimed. 'It's wonderful!'

'You like it?' Kitty said, looking modest and pleased. 'I must say I'm rather pleased with it – though there are things I'd like to change. But one always feels that about one's garden. It wouldn't be the same without a project.'

'You ought to open it to the public,' Jenna said.

'We used to have an open day years ago, when Peter was alive,' Kitty said. 'Once a year, in the summer, when the village had its annual fête, we used to open the grounds and take a collection for Princess Alexandra's fund. We used to do quite well. Goodness, it all seems so long ago now.'

'Does the village still have a fête?' Jenna asked.

'No, sadly it lapsed. I wish someone would start it up again.' She looked round as someone came in through the doorway. 'Oh, here's Fatty.'

It was a plump, olive-skinned woman, with dark eyes and black curly hair and a look of contentment which gave her face beauty, though it was not strictly pretty. She was wearing a pale green cleaner's overall over her summer dress, but her legs and feet were bare, and she had silver rings on four of her toes, a nice mixture of the prosaic and the exotic.

'Visitor for you, Miss Kitty,' she said, in a soft and liquid accent.

'Fatty, dear, this is Jenna, who's come to help me with the cataloguing.'

'How do you do,' Jenna said, and the woman smiled shyly and ducked her head in greeting.

'Who's the visitor?' Kitty asked.

'Mr Alexander,' Fatty said, though as she pronounced it, it sounded like 'Sikander'.

'Oh, good,' said Kitty.

Fatty nodded, and then added, rather like someone slipping a dose of medicine into the honey, 'And Miss Caroline is with him.'

'Ah. Good,' said Kitty, but it sounded quite different from the first one.

Seven

'Nice wheels,' Jenna commented. A black drophead coupé with the roof down was parked on the gravel before the front door. Watch and Barney sniffed round it and then urinated lavishly on the rear tyres.

'Caroline's,' Kitty said briefly. 'Xander drives a Volvo estate – he needs it for his work.'

'What is his work?' Jenna asked, picking out one of the many questions she wanted to ask before they got inside.

'Oh, didn't I tell you? He has a shop in the village, selling antique and reproduction furniture, with a workshop behind it for repairs and restorations. He does all the big antique fairs and finds pieces on commission. He does some restoration work for the National Trust as well, so it all keeps him busy.' She seemed almost defensive about it, as if someone had questioned his choice of career. Jenna was piqued as to why. It seemed perfectly respectable to her.

'It sounds interesting,' she said encouragingly.

'Well, *I* think so,' Kitty said.

There was no time for more as they were entering the drawing room. The female half of the visiting pair was at the window with her back to them, and the male half was standing in front of the fireplace. Jenna stopped at the doorway in sheer surprise, for he was tall, dark and so absolutely gorgeous it was impossible for a moment to look anywhere else. A wave of pure pheromones seemed to come from him and set Jenna's receptors twitching. He was mid-thirties, his chiselled features were firm, his dark hair exquisitely cut and just wavy enough to be interesting, and his eyes, in exciting contrast, were swooning blue. He was wearing a very formal charcoal business suit, but his tie was well judged, modern without being too challenging.

He also looked cross, and in the split instant before anyone said anything, Jenna put that together with the woman's turned back and decided they had been quarrelling.

'Xander,' Kitty cried, and there was no doubting the pleasure and affection she invested in the word. She went to him and rose on tiptoes to kiss his cheek. His cross look disappeared into neutrality and he stooped to return the kiss.

'Hello, Kitty. We were just passing so I thought you wouldn't mind if we popped in.'

'It's lovely to see you any time, darling,' Kitty said. 'My godson Alexander Latham – Jenna Freemont.'

He looked down at Jenna with an arrested look, almost of surprise, in his face; sadly, she thought, it was a surprise that seemed to give no pleasure. She didn't know what there was to disapprove of in her appearance, but he seemed to find something. He recovered himself and smiled slightly as he said, 'How do you do,' but it was a professional smile with no warmth behind it. She adjusted her own to match and they shook hands. His was warm, firm and dry, and standing close to him there was something still very agreeable about the experience, despite the disapproval. She was confused.

An annoyed throat-clearing reminded them of the presence of the woman at the window, who had turned and was watching them. Alexander let go of Jenna's hand and said, 'And this is Caroline, Caroline Russell.'

She came forward to join them: tall, willowy, in a beige silk suit and cream blouse, pearls at ears and neck, perfectly enamelled make-up and corn-blonde hair in a bob with not a strand out of place despite the open car: she must have tidied up before she came in, or worn a scarf.

It was, Jenna saw with a sense of inevitability, the rider from the day before. Out of the corner of her mind she noticed that Watch, who had followed them in, went up to greet Alexander with lavish wagging and a few half hops, as if he wanted to rear up and plant his feet on the man's chest, but was too well bred to do so; but he didn't go on to greet the woman. In fact, having finished with Alexander he went out again without having so much as looked at her. Don't blame you, boyo, Jenna thought, and went to meet her fate.

'How do you do,' the woman said, extending her perfectly-manicured hand, while her hard grey eyes bored into Jenna and reduced her casual clothes, messy hair and lack of make-up to shreds. Suddenly Jenna felt underdressed for a walk in the garden.

'Caroline is Xander's fiancée,' Kitty added.

Another inevitability, Jenna thought, though still with a slight sinking of the heart. Not that she was interested, of course, but it was always a shame when a perfectly presentable man turned out to be taken – and by the wrong woman. 'We've met,' she said.

'Have you?' Kitty said, surprised.

'I wouldn't call it a meeting,' Caroline said in crisp tones and a cut-glass accent. Everything about her screamed County and Public School. 'There was no introduction. She was looking at me over your hedge into the lane, and failed to account for herself.'

Alexander seemed to think this was quite rude enough for starters, and stirred uncomfortably. 'Have you been showing her round, Kitty? I hope you showed her your lovely flower-garden,' he said. And to Jenna, 'What do you think of Holtby House so far?'

'It's lovely,' Jenna said. 'And full of such interesting things.' One more than there was this morning, in fact – but enough of that!

He nodded and then, his social duty done, turned his attention to Kitty. 'By the way, that planning appeal of old Benson's – it's to be on Tuesday the week after next.'

They plunged into conversation, leaving Jenna to the mercy of the ice queen, who looked down at her with the superior faint contempt of a cat and said, 'So, do you do a lot of this sort of thing?'

'What sort of thing would that be?' Jenna replied, trying to be polite for Kitty's sake.

'Cataloguing,' Caroline said shortly. 'I suppose you worked for an auction house before?'

'No, I was a features editor for a magazine.'

'Oh, really? And what did that involve?'

'Researching and writing articles on whatever subject was chosen for that week.'

Caroline looked artificially puzzled. 'So, in fact, you have no qualifications or experience for this job at all?'

What was the woman's problem? Did she think Jenna was in league with a gang of house-robbers? 'I believe I'm quite capable of doing what Kitty wants. Anyway, she thinks so, so that's all that matters, isn't it?' She thought that was direct enough a snub, but Caroline was made of sterner stuff.

'Perhaps that's all that matters to *you*, but not Kitty's *friends*, who care about her. One wouldn't want her to be – *disappointed*.'

The hesitation seemed meant to suggest the words 'taken for a ride' or 'robbed blind' had been considered and discarded only for the sake of politeness.

At that moment Fatty, who was a much slower walker, appeared in the doorway, with a questioning look towards Kitty, to see if anything was wanted. Kitty broke off her conversation with her godson to say, 'Oh, Fatty, dear, would you make some coffee?' And to her visitors, 'You'll have some coffee, won't you?'

Caroline said, 'I'm sure Jennifer will help – won't you, Jennifer? Why don't you go and help Fatima carry things in.'

Fatty had already disappeared and Kitty had gone back to her conversation with Alexander – nothing exercises country people more than planning applications – so the words, and the implied insult, were only for Jenna, who took them in the spirit intended.

'I'm sure Fatty can manage,' she said. 'And my name is Jenna. It isn't short for anything,' she explained kindly. 'Just J – E – N – N – A.'

'Is that a real name?' Caroline said with a slight curl of the lip. 'I've never heard of it before. It must be so uncomfortable to have a made-up name.'

Jenna gave her a smile of tooth-aching sweetness. 'Then you must be so relieved that Caroline is such a *common* name.'

So battle was declared.

★　　★　　★

That afternoon, Kitty said she had things to do, and suggested Jenna take a walk into the village to get her bearings.

'We'll start work tomorrow,' she promised, when Jenna protested that she wasn't earning her keep. 'I really can't concentrate today. I don't know if you heard Xander telling me, but there's a dreadful man called Benson who owns the piece of land opposite the end of my grounds. He's applied for planning permission to build ten holiday chalets, right between me and that lovely view of the hills – can you imagine? It's been turned down by the planning office, but he's appealed. And the thing is, he doesn't even want to build them himself – he wants to sell the land, but with planning permission it would be worth infinitely more. I suppose one can't blame him for trying to increase the value of his assets, but he knows everyone in the village is against it, and if he gets his way he'll use the money to retire to Spain, leaving us with the ghastly mess on our doorsteps. So annoying and unscrupulous of him. Go and have a nice walk, darling, while I do the rounds of my friends and rally the defences. We'll need a good turn out at the hearing.'

So Jenna changed her shoes and strolled down the gravel drive, turned Barney and Watch back at the gate and slipped through into a green lane which after a few yards developed houses first on one side and then on both, and then emerged on to the village on the opposite side of the green from the pub. The sunlight was streaming through the chestnuts, two elderly women were sitting on a bench feeding the pigeons, and two girls on glossy ponies were watering them at the horse-trough. It was an idyllic scene.

She examined the shops: a bakery and sandwich shop, a very upmarket deli, a butcher, the post office – which doubled as a hardware shop – and a newsagent-cum-sweetshop which had some aisles of general groceries. At the end of the green the road forked and there were more shops down one of branches. There was a second pub, she discovered, a rather plainer, darts-and-bitter effort called The Castle; *two* dress shops, displaying the sort of frightfully expensive and yet terminally ugly clothes in floral print that you could never imagine anyone buying; and The Castle Tea Rooms (morning coffee, light lunches, afternoon tea) with rather home-made looking cakes on the counter, and a ginger cat basking on the window sill. One medieval building was sliced into two down the middle to make a tiny wool shop with embroidery canvases in the window, and an equally tiny art gallery, displaying what were obviously a local artist's efforts at watercolours, and some blobby oils of holiday destinations with the paint put on in chunks and very indigo shadows under everything to make it look as if the sun was shining brightly. A sign in the window said PICTURE FRAMING and PASSPORT PHOTO-GRAPHS WHILE YOU WAIT.

There was just about everything you might want day to day, she thought, except for fresh fruit and veg, but she would bet twenty quid there was a farm shop somewhere nearby. She returned to the main drag alongside the village green to look at the shop she had really wanted to see. A large window had the sign above it, LATHAM FURNITURE, and in smaller, curly letters, on one side *ANTIQUES* and on the other *RESTORATIONS*. In the window was a wing-backed chair, a drum-table bearing a silver tray and a cut glass decanter, and a pair of Georgian wine-coolers. Peering in, she saw other furniture nicely displayed and well polished. The shop was on a corner, and looking down the side turning she could see the workshop behind it with a big gated yard opening on to the side street. A roller-back van was parked inside the yard, and there was a maroon Volvo at the kerb outside. So he was in there, she thought. She resisted the urge to go and see him at his work, hesitated a moment, and then decided to go and have a look at the church instead.

As she was about to cross the road, the roar of an approaching car made her stop and look around. It whizzed past her, making her jump back – though it wouldn't have touched her: a bright red, sporty little Mazda MX5 with the window down, and a glimpse of a young man inside. It performed a U-turn round the end of the green and came to a halt outside the pub, opposite where Jenna stood. The driver stuck his elbow on the window, leaned out and grinned at her.

'Hey, Red!' he called.

He looked to be late twenties, fair-haired, good-looking, in a dark blue shirt open at the neck, the sleeve rolled up to the elbow. His forearm was tanned, and decorated with a very nice-looking watch.

'Sorry I made you jump,' he called, with a mischievous grin.

'No, you're not,' she called back.

'Don't buy furniture in there,' he said, pointing at Latham's. 'You'll be robbed and cheated. Terrible crooks, they are.'

'I promise I won't,' she said.

He eyed her with interest. 'Fancy a drive? You're new round here, aren't you? I'll show you the countryside. Hop in.'

'With you? Dream on!'

He grinned, completely undiscouraged. 'It's a small place, y'know, Red. We're bound to meet again.'

'Then you've nothing to worry about,' she said. She waved goodbye with the tips of her fingers. 'Got to go.'

He waved and returned his hand to the wheel. 'See yah!' And drove away with a show-offy roar.

She grinned to herself, much refreshed by the exchange, and went on to look at the church, which she found, to her disappointment, was locked.

'Well, talk about trusting your fellow man,' she grumbled. She made do instead with walking on up the road until she had passed out of the village and into the country. A short way further on there was a large white gate with a sign on it saying HOME FARM and an A-board advertising PARKER'S FARM SHOP, listing underneath milk, eggs, fresh fruit and vegetables, local honey, and home-made preserves.

'I owe myself twenty quid,' she said aloud. 'Now, what shall I spend it on?'

Oliver rang that evening to find out how she was getting on.

'The place is amazing,' Jenna said. 'Just stuffed with brilliant things. Like the best-ever antique market. And Kitty's an absolute dear. She and I hit it off right away.'

'Michael said she was nice,' Oliver said. 'But are you comfortable?'

'Goodness, lap of luxury!'

'Sybil was afraid it would be all decaying gentry, damp sheets and no hot water, mouldy bread and mice in the kitchen.'

'I have a bedroom with en-suite bathroom straight out of the Hilton, only nicer, and Kitty has a lady to cook for her, who stuffs me with tremendous food.'

'Well, you have landed on your feet, then! I'll tell Syb – she was worried you'd fade away or go into a decline or something.'

'Has Patrick phoned?' Jenna asked wistfully, following the logic trail.

'Three times. I made Syb answer so that she could tell him with a clear conscience that you'd gone and she didn't know where. He didn't entirely believe her, which accounted for the second and third calls. I dare say he'll call again. Shall we keep on denying you? The cock crowed thrice this morning.'

'I still don't want to talk to him,' Jenna said, though even she heard the hint of wistfulness in her voice. She braced it to add, 'He probably only wants Charlotte's watch back. Well, he's not having it.'

'Why don't you switch on your mobile and tell him that yourself? You don't need to tell him where you are.'

'I told you, I don't want to talk to him.'

'But it's very inconvenient for the rest of us, not to mention your friends. Why don't you get one of those cheap pay-as-you-go jobs, and give everyone except Patrick the number.'

'I might do that,' Jenna said. 'At the moment, though, I'm going to be confined to the house most of the time. There's a huge amount to do.'

'Have you found out what it's all about?'

'Yes, and it's awfully sad. Kitty says she can't afford to live here any more, because of what it costs to maintain the house, so she's selling the contents in the hope of making enough to stay on a bit longer. She loves the house so much, she was hoping to stay here till she died.'

'Who does it go to after her? Her children? Can't they help?'

'She and Peter never had any children, his brothers are dead and his nephews are scattered to the four winds. The house isn't entailed. And anyway, no one else would want it.'

'I wouldn't bank on that. But you mean she hasn't got any family?'

'None at all. I think Ma is her nearest relly, in fact.'

'God help her then!' said Oliver, and she could imagine him rolling his eyes.

'She has a godson who lives locally, but he obviously hasn't offered to help her in any way or she'd have told me. He's a bit of a stuffed shirt, but she adores him.'

'What does he do?'

'Furniture restorer.'

'Oh. Tradesman, then?'

Jenna laughed. 'Is that why she sounded defensive? But he's terribly posh.'

'How posh? Trevor Howard or Leslie Phillips?'

'Trevor Howard, but taller. But he has this ghastly fiancée, Caroline, who's taken agin me for some reason. I met them today, and she was poisonously rude, in that icily correct way that you can't openly object to.'

'Oh, good. I'm glad she's a bitch.'

'How so?'

'Well, every Eden has to have a serpent. If you hadn't identified it, it would mean it was still out there somewhere. You might have stepped on it at any moment. This way, you know where it is and you can avoid it.'

'You're such a comfort to me,' Jenna said, suddenly missing him. She was getting really into Holtby House and Kitty's problems, but home was home all the same, and there was no one like Olly.

'No mush, old thing. Anyway, it's obvious what you must do.'

'It is?'

'Yes, you must find a way for Kitty to stay on without selling everything.'

'It really would be a shame if she had to, because all the stuff is packed with history and it belongs here. But it'd be even worse if she had to leave the house. But what can I do?'

'Think of a way she can make money out of the house, enough to keep it going. Make an income from it. There must be loads of things you can do with a big house. Michael says it's like a mini-stately?'

'Kind of like that, only messier.'

'Well, then. Thinking cap on, darling. And I'll brainstorm with Syb, and maybe get the others in on it. It's just the sort of problem the family will like. I'll let you know if we come up with anything. Or they'll let you know themselves.'

She imagined the family ringing her up with their usual useful contributions. 'I'm sure they will.'

'Between us we ought to be able to bust it,' Oliver said breezily.

'Meanwhile, nil desperandum. Chin up, best foot forward and so on. Faint heart never won fair hearing. And watch out for the snakes.'

Later that evening, Kitty came back into the sitting room, where they had retired as darkness fell, from making a phone call out in the hall. She looked a little pink in the face, and her eyes were bright.

'I've had an idea – in fact, it's more than an idea, because I've already begun to work on it, so I hope you don't mind. I'm going to have a dinner party on Saturday.'

'How lovely,' Jenna said.

'Do you think so? I'm so glad. Looking at the dining room this morning and thinking how long it is since I used the table made me feel guilty, so I thought, why not have a dinner party in your honour, to introduce you to the neighbourhood?'

Jenna felt embarrassed. 'Really, there's no need—' she began.

'Oh, but I want to,' Kitty said. 'And you just said it would be lovely. It won't be _terribly_ formal, because no one does formal any more, but it will be fun. It's really just an excuse to entertain again, like the old days. You will help me, won't you? I can't do it without you.'

'Of course I'll help – anything you like. Though I'm not brilliant at cooking. But I can boil water without burning it.'

Kitty laughed. 'Oh, my dear, Mrs Phillips will do the cooking. She'd never let anyone else use her kitchen. And Fatty will serve, and Bill will see to drinks. But I need you to help me greet people and chat to them. I'm not very good at circulating. Peter used to do all that. I tend to get buttonholed by someone who won't stop talking, and I can't seem to find a polite way to get away, which means the other guests are neglected. But I just know you'll be brilliant at it.'

'I don't know about brilliant, but I'll do my best.'

'Any daughter of Annabel's is bound to be good in company. Now, we'll have Xander and Caroline, of course, and I thought I'd ask Harry for you – Caroline's brother. He's about your age.'

Jenna imagined what a brother of the Ice Queen would be like and said, 'Oh, that's not necessary—'

But Kitty was firm. 'It's nicer if the numbers are even. I thought

I'd ask four other couples, so we'd be fourteen in all, not too many, but enough for variety. Oh, I'm quite excited about it – I'm so glad you came and gave me the excuse! We'll have to plan a menu. Of course, whatever we choose, Mrs Phillips will want to do something different, but she likes to make believe she just cooks what she's asked to cook, so we go through the motions. Are you good with wine? That's one area she won't argue about. I'll show you the wine cellars when the menu's set. Peter laid down a lot – he was the great wine buff. I just know what I like.'

'I haven't anything to wear,' Jenna said.

'It won't be terribly formal,' Kitty assured her.

But Jenna thought that if Caroline was coming, it wouldn't be the most relaxed occasion. 'I've only got cotton trousers and jeans and things,' she said. 'Nothing remotely suitable for dinner.'

'There are a couple of dress shops in the village,' Kitty offered helpfully.

'Yes, I saw them,' Jenna said. Well, the town was only five miles away. She'd have to manage a trip there some time before the fatal night.

It was only later, in bed, that she returned to Kitty's arithmetic and realized that 'fourteen' meant Kitty was going to invite someone 'for' herself. She was intrigued; but after the Bill Bennett debacle, she refused to allow herself to speculate in Emma Woodhouse style. She'd find out soon enough.

Eight

The next day, Jenna made a start. It was wonderful to wake up in that lovely room, to get up in her own time, to dress how she liked and go down to a grand breakfast that she hadn't had to get for herself. No dashing out of the house, through the din of rush-hour traffic, cramming herself into a train and strap-hanging into the crowded, stifling city. She had felt part of an elite when she commuted; now, breakfasting on the terrace with nothing but birdsong in her ears, and with only a few steps to take to her place of work, she wondered how she had ever stood it.

Kitty left her at the big table in the library, where the computer also lived, with a heap of books, photo albums, journals, diaries and other papers, to start making out a simple timeline on the house, to be filled in later with the most interesting details. It was tremendously absorbing, and she hadn't even got beyond the building of the house (there were original letters between the owner and the builder, early sketches and plans, and invoices for materials and labour that gave a wonderful insight into what people earned and how hard it was to transport goods in those horse-drawn days) when Fatty, who was cleaning that morning, stuck her head round the door to say she was making coffee and did Jenna want a cup.

When she brought the coffee she said, 'You should go outside for a bit, while the sun shine. Too nice to be indoor.' And when Jenna hesitated, she added, as if it were her primary concern, 'While you out I dust library.'

So Jenna drank her coffee (Fatty's was even better than Mrs Phillips's) and went out through the open front door. The dogs were hanging around looking bored, and were only too glad to accompany her. She went to the first walled garden, wanting another look at the fabulously ordered vegetables and perhaps a poke around in those marvellous old greenhouses, and found Bill Bennett there, tying in his espaliered fruit trees.

'Hello,' he said, instantly putting down his twine and scissors, evidently ready for a chat. 'How are you getting on?'

'Very badly,' Jenna said. 'I've only done a couple of hours work, and here I am skiving off again.'

'You'll work better for a breath of fresh air,' he said comfortably.

'Fatty said she wanted to dust the library. I don't know how long that gives me.'

'As long as you like,' he said, laughing. 'She just wanted to get you out of doors. She thinks you're too pale.'

'But I'm not supposed to be here for a rest cure,' Jenna said.

'I thought that was exactly what you were here for. But don't worry – you'll get the work done. Every job has its rhythm. Once you find it, it'll romp away.'

It was a nice philosophy, which office life in the great metropolis had entirely failed to mention to her. 'What are these?' she asked of his trees, taking a reciprocal interest.

'Plums,' he said. 'This one is Czar. He's an old variety, good for pollinating others. I grow him among the greengages. Plums and gages can be tricky if they're not self-fertile, like Blue-tit over there, or good old Victoria. They only have a window of about ten days when they can be pollinated, and if they don't get fertilized in that time, that's it.'

'I know how they feel,' Jenna said.

He looked amused. 'But you're so young!'

'Maybe, but you've got to meet a man first, which is hard enough, then go on dates, get to know him, build a relationship and wait for him to ask you to marry him, and all that takes years. It took me four years to get to where I was with Patrick, and now I've got to start all over again from scratch. Not even a suitable man on the horizon, and the biological clock ticking away like a metronome on speed. I'd sooner be a plum any day! I wish I was self-fertile.'

'Oh, poor girl!' He laughed, but kindly. 'Don't despair. The thing about life is that everything can change in an instant.'

'I know that. A couple of weeks ago I thought I was sitting pretty.'

'Yes, but it can change for the better just as quickly. I thought my love life was over when Gill, my first wife, died. I thought no woman would ever look at me again. And then I went with a friend — just to please him — into the last place I would ever think of looking for a bride, and met Fatty. Six weeks later we were married.'

'Really? Six weeks?'

'Well, it was dark in that club, so she probably didn't realize what I looked like,' he said. 'And by the time she saw me in daylight, she was too kind-hearted to say she'd made a mistake.'

Now Jenna laughed. 'You don't fool me! You're bloody good-looking and I bet you've had women falling over you all your life. I even thought—' She caught herself up and blushed to her hair roots.

He eyed her knowingly. 'Thought what?'

'Nothing,' she said. 'Golly, look at the size of that bumblebee.'

'Come on, what did you think?' he insisted. 'That Kitty and I had something going?'

She yielded. 'Well, I didn't know you were married. She showed me the door to your house and said you both had a key.' He was laughing again. 'Listen, it was just because I like her so much and I wanted her to have a love interest, that's all.'

'She does have one, don't worry. It just isn't me.'

Jenna seized the moment. 'I *did* wonder, because when we were talking about the dinner party she said it was nicer if the numbers were even so I thought she *must* have invited someone for herself. But she didn't say who it was, so it's a mystery.'

'Not to me,' Bill said. 'Though she does try to keep it quiet, so don't talk about it to anyone else, will you? Here, catch hold of that twine for me, and I'll tell you about him while I work.'

Jenna picked up the ball of twine and handed it to him. 'Fire away.'

'His name's Jim Lancaster. He was a sea officer, and he lives in Barford, the next village, in a house called Barford Lodge. If you go out from here towards Belminster, you'll see it on the right-hand side as you go through Barford. He's a really nice chap, retired from the Navy now, of course, but he does a bit of consultancy work for the Admiralty now and then, which gives him trips up to town, all expenses paid. He makes ships in bottles for a hobby, and tends his garden. He's got a nice garden at the Lodge – only about half an acre, but he's crammed a lot in. Mad about it. He and Kitty can talk gardening for hours together.'

'I was wondering when you'd get on to Kitty. If he's so nice and wonderful and comfortably off, what's the problem? Why does she have to keep him a secret?'

'Well, it's not a secret that they're friends, of course,' Bill said, 'but they don't want it known that it's more than that, because there'd be a scandal. He's married, you see.'

Jenna's heart sank. 'Oh no! Poor Kitty!'

'Wait, it isn't what you think. His wife, Rose, has Alzheimer's disease, poor thing. She's in a home, in Belminster. Been there, oh, six years now. She doesn't remember anything or know anyone. She hasn't a clue who Jim is when he goes and visits her.'

'How sad. But can't he divorce her?'

'He's too nice. He thinks it would be letting her down.'

'If she doesn't know him, how would it hurt her? He could still go and visit her.'

Bill shook his head. 'I know, but he still won't do it. Besides, the County would never forgive him. They'd think it was too tacky by half. Especially if he did it to hook up with another woman. Poor Kitty would cop it worse than him if he went that route.'

'Surely not?'

Bill grimaced. 'You don't know country communities. She'd be labelled the scarlet woman who dragged a good man from the paths of rectitude, and betrayed a helpless invalid in the process. She'd be ostracized. They both would, but she'd be the one who was blamed. It doesn't help that Jim has a daughter. Erica. She's grown up, of course, and married, with children of her own, but she's still a daddy's girl, and jealous of any other female. She looks pretty sharply at his friends to make sure no one's going to take her mother's place.'

'Ridiculous! How old is she?'

'Oh, forty-ish, I suppose. One of those big-boned, lanky girls who was never popular at school. I suppose she was sort of in love with her father when he was a glamorous sea-captain, coming and going, and never grew out of it. She'd kick up a stink if he ever hinted at divorcing her mother or bringing a new woman into the house. So Kitty and Jim keep it quiet. Just good friends, who only meet at church, and village do's, and other people's dinner parties – all above board.'

Jenna frowned. 'Then how do you know there *is* anything else?'

'I saw them together one day in London. Jim had gone up on one of his consultancy things, and Kitty officially went up to stay with an old school-friend. Unofficially, of course, they were having a dirty weekend – except that it was midweek. Well, seeing the cat was out of the bag, Kitty confided in me, and told me all. They meet up in town a few times a year, and manage on away-days otherwise, and simply hope not to get spotted. And try not to hope that poor Rose dies – though who could blame them if they did? But Alzheimer's victims seem to live for ever, and Rose is only the same age as Kitty.'

'Oh, poor Kitty! What a tragedy,' Jenna cried, really distressed. Then she thought of something. 'But should you have told me, if it was a secret?'

'Oh, don't worry, I haven't betrayed anything. The other way they meet is for him to slip over here now and then under cover of darkness, so Kitty told me she was going to tell you, because you'd be bound to find out anyway. She was agonizing over how to spill it to you – worried you'd disapprove, you see – so she'll be relieved I've done the job for her. Don't worry, I know Kitty very well.' He smiled. 'In fact, if it weren't for Fatty, I could have given the Admiral a run for his money. In another life. I'm very fond of her.'

'I'm glad. So am I.'

'I'll tell her I've told you, so don't worry about it. Just don't say anything to anyone else.'

'Of course I won't. And I suppose I'd better get back to work now.'

'If you insist. What are you working on?'

'History of the house.'

'Oh, that'll take you a while! A lot went on in this place. A lot of famous people came here, one way and another – as you can tell from the artefacts around the house. Have you come across Churchill's inkstand? That's in the library somewhere.'

'Churchill came here?' Jenna exclaimed.

'Oh yes. You obviously haven't got up to the Second World War yet.'

'I haven't even left the eighteenth century. What happened in the Second World War?'

'Holtby House was a spy school,' Bill said, with a tight, teasing smile. 'But I won't spoil it for you.'

'Oh, no, of course I don't mind Bill telling you. I was going to myself this evening. I should have said something last night when we were talking about the party, but I – well, chickened out.' Kitty looked up at her appealingly. 'I was afraid you'd think badly of me.'

'Of course I don't!' Jenna exclaimed. 'It's perfectly understandable, just very sad for both of you.'

'We ought to have waited,' Kitty went on sadly, 'but there's no hope that poor Rose will ever recover, and at our time of life, one feels the need to seize happiness. I know that's wrong—'

'I don't think there's anyone who would condemn you for that,' Jenna said.

Kitty laughed, breaking the mood. 'Oh my dear, you clearly don't know country people!' she said, echoing Bill. 'Condemning others is exactly what they like best. What else is there to do, after all? It isn't like London, you know. Country life, especially village life, is one long soap opera. Well, now you know about Jim, I can feel more comfortable – oh, except, you won't mention anything to Mrs Phillips? Fatty knows, of course, but Mrs Phillips only knows Jim and I are friends. She wouldn't approve of anything else. She's Nonconformist. They're terribly strict.'

'I shan't say a word.'

'How did you get on today?'

'I found I was reading everything in too much detail for a first pass,' Jenna said. 'It was all so interesting. So I made myself skip on a bit, and I've got up to Disraeli.'

'Oh yes. He came here quite often. He gave the Lady Everest of the time a book of poetry, inscribed and dated. It's in the library somewhere.'

'I'd like to see it,' Jenna said.

'I'll find it for you later. Now –' Kitty sighed – 'if it had been a first edition of one of his *own* books, it might have been worth something. But it's just a collection of English poetry. He was a tremendous gallant, so even the romantic inscription doesn't mean much. There must be thousands of them all over the country.'

'One thing puzzled me,' Jenna said. 'There was a reference in one of the journals to the Centurion's Grave. Did they find Roman remains here at some point? I know they've dug up some mosaic floors and so on in the area. And isn't there a Roman villa at Belminster?'

'Yes, they've got footings, a hypocaust and part of a bath house, and a rather lovely bird mosaic. But we don't have any Roman remains here,' said Kitty. Her eyes were dancing. 'I'm afraid you misread it. It's not *the* Centurion's Grave or even *a* Centurion's Grave. Centurion was a horse. Have you noticed that rather ghastly ink-pot made out of a hoof on the table in the sitting room?'

'Yes – I did think it was a bit gruesome,' Jenna said.

'It wasn't meant to be at the time. Sir Edward Everest was in the Tenth Hussars during the Crimean War. That's his portrait in the library, in the left-hand alcove, in the blue coat. He took part in the Charge of the Light Brigade – one of Lord Cardigan's staff. He was wounded in the thigh but his horse, Centurion, carried him safely back.'

'Don't tell me! Centurion was killed?'

'No, no, they both survived. They fought the rest of the war together, then Sir Edward brought Centurion back here and retired him in a field down by the river. Holtby had a lot more land then – it was all sold off between the wars. Sir Edward was devoted to the horse, and went down to visit him most days. Centurion lived to be thirty, which is a good age for a horse, as you know. After he died, Sir Edward had one of his hooves made into an inkstand – which he used every day until *he* died – and he buried the old boy in the garden. The grave is down in that rough area between the woodland and the bottom hedge – what we call the wilderness. There's a cairn over the grave and a folly next to it. You evidently didn't get that far when you were exploring.'

'It looks a bit overgrown, and I haven't been in bushwhacking mode,' Jenna confessed.

'Well, you must go and see. The inscription on the cairn is very touching. It always makes me cry. And the folly's most entertaining. If you didn't know, you'd think it was a medieval ruin. They knew how to build in those days.'

'I'm beginning to feel that nothing in this place is what it seems,' Jenna said.

'Oh dear, don't say so. Are we disappointing you?'

'No, just the opposite. It's all very stimulating. I can't wait to find the secret passage behind the panelling that leads to the ruined abbey. And to have the ancient treasure map fall out of an old book.'

'And meet the mysterious stranger who takes such an interest in Uncle Quentin's work? Or didn't you read the Famous Five when you were a girl?'

'Couldn't get enough of them.'

'Well, then perhaps you'll come with me to interview Mrs Phillips about the dinner, and then she'll give us a magnificent tea with lashings of ginger beer.'

Jenna laughed. 'Whatever you say.'

*　　*　　*

The following afternoon, having done a good bit of work to appease her conscience, Jenna drove, with Kitty's blessing, into Belminster to buy a dress. 'You should have a look at it anyway, while you're here. It's an interesting town,' she had said.

The road from Holtby ran north and slightly west through Barford (she slowed for a look at Barford Lodge as she passed – Victorian Tudoresque with maroon paintwork) and Chidding, and ran into the southerly outskirts of Belminster through wide avenues of detached Edwardian houses with large gardens. Then there were narrower streets of Victorian brick terraces and little corner shops. Before the inevitable one-way system, Jenna followed signs for a car park, which shunted her westwards towards the railway station, where she dumped Florence in a pay-and-display, and walked down Station Road and through Horsefair into the town centre.

Belminster was an old market town, and the centre was quite grand, with the wide-open Market Square surrounded by tall, handsome stone buildings. On one side there was a solid-looking hotel, the Red Lion, with stone pillars and a porch, and there was a town hall at one end of the square and a church at the other. The side streets were a mixture of medieval frontages and later stone and brick buildings, and there was every kind of shop and service you could need, restaurants, coffee shops and more pubs. She learned from notices that there was still a market in the square on Fridays and Saturdays. There was also a cattle market on the first Thursday of every month, but the cattle market was a separate place, down near the station. The place was obviously very much alive, and most of the people she saw walking about looked busy and prosperous.

She enjoyed wandering up one street and down another, looking at the shops and the architecture, discovering where the library was, deciding she liked the look of The Bell, a small pub housed in a beamed and crooked building with pretty hanging baskets, and noting which dress shops to investigate. She found herself back in Market Square, and suddenly noticed a red Mazda sports car parked at the kerb a little further along. Of course, there must be plenty of them around, but it struck her as a coincidence, so she turned her steps in idle curiosity towards it.

It was parked outside one of the tall, handsome houses with

stone steps up to a huge front door under a pillared portico. All
these converted houses had plates beside the door with the names
of the businesses now occupying them, many of them solicitors,
but with accountants, PR firms and even dentists among them.
This door, which was standing open, had only one plate, and she
had only just had time to read the name *Beale Cartwright* – which
she assumed was a firm of solicitors – when someone came out
of the door and was running down the steps.

He jumped the last three to land in front of her with a delighted
grin. 'Hey, Red!' he said. 'I told you we'd meet again. What are
you doing here?'

'Shopping. What are *you* doing here?'

'I live here,' he said. He was smiling down at her with what
looked like genuine pleasure in the meeting, which warmed
her heart considerably. Perhaps Patrick was not the only man
in the world who would ever find her attractive. 'I've got a
flat in St George's.'

'What's St George's?' she asked.

'You *are* new to town,' he said. 'It's a development, a bunch
of old warehouses down by the river that've been converted into
flats. It's the swishest place to live in Belminster, and I was trying
to impress you.'

'Sorry. Shall we do it again?'

'Too late now,' he said, with a comical pout. 'I'll have to try
something else. I'll ask you to dinner and take you to the smartest,
cleverest, coolest restaurant in the county.'

'Which is?'

'Mazo's. It's so fashionable it hurts. It's so rocking you'll get
seasick. It's so hip it can't see over its own pelvis. Listen, it does
Congolese food!'

'Congolese? Why?'

'Why not?'

'I don't know what Congolese food is.'

He grinned. 'Nor does anyone. That's the beauty of it. It's
new. It's so new it makes a day-old chick look like Michael
Parkinson. Don't you want to be at the cutting edge of the trend?'

'It's my life's ambition,' she said solemnly.

'Then hitch a ride with me, babe, and I'll take you to the
stars. OK, Red, when's good for you?'

She laughed. 'Boy, you've got enough brass to start a foundry!'

'You don't get anything by not asking. Tonight?'

'I can't.'

'Tomorrow night?'

'Look—'

'Don't tell me – all booked up until the Second Coming?'

'I'm very busy at the moment.'

'Next week?'

'Why do you *want* to go out with me?' she asked suddenly, intrigued.

'You laugh in the right places. Some people – you may have difficulty believing this – some people don't find me funny at all. Shocking, isn't it? So, dinner next week? How about Thursday?'

'Look, I genuinely don't know how I'm fixed at the moment,' Jenna said. She wasn't sure how being a live-in affected her dating rights. Kitty obviously liked her company in the evening. She needed to settle in before she could find out what the unwritten rules were. 'Give me your number, and I'll ring you.'

He shoved a hand into his pocket and pulled out a bill of some sort, scribbled a number on the edge of it, tore off the strip, and handed it to her. 'Don't lose it,' he said.

'Why so nervous? You said it was a small place. You'd find me again.'

'True,' he said. 'But call me, all the same.' He gave her a farewell grin, jumped into the red car, and buzzed off, leaving Jenna feeling stimulated by the exchange. She put the scrap of paper into her purse for safe keeping, thinking that she really wouldn't mind a date with him next week, as long as Kitty didn't mind. Meanwhile, there was the agreeable business of buying a dress ahead of her. She headed down the Market Square towards Church Street where she had noted a couple of likely shops.

Nine

Jenna was up early on Saturday morning, ready to help out in any way she could. When she got downstairs, Fatty was already busy in the dining room. Jenna popped her head round the door to say good morning and found her preparing to polish the great table. 'Quite a job,' she commented.

Fatty smiled, her sleeves rolled up to the elbows, revealing her strong forearms. 'Nice job,' she said. 'Nice to see old table shining. Nice to have lots of people come. I like very much parties.'

Jenna left her to it. Breakfast was laid outside on the terrace. It was cooler this morning and the sunshine was hazy.

'Weather's changing,' said Bill, arriving with a huge basket of vegetables pulled from his garden for the occasion. 'We'll have rain tomorrow. There's everything here but the asparagus,' he told Kitty, resting the edge of the basket a moment on the corner of the table. 'I'll cut that later. If you need any help with the flowers, let me know.'

'Thanks, Bill.'

He heaved the basket back on to his arm and went along the terrace towards the back door.

'You must tell me what I can do to help,' Jenna said, sitting down to scrambled eggs and sausages. They were being kept hot in a chafing dish for self-service – Mrs Phillips was already busy on the dinner.

'Thank you, dear. There are one or two things,' said Kitty, poring over the list she had made in her methodical way. It was a revelation to Jenna, who had never thought of applying method when she entertained. She had placed her faith in Chaos Theory – that in dynamic states the final shape is predetermined. Of course, she had never given a formal, sit-down dinner for fourteen. And Kitty's plans had started developing even as she made them: now half a dozen people were coming for pre-dinner drinks (how did you get rid of them when it was time to eat, Jenna wondered) and they were being 'joined for coffee' after dinner by some neighbours. Altogether there was a lot of organization involved, which Kitty obviously relished, and a lot of work, with which she had expert help.

Thinking of the help, and watching Bill disappear into the kitchen lobby, Jenna said tentatively, 'It seems a shame that Bill and Fatty will have so much hard work and none of the pleasure.'

Kitty looked up. 'But they *will* have pleasure. Bill loves being butler and barman, and Fatty likes serving, and they both like seeing me surrounded by guests.' She gave Jenna a shrewd look. 'You mustn't think they ought to have been invited to dinner. I promise you, they'd absolutely hate to have to sit down with us. They'd refuse with all four feet. Did you think I was ashamed of them?'

Jenna blushed, her mind full of incoherent thoughts about servants and masters and social orders the modern world disapproved of. 'No, not that, of course, but—'

'They like to eat together in their own home. I've tried in the past to get them to join in, but they don't like it. Fatty's paralysingly shy, and while Bill is a good raconteur one to one, he clams up in company, and he's not happy if Fatty's uncomfortable, so there's no point in trying to force the issue for one's own selfish ends.'

Selfish? Jenna thought. That put it in a different light. She dipped a piece of sausage in mustard and said, 'I was being selfish – I hoped to get Bill next to me at the table. Now, what can I do to help? Do you think Mrs Phillips would like me to peel the potatoes? I can't believe any cook enjoys that, however autocratic they are.'

Kitty laughed. 'We'll ask her later. But first, after breakfast, I'd be grateful if you'd drive down to Parker's for the duck's eggs – you know, the farm shop just outside the village? They've put them aside for us. Mrs Phillips won't rest until she knows they're safely in the house. And then I'd like your help getting the glasses up from the cellar and washing them. And there'll be the flowers to do. I'd appreciate your help with that.'

'I'll be happy to do anything you want. But didn't Bill offer to help with the flowers? I wouldn't like to tread on his toes,' Jenna said, with her new sensitivity. Having domestic help seemed like a minefield.

'He meant he'd help me carry them,' Kitty said with a smile, 'not choose and arrange them. We'll have to get the extra vases up too. I'm afraid they'll be dusty. I hope you have some old clothes you can put on.'

'I don't own anything that dirt can harm,' Jenna assured her.

It was a nice, busy, useful day. Jenna drove out to Parker's, where a smart middle-aged woman, with an all-weather complexion and scarlet lipstick, pounced on her. 'You're Kitty Everest's new help, aren't you?' She had two jolly little Border terriers, who dashed up to greet Jenna, dancing on their hind legs. 'That one's Lucy, and that one's Juicy. He's Lucy's son. Starting to take an unfilial interest in her. We'll have to have him fixed. Shove them off if they're a nuisance. I've been hoping to meet you. Everyone's wild to get a squint at you, you know. How long are you staying? You've done some good already – Kitty hasn't given a party for I don't know how long. I heard that Bill said you've really perked her up. You'll be popular in the neighbourhood if you can persuade her to start entertaining again, like the old days. A village needs the Big House to put out, or there's a hole in the middle of it. The summer fête, for instance – everyone would like to have it start up again. And there always used to be a lawn meet at Holtby House on Boxing Day. Highlight of the year, that was. Do you hunt?'

Jenna answered as best she could, collected a dozen and a half duck eggs and two pints of cream and took them home. Mrs Phillips received them gratefully at the kitchen door, beyond which Jenna could see every surface covered with the preliminary labours for the dinner. She graciously agreed that Jenna could peel the potatoes, and set her up for the task in one of the sculleries, but she hovered and watched until Jenna had peeled and cut two to her satisfaction before she would leave her alone with the job.

With Kitty she hauled up boxes of glasses, and they set up in the larger scullery, with Jenna washing and Kitty rinsing and drying. There was a spectacular number of them: champagne glasses, red wine, white wine, water tumblers, whisky glasses, brandy glasses, liqueur glasses. They were all loaded on trays and had to be carried out to a big stone room which Kitty said had been the game larder, and which would act as the butler's pantry for the evening. It contained a large refrigerator which Kitty said was 'the spare' and was only used when they entertained. She had switched it on rather anxiously that morning, hoping it would still work. 'It's one thing I didn't have on my list, to check the fridge,' she confessed. 'We'll never have room for the champagne and everything if it doesn't.' But fortunately, though it rattled and vibrated alarmingly at first, it settled down to a steady chug, and when they carried in the last glasses, Kitty checked it again and it was down to temperature. 'I'll tell Bill – he'd better get the champagne in now or it won't chill enough.'

They left Bill hauling up bottles, and went down together to the walled garden to cut flowers. Jenna had not understood why Bill had offered to help carry them. How much help was needed for a couple of posies? But Kitty's flowers, she discovered, were on a very different scale. The drawing room and the dining room would be decorated, plus a big arrangement in the hall, and three low ones on the dining table. By the time they'd brought back what Kitty wanted, it was time to snatch a quick lunch – cheese and crackers, since the kitchen was otherwise occupied. After lunch they did the flowers and laid the table, moved the furniture around in the drawing room and introduced some extra little tables from elsewhere in the house for people's drinks, and then it was time to go upstairs for a bath, and to change for the evening.

Jenna was quite tired after the day's activity, and was looking forward to the evening with mixed feelings. On the one hand, she was a social soul, and it was her first party for ages; and every girl liked dressing up and putting on her warpaint. It was exciting to be going to a dinner party which promised to be unlike anything she had attended before, and she could be sure the food and drink would be good. On the other hand, she was going to have to be presented to a lot of strangers, probably all much older than her, who might very well be achingly dull; and the highlight of the evening was going to be another meeting with the Ice Queen, with lots more opportunities to be insulted, snubbed and generally looked down upon. Oh yes, and the Ice Queen was bound to have given her ghastly brother a poisoned report of her, so he was going to be furious that he'd been asked 'for' her and would spend the evening making her uncomfortable. Yippee!

She had been in a quandary when choosing a dress, having no idea what everyone else would be wearing. She didn't even know whether the women would be in 'short' or 'long'. Kitty had said it wouldn't be very formal, but she had no idea what Kitty's baseline was, so 'not very' wasn't much help. In the end she had decided to look for calf-length, which would pinch-hit either way, and for something reasonably plain, feeling that being overdressed would be much more embarrassing than being underdressed.

She had found a dress the right length with a full skirt and a fitted bodice, which the shop had in black, blue and cyclamen pink. Hair the colour of hers had to be catered to: since you couldn't disguise it or tone it down, you had to make a feature of it. The blue she discarded at once. Some shades of blue just made her look washed out. The black was superb, and her hair showed up wonderfully against it. She had thought the cyclamen wouldn't work, but when she put it on, it was amazing. The colour didn't clash with her hair; it was a statement in itself. She hesitated a long time between the two. The black was the safe choice: nobody could criticize black. On the other hand, she would knock the Ice Queen's eye out in the cyclamen. If she was going to be sneered at, she might as well go down with her colours flying.

In the end, she'd chosen the cyclamen just because she loved it so much. She wasn't going to be at Holtby House for ever, so she might as well have something she was going to want to wear again back in the real world. When she put it on in her bedroom, however, she felt a qualm. It was very eye-catching, and with her hair brushed out into a red-gold cloud it was even more so. Not only that, it was much lower cut than she had realized in the shop. With the proper bra on, it pushed up her bust into quite an interesting display – not vulgar, by any means, but – well, let's say you could tell she wasn't on her way to Sainsbury's to do the shopping. *Hello, boys!*

She looked at herself in the mirror for a moment, liking what she saw, but wondering how it would go down with Holtby's elite. But then she thought, what the hay, it *was* a dinner party.

If they couldn't cope with a bit of décolletage, to hell with them. She caught up the sides of her hair with glittery clips so that it rampaged down the back, put on plain gold earrings and a thin gold chain round her neck. She inspected her make-up (not the full warpaint – after all, she wasn't going on the pull, given that the only two unmarried males were going to be the Ice Queen's snotty fiancé and her probably even snottier brother – but enough for her self-respect, and to balance out the dress) and went downstairs.

'You look wonderful,' Kitty said. 'Quite dazzling.'

Kitty was wearing a skirt and matching top in dark-blue silk crêpe figured with grey – elegant but not very exciting. Jenna was relieved to see it was the same length as hers – so that was one less thing to worry about – but beside her she looked like a petunia in an onion patch. 'You don't think I'm too garish?' she said doubtfully.

'Not at all. You'll perk us all up,' Kitty said, which Jenna didn't find entirely comforting. 'And you got it in Belminster? I had no idea you could get anything so pretty there.'

'It was a branch of Hobbs, in Mill Street. I know them from London, so I thought they might have something. The shops in Belminster are very good, aren't they?'

'I can't say I've had much call to notice lately,' said Kitty. 'But perhaps your coming will shake me out of my rut. I ought to have a new wardrobe. I can't even remember how old this thing is. I simply haven't thought about clothes since Peter died – isn't that dreadful of me? But you know how one invitation always sparks off another. Perhaps this is the beginning of a whole new social life.' She didn't sound unhappy at the prospect. 'Is that a car?'

There was the sound of wheels approaching over the gravel, as the first guests arrived, and the evening began. There was an influx of people, cheerful greeting, introductions, and Bill popped up like a genie with glasses of champagne on a tray. She caught his eye as he withdrew, and he winked at her, which warmed her. The arrivals were the pre-dinner-drinks crowd, late-middle-aged and elderly local people, solid, respectable and wealthy, and their interests were County and political. They were soberly and plainly dressed, the men in suits and the women in ordinary-length dresses that might have been Marks and Spencer had they not been obviously more expensive. Jenna felt out of place, but comforted herself that they were not, of course, dressed for a dinner party. They spoke kindly to her, but it seemed an effort, since she did not share any of their interests, and they soon slipped with relief back to talking to Kitty and each other. Jenna smiled and drank more champagne. At least this bit wouldn't last long.

Before they left, the dinner guests started arriving, so there was an overlap. The first in was the woman from Parker's Farm, in ankle-length floral, full warpaint and the sort of chunky costume jewellery that Jenna had seen in department stores. She'd always wondered who bought it. When introduced to Jenna ('Madeleine Enderby – she and Simon have Home Farm and keep the farm shop') she clamped a hard hand round Jenna's wrist and said, 'Oh, we're old friends! We had quite a chin at the shop this morning, so we're practically sisters now! But you haven't met the Hub – Simon, this is Jenna that I was telling you about.'

He was a red-faced, well-fleshed, genial man, evidently pleased with life and proud of his wife. They called each other Mad and Si, and occasionally Hub and Wifey. She did the talking, and he laughed at her jokes. They were refreshingly easy to get along with, especially Mad, since she was happy to talk without requiring answers.

Jenna drank more champagne, and when a pause for breath occurred she asked why the shop was called Parker's.

'Oh, the Parkers had Home Farm before us, and they started the farm shop back in – what was it, Si? Nineteen seventy-four?'

'Nineteen seventy-three – but they'd been at Home Farm for generations,' Simon managed to get in before she was off again.

'So Home Farm was just as often called Parker's Farm. You've probably noticed the lane a bit further along is called Parker's Lane. Anyway, when we took it over we decided to keep the shop, and we tried changing the name but it never took. Everyone kept calling it Parker's, and we were losing passing trade because people were telling them to go to Parker's and there was our shop called Enderby's, so they were going straight past. So in the end we gave in—'

'To overwhelming pressure—'

'And put up a new sign with the old name on it, and everyone was happy. But it's like that here,' she added, leaning a little forwards so Jenna could see where the perma-tan of her upper bosom ended down in the vee of her dress. 'Sacred traditions and so on. Mustn't be trampled on. Which reminds me – what have you done to upset Caroline Russell?'

'Now, Mad, no gossip,' Simon said unconvincingly.

'It's not gossip. I got it from Abigail Turner – is she coming tonight?'

'I think I saw that name on the guest list,' Jenna said.

'Of course, you don't know any of these people yet. Poor you. Or maybe it's lucky you! Well, let me warn you, some of them are pure poison.'

'Come on, Wifey, don't put the poor kid off,' Simon said. 'It's not that bad,' he added to Jenna. 'It's just that some of these locals are slow to take to new faces. Mad and I have been at Home Farm for twenty years—'

'Nearer thirty. We came in 1980.'

'And some of them still think of us as newcomers.'

'Well, I won't be staying long enough to cause anyone any heartache,' Jenna said. 'I'm strictly temporary.'

They looked at each other. '*Really*?' said Mad. 'That's not what I heard. Hmm. Well, anyway, just a word to the wise – keep on your toes.'

Jenna was hauled away then to meet other dinner guests. The pre-dinner people were obediently taking their leave, so the sartorial soup was now undiluted. All the men were in dinner jackets and the women were in long dresses, mostly floral prints or small figured patterns on backgrounds of black, grey, maroon or dark blue. They were elderly, kindly and dull, and spoke to Jenna as the liberal headmaster of a top public school might speak to the village girl who had been chosen to present a bouquet to the wife of the Lord Lieutenant: they tried to put her at her ease, without the faintest idea of what subject might engage her. Jenna felt surreally out of place, and drank more champagne.

Fatty was circulating now with plates of canapés, which Jenna eyed with amazement. When she found herself next to Kitty she murmured, 'How did Mrs Phillips have *time*?'

Kitty whispered back, 'She didn't. I went to Marks and Sparks in Wenchester yesterday.' And then she took Jenna's arm and turned her and said, 'I do want you to meet Jim Lancaster. Jim, this is Jenna Freemont, my much-removed cousin.'

Jenna found her hand engulfed in a strong, warm one, and looked into the face of a man who had been to hell and back and therefore knew a thing or two about the importance of love. He was in his vigorous sixties, with bushy grey hair and eyebrows that would defy taming, and blue eyes used to long horizons, and a mouth made for smiling. And kissing. *Goodness*, Jenna thought, *I have had a lot of champagne.*

'Jenna – delighted to meet you,' he said. He had a delicious, rich, warm voice, and Jenna felt a frisson that told her if she was Kitty's age she'd be leaping into bed with him at the slightest encouragement. Oh, what a terrible, *terrible* shame it was about the wife! And she appreciated for the first time how ghastly it must be to have to wait for someone to die before you could have what you wanted and needed; and how doubly ghastly to have to keep from *wanting* her to die.

She pressed his hand and said, 'I'm delighted to meet you, too,' and tried to put into her voice the sympathy she felt, the wish to be friends, and the message that she didn't mind in the least if he slipped in to Kitty's room after dark. 'Kitty's told me about you,' she said. 'And Bill says that you have a lovely garden.'

He smiled. 'Well, *I* think my garden's lovely. One always thinks one's own child is, whatever outsiders may think. Are you interested in gardening?'

'I wasn't before. I lived in a flat in London. But seeing this place, I think I could be.'

'Kitty has a genius with flowers. Her eye for colour is remarkable.'

Impulsively, probably because of the champagne, Jenna said, 'I wish mine was.' She gestured to her dress. 'I feel so out of place.'

His eyebrows went up. 'But you mustn't! Because *we're* all dull, it doesn't mean you have to be. And only a genius would have known that pink would work so well with your glorious hair. You look ravishing, my dear, and I feel privileged to be talking to you.'

She smiled. 'Thank you. You're very kind. But—'

'No buts! No one here tried very hard tonight, because they didn't know what it would be like. It's Kitty's first party for a very long time, so they just dragged out the old rag they've worn a dozen times. But you've gingered them all up. The next party someone gives, you'll see the difference. They'll all have new dresses, and we'll all be much more cheerful for it.'

She laughed. 'How do you know so much about female psychology?'

He twinkled. 'I was a sailor. I spent my whole life in the navy. A girl in every port, and a port in every girl.'

'I wish—' Jenna began, but was interrupted by the arrival – perilously close to being late – of the last guests: Caroline Russell, her brother, and Alexander Latham. All conversation ceased and everyone turned towards the door, where Caroline had paused, and stood framed.

'Pure theatre,' Jim murmured wickedly to Jenna. 'How that girl loves to make an entrance!' Jenna glanced at him, startled, and he grinned and mimed smacking his own hand. It made her giggle.

Kitty hurried forward to greet her. Caroline was in pale blue chiffon, floor-length, with loose half-sleeves and a décolletage nicely judged to show just the proper hint of cleavage. Her corn-gold hair was piled up and she wore two rows of pearls round her neck, while the ones in her ears were surrounded by diamonds, which caught the light as she moved her head. She looked like a queen. Alexander appeared, tall and dark and gorgeous in the crisp black-and-white setting of dinner jacket, the perfect foil to her bright pallor.

He looked at Jenna over Caroline's shoulder with what seemed to be a forbidding frown. It must be disapproval, she thought. She felt suddenly that they were the real grown-ups, rich, confident, cosmopolitan, far out of her sphere. She felt ridiculous in her too bright, too short Hobbs dress, shimmery pearlized tights and strappy, tottery sandals. The only thing that glinted when *she* moved were the sparkly hair slides, which were entirely made of plastic.

She found herself walking forward, all the same (had Jim given her a discreet shove in the back to get her started?), to do the

pretty, as Kitty wanted her to. They exchanged meaningless greet-
ings. Caroline looked down on her with a brief curl of the lip
before she fixed the icy smile into place, and said, 'Goodness,
what an intriguing dress, Jenny. You must have brought that with
you from London. I'm sure you couldn't get anything like that
down here. It's – how would you describe it, darling?' She turned
her perfect profile towards Alexander.

'Pink,' he said tersely. 'Hello, Jenna. Are you settling in?'

There was no friendliness in his tone, but at least he got her
name right.

'Yes, thank you. And I've started work,' she added, to let him
know she was not merely a ligger.

'I'm sure you have,' Caroline said grimly, as though she had a
whole different definition of 'work' to apply to Jenna. 'But we
won't talk about that. This is a social occasion. Allow me to
introduce my brother Henry. Henry Beale. Harry, this is Jenna.'

She unblocked the doorway at last and Alexander stood aside
to allow the figure behind him to be seen. Though smaller than
Alexander he was still taller than Jenna, and as he took her hand
he could look right down the front of her dress, which he did
with gleeful frankness.

'Hello, Red,' he said with a grin. 'I see you've thrown yourself
open to the public!'

Ten

'You!' said Jenna.

He grinned. 'I kind of guessed it was you. Didn't you guess
it was me?'

'Not at all. When Kitty said she'd invited Caroline's brother
for me, I thought—' She stopped, realizing the champagne was
leading her into indiscretion.

'Go on,' he urged. 'You thought what?'

'Well, I thought you'd be a stuffed shirt,' she confessed.

'Like old Xander, eh? Look at him scowling at us. Doesn't
approve of the young entry having fun! Poor old guy.'

'*Old* guy?' Jenna was amused. 'He can't be more than thirty-five, six.'

'Seven. Eight. Who knows? But that's ten years older than me. You can't expect me to see him as a young guy, especially the way he acts. I can't think what Caro sees in him. If he keeps on looking this way, though, he'll be in trouble with her. That's why I thought it was you, by the way – in case you were interested.'

'Thought what was me? What?' She was confused.

'Thought the newbie at Holtby House was the gorgeous redhead I kept bumping into. From the way old Caroline was spitting tacks about this young thruster who's taking advantage of dear old Kitty.'

'She wasn't! Was she?' Jenna was disconcerted.

'She implied you were a bit of an outsider, all right,' he said. 'And usually when she gets a down on someone from the word go, it's because they're prettier than her. Especially if they're also younger. So when I saw you swanning about Holtby, I thought, "I wonder." And now I know. And here you are, knocking her eye out again in that dress.' He made an encompassing gesture of his hand.

'Oh, don't,' Jenna moaned. 'This dress is a disaster.'

'Is that what you were in Belminster for? Hobbs, isn't it?'

'How on earth do you know that?'

'I know other females apart from you. So why don't you like it? I think it's brilliant.'

'I had no idea what everyone else would be wearing tonight. And everyone else is in full length and muted colours. I stick out like a sore thumb.'

'If that's a sore thumb,' he said, looking at her admiringly, 'then – whack my opposable digit with a hammer, baby, cos I'm *on* with that.'

She laughed, feeling a bit better. He really was extremely good looking, with hair a shade darker than his sister's, and a fine, straight-nosed, classy sort of face, not quite as chiselled as Caroline's and, instead of her cool blue eyes, rather fascinating hazel ones. And she always liked men who made her laugh. That's why it was such a mystery that Patrick had stolen her heart. Oh Patrick! But she mustn't think about him now. 'Well,' she said, 'I did think

I might as well have something I'd wear when I go back to the real world. They had it in black, but I like this colour.'

'It's genius to wear something like that with red hair. What do you mean, the real world?'

'Oh, I don't mean it insultingly,' she said hastily. 'I suppose I've been in London so long everything else seems a bit surreal.'

'I always feel that way when I'm *in* London. Oh, hello, Helen. How are you?' He turned politely as one of the other guests came up to him, and Jenna, remembering what Kitty had wanted of her, moved away to circulate and speak to everyone else in turn.

In this way, she found herself eventually with Alexander, detached for the moment from Caroline, who was talking to a thin elderly man that Central Casting would have snapped up for rector parts.

'Hello,' Jenna said politely.

He didn't smile.

'Problem?' she asked brightly.

'If you must know,' he said, 'I don't think that dress is at all suitable.'

She wasn't entirely surprised. 'Kitty loves it,' she said. 'And it's her party.'

'Kitty's polite.'

'So what's wrong with it?'

'You know perfectly well,' he said, glaring at her cleavage.

She had felt uneasy about it all along, but she wasn't going to let him criticize her. 'I can see you enjoy looking down on me,' she said.

Two spots of colour appeared in his cheeks and he looked away.

'Look,' she said, 'I don't know what your problem is with me, but I'm just here, at Kitty's request, to do a job. I'm not part of your local society, and I don't have to fit in with it. When the job's done, I'll be off, and out of your hair.'

His eyes returned to her face. 'Is that what you think? Then you must be extremely un-noticing. Kitty's very taken with you, and she's enjoying having you here.'

'Well, what's wrong with that?' Jenna said indignantly. 'I just don't get what you're in a state about.'

His nostrils flared. 'I'm not in a state. I never get in a state—'

'*That* I can believe,' Jenna said.

He breathed hard. 'I'm very fond of Kitty, and as her godson I have every right to be concerned about her. I don't want her to be hurt, and I don't want her to be exploited.'

She lost her temper a little bit. 'I don't know what the hell you think it is I'm doing here,' she began, managing to keep her voice to a low hiss, 'but you've got some cheek coming here criticizing my appearance and implying – well, I don't know what you *are* implying. That I'm some kind of crook?'

'I didn't say that. But this so-called *job* of yours—'

'It's something Kitty wants doing – which, by the way, I would have thought *you* were the ideal person to do, if you could have been bothered.'

'I couldn't possibly find the time,' he said, indignant in his turn. 'I have a business to run and it's full-time work. But even if Kitty does want you to do this, you don't have to embarrass her at her party by turning up looking like a—'

Fortunately, since Jenna had a half-full glass of champagne in her hand, he didn't finish the sentence. 'Like a what?' she demanded.

He waved a hand. 'Shocking pink and slashed to the navel—' He took a breath and started again. 'You must *see* it isn't appropriate,' he added, his tone more propitiating.

'But you didn't say what you think I am,' Jenna growled menacingly. *She* wasn't ready to fold. 'What am I?'

'I think you're just like your mother,' he said coldly.

At that moment Jim appeared between them and said cheerily, 'Good party, isn't it? Wonderful to see Kitty entertaining again. And Mrs Phillips cooks like an angel. You must have the inside track on what delights are before us, Jenna. Care to give us a preview?'

It was like coming down to earth again with a solid bump. The rest of the room tuned in around her, and she blinked like someone waking. What on earth had been going on? Why had she and Alexander been at each other's throats? She didn't know the man from Adam. She looked round furtively, hoping no one else had noticed, as Jim obviously had. He had come to throw cold water on them like fighting dogs.

'Oh, I couldn't possibly spoil the surprise,' she said lightly, managing to smile nearly normally. 'But from the little I know, Mrs Phillips ought to be in the Michelin Guide.' She risked a glance up at Alexander, who was looking almost as bemused as she felt. She tried an apologetic smile on him and got a twitch of the lips in response. 'You must have tasted more of her dinners than I have. How many stars do you think she should get?'

'Oh, four, I'd say,' Alexander said. 'Excuse me, I must circulate.' He gave them a nod that was almost a bow and moved away.

Jenna turned to Jim, wondering what he'd say, prepared to thank him for intervening, but he was too well behaved to allow her to mention it. 'I think the waiting is almost over, anyway,' he said cheerfully. 'I just saw Bill appear in the doorway, and it looks as though Kitty's gathering her chicks. Allow me to escort you to your escort. Young Henry's taking you in, isn't he?'

'Yes – he's over there.'

'You'll have a lively dinner companion, anyway. I think I've got Jean Longhurst on my other side, and she's very deaf, poor thing. It must be an awful affliction.'

He had talked her down to earth by the time he presented her to Harry, but he did it so naturally that she would have been left to wonder whether he really *had* effected a rescue, or whether it was pure chance, except at the last moment before he turned away, he whisked her champagne glass out of her hand and bestowed a fatherly wink on her.

The food was delicious. They started with a cold watercress soup, then went on to the duck eggs, poached, with the asparagus and a hollandaise sauce.

'My first grass this year,' Harry said. 'Bill always gets ahead in that walled garden of his.'

'Microclimate,' Jenna said.

'Are you a gardener?' he asked doubtfully.

'Do I look like a gardener? But I can read. And we did a feature on walled gardens a couple of years ago, as I remember.'

'What do you mean, "did a feature"?'

She told him about her job, in which he seemed interested enough to keep the topic going to the end of the course. Then some movement seemed to ripple round the table, and Harry, who had turned away from her, turned back to explain in a whisper, 'You have to talk to your other side now. It's the rule.'

Everyone had turned to talk to the person on their other side. It seemed a nice, polite thing to do, she thought, but fancy there being an absolute rule about it! And fancy that everyone knew the rule! So she got a go of her other dinner partner, a spritely old man who turned out to be called Brian and to be married to the deaf Jean Longhurst. Perhaps this accounted for the fact that he was bursting to talk, and also that he didn't seem to require answers. He ran his sentences so seamlessly together, segueing from how jolly it was to be dining at Holtby House again, to how his dogs hated being left alone in the evenings and seemed to have a sixth sense about when it was going to happen, to the lunatic neighbours who had started *feeding* foxes at the back door and how they must be town people, to the shocking numbers of weekend homes there were nowadays and something ought to be done about it, to how the government interfered too much and didn't understand the countryside. Jenna had only to nod and murmur agreement, which left her free to enjoy the next course, which was stuffed roast leg of lamb, which Bill brought in on a trolley and carved in front of them while Fatty carried the plates round. The lamb was delectable, the stuffing piquant, and the gravy could have got up and sung opera, it was so artistic.

When the plates were cleared, Brian Longhurst laid a chalky hand over Jenna's and said, 'I've enjoyed our little chat. It's a long time since I had the undivided attention of such a pretty woman. And your dress is beautiful, my dear.' Then he turned away to his other neighbour, leaving Jenna to realize that he wouldn't have said the last bit had someone not been criticizing it. She had a fair idea who it was. Caroline had been shooting ferocious glares at her down the table. Across from Jenna, Alexander had been giving her the occasional glance, which she was piercingly aware of even when she was looking elsewhere. Now and then, when she thought he wasn't looking, she stole a glance at him. He was still shiveringly attractive – but what a stiff! Once when she was looking he moved his head and their eyes met, and it was like an electric shock. She jerked hers away, and felt herself blushing. She wished she were down the other end of the table, where things were much livelier, and Mad Enderby was defying protocol and talking to a whole group of people at once, interspersing her remarks with jolly laughter.

'So,' said Harry when they had settled down again, 'why did you leave this job of yours? It sounds as if you enjoyed it.'

'I did. But I got downsized.'

'Wow.' He looked down her cleavage. 'I wish I'd met you before.'

'Don't be rude.'

'Sorry,' he said with a grin, not seeming it. 'And why did you leave London, that you say you've always lived in?'

'Lost my job, lost my flat, needed a holiday but couldn't afford it. My brother said what you need is a job that's like a holiday, and my other brother found me this.'

'Ah, that accounts for the rumours that you're here on a rest cure. I was imagining tuberculosis or a nervous breakdown at least.'

'Do I look—?'

'Of course not,' he interrupted hastily. 'But it's better than Caro's theory, that you're here to lead Kitty to ruin.'

'What *has* she got against me?'

'You're a rival.'

'What, for Alexander? No thank you!'

'Just generally. She's used to being the centre of attention, the Belle of the County. Though it has to be said old Xander does keep looking at you an awful lot.'

'Pure disapproval,' said Jenna. 'Why did you say you didn't know what Caroline saw in him? He *is* terrifically good looking.'

'But Caro's never cared about that. What she wants in her men is wealth and power. You should have seen some of her past efforts! Gruesome in the extreme. No, Xander's not rich or posh enough, with his piddling little furniture business, and his parents weren't anyone. And I can't believe she's in love. So what's she up to?'

'You don't like her much, do you? Shouldn't you be loyal to your sister?'

'Are you loyal to yours?'

'I've two sisters and two brothers, and I adore them all, and we're all loyal to each other. That's what families are for.'

'Someone forgot to tell mine that,' Harry said lightly. 'There's only the two of us. And she's only my stepsister, anyway.'

'Really? And I was thinking you looked so alike.'

'Her mother divorced her father and married my dad. She doesn't look like her mother and I do look like my father, so I suppose her mother had a fixed taste in men.'

'Hang on, I need a minute to work that out.'

'Anyway, she was ten when I was born, so by the time the folks got together she was away at boarding school. I never really had much to do with her. She was just this bossy thing that appeared in holidays and nagged me for being dirty and noisy and annoying.' He grinned. 'So I've made a career out of being annoying to her ever since.'

'What happened to your mother?'

'Died,' he said shortly. 'I was just a baby, so you don't have to say "sorry".'

'If Caroline's mother married your father, how come you've got different surnames?'

'Caro never dropped the Russell. Posher name, you see, and she needed that at boarding school, to keep her end up. Benenden – frightfully posh.'

'I should have thought your father would have made her change.'

'Oh, Dad didn't care. He soon divorced Caro's mum anyway, so it was just as well she stuck with the first name. Funny, though, even after the divorce Caro stayed friends with my dad. I think she spends more time with him than with her mum. Like calls to like, so they say.'

Before Jenna could ask more, the course came to an end. They had been eating poached pears with meringue and warm coffee-chocolate sauce. The pears seemed to have been poached in Poire William liqueur, to judge by their boozy taste. Now as the dishes were cleared, she asked, 'What's next?'

'Dessert,' Harry said.

'We just had that.'

'No, dear, that was pudding. Dessert is cheese and fruit,' he told her kindly.

'God, the minefields!' she exclaimed. 'I'm getting fork anxiety. And to think a couple of weeks ago I was sitting on the sofa in front of the telly eating rice pudding out of the tin.'

'Sounds like heaven to me!' He grinned. 'You mustn't think we go on like this all the time. Everyone enjoys the full fig now and then, but there are kitchen suppers too, with a huge bowl of spaghetti in the middle and help-yourself, and the Enderbys' barbecue in the summer.'

'It must be nice to live in a place with a real community,' Jenna said. 'In London you take your friends where you find them, and you hardly know your neighbours.'

'Well, it's good and it's bad. You can't keep anything secret,' Harry said. 'For instance, when you and I go out for dinner on Thursday next week, everyone within a ten mile radius will know about it.'

'I haven't said I'll go out with you yet.'

'Congolese food,' he reminded her seductively. 'You can't go to your grave never having found out what it is.'

She laughed. 'Oh, all right, if Kitty doesn't mind. Shouldn't we change sides again?'

'Once dessert's on it's a free for all. But I think poor old Brian Longhurst would love another go of you, if you're feeling charitable.'

So she turned and talked to her other neighbour, who did seem delighted; and while she listened and nodded she thought that Harry was really rather sweet. He pretended to be terribly hip and cool and careless, but he was kind and thoughtful towards an old man who was nothing to him but a neighbour. Maybe there was something in this country living.

The dessert stage didn't last long, as there were after-dinner guests coming, and everyone soon decamped into the drawing room for coffee and a welcome injection of new conversation.

Suddenly and surprisingly, Jenna found Alexander standing before her again. 'How times have changed,' he said. 'Just a few years ago, this stage of the evening would have included the smoking of cigars. Now nobody except a few of the farm workers smokes.'

'And presumably they don't smoke cigars,' Jenna offered. His tone had been pleasant, social, and he was obviously trying to make amends, so she did the same.

'Maybe they do, in the privacy of their homes, but I've never seen them do it in public,' he said. He smiled. It was a cautious, wary smile, but a smile nonetheless, and it transformed his face. Jenna had to take a deep breath to withstand it. 'I'm sorry about earlier,' he said. 'That was bad form.'

'I don't know what happened,' Jenna said. 'I've absolutely no desire to quarrel with you.'

'One thing you said did hurt me,' he said gravely. 'About my not helping Kitty with the cataloguing.'

Jenna waved it away. 'Not my business. I shouldn't have said it.'

'You were entitled to wonder. But my own business takes up all my time. And my expertise is strictly with furniture. Of course, when the time comes, I'll help her to sell the better pieces of furniture – though the market's depressed at the moment and prices are down. And some of the items, like that dining table, will be very hard to find a buyer for. Nobody wants these big pieces nowadays.'

'It's a terrible shame to think of selling them anyway,' Jenna said more warmly. 'They should stay where they are, where they belong. And Kitty should stay, too. It's what she wants.'

He cooled a little, seeming to take that as a criticism. 'You have no idea how much it costs to maintain a house like this. Nobody wants them any more. They're a millstone round people's necks.'

'But surely there are rich people always looking for big houses – footballers and pop stars and Arab sheikhs, anyway. Millionaires have to live somewhere.'

'These days, millionaires want to build their own houses, from scratch. New house, new furniture. They don't want antiques.' There was a hint of bitterness in his voice now. 'They want everything new. Haven't you seen them popping up everywhere, these ghastly gin-palaces with their electronic gates and flood-lighting and indoor swimming pools and gyms? Horrible blots on the landscape.'

Jenna said, 'Well, it's sad, but if that's what they want, aren't they entitled to have it?'

'The wrong people have the money these days,' he said.

She laughed. 'Meaning, not you or me? Well, I agree with that.'

They seemed to be getting along quite well, but just then one side of Jenna went cold all the way down to her ankles, and Caroline was there, the mobile open freezer. 'Agree with what?' she asked brittlely. 'You two are having quite a chinwag, it seems.'

She slipped her hand through Alexander's arm as she spoke, and his face seemed to cool and set, too, into the old mask of faint disapproval. Jenna shivered involuntarily.

It gave Caroline her opening. 'I'm not surprised you're cold. There isn't much to that dress, is there, Jenny? Shouldn't you go and get a cardigan? It would make things very difficult for Kitty if you were to get ill. It would be inconsiderate of you to expect her to nurse you.'

'My name's Jenna, as I told you before,' Jenna snapped.

'So you did,' Caroline said in a kindly voice. 'I have difficulty remembering it, because it's not a proper name, is it? It must be so annoying for you when people keep getting it wrong. Perhaps you should think about changing it by deed poll.'

Harry joined them at that moment, and Jenna looked at him gratefully and fought down the urge to say, 'Get me out of here.'

'Admiring Jenna's dress, Sissy?' he asked of Caroline. 'Something like this would suit you, you know. But you'd have to wear a padded bra, of course.'

'Don't be vulgar,' she snapped. 'And don't call me Sissy.'

Jenna made the mistake of laughing, and the freezing air now coming from the two of them was making her nipples stand up. She slipped her arm through Harry's and leaned against him, and was gratified to see Caroline's nostrils flare in annoyance.

'Oh, I don't think this dress would suit your sister at all,' she told him. And to Caroline: 'It really isn't your style. You're much more—' She paused, as if searching for the right word, giving her the opportunity to look Caroline up and down consideringly. The nostrils began to resemble the entrance to the Channel Tunnel. She felt Harry holding his breath. Alexander was beginning to look alarmed. 'Grecian,' she concluded pleasantly.

Harry let out his breath in a snort of laughter, and Jenna took the opportunity to say, 'Excuse me, I must go and see what Kitty wants,' and take her leave. *Pure theatre*, she thought, using Jim's words. *That girl loves to make an exit.*

She hoped she hadn't gone too far. But she was only going to be here a month, so it was hard to care.

Eleven

The rain Bill promised arrived as the last guests were leaving, and Jenna woke the next morning to a misty world of gurgling gutters and dripping trees. After all the excitement – and, it had to be said, all the wine – of the previous evening, she had slept later than usual, and went downstairs to find the place empty except for the two dogs, sitting by the front door looking hopeful. *What's a bit of rain*, they urged, wagging their extremities and making little suggestive movements towards the outside world.

'Where's the missus?' she asked them. They weren't telling, but she found a note Sellotaped to the sitting-room door. *Gone to church. Didn't want to wake you. Back about 9.30. Don't wait to eat if you're hungry. No Mrs P today, so it's cornflakes, I'm afraid!*

It was a quarter past nine already. Feeling guilty, Jenna went along to the kitchen – which was spotless, though the sculleries were still piled with things for washing-up – and by the time Kitty got back she had breakfast almost ready.

'What's that nice smell?' Kitty said, stepping into the back lobby and starting to shed wax jacket, shapeless hat, welly boots and dripping umbrella, every movement hampered by joyfully bouncing dogs. 'Can it be toast?'

'I couldn't let you come back to cold cornflakes,' Jenna said. 'I'm doing us scrambled eggs, toast and coffee.'

'What a rock of a girl you are,' Kitty said, seeming more delighted than the small service warranted. 'I knew I was right to ask you here.'

'Isn't it early for church? I thought services started about half past nine or ten,' Jenna said, stirring the eggs.

'There's Matins at ten o'clock, but I like to go to the eight o'clock service. There's something about being out early on a Sunday. The feeling that you have the world to yourself.'

'I must come with you next week,' Jenna said. 'I'm sorry I

slept in this morning. The eggs are ready now. Do you like them *on* the toast, or to the side?'

They carried everything through on two trays and ate in the conservatory, with the rain pattering steadily on the roof above. Kitty opened the door so that the smell of the wet world could come in, and the dogs went and lay down by it with their paws on their noses. Only their eyebrows moved as they followed every movement of the human hands, but they sighed gustily from time to time.

'It was a marvellous do last night,' Jenna said.

'*Did* you enjoy it? There were times when I looked around and thought what a dull lot of friends I have. Of course, they're my age and not yours, which is only natural. Next time we entertain, we must do something we can invite more young people to. But Harry seemed to be entertaining you all right?' There was a faint question mark at the end of the statement, and Jenna responded to it.

'He was fun. He's very different from his sister, isn't he?' she asked cautiously. She really wanted to know what Kitty thought of the Ice Queen.

'Well, they're only *step*brother and sister, of course,' Kitty said. She hesitated, as if on the brink of something, and then took another forkful of egg instead of speaking.

Jenna tried: 'I don't think Caroline approved of my dress. I'm afraid perhaps it *was* a bit over the top, but you see I had no idea what people would be wearing. I had to guess, and I guessed wrong.'

Kitty was suddenly fierce. 'Oh my dear, there was nothing wrong with your dress! It was delightful, and such a pretty colour.' Red patches of annoyance coloured her cheeks. 'I wasn't sure whether to tell you, because I don't want to stir anything up, but Caroline came to early service this morning *on purpose* to complain about you. I know it was deliberate, because she *always* goes to the ten o'clock, and she waylaid me on my way out and walked with me to the gate so I couldn't avoid her. Made me miss speaking to the vicar, too,' she added wrathfully, 'which I was intending to do.'

'What did she say?'

'Well, I couldn't really get a handle on what it was she objected to, apart from your dress. She seemed to think it was proof that you were a woman of easy virtue, or something like that. I don't know *who* she thinks you could debauch around here. Poor Brian Longhurst, perhaps! She seemed to be trying to put me on my guard against you, without saying what it was you might try to do to me.' A gleam of humour came into her eyes as her wrath faded. 'Now, promise to tell me if you decide to hit me over the head and steal my purse, because I do hate surprises.'

'I'd never hit you on the head,' Jenna said solemnly. 'I hate unnecessary violence. I'd just steal your purse in the night and slip away under cover of darkness.'

Kitty smiled. 'Such a lot of nonsense! I'm so glad you aren't offended.'

'Oh no. She made it pretty clear last night she didn't like me, though I can't think why.'

'I'm so sorry. You were supposed to enjoy yourself.'

'I did. Don't worry, she didn't upset me. I'm only sorry to be the cause of friction in your life. After all, she and Alexander *are* going to marry, so it's more important that she gets on with you than with me.'

'Poor Xander,' Kitty said abruptly. 'I can't believe he'll be happy with her. I'm rather afraid she found him when he was vulnerable, and he didn't entirely realize what he was getting into.'

'How was he vulnerable?'

'Oh, he was just out of a relationship that broke down. Like you. He and Stephanie had been together for years, and we all thought they'd get married, but then she went off with someone else and broke his heart. And it seems almost before he could draw breath, there was Caroline. Suddenly they were seen everywhere together. It all happened much too quickly. Within a matter of months they were engaged. He bought her a huge ring – I can't think how he afforded it, because all his money's tied up in his business.'

'It does sound a bit as if she "caught" him. But that's no reason for him to marry her if he doesn't want to.'

'Well, perhaps he does. I can't answer for his inner feelings, of course. I just feel they aren't suited, and I'm so very fond of him, I really want him to be happy.'

'Then I'd better keep out of the way as much as possible. After all, you'll have her around for the rest of your life, but I'm only going to be here for a month.'

Kitty looked bleak. 'What a horrid prospect. I wish you hadn't reminded me. I do so like having you here.'

'Well, I can always come and visit,' Jenna said. 'When Caroline's not about. By the way,' she added as she remembered something, 'Alexander said something last night that intrigued me. He said I was just like my mother. Did he know her?'

Kitty frowned. 'Well, of course, Peter and I were close friends with Xenia and Geoffrey – Xander's parents – during the time that your mother and father used to come to visit, and we all six used to get together, in this house or theirs. But Xander was only a schoolboy, and I can't believe he really noticed your mother very much. Children don't take that much interest in grown-ups, do they? Perhaps he's seen a photograph of her, and meant you look like her – which you do, quite a bit. Though you're prettier than Annabel. She wasn't a classical beauty: more what I would call striking. And she was a wonderful dresser, always looked sensational. I never really had much dress sense. And frankly –' she smiled – 'I've never cared that much about clothes anyway. I was always too interested in being comfortable. I suppose that's living in bad climates so much. Well, what are you going to do today? Rather sorry weather, but it's good for the garden. Especially the veg. Bill's ecstatic about the rain.'

'There must be a lot of clearing up to do from the party,' Jenna said.

'There's a bit. Mrs Phillips did the crockery last night – one load in the dishwasher while we were still eating, and another load afterwards, before she went home. But there are the glasses and cutlery still to do. But you don't need to bother with it. I can manage.'

'I wouldn't think of leaving you to do it alone,' Jenna said. 'Of course I'll help. And afterwards, I might as well do a bit of work. If you're up for it, we could go through the photographs and pick out the ones you want included in the house history.'

Kitty brightened. 'There's nothing I like more than looking at old photographs, as long as I've got someone to look at them with. I might find some of your parents, if you're interested. And there are some very sweet ones of Xander as a little boy. He was quite enchanting, as beautiful as an angel. His mother used to call him her little star.'

'How sweet,' Jenna said, thinking that was something to store up as possible ammunition, should the need arise.

They lunched on cold-lamb-and-stuffing sandwiches, and afterwards Jenna said she needed to stretch her legs before settling down to work. 'The rain seems to be easing off a bit,' she said. 'I think I'll go for a walk.' She hesitated. 'Do you think I could take the dogs with me? Would they like it? They look awfully bored.'

'They'd love it,' Kitty said. 'They go shamefully short of walks, because there's so much room for them to roam around here, but of course that's not the same thing to a dog.'

'Will they go with me all right?'

'Oh yes, they know you now. And they're very good on a leash.'

So a short while later, Jenna was heading out of the back door, clad in Kitty's wax jacket and shapeless hat, with a joyful dog on either side. They said this was just what they wanted, and commended her for her very canine disregard of the rain.

As soon as she passed through the yard it came on more heavily again. Veils of it drifted across in front of her, the sky was low, wet and grey, and a mist of water seemed to hang about the green dripping hedges and trees. Suddenly the little cottage looked very inviting, with a light on inside and the smoke from the chimney suggesting a nice log fire. But she was restless for exercise, and she told herself the rain wasn't cold – just really, really wet. Besides, she couldn't possibly disappoint those two hopeful doggy faces, eagerly turned up at her. She went on out into the lane, and turned away from the village.

The dogs did walk well, trotting beside her and only occasionally pulling, their nostrils flaring to catch all the unfamiliar scents. She walked for ten minutes to establish discipline and then let them snuffle on a grass verge and relieve themselves. One car swished past, windows steamed up, throwing spray from its wheels. Wood-pigeons croodled liquidly from the trees above her, and somewhere a crow yarked repetitively, but otherwise she might have been alone in the world. She went from one lane into another, and realized the frustration of walking in this sort of country: you couldn't see over the hedges, so the scenery was rather monotonous.

The wax jacket kept her body dry and warm, and the hat seemed impervious to the weather, but her feet and lower legs gradually soaked through. She had refused the offer of Kitty's wellies – even if they had fitted, she was queasy about wearing someone else's footwear – and though her shoes were respectable flats, the long exposure to water and the occasional puddles she couldn't avoid proved too much for them, while the long wet grass of the verges soaked her jeans. She began to feel rather chilly, and the rain didn't seem to have any intention of stopping or even slowing: the sky was invisible beyond the low veils of grey. The dogs had stopped frisking, though when she addressed them they looked up at her and wagged in a way that suggested they would go on as long as she could.

'Oh, we'll go back,' she said aloud, turning around. 'It'll take the rest of the day to get you guys dry.'

Another car went by, spraying her lightly and disappearing round the bend with a brief flash of red brake-lights, prismed through the falling water. The world seemed deserted. Even the birds had stopped, and there was no sound but the endless patter of the rain on the road and hedges. Jenna shivered, and thought of home, getting dry, having a cup of tea – and maybe a piece of Mrs P's shortbread, if there was any left. The lamb sandwich seemed a distant memory now. She was developing a real outdoor-girl appetite these days.

Then she heard the sound of hoof-beats coming towards her, and she pulled the dogs over on to the verge as a big bay came into sight, ridden by a man in a riding mac and a crash cap with a waterproof cover. As they came closer she reckoned the bay was easily sixteen hands, and very well bred, going at a collected trot on a double bridle, its tack expensive and beautifully kept. She couldn't see much of the man's face between the brim of his cap and the turned-up collar of his mac; but as he approached he pulled the horse down to a walk, and she realized as he stopped beside her that it was Alexander.

'Hello,' she said cheerfully. 'Lovely weather for ducks.'

The horse didn't seem to be bothered by the dogs, so she drew closer to get a bit of relief from the rain in the lee of the big animal. It was so tall that she was on a level with the rider's booted leg (not rubber but real leather – oh posh!) and behind it the gleamingly-polished saddle flap and the steaming bay flank. Alexander's leather-gloved hands were quiet on the reins; looking up further, flinching as the raindrops hit her face, she saw that glorious face looking down at her, and – would wonders never cease? – it was with a smile of friendliness and approval.

'Aren't you the intrepid one?' he said pleasantly. 'Braving all this for the sake of the dogs! Not what one expects from a townie at all.'

'Oh, it's a mistake to underestimate me,' she said lightly. 'I'm a very unusual person.'

'I'm beginning to realize that,' he said.

The words warmed, but disconcerted her. Where was the disapproval of yesteryear? 'I suppose you recognized the dogs,' she said, for something to say. The smile was throwing her out. She wasn't used to it. And it made him look all too attractive.

'And Kitty's hat,' he said. 'But why didn't you borrow some boots? Kitty's would be too small for you, I expect, but there are dozens of pairs knocking around, I know for a fact.'

'I'm squeamish about other people's shoes,' she admitted. 'Foolish, I know, but I can't help it.'

'Well, be sure and get your feet properly dry when you get home,' he said. 'Don't go around all evening in damp socks.'

So solicitous, she thought. The horse eased his weight from foot to foot, and turned his nose to see who she was. She let him sniff her fingers and then patted his neck. 'Nice horse,' she said. 'Is he yours?'

'Yes. He's called Victor.'

'He's got a terrific crest on him. You obviously keep him fit.'

'We do a bit of cross-country. I'd like to event, but I never really have time. You obviously know something about horses. Do you ride?'

'When I can. Not so many opportunities in London, but when I was a girl I was horse mad. It was my thing. Harriet wanted to be a ballerina and Rachel wanted to be a nun, but I wanted to be a girl groom.'

'Not a showjumper?'

'I had very modest ambitions,' she said, laughing.

'You should get some riding in while you're here,' he said. 'It's lovely country, and of course you can't really see it on foot. The hedges are too high.'

'I was thinking the same thing only a minute ago,' Jenna said.

'Well, look here,' he said. 'Would you like to go for a ride tomorrow evening, after I close the shop? I know of a horse I can borrow for you, and I can show you a bit of the countryside around here.'

'I'd love it,' Jenna said, surprised and pleased at the overture of friendship. She supposed it was for Kitty's sake, but was perfectly willing to go along with it – especially if it meant a ride. 'But I don't have any riding clothes with me. I'd have to ride in jeans.'

'I don't mind if you don't,' he said. 'Are you on, then?'

'Definitely. Though we won't see much if it's raining like this.'

'Oh, this will have passed over by tomorrow,' he said, glancing around.

She laughed. 'Do all country people know exactly what the weather's going to do?'

'Of course!' He smiled. 'It's God's compensation for having no cinemas and theatres and concert halls.'

The horse sneezed lavishly.

'Now you'd better get home before you drown,' he said.

'That was the horse, not me,' she pointed out, and he laughed, making her shiver, because she saw for an instant how utterly gorgeous he could be when he did it.

'I know that! Go on, off you go. I'll come and collect you around half past five tomorrow, if that's all right? I close up early on a Monday – there's never much trade.'

Kitty was delighted with the news. As they crouched in the rear lobby towelling a dog each, she said, 'I'm so glad he's making an effort to get to know you. I really want you two to be friends. But he's terribly shy, you know, which makes it difficult for him to get on with strangers.'

'Shy?' Jenna said. That was the last thing she'd have accused him of.

'Yes, and it makes him rather stiff with people, and they take it the wrong way and decide they don't like him, so they never get the chance to know the real person.'

'I should think being stiff with strangers would be a disadvantage in his trade,' Jenna remarked.

'Oh, he's fine with customers, because that's business, and you never have to let them inside your guard,' Kitty said. 'It's getting personal with people he has a problem with. Anyway, the antique trade is full of stiff people, and the fine furniture people are the stiffest of all, so he fits in perfectly well at the trade fairs and country house auctions.'

'Maybe Caroline really suits him after all, then,' Jenna said. 'She's stiff too.'

'Yes, but Xander's only stiff on the outside. She's stiff all the way through. I think Barney's as dry as I'm going to get him. How's Watch?'

'Like a soggy lambswool cardigan, and he smells just the same,' Jenna said.

'They'll do for now. And you must get out of those wet things before you catch cold. Why don't you have a nice hot bath?'

'That sounds lovely. I am feeling a bit chilly.'

'Yes, it's a nasty dank sort of afternoon. Why don't I light the fire in the sitting room, and we can cosy in for the evening?'

'That sounds like heaven.'

'It's only cold lamb again for supper, but we can cheer it up with a nice bottle of wine, and have a cocktail beforehand. Or would you like your cocktail in the bath?'

'Wouldn't that be the depths of decadence?'

'The heights, rather,' Kitty said, smiling. 'I like to take my baths seriously, with a good book and preferably something agreeable to drink. Shall I bring you one up? I make rather a wicked Martini.'

So in short order Jenna found herself lying full length in the massive bath, up to her neck in hot water, with a dry Martini gathering dew beads on its glass. The Martini had a wonderfully fragrant, floral overtone: 'A dash of elderflower cordial,' Kitty had told her. 'It's my special recipe. I can't cook, but I can make a cocktail.'

This is the life, Jenna thought with a sigh of content. Oliver was right, it was just what she needed, a job that was like a holiday. This was almost too much like a holiday for her conscience. But it was a mistake to think about Oliver, because that reminded her of her old life, which she had lost so completely. Patrick's face came before her eyes. She felt a pang of loneliness and loss, and her body ached for the touch of a man, and for that wonderful intimacy, the cosiness of belonging, of not having to do things by yourself.

A tear trickled down her face and mixed with the steam dripping off her chin. Oh Patrick! Why? She took an incautious swig at the Martini, which made her cough – Kitty had no inhibitions when it came to the use of gin – and it broke the mood and made her pull herself together. This was supposed to be a moment of sublime pleasure, and she wasn't going to spoil it with yearning for that worthless swine who had taken another woman into *her* bed. She was going to enjoy her bath and her cocktail, and after supper she and Kitty would sit by the fire and look at photographs and maybe find some of her parents when they were young. She'd love to see some new photos of Daddy.

And there would surely be some of the 'angelic' child who had grown up to be Alexander. Now there was a thing!

Twelve

It was the most beautiful morning she had ever seen. Jenna bounced out of bed to dash to the window and push it up. The smell that rollicked in was so heady and full of life it almost knocked her over. The sky was a perfect, newly-washed blue, the sun jinked on a gazillion diamonds carpeting the grass and decking the trees. Everything seemed to have grown six inches in one day. Now Jenna could see why people like Kitty and Bill said 'lovely rain'. In town, rain was just an unmitigated nuisance. Here it was beautiful and life-giving. She felt she had misjudged it all her life. She leaned out of the window and said, 'Sorry, rain.'

Below her, on the turnaround, Watch looked up and gave a single bark in reply. Barney only gave her a sultry glance and then rolled on his back on the warm gravel in a very kittenish way with his paws paddling in the air. Watch clearly thought this was going too far. He turned his back on Barney, hoicked up a hind leg and scratched thoroughly behind one ear, shook himself violently all over, then looked up at Jenna again and gave another bark, which obviously meant, 'What are you hanging about up there for? Hurry down!'

She sang in the shower, something she didn't remember ever doing before (you could make some interesting gurgling noises when the water ran into your mouth), and ran down the stairs two at a time to breakfast on the terrace.

Mrs Phillips was just putting a hot dish on the table. 'I didn't know if you ate kippers,' she said to Jenna by way of greeting, 'so I made kedigree.'

The logic of this passed Jenna by, but she said, 'I love kedgeree, thanks.' And then had a moment of panic as she couldn't remember whether it really was kedgeree or kedigree. They both sounded right.

Mrs Phillips lingered. 'I thought that all went off all right, Mrs Everest, dear,' she said. 'One of my duck eggs was a bit hard but I told Fatty to give that one to you.'

'Quite right,' Kitty said. 'She did. And it was delicious anyway. No one makes Hollandaise sauce like you.'

'And my lamb came out just right,' Mrs Phillips went on.

'Perfect. Just pink enough, and beautifully tender and moist,' said Kitty.

'I wasn't sure if I'd put too much coffee in the chocolate sauce.'

Jenna listened in amusement as the whole menu was gone through and praise garnered for each dish. From Kitty's expression this was obviously a familiar ritual, which ended with deep and heartfelt thanks for 'all your efforts and your great skill', upon which Mrs Phillips said, 'Oh, as long as you're happy, Mrs Everest, that's all that matters. I'm not one to fish for compliments, believe you me.' And she took herself off to make shepherd's pie for their supper from the seemingly endless cold lamb.

'Bless her,' Kitty said when she was out of earshot. 'We always have to go through that. I thanked her in loving detail on Sunday night, but she likes to come back for more on a daily basis.'

'It's the most evanescent of art forms,' Jenna said. 'A painter or sculptor has something to show for his art, but a cook's gets eaten right there and then, and it's gone.'

'True. It should be looked upon as performance art, really, like theatre.'

'But even actors have their performances remembered and talked about. Who will ever mention Mrs Phillips's roast lamb of the twelfth of May again?'

After breakfast, Jenna refused all beguilements and got straight down to work, and put in a solid day to ease her conscience. She was beginning to get some idea of the size of the task, and to doubt that she could get it done in the time allotted. But on this glorious morning she didn't feel it was all that essential to be getting back to the Smoke and her career as soon as possible.

Kitty spent much of the day on the phone, as everyone rang up to say thank you, and how wonderful it was that she was entertaining again, and wouldn't it be lovely to get back to the old routine. She also, as she told Jenna at lunchtime, had wistful calls from people who hadn't been there but had heard about it, and were probably hoping to be on the guest list next time.

'And we've had two return invitations already,' she concluded. 'To dinner with the Buckminsters, and Dolly Cornwall has asked us to lunch one Sunday because she has a lot of young people coming to play tennis. Do you play tennis?'

'Not worth mentioning,' Jenna said.

'Well, you needn't play, of course, but it will be a nice occasion, in the garden if it's fine, so I said yes. And to the Buckminsters. I hope that's all right.'

Jenna was embarrassed. 'Really, you don't have to make a social life for me. I'm here to work.'

'I know,' Kitty said, 'but I want you to enjoy yourself as well. Of course I don't want to impose my friends on you, so you must say yes or no absolutely freely. You won't hurt my feelings, I promise.'

'If you think it'll be fun, that's fine with me,' Jenna said.

Jenna felt almost fluttery as she went upstairs to get ready for her ride – almost as if it were a date. You'd better stop that, and stop it right now, she told herself sternly. He's only being nice to you for Kitty's sake, and it's probably a huge effort for him. Remember how he looked at you in The Dress? You come from different worlds. You are universes apart in character and everything else. And he's taken. Let's face it, the man who could stay engaged to Caroline Russell can't be all good.

Calm down, she replied to herself as she reached her bedroom. It's only the ride you're excited about. It'd be grand to be on a horse again. She only hoped it was a nice, well-mannered horse, since she was out of practice. She stopped short for a moment with a cold thought – it wouldn't be Caroline's, would it? No, she'd never lend her horse to a fallen woman.

Or *would* she? A scenario sprang into her mind: a needle concealed in the underside of the saddle so that only when the rider's weight came down on it would the needle prick the horse and drive it mad. Horse bucking wildly and then bolting. Red-haired rival tossed into the unforgiving road, or even into the path of an oncoming car. Ambulance summoned, but too late. Hospital so far away when you live in the country. Redhead pronounced dead on arrival. Crocodile tears. 'Oh, if only she hadn't pretended to be able to ride!'

What's wrong with this picture? Jenna asked herself derisively as she stripped off her working trousers. Yes, you got it: Jenna is not a rival. It gave her pause for a moment, though. Was it possible that that was why Caroline instantly disliked her – that she was female, passably attractive and being thrown in Alexander's path? She shrugged. He had made it clear enough at the party that he *wasn't* attracted to her, so Caroline oughtn't to have any fears on that score.

Probably it was just the country person's legendary resistance to incomers. Anyway, she was getting a ride out of it, and she was going to enjoy it. She put on her jeans, her chambray shirt and her sensible shoes (which had been stuffed with paper and put before the fire last night to dry, and which someone had taken away in the night and polished to within an inch of their life – she suspected Fatty, bless her – so that they were supple and gleaming again). Then, in honour of that noble creature, the horse, she brushed out her hair and plaited it neatly into one fat tail to hang down between her shoulder blades. Touch of lippy and mascara – just enough for self-respect but not enough to show – and she was ready.

Downstairs, Kitty was waiting with a beam of pleasure about the whole thing. 'I'm so pleased you're going to have a ride,' she said. 'I thought you might like this.' She handed over a carrot chopped into chunks. 'For establishing good relations. I don't know which horse he's borrowing for you, but a little upfront bribery never goes amiss.'

'Thanks,' said Jenna.

'And these,' she went on, 'as your hands will probably be soft if you haven't ridden for a while.' It was a pair of fingerless leather gloves, worn, but obviously originally expensive.

'Thanks. That's very thoughtful of you.'

'I want you to have a good time,' Kitty said, turning away not quite soon enough to hide a little, secret smile. Now what was she up to? 'It's almost half past. Xander's always punctual, so perhaps you'd better go and wait in the yard, to save him having to dismount and tie them up.'

'OK,' said Jenna. 'See you later.'

It was, indeed, on the stroke of half past by Jenna's watch that there was the sound of multiple hoofs and Alexander rode into the yard on his big bay, which looked even more magnificent in the clear light of a golden afternoon. Actually, it had to be admitted that the rider looked pretty good, too. Without the riding mac, his body showed to advantage, the taut thighs and abdomen in the close-fitting breeches, the long, strong legs in the leather boots. Jenna tried to imagine Patrick in the same clothes and position and felt he would not have shone: he was more the lean and languid type, definitely cosmopolitan, fitted for lounging against bars and beside pools. There was a certain power to Alexander's shoulders, while Patrick's were more in the slim and neat class. Alexander was wearing a khaki shirt with the sleeves rolled up. His muscular forearms were nicely brown, and his watch was a surprisingly plain and battered-looking aviator on a leather strap. Patrick was an aficionado of expensive Tag Heuers and Rolexes – Jenna wondered suddenly if Charlotte's Cartier had been a present from him. That was his style. She banished Patrick and his floozie hastily from her mind, and arranged a smile for the nice man who was going to take her for a ride.

'Hi,' she said. 'You're very punctual.'

'Punctuality is basic good manners,' he said, to which there didn't seem to be any answer. 'This is Tabitha. Sorry about the name, but she's a nice ride.'

Jenna dragged her eyes from him to the mare he was leading. She was about fifteen hands, part Arab, milky white with a little dappling over the quarters. Her dark, expressive eyes were looking about her with interest; her goose rump and very long pasterns suggested that she would be fast, and could jump. 'She looks lovely,' Jenna said. 'I forgive the name. We all have our weak moments. Whose is she?'

'She belongs to Anne Tyler from Grey's Farm over at Burholt. She's away at university and her mother has difficulty finding time to exercise her, so she was happy to let me borrow her.' He looked down at her seriously. 'I'm to watch you carefully, and if you really *can* ride and have light hands, I'm to tell you you can borrow her as often as you like.'

'How indiscreet of you to tell me I'm on trial,' Jenna said. 'Though I probably would have guessed it from your gimlet eyes, and tooth-sucking of disapproval when I fall off at the walk.'

'If you do that I'll abandon you. Nice-looking mare, isn't she?'

'She looks like a jumper.'

'Anne does jump her,' he admitted. 'Or she did, until she went to university. Who knows how she'll feel when she gets back? University does change people, especially horse-mad girls.'

'What's she reading?'

'Chemistry.'

'Oh, she'll be fine, then. Male science undergrads are too dull to replace horses as a passion. Now if it had been English or drama . . .'

He laughed. 'You do say the most peculiar things.'

'I'm a most peculiar person,' she said solemnly.

He looked embarrassed. 'Oh, I didn't mean it as a criticism.'

'I know.' She smiled up at him. 'Shall we get going?'

The mare was wearing a halter under her bridle and he was leading her by its rope. Actually, she noticed that Victor also had a halter on, the rope tied round his neck. It struck her as unusually informal for such a formal man.

He handed her the lead rope and said, 'Will you be able to manage to mount on your own? Do you want me to get down and help you?'

'I'll be fine,' she said.

'I don't know how long it is since you last rode.'

'A couple of years,' she said. She brought out carrot chunks and the mare took them eagerly, and tossed her head up and down with pleasure as she crunched them. Jenna tied the halter rope loosely round the grey neck, and took the rein.

'Check your girth,' Alexander said.

'Yes, I will,' Jenna said. It was second nature always to check the girth, but he seemed to have doubts about a townie's first nature, let alone her second. She stuck her head under the saddle flap and hauled in the girth a couple of notches. Tabitha hitched her back up skittishly and kicked, but it was a very mild protest, not meant to do damage, and Jenna heeded it not.

'She might be a bit lively,' he said anxiously. 'Perhaps I ought to give you a hand to get settled.'

'I'm fine,' she said, pulling down the stirrup.

'Keep your nearside rein short,' he advised.

'Yes,' she said patiently. She was on her mettle now – no fumbling the mount! She got her foot in the stirrup – jeans were not ideal, being tight in the knee just where you needed flexibility – gathered herself, and with a great effort, managed to make it look as if it was not an effort, and was up and across. The mare wanted to move off straight away, but with the rein short on the nearside she could only turn a circle.

'Can you adjust your own stirrups?' he asked.

She looked up at him. 'Yes, Daddy,' she said.

He blushed slightly. 'Sorry. Am I being a bore? I feel a bit responsible for your well-being.'

'My being is quite well, thank you. Don't worry.' The unknown Anne's stirrup length worked all right for her, so she didn't adjust them. She settled herself, feeling the old thrill of being astride a horse, with all that power and potential beneath her. Tabitha was comfortably narrow, and her mouth was responsive at the end of the reins. 'Ready?' Jenna said.

'Oh, Lord, I almost forgot.' He reached to his offside, and produced a crash cap. 'I hope this fits all right. I've got a hand-kerchief to stuff it with if it's too big, but I don't know what we'll do if it's too small.' Jenna urged Tabitha closer and took it from him. 'I hope you're not squeamish about hats as well as boots.'

'I am,' she said, 'but I'm guessing you'll refuse to take me out without one, so I'll suffer in silence.' It was an adequate fit – good enough for someone who didn't intend to fall off, anyway. She'd always had serious doubts as to whether a hat would really protect you much, but it was the done thing to wear them.

'All set?' He gathered his reins and turned Victor. 'Stay behind me on the lane, and we'll get off it and on to a track quite soon. Then we can ride side by side.'

Tabitha jostled and jogged a bit, but Jenna felt quite comfortable. Her paces were wonderfully smooth and sittable, and she was obviously only eager – there was no vice in her. She followed Alexander's broad back and Victor's shiny rump up the lane and after a couple of hundred yards he turned left on to a track between the hedges and she came up alongside him. Both horses were flicking their ears back and forward excitedly, and Tabitha was pulling a little.

'All right?' he asked.

'Fine.'

'How about a canter to settle them down?'

'And to check if I really can ride?'

'Don't take it to heart. I am responsible for you and the mare.'

'Up to a point, Lord Copper,' she said, grinning.

He smiled too. 'All right, then. You go first, or she'll try and race. There's a gate at the end of the lane that'll stop you if she gets away from you.' .

'She won't,' Jenna said, and gave the mare the office. She sprang into a rocking-horse canter which Jenna had no difficulty in sitting, and after the first few paces she settled down and stopped trying to gallop. She *was* fast! The hedges whipped by, the sweet air buffeted her cheeks, and she felt her plait thumping her back rhythmically. It was heaven! After about a mile – all too soon – the gate appeared up ahead, and she sat down and slowed the mare, who came back to hand very well, though she didn't want to stop cantering, and halted with a couple of bounces in front of the gate. Jenna turned her head to see Alexander – who had been keeping well back so as not to encourage the mare to race – pull down into a trot and then a walk as he approached them.

'That was great!' Jenna said.

'You looked comfortable,' he said, with a slight question in it.

'She's lovely. An armchair ride. Did I pass muster, then?'

'You have a nice seat,' he said. 'I'm sorry if I've been a bit—'

'Magisterial?'

'Is that how it seemed to you? I'm glad you didn't say bossy. But I really didn't know how much riding you'd done, and you could have been—'

'Boasting? Lying?'

'I didn't say either of those things. Can we call a truce?'

'Consider it called. I'll let you open the gate, though. I was never very good at that.'

He opened the gate with a masterly ease, and they passed through on to another track at right angles to the first. It had trees to its right and a low hedge to the left, beyond which was a stretch of open, rolling fields and a fine view of the hills.

'Oh, this is better,' she said. He came up alongside her, and the horses adjusted their pace to each other, and walked along, heads bobbing, hooves making a soft thub-dub on the bare earth. The evening was clear and beautiful, the sunlight slanting and golden across the fields, illuminating a carpet of buttercups, and a million tiny flying things dithering in the warm air. Chaffinches and blackbirds were making their evening claim to territory, great tits were shouting *me too, me too!* from tree to tree, and now and then a robin thrilled the air with its wistful falling cadence.

'What a perfect evening,' Jenna said, enjoying the rocking motion of Tabitha's long stride. 'You were right about the weather.'

'Of course I was,' he said.

'Well, you needn't be too smug,' she said. 'We had a pretty infallible way of telling the weather in Muswell Hill when I was a kid.'

'You did?' he indulged her.

'Absolutely. It was a special piece of seaweed.'

'Oh, I've heard of the seaweed test,' he said, 'but never understood it. How does it work, exactly?'

'You put the seaweed outside on the window sill, and you look at it first thing every morning.'

'And?'

'If the seaweed's wet, it means it's raining. If it's dry, it means it's sunny. And if you can't see it, it means it's foggy.'

He smiling, shaking his head. 'You do say the—'

'Strangest things?'

'Well, you do, I've never met anyone like you.'

'Oh, I'm pretty normal,' she said. 'It's the rest of the world that's odd.'

'There you go again.'

'Shall I stop talking?'

'No, I like it. Everyone else I know is so – predictable.'

'Not Kitty.'

'No, she's an original all right,' he said. 'I suppose that's why you and she get on so well.'

'You think we do?'

'I've never seen her take to anyone as quickly. I suppose—' He stopped.

'You have a terrific line in unfinished sentences.'

He looked embarrassed.

'Did you think that the fact I was able to charm her meant I was a con man? Or con woman?'

'I didn't think that.'

'But you worried that I might be.'

He didn't precisely deny it. 'I'm very fond of Kitty. And she is all alone.'

'Well, up to a point, Lord Copper.'

'Why do you say that? That's the second time.'

'It's a quotation. From Evelyn Waugh.'

'I've never read him.'

'At least you knew he was a him,' she said with a grin.

'Thanks! I'm not a complete philistine. But what does it mean? The Lord Copper thing.'

'He was an autocratic employer. It was his employee's way of disagreeing with him. He couldn't say outright to his boss "you're wrong", so he said he was right "up to a point".'

'All right – setting aside the "autocratic" insult – what was I wrong about then?'

'You said Kitty was all alone. But she has Bill and Fatty and Mrs Phillips.' She didn't add Jim in case he didn't know about that. 'And you.'

'It's not the same, though,' he said. The smile faded from his face. 'It's not like being married.'

'No,' she said, having been thinking exactly the same in the bath the day before. 'Nothing replaces that.' She wanted to ask him about Stephanie, but didn't quite like to. He didn't seem the sort of person who would like knowing that two women had been discussing his broken heart behind his back.

'So what are you *doing* here?' he asked after a moment.

'You know that. Cataloguing for Kitty. And the longer I'm here, the more it seems the most terrible shame to think of her selling up and having to move. There *must* be a solution.'

'Do you think no one but you has ever tried to think of one?' he said, sounding cold and annoyed.

Oops! 'Of course not, but sometimes when a problem's under your nose it's harder to think clearly about it.'

'So I'm not a clear thinker?'

Oh, do stop being touchy, she begged inwardly. The stuffed shirt was back. 'I'm not trying to insult you. I'm just concerned for Kitty.'

'Oddly enough, so am I.'

Was there no way not to tread on this man's toes? 'I was wondering,' she said, cutting to the chase, 'about the National Trust. Couldn't she give the house to them, on condition that she was allowed to keep living there?'

'The National Trust doesn't take on properties any more, unless they have a large endowment attached to them. They don't want the expense of upkeep any more than the owners do.'

'Oh dear,' said Jenna. 'Another fine idea crashes and burns.'

'I can't believe you don't realize that we've considered all options. Do you think we're all rustic idiots?'

'No, I don't think that, and can we call another truce? I was so enjoying the ride, and I've no wish to quarrel with you.'

He was silent a moment, his nostrils expressive, and then he said stiffly, 'Truce is duly called. I've no wish to quarrel with you, either.' He visibly sought for something neutral to say. 'I like your hair done like that. Not everyone can wear a plait.'

'Thank you. It needs bushy hair to give it substance, that's all. Thin hair makes a thin plait and you end up looking like one of Nelson's ratings.'

He managed a smile. 'I don't see you as a jolly tar, somehow,' he said. 'Caroline wears a plait sometimes, but it's the other sort

– I don't know what you call it, but the plaiting goes inward rather than outward, if you know what I mean.'

'Yes,' Jenna said. One thing she *didn't* want to talk about was Caroline. New subject needed. 'You're supposed to be showing me the countryside. Tell me about the view. What are those hills over there?'

'Oh, they're part of a larger range, but they're called the Black Hills locally. We'll go there another day, if you like – it's a bit far for an evening ride, but there are some good tracks up there, and the view is wonderful. There's a monument on the top – can you see it?'

'Oh yes,' she said, digesting the fact that he was proposing another engagement. So he couldn't hate her entirely. More Tabitha – yippee! 'What is it?'

'Just a stone column. Everyone thinks it's a war memorial or something, but it marks the place where there was a Roman beacon. Some eccentric local landlord in the eighteenth century thought it was worth marking. How he knew there was a beacon there, I've no idea.'

'And what's that cluster of roofs over there? I think I see a church spire. Is it a village?'

'Yes, that's Chidding. That's where we're heading. Are you ready for another canter? There's a nice open stretch just along here – and a couple of jumpable logs, if you fancy it.'

'I bet Tabitha does. She's got jumper's hocks if ever I saw them.'

'You know a bit about horses, don't you?' he said with faint surprise.

'Just enough,' she said.

He was smiling again. He was like one of those spring days with sunshine, fast-moving clouds and occasional showers. He was a bit of a challenge, and no mistake; but she liked a challenge. And Kitty wanted them to be friends, so she determined to put her best foot forward and try to avoid tricky subjects for the rest of the ride. Given her normal nature, it wasn't like her to take so much trouble. Kitty should be grateful. It could only be for love of Kitty she contemplated it.

When they reached Chidding – a nice little village of pretty stone cottages, and a tiny church with an oversized spire – she discovered the reason for the halters under the bridles. Alexander led the way to the village pub, The Hart In Hand, and rode down the side of it to a tarmacked car park, at the far end of which was a patch of grass, a few apple trees still casting the last of their blossom, and a stout wooden fence with a wooden horse-trough standing against it.

He halted and dismounted in one fluid movement, and caught Tabitha's rein as Jenna came up beside him. 'It's such a nice evening I thought you might like to stop for a drink,' he said, looking up at her. 'They're used to horses here – they keep this patch of grass for the purpose. Is that OK with you?'

'Lovely,' Jenna said. 'What a nice idea.'

She jumped down, and they ran up the stirrups, loosened the girths, and tied the horses to the fence with the halter ropes. Then together they walked towards the back door of the crooked little inn, and ducked in to the low-beamed bar, where the light from the tiny windows bounced companionably off a large collection of brass and copper objects, and the metal bits of horse collars and the like. There were only two other customers in there, young men who looked like farm workers from their red faces and knotty forearms, who were having a game of darts.

The bartender came forward to greet them. 'Evening, Mr Latham. Nice evening for a ride.'

'Evening, Ted. Two tied up out the back – all right?'

'That's what it's there for. What'll it be?'

'What will you have?' Alexander asked Jenna.

Jenna surveyed the taps. 'Oh, a pint of best, I think, thank you.'

'A pint?' Alexander said with faint surprise.

Jenna's nostrils flared. No doubt Caroline would never do anything so unladylike as drink beer, let alone in a pint glass. But she bit down any such comment. 'It doesn't taste the same in a small glass,' she said pleasantly.

Ted laughed. 'A girl after my own heart,' he said. 'You're not wrong, either. Two pints, then, is it?'

When they were pulled, Jenna took hers from the bar and said, 'Thank you, Alexander.'

'Oh, please,' he said, 'call me Xander. All my friends do.'

'Well,' she said, 'I'd certainly like to be numbered among your friends, so: thank you Xander.'

'Thank *you*,' he said. 'I'd like to count you among mine, too.'

And they exchanged a look which was tentative, enquiring, invested with good will; and, if it was also a little speculative, who could blame them? A ride on a gorgeous summer evening can have that effect.

Thirteen

They went and sat on a wooden bench in an alcove by one of the little crooked casements, put their pints on a round wooden table before them and leaned back against the ancient oak wainscoting. The low beams emphasized Xander's height and size – medieval buildings like this were designed for a race of smaller beings.

Jenna said, 'Cheers!' supped some of her pint and remarked: 'Nice place.'

'Glad you like it,' he said. 'It's my local, more or less. At least, there is another pub slightly closer to me, but there's no place to tie up a horse, so The Hart wins on points. Besides, the other pub's called The Silent Woman, and the pub sign shows a coffin, so you have to be careful who you take there.'

'I can see that,' Jenna said. 'How did that get past the PC brigade? I didn't know you lived in Chidding,' she commented. 'Well, I had no idea where you lived, so I don't know why I'm sounding surprised.'

'I've got a little place here – just a tiny cottage. It isn't anything, not even especially nice, but it was all I could afford. I put all my money into the business. I don't have any to waste on home-making.' There was a bleakness to his tone when he said this that warned her they were probably near Stephanie-territory.

'I don't think being comfortable is ever wasted,' she said lightly. 'Where do you live in London?'

'Nowhere, at the moment. I was sharing a flat with a man, and we split up in painful circumstances, so in fact I'm homeless. Fortunately I was able to stay with my brother in the short term. Didn't Kitty tell you my story?'

'Kitty's very discreet,' he said – which wasn't saying yes and wasn't saying no. But if Kitty hadn't explained, it was no wonder he was wary of her for turning up out of nowhere.

'Well, it worked out nicely for both of us. I was made redundant at the same time, so I needed a temporary live-in job, and Kitty wanted a temporary helper, so we dovetailed.'

'Hmm,' he said, and she sensed reservations. He was frowning. Discretion lapsed. 'Now what have I said?'

'I'm sorry?'

'You've got that "she's probably a con artist" look again.' She stroked her chin, did a parody of his scowl, and said in a put-on gruff voice, 'Something in her story doesn't add up.'

He laughed, perhaps a little uncomfortably. 'You *are* a strange person! I wasn't thinking that at all. Just how unpleasant it must be not to have a place to live. My cottage is no great shakes, but at least it's mine.'

'Well, my flat was Patrick's, and I ain't livin' there no more. But look on the bright side.'

'There's a bright side?'

'Yes!' she said with more enthusiasm than she really felt. 'I have a whole fresh start. I can go anywhere, do anything, become anyone. How many people get to start all over at my age? Sweep away the mistakes of the past, reinvent yourself. The world is your oyster. Actually—' she short-circuited herself – 'I've never really understood that expression. I mean, an oyster shell's a pretty tight fit, even for an oyster. It doesn't really represent boundless freedom, does it?'

'It *is* strange, now you mention it,' he said, and thought a moment. She liked him for taking the mystery seriously. Patrick was always impatient of her 'flights'. Then he dismissed it with a shake of the head. 'I can't think what it really means. But what *are* you going to do with your life?'

'Dunno,' she said. 'Make myself open to offers, is all. Anyway, I don't need to think about it now, thanks to darling Kitty. Tell me, has your cottage got stables attached?'

'No, sadly. It could hardly be more basic. I keep Victor at livery, at Grey's Farm.'

'Ah, hence your intimate knowledge of Tabitha's situation.'

'Well, everyone knows everyone else,' he said, 'so I'd have known about Anne going to university anyway. Everyone knows everyone else's horses, too, in a small community like this.'

'Don't you mind that?' she asked, really curious. 'Living in a goldfish bowl?'

'Sometimes,' he said. 'Mostly it's a case of "if you have nothing to hide you have nothing to fear". And it's nice to know people care about you.'

'Do they?'

'In a basic way – yes. One thing, you wouldn't lie dead in your flat for a month until the smell gave you away, like a town dweller.'

She threw back her head with laughter. 'Oh, make room for me at once! That's been my overmastering fear ever since I left school!'

He smiled sheepishly. 'I don't say I brood about it. But it must be much lonelier living alone in the town than it is living alone in the country.'

'Well, probably,' she said, thinking suddenly that that would be her fate, when this country gig was over – living alone in town. 'Although it must be tiresome having everyone feel sorry for you, and telling you so every time you meet them.'

He stiffened. 'Why should you think anyone feels sorry for me?'

'Oh, I didn't mean you specifically,' she said hastily. 'I meant "one". Or me, even. Having my family commiserate with me about Patrick was nice to begin with, but I wouldn't want to hang around when they got to that stage of inviting "awfully nice men" to dinner on my behalf.'

He didn't laugh, as she had meant him to. He said, 'What does he do – Patrick?'

She didn't really want to talk about him, but she thought he might open up about his ex if she did about hers, so she said, 'He's an architect. Very successful. And he traded me in for a newer model.'

'I'm sorry,' he said. 'I can't imagine why he'd want to. You seem to me—'

'Yes?' she urged at last. 'You do pause in the most perplexing places.'

'Perplexing,' he said. 'There's a word you don't hear very often.'

'Prevarication is another,' she said, but he wouldn't be drawn. He didn't open up about Stephanie, but instead changed the subject rather clunkily to ask her what books she liked reading, 'besides Evelyn Waugh'.

So she shrugged inwardly and talked about favourite books, and then favourite old movies, since he didn't seem to have seen any new ones – 'Not since the Regent in Belminster closed down, and that must be – oh – five years ago.'

'Haven't you heard of Love Film?' she demanded, and it turned out that he didn't even have a DVD player.

'When would I get time to watch one?' he said. 'I'm hardly ever at home, except to bathe and sleep.'

And it occurred to her that he was leading a much more fulfilling life than anyone she knew in London, and she had nothing to feel sorry for him about. But he did have a list of old movies he liked from his younger days, and the subject kept them occupied until their pints were drained.

'I'd love to buy you another,' she said, 'but I didn't bring any money with me.'

'Thanks, but one's enough anyway. And I ought to get you back to supper. I expect Kitty's waiting it until you get home.'

'I expect she is. Well, it'll be my treat next time, then,' Jenna said, standing up. 'I haven't forgotten you said you'd show me the hills.'

He stood too, and looked down at her, his dark head bent a little under the ceiling beams, too tall and big for this cramped space, his face half hidden in the shadow. 'I'll do that with pleasure,' he said quietly, and a strange little thrill ran through her like a shiver as she looked up at him. *Pleasure*. Yes, it had been a pleasure, this time with him – most of it. When she wasn't treading eggshells. Perhaps when he knew her better he wouldn't be so reserved and difficult on certain subjects. He would learn that he could trust her.

Ha! And when was he going to get the chance to know her better? she demanded of herself derisively. In the remaining three weeks of her visit? And, naturally, it would have to be before he married Lady Caroline, Ice Queen extraordinaire. *Married*, remember that word? She had to break the moment. 'I've heard there are a lot of Roman remains around these parts too,' she said, pretty much at random. 'I ought to try and see some of them before I leave.'

He seemed to cool as well, on the word 'leave'. 'Not suitable for visiting on horseback,' he said. 'Talking of which, we'd better get back to our nags before they throw a leg over the rope.'

She led the way out, calling a cheery goodbye to the landlord, who returned it with, she thought, a speculative look. It cheered her up. In a place where everyone knew everything, it would surely not be long before someone told Caroline about how chummy her fiancé had been with the Scarlet Woman in The Hart In Hand at Chidding. *Eat my dust, sucker!*

She had underestimated the determination of the Russells. They hadn't long got back on to the track from the village road, and were walking side by side again, when there was a sound of trotting hoof-beats behind them. Xander looked round and said, 'Oh, it's Midnight.'

'Not by my watch,' Jenna said.

'Midnight's Caroline's horse,' he said, faintly impatient, as if she should have known.

She thought it was interesting that he had identified the horse first, rather than the rider, but forbore to say so. Instead she said, 'What a coincidence.'

He frowned. 'I'm sure it isn't,' he said shortly. 'She's joining us on our ride, I expect.'

They halted, and Jenna turned to look. Caroline posted towards them, looking to-a-hair perfect as though she'd been painted on the horse. Midnight was rather over-curbed and was spilling foam down his gorgeous back chest. He was a true black, with a white star so perfect Jenna would have bet Caroline had scoured the country for him; whether his performance would match his looks, she couldn't say. 'He dishes with his off fore,' she commented. She probably shouldn't have said it aloud, because it sounded like a criticism – which it was, of course.

Xander was silent a beat, and then said, 'A little, perhaps,' in a tone of voice that said, *that's enough from you, thank you very much.*

Caroline pulled down to a walk and joined them. Midnight smelled hot, and threw his head up and down, spattering the other horses with foam. She looked annoyed, and darted glances from Jenna's face to Xander's and back again, but with a visible effort composed her expression into a rather brittle smile. 'Fancy meeting you here,' she said.

'I told you I was taking Jenna out to show her some of the country,' Xander said, sounding annoyed-but-controlled in his turn.

'Yes, but I didn't realize you'd be riding over to Chidding,' she said. 'If I'd known I might have asked to join you.'

'I thought you were busy this evening,' he said, revealing far more than he was probably aware of.

Jenna could imagine the scene.

Why do you have to take this girl out?

It's only polite. And she likes riding.

Well, let her organize it for herself. You don't have to be involved.

Kitty asked me. I can't say no.

You'd say no fast enough if she was a man.

It's not like that. I'm just doing it for Kitty. Why don't you come with us, then you'll see for yourself?

No thank you very much! Anyway, I'm busy.

You didn't tell me.

I'm telling you now.

And so on. And Xander, the poor male fish, couldn't understand why, having resolutely refused to come on the outing, Caroline had now turned up, looking as if she'd been bashing about the country searching for them for the past two hours.

Caroline made the best of it. 'Oh, my engagement was cancelled at the last moment,' she said airily, 'so I thought I'd have a ride, as it's such a lovely evening. How are you liking Tabitha?' she addressed Jenna. 'I hope she's not too much for you? She hasn't been having much exercise recently. She's quite a handful, and I don't expect you've ridden much.'

Jenna could see Xander was on the verge of defending her, suicidally, as a good rider, and out of the kindness of her heart she stepped in and saved him. 'Oh, I'm just about managing,' she said humbly. 'Of course, I don't ride as well as you, but she's a forgiving horse, and she's taking care of me.'

Caroline was mollified. 'She's not a horse, she's a mare,' she informed kindly. 'But I wouldn't expect you to ride as well as me. I expect you'd ride quite nicely if you had the opportunity. Pity you won't be here long enough to get into practice. But as long as you're having a nice time tonight, that's all that matters. You haven't fallen off?'

'Not yet,' Jenna said, with a rueful laugh to suggest it was only a matter of time. Xander might be a man, but he wasn't completely daft, and he looked at her with a surprise that could have given the game away, had Caroline been looking at him just then. So she went on quickly, 'We were thinking we ought to be getting home – Kitty will probably be keeping supper till I get there.'

'I'll ride with you,' Caroline said magnanimously, 'and then Xander and I can ride home together when we've dropped you off.'

'Oh, do you live in Chidding too?' Jenna asked.

'No, but I keep Midnight at Grey's as well.' She smiled at Xander. 'I've left the car there, of course. We could go on somewhere for supper, if you like. There's that seafood place in Wenham St Stephen we were thinking of trying.'

If you could slip your arm through someone else's while on horseback she would have done it.

'Ah, the world is your oyster,' Jenna murmured wickedly, and was gratified to see Xander's ears go pink.

'We're not dressed for it,' he said tersely. 'Another time, perhaps.'

'All right. Toasted cheese at your place is fine by me,' Caroline said with a gay laugh.

They started for home. The path wasn't wide enough for three horses abreast, and Caroline got Midnight next to Victor before anyone else had time even to wonder what the order would be. She occupied Xander's attention ruthlessly, though she did turn back to address the occasional comment to Jenna, pointing out landmarks to her, giving her helpful hints about her riding, and telling her encouragingly that she was 'doing really very well – I'm pleasantly surprised'.

Then after a time she asked kindly if Jenna 'felt up to' a canter, and before she could answer, jabbed Midnight straight into a full gallop, presumably in the hope that Tabitha would dash after her and Jenna would be sufficiently taken by surprise to fall off. Victor and Tabitha both flung their heads up and pulled and jostled, but neither got away from their riders. Xander gave Jenna a glance to see if she was all right, and with a face like thunder put Victor into a canter. Jenna followed slowly, letting him get ahead in case he wanted to remonstrate with his beloved at the other end. Caroline was already out of sight, so there would be plenty of time. Once Victor was well ahead, Tabitha stopped worrying and was content to canter along and enjoy the evening – she had a nice way of looking around her all the time, as if she was admiring the scenery, that made her a very pleasant ride – and Jenna took her off the main path to jump the 'jumpable' logs again, which the mare cleared each time with extravagant ease.

By the time the other two came in sight, waiting for her in the middle of the path, any words they might have had were over, and they were both determinedly social. Caroline perhaps looked slightly disappointed that Jenna was still aboard and showing no signs of mud about her person, and Xander was wearing his most impenetrable look, but they both greeted her lightly and chatted about neutral subjects for the rest of the ride.

Back in the stable yard, Xander dismounted quickly and gave Caroline Victor's rein so he could come and help Jenna down. 'You'll be very stiff tomorrow, if you haven't ridden for years,' he said quietly, untying Tabitha's rope. 'Have a good, hot bath as soon as you can, and ask Kitty for some liniment. She's got a really good one for sore muscles.'

'Thanks,' she said. He was being kind, and she invested her voice with real gratitude. 'And thank you for such a lovely ride. I've enjoyed it very much.'

He didn't smile, but searched her face a moment as if making sure she really had enjoyed it. 'We must do it again,' he said. He hesitated. 'I'm sorry—'

She waited. *Surely* he wasn't going to apologize for Caroline?

But he didn't. 'I'm sorry you'll be leaving so soon. There are a lot of good rides round here. And I'd have liked to show you Carbury Sands.'

'Is that "sands" as in "by the sea"? I've never ridden on a beach,' she said, as encouragingly as she dared.

'Yes. But it's too far for a normal hack. You have to make it an all-day ride, or box the horses over. I usually box over. It's good for the horses' legs to sea-bathe. I suppose—?'

Caroline coughed meaningfully. He abandoned this line of thought and said briskly, 'Tell Kitty I got you back in one piece,' and turned away.

Jenna watched while he took back Victor's reins, and managed to mount neatly while holding Tabitha's rope as well. He nodded farewell, Caroline gave her a tight kind of smile, and the three horses clattered out of the yard.

Almost instantly, Bill was beside her. 'So she found you?'

'Caroline?' Jenna said in surprise. 'How did you know about her?'

'She came here looking for you. I guessed he'd take the tracks to Chidding, because it's a safe ride and he didn't know if you were any good.'

'The minx! She pretended it was coincidence, meeting us,' Jenna said.

He looked down at her. 'Don't get in between them,' he said seriously. 'She's not one to be taken lightly.'

'I don't want to take her any way,' Jenna said. 'And I've no interest in Xander. Don't worry.'

He nodded, patted her shoulder, and then smiled. 'You'll be stiff as a board tomorrow,' he said.

'Turpitude has its own reward,' she said, smiling back, and started for the house. Even standing still those few moments had stiffened her up. Bloody hell! Never mind tomorrow, she'd be lucky to get up the stairs tonight.

Kitty wanted to know all about it.

'Do you ride?' Jenna asked.

'Oh, I used to. I used to love it. I had my own horse in Kenya. And I used to exercise racehorses when we were in Hong Kong. But I'm too old now. Still, I love to see them, and talk about them. I want every detail. How did you like Tabitha?'

They ate in the conservatory and had the shepherd's pie with peas and baby carrots – 'Thinnings,' Kitty said – and Jenna told her about the ride in as much detail as she wanted, and the pub stop in Chidding.

'Oh, I'm glad he took you there. The Hart In Hand is a nice little place. I haven't been there for a while, but they used to do good pub grub. Xander lives just nearby.'

'Yes, he told me that. In a horrid little cottage, apparently.'

'Not horrid, really, just rather basic and, well, comfortless. It's a simple one-up-one-down labourer's cottage – quite picturesque in its way, stone, with a thatched roof, and roses climbing over it – but it strikes me as cold and damp and too dark inside – those little windows! I'm not a cottage person, really. I like high ceilings and big windows. And the bathroom's in a lean-to at the back and the kitchen in another. Rather primitive. It could be nice – or nice-ish, anyway – with some money spent on it, but he won't put a penny into it.'

'He said he doesn't care about comfort,' Jenna said.

'Oh dear, did he? I'm afraid he's been rather stern and self-punishing since he broke up with Stephanie. They'd been saving for ages for a house, and when they split up he insisted on dividing the money evenly, though I'm sure he'd put in much more than her. All he could afford after that was Ford Cottage. Can you reach the wine? Do refill our glasses, won't you?'

'Perhaps he really doesn't mind, though,' Jenna said hopefully. 'Men can be amazingly indifferent to the place they live in. I was rather spoiled, living with an architect, but other boyfriends I've had – well, they might notice if a wall fell out, but nothing much less drastic would impinge on them.'

'I know what you mean. And perhaps he really doesn't mind. But he was always so tidy and meticulous as a child, and even as a young man. He used to do beautiful watercolours. I have some somewhere – I must get them out and show you.'

'Watercolours?' Jenna was surprised. 'We didn't talk about art. We discussed books and films, but we didn't get on to paintings.'

'I don't think he does it any more,' Kitty said, sipping her claret. 'This is rather good, isn't it? I'm quite pleased – I chose it myself, and bought two dozen, so it's a good job it turned out all right. Where was I?'

'Xander doesn't paint any more?'

'I don't think so. Well, one doesn't do those sorts of things, does one, when one grows up and goes out to work. And he did rather have the – shall we say, lyricism? – knocked out of him.'

'By Stephanie?'

'Oh no, before that – by his parents divorcing. He took it rather hard. He was an only child, and they treated him very much like a grown-up, so he was devoted to both of them. But

I suppose particularly to his mother. He looks very like her, you know. Well, in fact, there's her portrait in the sitting room, so you can judge for yourself.'

They got up and Kitty led her to a painting on the wall, among many others, of a woman with thick dark wavy hair hanging loose over her shoulders, and a fine, high-cheekboned face that did have a certain look of Xander about it – though her eyes were not blue but very dark. 'She's lovely,' Jenna said. 'I can see where he got his good looks.'

'Well, Geoffrey was handsome, too. But he does look more like Xenia. She was Russian, you know. Well, Russian blood – she was born in England. I sometimes wonder if that's where he gets his melancholy streak. Not that she was melancholy – well, not without cause – but Russians are supposed to be that way, aren't they?'

They went back to their supper. 'So what happened?' Jenna asked. 'Why did they divorce?'

'Oh, the usual thing,' Kitty said sadly. 'Another woman. I must say I was astonished at the time because they were a devoted couple, and Geoffrey adored her. He was the last person I could imagine wanting anyone else. I think he had one of these moments of madness with a young girl – male menopause they call it nowadays. It didn't last, but it broke Xenia's heart when she found out about it, and even though he apologized and begged her to forgive him, she never could. For years he tried to get back together with her, but she wouldn't have him. That was the Russian temperament coming out, perhaps.'

'And what happened to Xander?'

'He stayed with her, of course. Well, he was at school much of the time, but he went to her in school holidays. And I imagine she tried to keep him away from Geoffrey when she could. She was very vengeful. In fact,' she pondered, 'he didn't really see much of his father until after Xenia's funeral.'

'She died?'

'Yes, of cancer. Tragically young.'

'How very sad,' Jenna said. 'Poor Xander!' She wondered if it didn't explain a lot.

'Yes, poor indeed. Fifteen, sixteen is a bad time in a boy's life for an upheaval like that. He ended up losing both parents. He coped remarkably well, but one can see that he must have pushed a lot of things inward.' She stared into the depth of her glass for a moment, and then said briskly, 'But he wouldn't thank you for pity. He picks himself up and gets on with things, and doesn't feel sorry for himself, so he doesn't want anyone else to feel sorry for him either. But I think, in a way, that's why he's fond of me – as a sort of substitute mother. Well, not that I can be a substitute for poor Xenia, but you know what I mean. I'm the same generation, and I was always *there*. It counts a lot to a child to have someone *there*.'

Jenna nodded. 'And then,' she added, thinking about it, 'to have the Stephanie thing on top of that.' Moody, difficult and damaged: however handsome he was, she was glad he was someone else's problem.

'Yes,' Kitty said. 'It couldn't have happened more unfortunately. But perhaps he had invested too much in it, you know. It would have been a big responsibility for Stephanie, to live up to expectations of that order. Perhaps in the end she couldn't take it. She was a lovely girl, but – rather ordinary, when it came to it. I think he saw more in her than perhaps was there; and in the end, maybe she realized that too. She ran off with a very ordinary man, so I expect she'll be happy. Of course, that only made it worse for Xander. If he could have seen that his rival was superior to him, he might not have minded so much. He's not,' she added, looking up at Jenna, 'a man to bear humiliation.'

Jenna thought of Patrick and his blonde in her bed. 'Which of us is?' she said lightly.

Fourteen

They had just about finished supper when the phone rang. Kitty went to answer it, and came back to say it was for Jenna. The phone was out in the hall, a wonderful old ivory Bakelite job from the 1970s, practically an antique; but if ever a house needed roamer handsets it was this one, Jenna thought as she went out to take the call.

It was – big surprise – Rock. 'Darling, how are you? Settling in?'

'The line's crystal clear,' Jenna said. 'You don't have to shout.'

'I'm in LA,' Rock said, very slightly lower. 'Everyone shouts here. The person who gets heard is the person who shouts loudest.'

'I'm betting you get heard,' Jenna said, grinning.

'It's my job to. Actors' lives depend on me.'

'It's so nice to hear from you. An unexpected honour.'

'Oh, I know, I'm not the best at keeping in touch, but I do think often about all you little ones back home. Big nostalgia trip. Especially you. I played with you instead of a doll, you know.'

'So what made you call suddenly?'

'Olly told me about your mission, and I must say I think it's wonderful that you're doing this for Aunty Kitty. Was that her who answered the phone?'

'Yes – why didn't you talk to her?'

'I wasn't sure it was her. It might have been the housekeeper or the maid or someone, and that would have been embarrassing. Anyway, I haven't seen her since I was a kid. What would I say to her? But I remember liking her. She used to give me cookies. And Uncle Peter used to do that trick finding a coin behind your ear.'

'Sure-fire stuff for kids.'

'Especially when he gives you the coin,' Rock said.

'So why did the Aged Ps drift apart from them?'

'Oh, the usual, I expect. Too much to do and too little time. Also they never had any kids, and in my experience people with kids tend to stick with other people who have kids, and vice versa. If you're sprogless, it's a great big bore listening to nanny-horrors and school-horrors and all the rest of it. Greg and I hardly know anyone with kids – except one or two of the big names, who keep their rugrats completely separate. Margie and Anton even have a separate *house* for theirs.'

Jenna loved the way Rock called international movie stars casually by their first names. Oh, the glamour! 'I thought you were toying with the idea of adopting?' she queried.

'Did Olly tell you that? He was winding you up. He knows it was totally a publicity thing. Emilia Estragona was trying for one, and she wanted me to do it with her. We got some good column inches out of it, and then I quietly dropped out. Of course, Emilia didn't get one in the end. They're really clamping down over there now, God knows why. Too much shoving from Madge, blast her. Why did she have to go on this African gig? The East Europeans are much more accommodating. You can get all the nice little Romanian babies you want – though I suppose they're not *quite* as camera-cute as the black ones.'

'Rock, you are a complete moral vacuum!'

'Hey! If an abandoned kid gets a nice home and an adoring mom, who's the loser? But I'm amazed you believed I'd be into that shtick. You know Greg and I have all we can handle with the doggies. You wouldn't believe what dog walkers charge in LA these days, and vet bills are truly terrifying! Just getting the new one chipped – oh, did Olly tell you we'd got a schnoodle?'

'Yes, he did mention.'

'You never saw anything so cute! We called him Smitty – Billy Smith is gonna be his godfather. Did Olly tell you Greg's got him for his new movie, opposite Julia?'

'You mean Billy Smith, now, not the dog?'

'Of course not the dog! Though come to think of it . . .' she mused. 'Julia and Smitty? I love that! I wonder if we could work it in?' She snapped back into brisk mode. 'But it was a terrific coup getting the part for Billy – and everyone says he's just ready for a big, big break.'

'I loved him in that political thing on the telly – what was it called?'

'*Governing Party*? Darling, that's years old! Of course, I forget you don't get stuff over there until it's growing whiskers. You haven't seen *The Room*, I guess?'

'The hospital drama? No, it's not over here yet, but I've read about it.'

'It's topping all the charts here, and Billy's huge in it. They've just signed up for a second series, so Greg's thrilled to have got him for *Stay of Execution*. He's just about going to squeeze the movie in before filming starts on *The Room* this autumn.'

'Well, congratulations. To both of you. And I hope Smitty gets his cameo role. Hey, that's a great name for dog food. Cameo Roll – just slice, and delight your dog.'

Rock laughed. 'You ought to go into advertising. You've got

an ear for it. Sweetie, it's been lovely chatting to you, but I've got to go. My other phone's been ringing itself off the hook.'

'It's been lovely talking to you, too. I don't remember when we last had a chat. You didn't ring for anything in particular, then?'

'Christ! Yes. I'd completely forgotten. About Aunty Kitty's house. I think it's great that you're trying to save it for her. Olly's brainstorming the family for ideas to make some money out of it, and it came to me: these stately homes are all the rage for movie sets. There's an agency over there that arranges it all. I'll send you the URL of the website. You can get five hundred a day for using the grounds, and fifteen hundred a day for interiors.'

'That sounds interesting. But wouldn't it be a huge amount of work, clearing the rooms out and putting it all back? I mean, Kitty's not young, and there's a heck of a lot of stuff in here.'

'Oh, no, they do all that themselves, and clean up afterwards and put everything back the way it was. You don't have to do a thing except keep out of the way.'

'Well, I'll certainly look into that,' Jenna said. 'Thanks, Rock, that's a brill idea.'

'OK, sweetie. It's been great, but I gotta go.' She became suddenly serious, quieter and much more English. 'Jen, I'm sorry about you and Patrick. And the job and everything. When you're done with Aunty Kitty, why don't you come out here? You could make a great new life for yourself, have a lot of fun, maybe meet someone. I can get you work with Greg's company as a runner to start you off, and you can stay in our apartment until you get settled.'

For a moment, LA twinkled and beckoned like a constellation. But the upheaval, and the loneliness of a strange city where you don't know a soul . . . 'It sounds great,' she began hesitantly.

'Think about it. No need to decide now. The offer stands. Give Aunty Kitty my love. Kiss kiss, babe.' And she was gone.

She had been peripherally aware, while talking to Rock, that something had been going on in the background – the sound of a female voice which, by its pitch and rapid delivery, could not have been Kitty's. Returning to the sitting room she found

Madeleine Enderby there, still on her feet, talking seamlessly. She must have come in through the garden – country people never seemed to use the front door. Juicy and Lucy were playing a rough and tumble game in the conservatory with Watch and Barney, with much wagging of tails and many play-bows to show it was friendly.

'Hi, Jenna,' Madeleine interrupted herself. 'How was your ride? How did you like Tabitha? Anne Tyler got a first with her in the juvenile jumping at the County Show last summer. Betty Tyler's so grateful to have her exercised, you could go out every day if you wanted. The Hart's a nice little pub, isn't it? They used to do good pub-grub there, but I haven't been in ages. Hub and I never seem to go out anywhere any more. That's why it was so great that Kitty had her party. I was just telling her what a great time everybody had. Just like the old days! We used to be in and out of each other's houses all the time. So when I took the dogs out for their constitutional I thought, instead of just tramping up the lane, why don't I pop over to Holtby House and thank Kitty in person?'

'There was no need,' Kitty said. 'You'd already thanked me over the phone.'

'Oh, but it's much more neighbourly this way,' said Mad.

'Won't you sit down, anyway,' Kitty said, 'and have a drink?'

'Love to, but this is only a fleeting visit. I only just popped in, as I said. Really can't stay, because I've got a mass of paperwork to do, and I only left it because the dogs had to go out and Si couldn't take 'em because he's gone over to Wenham St James about some feed – you know the Coopers at Yew Tree Farm are selling up?'

'I had heard a rumour,' Kitty said.

'Can't make a go of it, poor things, and they've got a load of feed they want to sell off at a bargain price to get rid of it, so Si took the pick-up and went to make them an offer. At least that way they'll get cash in the hand, otherwise the bank will probably end up with it. Their boy Jason going off to join the navy was the last straw. They always thought he'd make a career of the farm, but he wants the bright lights – they all do, don't they? Kids! Who'd have 'em? And Bob Cooper says what's the point of going on, even if they could, without someone to leave the farm to? I mean, it was his father's and grandfather's before him.

It's breaking his heart, but if they're going to have to sell it they might as well sell it now as later, he says, and at least have a few years taking it easy, without having to get up at four in the morning to milk the cows. Can't say I blame them. So that's another one gone.' She sighed. 'Soon there won't be any real farms left. And I've heard a rumour that someone from London's looking at Yew Tree as a weekend home, only of course they'll sell off the land and convert the barns, and knock the farmhouse down and build something new on the spot, which is a crying shame, because Joan Cooper says part of that house goes back to Charles the First or Charles the Second or someone, or was it Queen Elizabeth? Only it's not listed of course, so it's only a matter of getting planning permission, and that Ralph Puddephat – you know, the planning officer in Wenchester? – he'd give anyone permission for anything if you winked at him the right way. Not that I'm saying he takes bribes or anything, obviously that would be defamation, but he's a lot too chummy with certain business interests, Simon says, and there's more to that St George's development in Belminster than meets the eye! It's such a shame about the Coopers, but farming alone doesn't pay, unless you've got thousands of acres, and they felt they were too old to diversify. I mean you have to diversify if you want to survive these days. There's the Tylers doing livery and the Garnetts with their caravan park, and we've got the farm shop. And we're thinking we might go in for some holiday cottages too, because there's the old pigsties doing nothing, not that you could convert them of course, but we'd pull them down and build new and Si says as long as the footprint's the same, or not more than ten per cent larger, you can get permission all right, even without slipping old Puddephat something!' She twinkled. 'And we could get four in the space, enough to make it worthwhile. So it would just be a matter of getting a bridging loan for the building work, because Si's got some money coming in next year from an investment he made before he met me, clever man, which should be just about enough to do the work, and those cottages bring in quite a good return, I've heard, as long as you don't have a mortgage on them. Anyway, it's worth looking at. We all have to turn our hands to everything these days, don't we? Diversify, that's the secret. You can't make a living out of just one thing any more.'

She paused for breath, and Kitty said, 'Do let me get you a drink, and sit down and be comfortable.'

Mad beamed. 'You're so kind. But I really only popped in for a second, just to say thank you for the party, and to ask you about the asparagus.'

'The asparagus?'

'Didn't I mention it yet? God, talk about head like a sieve! The thing is—Juicy, get *off* her! *Bad* dog! I'm going to have to get him seen to, you know, and she does nothing to discourage him, the awful slut. *Juicy!* Mind you—'

'What was it about the asparagus?' Kitty nudged her desperately.

'Oh yes. Well, the asparagus you served us on Saturday was so fresh and delicious, I wondered if you had any surplus, and if so, whether I could sell it in the shop. Everyone loves asparagus, particularly the passing trade. Luxury items like that sell really well and bring people in. Asparagus and artichokes and strawberries – particularly strawberries. Have it on a chalk board outside and people stop and come in, and once they're in they buy other things. Now of course I can get them from our suppliers, but yours would be much fresher and nicer, and it's nice to be able to say it's really locally grown. And it would keep it in the family, wouldn't it? The village, I mean. I'd sooner you and I made a bit of profit from it than some bloke in Wenchester with twenty acres of glass. Of course, assuming you wanted to sell. And that you had some to sell.'

'It's very kind of you to think of me,' Kitty said, 'but in fact all the vegetables belong to Bill. He takes care of the kitchen garden, and he does jobs for me, like the lawns and hedges, in return for the produce. What he doesn't eat, I think he gives to friends. So, though it's a lovely idea, I'm afraid it's not on.'

'Wouldn't you need much larger amounts, anyway?' Jenna said. 'And an assured supply?'

'That's the beauty of a place like ours,' Mad said. 'You can be flexible, and sell what you want or you happen to have. Of course, some of the basics we have to get in bulk, but the luxuries we can slip in as they come. However, if it's not to be . . . It was just a thought, Kitty. I hope you're not offended?'

'My dear, of course not! Absolutely not! It was kind of you to think of me.'

'Oh, I was being kind to myself.' Mad smiled. 'That asparagus was the best I've ever tasted. Never mind. On with the circus. I must get back and fill in some forms. Bloody DEFRA. Come on, dogs! I'll see you around, Kitty – oh, and Jenna, if you want Tabitha again, I know Betty Tyler would be delighted. I had it from Cal Bateman, when he brought the milk, that Xander told her you had a good seat and nice light hands. And it would be a weight off her mind because Tabitha can jump anything and if she gets too bored in the field she just jumps out and then it's hell's own job to catch her again, to say nothing of the danger from the traffic, because people drive round these lanes like madmen. I don't know what it is about country people. You'd think you were at Brands Hatch sometimes. Honestly, this Focus went past me the other day. Must have been doing sixty, and I was in that narrow bit of Thorny Hedge Lane, you know, Kitty, where it makes practically a right angle round that big oak tree . . .'

Kitty came back in from showing Madeleine out, wiped imaginary sweat from her brow and rolled her eyes at Jenna.

Jenna laughed. 'She might as well have sat down and had the drink,' she said.

'Oh, she's a good soul, and as kind as they come, but her tongue's like a roller towel. I'm sorry you came in for that.'

'No, no, don't be. I like her. She's genuine.'

'I'm glad you like her, because I have a lot of time for her. Some people round here laugh at her, and avoid her because she talks too much, but I find it very restful.'

'I wouldn't have thought of "restful", exactly, in that context.'

'But you see, if she does the talking, it means I don't have to. I can just surf along on this lovely wave of words. It's effortless.'

'I see what you mean. By the way, that was Rock on the phone to me.'

'How delightful! How is she? It's such years since I last saw her.'

'She's fine. She sent you her love before she had to ring off because her other phone was going mad.'

'I'm sure she's tremendously busy.'

'If she ever isn't, she'll probably die of shock.' And she told Kitty Rock's idea.

She had thought Kitty would instantly dismiss it, but she listened carefully and asked a question or two, and then said, 'It certainly sounds like a possibility, though I fear a lot of clearing out would be needed, even if they did say they'd do it themselves, or they'd be two days before they could start. And the money would certainly come in handy. But I don't see how it could be the answer to my problem. I mean, even at fifteen hundred a day, there wouldn't be that many days a year you could get it, would there?'

'I don't know,' Jenna said.

'Well, there must be lots of properties competing for the bookings, and not all that many films and television programmes being made. I imagine if you could get two days a year you'd be doing well.'

'Yes, I see what you mean.'

'And three thousand pounds would be a wonderful addition to an income, but not enough in itself to keep the house going.'

'I think it's worth looking into, though, don't you?'

'Of course,' Kitty said. 'And thank you so much for thinking of it.'

'I'll look at the website and make some enquiries. I dare say someone from the agency has to come and inspect before they put you on the books. But I think this house has definite possibilities. The hall is beautiful, and so pure. And the grounds aren't overlooked – which means no modern housing or pylons in the background to be masked out.'

'I hadn't thought of that. You know a bit about it, don't you?'

'Oh, I've read some articles.' She smiled at Kitty. 'I'm getting so fond of this place I can't bear to think of you selling it.'

'I'm glad you like it. But let's not talk about selling – too gloomy. Do you know what I suddenly fancy? A cup of cocoa. Would you like one, or would you prefer a whisky, or something?'

'Cocoa sounds marvellous. And then can we watch *Governing Party*? They're repeating it on BBC Two, and Rock says Billy Smith, who stars in it, is the new hot property. I'd like to refresh my memory about him.'

'My dear, watch anything you like. I hardly watch any television, but I'm not beyond a hot property when there's one going.'

Jenna laughed. 'Well, he's Rock's new dog Smitty's godfather, so as Smitty's aunt, I'm a kind of relative of his now. I feel a family interest in him.'

'Well, as Rock's new dog's godfather's aunt's mother's cousin, I certainly have to be in on that,' Kitty said. 'Cocoa *and* biscuits called for, I think.'

Fifteen

Kitty was out working in her garden next morning, and Jenna was on the Internet looking up the difference between Chelsea and Rockingham figurines, when all the hair stood up on the back of her neck, and she jerked round to see Xander in the doorway of the library, watching her.

'How long have you been standing there?' she demanded.

'Oh, a few minutes. I was intrigued to see you so absorbed in your work you didn't hear me.'

'Those no-good dogs should have told me you'd arrived.' She pushed her chair out and stood up. It was good to see he was in his friendly mode. 'What time is it? Oh, nearly lunchtime. Are you staying?'

'I wish I could, but I've got to get to a sale in Wenham St Denis to bid for some things for a customer. Don't let me disturb you. I just dropped in to see if you were all right.'

'All right? As in . . .?'

'Not too stiff?'

'Oh! Well, I certainly felt it when I tried to get out of bed this morning – all down the inside of my thighs – but nothing life-threatening. I've loosened up now, anyway.'

'Good. I enjoyed our ride.'

'So did I. Thanks again for arranging it.'

'It was a pleasure. And you ride really well.'

She grinned. 'For a townie.'

'I didn't say that.'

'No, I heard you'd said nice things about me to Mrs Tyler.'

'Not nice things, true things,' he said. He was almost smiling.

'I won't ask how you know what I said to Mrs Tyler, but you can take it as an example of how everybody knows everything about everyone in a village community.'

'Actually, I can tell you exactly what the data trail was: the man who delivers the milk took it from Grey's Farm to Home Farm and Mad Enderby brought it here when she came to talk about asparagus. Disappointingly short and uncomplicated – no challenge to an experienced researcher like me. But no doubt you'll all do better another time. Anyway, I'm glad my riding style met with your approval.'

'So much so that I'd like to fix our ride to the hills with you. Sunday would be best from the traffic point of view, but I've already got plans, so I thought perhaps we could make it next Monday afternoon. If I get Fred to watch the shop – he's my restorer, who works in the back – I could get off a bit earlier. Would that work for you?'

'Oh – yes, as long as Kitty doesn't mind.'

'I'm sure she won't,' he said.

Jenna agreed with him. Kitty wanted them to be friends much more than she wanted her cataloguing done. Jenna did wonder what Caroline would think about it, but she wasn't going to ask him that and spoil the mood. He was looking at her with a faintly quizzical expression, as if he quite liked her, but was having difficulty working her out. She cocked her head at him. 'What?' she said.

'What do you mean, what?'

'You look as if you don't know what to think of me.'

He blushed a little. 'I'm sorry. I was just thinking—'

'There you go again, with the intriguing broken sentences.'

He shook his head. 'You do say such odd things. And I was going to say, I was thinking – that perhaps you aren't very like your mother after all.'

'And is that a good thing or a bad thing?' she asked. 'Or did you just mean in looks? I'm much scruffier than my mother – but you aren't seeing me at my best here, because Kitty keeps telling me to be comfortable and not to worry about what I wear.'

'You're perfectly suitably dressed for your job,' he said. 'By the way, Betty Tyler says that any time you want to ride Tabitha, you're welcome, just to give her a ring and she'll have her brought in and tacked up by the time you get over there. Kitty has her phone number. I thought you might want to have a couple more evening rides before Monday to get your muscles worked in. I'd like to come with you but I'm busy this week.'

'Thanks,' Jenna said, and had the feeling that by gabbling about clothes she had let him evade the question, and possibly missed out on some important information. *Damn you, unruly tongue!* 'I'll probably take her up on that.'

'All right. Now I really must go, or I'll miss the lots I'm interested in. Love to Kitty.' And he departed abruptly.

Jenna felt strangely unsettled both by his visit and his departure, as if things had been meant to be said that were not, and other things that had probably better not be said had been thought.

On Wednesday Jenna went into Wenchester to visit the reference library, and then went on to the museum, which had a good ceramics section. There was actually a curator there, rearranging one of the displays, and Jenna introduced herself and got into conversation with her.

She said her name was Nicola Pearson, and she seemed interested in Jenna's job, and practically salivated at the thought of all that chinaware. 'It must be a marvellous collection. It really ought to be shown,' she said. 'It's a shame that the public hasn't any chance to look at it.'

'It's not so much a collection at the moment as a diaspora,' Jenna said. 'But I'm doing my best to get it together. I've never really looked at ceramics before, but it's kind of interesting when you get into it. Why is there such a big department here, by the way? I mean, it's not a huge town.'

'Because of the local porcelain,' she said, and seeing that Jenna hadn't followed, added: 'You know, Wenchester china? You didn't know there was an eighteenth-century factory here?'

'Sorry,' said Jenna. 'I'm new to all this.'

'It's a small but important niche in the collectors' market, like Lowestoft, or Portland. Good early examples go for quite large figures now. It was only functioning for about fifty years, so the pieces have a rarity value, though in their time they weren't at the top of the range.' She smiled. 'Kitchen china, you might almost say. But anything becomes valuable if it's old enough and rare enough. We have some nice stuff here. I ought to show you what we've got so you can recognize it, in case there's any in your collection.'

What with an intensive lesson, combined with an interesting chat, the museum visit extended itself and Jenna finally came out into the street to discover it was lunchtime and she was starving. There was a café just across the road from which agreeable smells were issuing, so she went straight in. It was one of those whole-some and slightly amateurish places where well-spoken, grey-haired ladies in protective smocks served home-made soups, quiches and slightly lopsided cakes, and got into a muddle over the change. But the pea soup was delicious, accompanied by a hunk of rough granary bread, and Jenna enjoyed it so much she even went for a wedge of rhubarb pie afterwards with her coffee. It was nice to have a change of scene, and she enjoyed watching the people sitting at tables nearby and passing by in the sunny street. It was a pleasant way to spend three quarters of an hour.

She had just paid and was walking out into the street when her new cheapo mobile – bought in Belminster the same time as The Dress – rang.

It was Harriet. 'Hello. How's it going? Is your broken heart still aching?'

'They don't mend that quickly, you know.'

'I suppose not. Poor Jenna. But Olly says you like the place, and the old lady?'

'Don't call her that. She isn't a bit like one. And she's only the same age as Ma.'

'Well, I call Ma an old lady. You can't say she's young, can you? Or even middle-aged.'

'But "old" sounds condemnatory. Call her Kitty.'

'Whatever. Anyway, it's nice there?'

'Beautiful. And the garden's stunning – you'd love it.' Harriet was the only one of the family particularly interested in gardening.

'So Olly said, which was what gave me the idea. To make an income out of the place, I mean. Why not open the garden to the public? Lots of people go down to that part of the world specifically to look at gardens. They build their holidays around it. There's even something called the Garden Route – not that

I've ever done it, but I've heard of it. You'd only have to get on the right tourist board lists, get leaflets into the tourism offices, and you'd be on the circuit. How big is it?'

'The garden? Kitty says about four acres.'

'Oh, big enough, then.'

'But a lot of that is down to lawns, although there are two huge walled gardens and a woodland walk. And a wilderness. And some shrubbery and rhododendrons.'

'Well, that sounds all right. Especially if you can give them tea somewhere. People will always fork out for tea and cakes, especially when they've been on their feet for any length of time. It'll improve the profits.'

'There's the conservatory. It's pretty big,' Jenna mused. 'And the terrace if it's fine.'

'What you need is something to set you apart,' Harriet went on. 'Some element no one else has got, to make you a must see. She doesn't have the national collection of something, does she? A lake? Waterfalls? Or a folly, a grotto, something like that?'

'There's Centurion's grave,' Jenna said.

'What's that?'

Jenna explained. 'And the inscription is lovely: *beauty without vanity, strength without insolence, courage without ferocity, and all the virtues of man without his vices.*'

'That's so sweet!'

'It's taken from Lord Byron's tribute to his dog, apparently, but it works even better for a war horse in my opinion.'

'But it's perfect!' Harriet said. 'Sentiment and history combined! A dead animal and a brilliant story. You can't go wrong. People with children will love it, especially if you can dredge up lots of stuff about the horse, and maybe photos as well. Or did they have photography in those days?'

'The Crimean was the first war with photographs,' Jenna said. 'I don't know if there are any of him, but there's a portrait. And one of his hooves made into an inkstand.'

'Yuck! I'd leave that out, if I were you. Might put the wrong idea into young heads.'

'God, yes, they'd go home and make their hamsters into pencil cases.'

'Or their rabbits into fluffy slippers. But the grave and the inscription and everything are perfect. I'd happily bring Martha to see that.'

'Well, thanks for the idea,' Jenna said. 'I'll put it to Kitty and see what she thinks. She's very proud of her garden.'

'So, are there any cute men down there?' Harriet went off on another tack.

'I'm not here to date, I'm here to work,' Jenna said sternly.

'Ah, so there are some cute men!'

'How do you make that out?'

'You'd have said no if there weren't any.'

'Well, there's one who wants to take me out, and he is pretty cute, in his way.'

'Ha! Brilliant. You've got a date!'

'I didn't say that. I haven't completely made up my mind yet. I'm not sure I'm ready.'

'Ready? For heaven's sake, nobody's asking you to marry the bloke! Just go out with him. You have to get back on the horse, Jen.'

'And I haven't asked Kitty.'

'You're not thinking of taking her along?'

'Ha ha. But she likes my company of an evening.'

'God, I can just see the two of you, blankets over your knees, watching *Heartbeat* and drinking Horlicks. Get out there and live! Go on the date!'

Jenna laughed. 'All right, keep your hair on. Maybe I will.'

'I'll check up on you,' Harriet warned.

Kitty was out when Jenna got home, and she put in a few solid hours' work, undisturbed until Mrs Phillips put her head round the door to say she was leaving and that there was a bit of cold chicken and salad for their 'tea'. 'I didn't have time to cook anything, what with the mountain of ironing I had to do. All them double-damask dinner napkins – you've got to get 'em just right. Can't rush it. So salad it is.'

'Thanks, Mrs Phillips. What could be nicer than salad on a day like this?'

Mrs Phillips shook her head pityingly. 'Be a thunderstorm before long,' she said. 'You've got a lot to learn about weather.'

'Never mind. Whatever you've left'll be fine.'

Mrs Phillips nodded. 'And Bill Bennett brought up some strawberries, and there's cream left over in the fridge. You won't starve.' She disappeared.

Jenna worked for a bit longer, but her concentration was gone, so she decided to take the dogs out for a walk to stretch her legs. Only Barney appeared when she went looking for them, but he was willing as always for a jaunt. She made a circuit, finding a useful track between overgrown hedges that made a short cut into the back end of the village. The route home took her past Xander's shop, and she glanced at it, noting that his car was there, parked down the side street. She thought she saw someone moving about inside – the sun was shining on the windows so she couldn't see into the shop properly, just the ghost of a shape and a paler smudge of face – and hoped for Xander's sake it was a customer. Did someone wave, or was it a duster being flapped?

She walked on, noticing a change in the quality of the air. And there were clouds coming up, a particularly large, plummy-looking one in the west blocking the afternoon light, so that the declining sun made a liquid gold rim around its edges. Perhaps Mrs Phillips was right. A cold little wind fingered the back of her neck and she speeded up, suddenly eager to be indoors, and thinking about putting the kettle on.

Kitty got back just before the rain. 'Going to come down cats and dogs any minute,' she said, appearing in the doorway, slipping her silk scarf from around her neck. 'Will you help me check all the windows are closed? Fatty sometimes leaves them open to air the rooms, but the wind's getting up as well and the rain'll be the driving sort.'

By the time they reached the top floor, it was 'black as Newgate knocker' outside, as Kitty said. It was stifling up there, right under the roof tiles, even though several windows had indeed been left open, plus the skylight over the backstairs, and in the gloomy half light the big display cabinets in the corridor had a sinister look, as if they might start shuffling along on their bowed legs. Jenna told herself it was the rapid change of air pressure that led to fanciful ideas when a storm was brewing, and hurried after Kitty downstairs again. As they reached the hall there was a tremendous crack of thunder that sounded like a huge tree-trunk being split in half, and it made Jenna flinch.

'Do you mind thunderstorms?' Kitty asked, looking at her in concern.

'I don't mind them, really. It just took me by surprise,' Jenna said. 'Had we better close the conservatory doors?'

'Yes, better,' said Kitty. 'The wind's setting that way.' Watch was sitting just inside the door looking out mournfully at the unnaturally dark world. The rain started falling, in large, separated drops that smacked on to the terrace stones and bounced up like marbles. The dog jumped back, and whined. 'Poor chap,' Kitty said, stroking his head as she passed. Barney was nowhere in sight. 'He'll be under one of the beds by now. He doesn't like thunder.'

She took one door and Jenna took the other, and as they pulled them closed the heavens opened and the rain pelted down. At once the temperature fell ten degrees; outside a slash of lightning cut the sky, followed by a long-drawn-out rumble of thunder that sent Watch slinking away from the doors. It was almost as dark as night.

'Rather exciting in a way,' Kitty said hopefully. 'Raw nature in all its power. Gives you a perspective. Makes you realize how puny we really are.'

'Makes me realize that Mrs Phillips said she's left us salad,' Jenna said.

'Oh dear. Still, we can have a bottle of wine with it, to cheer it up. That's one of the many good things about having you here – that I can have wine with dinner every night.'

'You could anyway,' Jenna pointed out.

'I wouldn't enjoy it. I don't like to drink alone. Well, I shall go and change into something warmer, and then we'll see about the wine. Unless,' she added with a mischievous look, 'you're afraid to go down in the cellar in a thunderstorm.'

'You mean, because of that creature you've assembled down there out of body parts stolen from the graveyard? No, not a bit,' said Jenna serenely.

'The lightning will bring it to life, and it will be our slave and do our bidding,' Kitty said. 'Right up to the point when it murders us, that is.'

'I wonder if it can cook?' Jenna mused, following her to the stairs.

★   ★   ★

Jenna was down first, and almost jumped right out of her skin as a dark figure appeared before her in the twilit hall.

'Oh my God!' she said, clutching her heart. 'You almost killed me!'

'Sorry,' said Xander. 'I did call out, but I suppose nobody could hear over the noise of the storm.'

'I thought you were Boris Karloff, come up from the cellar.'

'Foolish mistake to make,' Xander said, deadpan. '*I* don't have bolts in my neck.'

'Now you mention it . . .' Jenna said. 'You're soaked,' she discovered.

'It's falling stair rods out there.'

'You got this wet just coming from the car?'

'Well – I thought one of my lights wasn't working.'

'And you couldn't wait until the rain stopped to check it? You men and your cars!'

'I'm not so very wet. It's mostly superficial – my jacket, and my hair.'

'Well, let's hang the jacket up in the kitchen where it can drip. And there's a towel in there for your hair,' said Jenna, getting briskly practical because there was something unfairly endearing about his sudden waif-status.

In the kitchen she took the coat hanger that the peg bag hung on and slipped it into Xander's suit jacket, and he reached up and hung it from the drying rack across the ceiling.

'The warmth from the Aga should do the trick,' she said, handing him the towel. He disappeared into it and rubbed his head vigorously, emerging with wildly ruffled hair and eyelashes stuck together with damp. They were amazingly long and thick for a man, she thought. For an instant the world seemed to stop turning, and she was painfully aware of his closeness, his height and weight filling her immediate horizon, blocking out everything but his presence. Her mouth was dry, and she felt a sort of distant shock, as if of recognition. 'You'll need something else to put on,' she heard her voice say, very far away. 'It's cold this evening.'

The click of nails heralded Watch's arrival, to thrust himself between them for comforting, and the world jolted and rolled on.

A moment later Kitty came in saying, 'There you are! I

wondered – oh, and Xander! I didn't hear you arrive – too much noise outside. I wasn't expecting you, was I? Dear boy, are you wet?'

'Not very,' Xander said, his eyes still on Jenna's. 'And we've taken care of that.'

She wrenched her gaze away. 'He'll need a jumper or something, Kitty. His jacket has to dry.'

'I'll get something,' Kitty said eagerly, turning away, but he stopped her.

'No need to go upstairs. There's that old gardening sweater you keep in the lobby. That will do.'

'Are you sure? Well, put it on quickly, before you catch cold. Your shirt isn't wet, is it?' She touched it to be sure, on the chest. Jenna watched her fingers make contact and imagined the heat of his skin through the fine cotton. 'Oh, look, it *is* damp,' Kitty said reproachfully. 'And your trousers too. They'll crease horribly. You really need a complete change. Are you going home?'

He seemed to hesitate, and Jenna knew he was looking at her, though her eyes were turned resolutely away. 'I suppose I should. I was actually on my way when I suddenly thought of that cold damp cottage, and spending the evening there alone and – well . . .'

'Darling, say no more,' Kitty said eagerly. 'You don't need to be invited to *this* house, you know that. Of course you must stay – but we'll have to get you a change, because the house is like a tomb and you'll catch your death sitting about in damp clothes.'

'Why don't I go and light the fire?' Jenna said, jerking herself out of her paralysis.

'*Would* you? Do you think you can manage?' Kitty asked.

'I've watched you do it. I'm sure I can work it out.'

'Oh good. And I'll go and bother Bill for something for Xander to wear.' She beamed. 'How *nice* it is to have unexpected visitors! What a good thought of yours, Xander.'

'My motives were entirely selfish,' he said. 'But I hope I'm not going to be a strain on the commissariat.'

Jenna was already heading out of the kitchen, but she paused long enough to call mischievously over her shoulder, 'You can't be much of a strain on chicken and salad. *Cold* chicken and *cold* salad, that is. Welcome to Liberty' All!'

★   ★   ★

Fortunately the fire had been laid ready by someone – probably Bill – and the fuel was all dry, so it caught easily and didn't present Jenna with any problems. Outside the thunder and lightning had passed and it was just pouring steadily out of a gunmetal sky, the unnatural dusk melding into real twilight now. The sound of the rain drumming on the conservatory roof was quite comforting in a way, but the room was still chilly and unwelcoming, so she left the fire to put on some lamps, and then turned on the CD player, which still had the disc in from last time. She closed the doors into the conservatory, and soon the crackling of the fire was mingling with a Chopin étude and the rain could be heard no more.

Kitty came back with Xander, now clad in tracksuit bottoms, a sweatshirt and a pair of thick, nubbly socks donated by Bill, his hair drying but still tousled. She had never seen him anything but elegantly garbed and unruffled, and it was almost like meeting a stranger for the first time. They had evidently come back via the cellar, for he was carrying a bottle and Kitty had a posy of glasses in her hand. Watch padded in behind them and made straight for the fire, almost shoving Jenna out of the way to sit down with a sigh, staring into the flames so that he didn't have to notice the weather beyond the windows.

'Sacrilege really,' Kitty said cheerfully, 'but I thought we could have a glass *before* supper. I know wine is for food, but this Mercurey is *very* soft, and Xander promises he won't tell anyone influential what we've done.'

'Who cares what people say?' said the new version Xander blithely, wielding the bottle opener.

'Well, you do, dear,' Kitty reminded him, 'because they have to think you have impeccable taste or they won't buy their furniture from you.'

'By the way,' he said to Jenna, 'I saw you go past the shop this afternoon. I waved to you, but you didn't come in.'

'The sun was reflecting off the glass. I couldn't really see you,' Jenna said. You *waved* to me? You waved to *me*? 'I think the fire's caught all right,' she said. 'Should I put more wood on yet?'

'Yes, now's the time,' Kitty said. 'Shall I do it?'

'Let me,' Xander said. 'You pour the wine.' He knelt down on the hearthrug beside Jenna and reached over the dog to reshape the fire and put more logs on. The borrowed clothes smelled slightly earthy – she supposed they were some of Bill's gardening kit – which made Xander's strangeness more real. He looked younger, too, with his hair unsleeked and the rosy firelight glowing in his face. The everyday stern, controlled lines had softened, and he looked – yes, *carefree*: as he must have been in the past before his troubles fell upon him. That was why he seemed younger.

He turned his head and caught her staring at him. She blushed, but he said easily, 'Do you know the old saying about making a log fire? "One can't, two won't, three might, four will, but it takes five to make a fire."'

'That's right,' Kitty said. 'You can't be stingy, or it just goes out. A wood fire needs to be big.'

'Needs to be good wood, as well,' Xander said. 'What's this – ash?'

'Yes, and some laurel and apple,' Kitty said. 'Ash is the best for fires – fortunately, since it grows so fast and seeds so far.'

'What's that old rhyme, Kitty, about firewood, that you used to say when I was young?' Xander asked, sitting back on his heels and taking the glass of wine she offered him.

'Rhyme?' Kitty said. 'Oh, I know what you mean.' And she quoted it.

> *Beechwood fires burn bright and clear*
> *If the logs are kept a year*
> *Birch and fir-wood burn too fast*
> *Blaze too bright and do not last*
> *Applewood will scent the room*
> *Pear wood smells like flowers in bloom*
> *But ash-wood wet and ash-wood dry*
> *A king may warm his slippers by.*

'Oh, I love that,' Jenna said, and made her say it again so she could remember it. Kitty and Xander remembered other old saws and country sayings for her amusement as the fire blazed up and the rain fell steadily outside, making the inside cosier by contrast. Barney appeared looking shamefaced and sneaked into the firelit circle, where he flopped down with relief. The level in the bottle went down. The wine was delicious, very soft, as Kitty had promised, and wonderfully scented – 'Almost like violet cachous,' Jenna said.

'You're exactly right,' said Xander. 'You have a good nose.'

'It would be fun to go through some of Peter's cellar with you,' Kitty said. 'Both of you, I mean. Three is just the right number to try out a bottle. With two, you get too drunk too soon.'

'Well, this one's nearly dead,' Xander said, holding the bottle up to the light. 'Lovely burgundy, Kitty.'

'We'll try something else with supper,' Kitty said, and then her face fell as she remembered. 'Oh dear, cold meat and salad. I really can't get enthused by salad, especially on an evening like this.'

Jenna said, 'Why don't we do something else with the chicken? I'm sure there are plenty of ingredients in the kitchen. I can cobble something together with onions and garlic and – what else?'

'Rice,' Xander said. 'There's bound to be rice.'

'A sort of risotto, then?'

'Pilaf,' Kitty said. 'Isn't it a pilaf if it has meat in it?'

'I don't care what it's called,' Jenna said, jumping up. 'It must be better than salad. Shall I have a go?'

'Can't let you labour all alone,' Xander said, getting up too. 'We'll all go.'

The cooking session turned out to be moderately hilarious, with only Kitty sounding a note of caution as she thought of what Mrs Phillips would say if anything in her precious kitchen was left less than immaculate. Kitty found some chicken stock in the freezer to cook the rice in. Xander insisted on chopping the onions and garlic, which he said was a matter of chivalry. 'Can't have a lady's dainty hands smelling of garlic. What happens when your knight comes back from the crusades and wants his brow caressed?'

'I'll wash my hands while he's looking for the key to the chastity belt,' Jenna answered.

She cut up the chicken, and chopped a couple of rashers of bacon from the fridge, and then found some mushrooms in the larder, which she sliced, while Kitty cooked the rice. Xander reached down the biggest frying pan and they started chucking things in, frying the bacon, onion and garlic first, then adding the rice, chicken and mushrooms. Various dried herbs, salt and pepper, and finally, from Kitty, who was really getting into the swing of it, a few shakes of Tabasco.

Kitty got out some big pasta bowls to eat it from, with smaller bowls for the despised salad, which was acceptable now as an accompaniment, and they carried it all back into the sitting room with another bottle of wine – a fat and peppery Rhone this time, which Xander said would stand up to the food.

'Delicious,' Jenna said, sampling the first mouthful.

'Delectable.' Kitty went one better.

'You can taste the cooperation,' said Xander.

'And the fellowship of joint effort,' Jenna added. 'We ought to give it a name.'

'Risotto Holtby,' Kitty suggested.

'I thought it was a pilaf,' said Jenna.

'All right, then,' said Xander, 'we'll call it Edith Pilaf.'

'I have to ask,' Jenna said. 'Why Edith?'

'Because it's so delicious and nutritious we'll have no regrets.'

'I think you must be very drunk.' Jenna smiled at him. 'Delicious and nutritious?'

'If I were drunk I couldn't say it,' he pointed out.

'Mrs Phillips said a good one today. "Double damask dinner napkins."'

'That *is* a good one. "Double danask danner nipkins."'

It just got sillier, as they drank the Rhone and ate the delicious Edith and thought of ever more difficult tongue-twisters, right up to and including the fiendish 'Amidst the mists and sharpest frosts . . .' Jenna's sides ached with laughing. Xander seemed to have abandoned every last shred of dignity.

The dogs dozed and twitched in the warmth of the fire, darkness fell and the rain stopped. The food was finished, Kitty put some more music on, and a quieter mood came over them. They listened and talked comfortably like the oldest of old friends. It was an evening so undemandingly pleasant it was almost blissful – like being back home, Jenna thought.

'It reminds me of when I was a child,' she said aloud at one point. 'With Olly and Harriet, playing ludo on the floor for hours and hours. It was my favourite game when I was about six. I used to think it was the greatest treat there was, playing ludo with my brothers and sisters.'

'My parents sadly didn't provide me with any of those,' Xander said. She looked at him quickly, but he hadn't said it bitterly, and indeed he was smiling and relaxed.

'I sometimes think,' she said carefully, 'that it's a mistake to have too happy a childhood. Nothing else in life ever matches up to it, so it's all downhill after that. You grow up, you all scatter, and suddenly you haven't got a family any more. What do you do then?'

Xander considered the question seriously, looking into the ruby glow of the last of his wine, held up against the firelight. 'Make a new one,' he said at last.

Sixteen

Oddly, after such a pleasurable evening, Jenna didn't sleep well. She had disjointed, uncomfortable dreams, and kept jerking awake as if she had been called, and being unable to remember just for a moment where she was. She fell into a heavy sleep at last just before dawn, when the first birds began their chorus, and woke finally to find it was after nine o'clock.

The first image that came to her waking mind as she sat up, yawning, was of Xander, so disarmingly different and approachable in his borrowed slobs and unruly hair. It gave her such a tug, somewhere deep inside her, that she drove it out briskly, jumped out of bed and dashed for the shower. Why, at some point under the streaming water (*Xander dripping wet from the rain – oh, stop it!*), she should have decided that she *would* go out with Harry that evening, she couldn't afterwards determine. Probably it had nothing to do with the strange and beguiling evening she had just spent. She had probably been moving towards that conclusion anyway.

To her surprise, she didn't get the immediate warm endorsement she had come to expect from Kitty when she ran it past

her. In fact, for an instant, Kitty's face actually fell, though she
hoicked up the smile immediately and said, 'Of course – you
don't need to ask my permission!'

'But you didn't look pleased about it,' Jenna pursued. 'What's
wrong? If you don't want me to go out in the evenings I won't
go. Really, it's not that important.'

Kitty looked alarmed. 'Goodness, I don't need a babysitter.
What *are* you thinking – that I asked you here to take care of
me in my dotage?'

'No, but we have enjoyed chatting in the evening over dinner—'

'Yes, I love your company, but I'm quite used to being on my
own, and I wouldn't dream of interfering in your social life.'

'Well, then, what was it? You looked as if you didn't like the
idea.'

'Oh, it isn't that. Well, if you insist, it's just that he has a bit
of a reputation as a tearaway. But that could just be unkind gossip.
And you're a grown woman – you can take care of yourself.'

'I can. But we're just going for a meal, that's all. I shan't get
into any trouble.' She looked seriously at Kitty, wondering what
else might be troubling her. 'And I shan't get my heart broken,'
she added. 'Remember, it already is. That's the best defence – I'm
completely immunized against charm at the moment!'

The residue of doubt disappeared from Kitty's face. 'I hope
you have a lovely time. I really mean it.'

'Thank you,' Jenna said. She reflected afterwards that it seemed
to have been fear for her heart rather than her body or reputation
that had bothered Kitty, and wondered why. Was it something to
do with Xander, who had rebounded disastrously from Stephanie
to Caroline? Was she afraid Jenna might rebound into the same
family? The pleasing thought came to her that if she did, she'd
end up as Xander's sister, ha ha. Now wouldn't that please the
Ice Queen!

'Hey, Red!' said Harry. 'I was afraid you weren't going to call.'

'Oh, you shouldn't say that. It makes it sound as if you didn't
have complete faith in your irresistibility,' said Jenna.

'Well, I didn't mean it, of course. I knew you *would* call –
couldn't help yourself. I was just flattering you by suggesting you
had a choice.'

'We could play that game all night. Is the offer of dinner still on?'

'I've already booked the table,' he said. 'That's how confident I was.'

'You have to *book*? For Congolese food?'

'I told you, this place is cutting edge. For this week and next week, anyway. Who know what will be hot after that? Hey baby, the Success Express is leaving the station – you gotta jump on board!'

'It sounds exhausting.'

'We could eat in at my place instead,' he said sinuously.

'No, thank you. I've been warned you have a reputation.'

'That's very hurtful,' he said in wounded tones; and then, in curious ones: 'Reputation for what?'

'Vanity, vanity! All I heard was that you were a tearaway, whatever that is.'

'Oh, that's just the car,' he said. 'I'm relieved. I was afraid people actually did know what I was up to.'

'And what *are* you up to?'

'Well, I'm not going to tell you just for the asking, am I? Forewarned would be forearmed. Talk sense, Red! Shall I pick you up at seven thirty? Best bib and tucker?'

'Fine. See you then.'

Oliver phoned around six o'clock. 'I'm off to Delhi tomorrow morning, so I thought I'd check in on you before I go.'

'How long this time?'

'Six weeks. And that ought to be the end of it – I hope, anyway. I certainly don't want to be out there in the middle of summer.'

'Do you know where next?'

'Well, there are talks of the Arctic circle, but I imagine that has to wait until the ice re-forms next winter. In the meantime, I might even get a home posting for a few months, which would be heaven.'

'Really?'

'Sit in an office doing paperwork and drinking coffee, like normal people? Are you kidding me?'

'*Chacun à son gout*. Dream that dream, boy.'

'So anyway, for the next few weeks, at least, I'll be leaving it to Sybil to keep an eye on you. How are you, baby sis? You're sounding quite bright.'

'I'm fine. Moments of gloom and despair, but there's so much to think about here, interesting things and interesting people. It keeps me from brooding.'

'Excellent. At the risk of introducing a topic for brooding, yon Patrick still keeps phoning.'

'Really?' Jenna felt a quickening of gratification.

'Every day. Syb's getting almost sympathetic to him, though she won't tell him anything, of course. But she says the poor bloke's falling apart. He's desperate to see you.'

'I'm glad. I really want him to suffer.'

'Do you? I'll take that as a healthy sign. You don't want us to pass on your address, then?'

'God, no! He's probably only wanting to get Charlotte's watch back, anyway.'

'According to Sybil, Charlotte's history and he wants you back.'

'Are you trying to get me back with him?'

'Don't be daft. I can't advise you either way. I'm just telling you the situation so you can make informed choices. You won't be staying in Holtby for ever.'

'No,' she said, with a pang of sadness at the thought. Whatever the situation down here, it was at least simpler than her life in London, where she'd have a home and job to find, as well as 'getting back on the horse' – made more difficult when it was metropolitan types like Patrick you had to cope with. Maybe she could marry a simple ploughman and stay here for ever – living in a damp two-room cottage like Xander's, no doubt, she added derisively. Love among the haystacks. 'Hey,' she said cheerfully, 'I've got a date!'

'Good for you,' said Oliver. 'Is he nice?'

'Amusing,' she said.

'It's good to keep your hand in,' he said approvingly. 'Just don't go falling for the simple life, will you? It's never as simple as it seems on the surface.'

'How do you always know what I'm thinking? I do love you, Olly. I miss you.'

'I haven't gone yet. And don't forget the real reason you're down there – to find a way for Kitty to make a living from the house. On the subject of which – Sybil tells me to say "weddings" to you. Apparently rich people will pay huge sums to hold their weddings in stately homes, which I gather Holtby almost is.'

'Stately enough – and yes, I had thought of weddings. It's on my list with the other ideas – though there are problems involved with wedding hosting.'

'There must be problems involved with any of the ideas.'

'Yes, you're right. But don't worry, I'm working on it. Just got a bit of research to do, and then I'll be ready to make my presentation. I have to have all my ducks in a row, so that Xander can't shoot them all down.'

'I thought ducks in a row was exactly what people did shoot down. And why would Xander? He's the godson, Alexander, I take it?'

'Because he's a stuffed shirt. Only he's sometimes not as stuffy as others,' she added, remembering the moment in The Hart in Hand when he looked down at her, and the fact that he wanted to take her riding again. And last night . . . She shook herself. 'But he's bound to be stuffy about any idea I have for Kitty. He seems to suspect me of some devious purpose concerning her.'

'No wonder you say it's keeping you occupied. But don't get sucked in, will you, Jen? These people have their own lives, and you're not part of them.'

'I know,' Jenna said, though it made her feel sad to realize it.

Thursday evening was cool and rather damp, and Jenna was glad that Harry arrived with the roof of the car up.

'You're wearing That Dress!' he exclaimed as she came out to him.

'You said best bib and tucker. This is all I have.'

'I want to be buried with That Dress,' he said reverently. 'You look gorgeous.'

'Thank you,' she said. It was nice to be appreciated. 'You get the full warpaint tonight. I pulled my punches at the dinner party.'

'Probably wise. Poor old Brian Longhurst has a dicky heart.'

They didn't talk much on the drive in to Belminster. He drove fast, and the engine was noisy, and she was not a good passenger. She spent the journey holding on to the sides of her seat and working the invisible pedals in her footwell at every bend and corner. But despite driving at a mad speed, like all country people, he handled the car skilfully and they had no near misses.

The town seemed lively, with crowds of young people wandering along the streets and going in and out of pubs and coffee shops. Mazo's was down the end of Mill Street, where there were a number of restaurants. It had a purple fascia with the name scrawled in dull gold, and the windows were obscured with wooden bead curtains over unbleached cotton blinds, so you couldn't see anything until you went in. Jenna expected it to be empty – she couldn't believe there were that many people in Belminster interested in cutting-edge cuisine – but when they opened the door, the dimly-lit interior, throbbing with African music, was heaving. A waiter came to meet them with a refusal in his eyes, until Harry gave his name, and then he beamed and led them to a barely adequate table for two in a crowded corner.

'If this is popularity . . .!' she shouted to him as they squeezed into their seats.

'Great, isn't it?' he shouted back, his eyes shining. The decor was simple: plain, square, pale wood tables and chairs, aubergine coloured walls with primitive paintings in black and white, and small downlighters in the black-painted ceiling, which entirely failed to give the impression of stars twinkling in the vast night sky of Africa. They had taken the last table, and at every other there were couples and groups of the well-to-do leaning forward and conversing in eager bellows against the music.

The waiter brought them menus and apparently asked what they wanted to drink, though she couldn't hear what he said. 'Red wine OK?' Harry asked her, and she nodded. 'Yeah, baby!' he said, when the waiter had gone. 'Now let's score some totally ethnic food.' She couldn't tell if he was joking or not.

The menu was not extensive and the food was entirely unfamiliar to her. 'The kossa kossa is a speciality,' he said helpfully. The menu said they were *giant spicy shrimps.*

'So nice they named it twice?' she hazarded.

'How about one kossa kossa and one fumbwa to start, and we share?' *Yam leaves cooked in peanut paste and smoked salted fish*, said the menu.

'Whatever you say,' she agreed, taking the path of least resistance.

There was a lot of salted fish on the menu, and something called *manioc leaves*. She thought you wouldn't have to be a manioc to leave this place. The non-fish main courses were goat stew, Congolese braised chicken, and white bean casserole with pigs' trotters (she tried imagining it and wished she hadn't – pale and glutinous, with the pig's toenails peeping gruesomely out). She chose the chicken for safety's sake, and Harry went for the goat. The wine came – South African: she supposed the Congo didn't have any vines – and Harry gave the order, and asked for steamed rice to go with it. It was that or fried yams, apparently.

'Well, what do you think?' he asked when the waiter had gone.

'Seriously?' she asked.

He looked hurt. 'You don't like it.'

She tried to put her feelings into words. 'Well, that menu – the food was just preserved fish and plantain leaves, gussied up a bit with a few aubergines and chillies and a bit of peanut paste. It's basic peasant food.'

'Yeah, well, that's cool, isn't it?'

'Except that the peasants concerned probably couldn't afford it back in the Congo. I mean, don't you think it's a bit distasteful for all us fat, rich people to scarf up a dish that would do a whole family out there – and they'd probably only have it on someone's birthday?'

He blinked. 'Blimey, lighten up, Red. We're not in the Congo now.'

'I know. That's kind of my point.'

'Look, the ingredients came from the market in Wenchester, and our waiter worked in the Golden Jasmine curry house in Church Street until last month. His name's Desmond and he was born and bred here. It's a restaurant, not a UNICEF camp. It's a place for parting lazy people from their cash in return for cooking them dinner. If anyone's being exploited, it's us.'

She laughed. 'All right. Fair comment. I just wish it weren't so fashionable. I don't like to think of people being excited by this sort of thing.'

'Who's excited?' he said.

'I thought you were.'

'Only by the thought of a date with you.'

'Aah, you're so sweet.'

'I thought I'd never get you if I didn't impress you with Mazo's, but if I'd known you were going to go all Bob Geldof on me, I'd have booked us in to the transport caff for sausage and chips.'

'Sos and chips? Pure heaven!'

'All right – the lentil bar in Church Street for a veggie burger.'

'Ah, now you've got me. But why did you want to go out with me so much?' she asked, her vanity wanting feeding.

'To annoy Caroline, of course,' he said, straight-faced.

'Ouch!' she said.

He grinned. 'Gotcha! But actually, I seem to have missed my mark, because she's changed her mind about you.'

'How do you mean? I thought she hated me for some reason.'

'So did I, but now she's actually encouraging me to "get to know you". She was all smiles and sweet words.' He shuddered. '*That* you don't want to see before breakfast.'

'Is it possible she's mad?' Jenna asked. 'I mean, bonkers, not angry.'

'Oh, more than possible. I think she's both, actually. Here's our starters. One good thing about peasant food – it doesn't take long to cook.'

In fact, the whole meal was so quick they were finished and out in the street by half past nine. 'The night is still young,' Harry said. 'What would you like to do now? Go out for dinner, perhaps?'

She laughed. 'It wasn't that bad. In fact, mostly it was quite tasty.'

'In a school canteen way. Do you fancy a drink?'

She hesitated. The pubs all looked crowded, with loud conversation and music spilling out of the open doors into the street. 'The noise in Mazo's has made my neck ache,' she said. 'I'd sooner go somewhere quiet.'

He looked pleased. 'Right,' he said, rather too promptly. 'Back to my place, then.'

'Oi! I didn't mean that.'

'You misjudge me again. I just meant for a quiet drink. And so I can show it off to you. I like showing off my flat, and I don't get many chances.'

'I find that hard to believe.'

'I have very high standards,' he said loftily. 'But if you don't want to see the famous St George's development in all its glory—'

'All right, I'll come – on the strict understanding that there's no hanky-panky.'

He snorted. 'Hanky-panky? *Hanky-panky*? Have we slipped into the 1950s without my noticing?'

'You'd better hope not,' she said, 'or your flat will still be a warehouse.'

The ex-warehouse stood on the edge of a canalized part of the river. The brickwork had been cleaned to pristine yellow, the new windows and balconies had been added in smart ironwork, and a new row of trees was struggling to look convincing on the opposite bank, while the non-canalside approach had been expensively land-scaped. Everything about it spoke of new, young money, and lots of it.

'Nice,' Jenna said politely as Harry tapped a number into the keypad at the security gates and they swung silently open to admit them. It could not have been more of a contrast to Holtby House – but variety was the spice of life, she thought. The lift shot them to the top floor, to a corridor where he unlocked a door on to a staircase leading up to – 'The penthouse. Nice,' she said again.

'Where else?' he said. 'Nothing but the best for me.'

He ushered her in, and at that point words failed her. The place was massive, a vast expanse of shiny wood flooring leading to a bank of floor-to-ceiling windows looking over the sparkly lights of Belminster and the dark country beyond. There was a terrace, she saw, with flowers and shrubs in pots and a glass windbreak sheltering a table and chairs. Inside there was the minimum of furniture, very modern and expensive. One end of the vast room was a gadgety steel-and-black-marble kitchen; the middle was a sitting area; and the other end sported a top-of-the-market range of entertainment items, including a huge plasma TV, and sound equipment that wouldn't have disgraced a recording studio.

'Wow,' she said at last, since he seemed to be waiting for her response.

'Thank heavens,' he said with relief. 'I was afraid you were going to go with "nice" again.'

'Oh, you've moved way past "nice" here,' she assured him. 'How do you *afford* a place like this? What is it you do?'

'Property search.'

'Oh, I've read about that. That must be interesting.' Forgetting she was out of a job, Jenna was automatically thinking how it would be a good subject for a feature. She shook herself. 'But does it really pay that well? Or are you a drug dealer or gun runner on the side?'

'None of the above. My dad's rich,' he said simply. 'And given that his business is construction and property development, it wouldn't look good if his son had anything but the best apartment in St George's, now, would it?'

She was remembering that day in Belminster. 'Beale Cartwright? That office I saw you coming out of? I assumed it was a firm of solicitors. Your father owns it?'

'Most of it. Uncle Ben owns a quarter. Ben Cartwright. He's no relation, but when we were kids we called him Uncle Ben and it sort of stuck. He's nice. Dad can be a bit of a tartar, so it's good to have a soft touch to appeal to.'

'But if your dad gave you this amazing flat, he must be pretty nice, too.'

'Well, partly I earned it. Commission, sort of.'

'Oh, you do the property search thing for the company? I was imagining you searching for rich couples getting out of the Smoke.' She looked around. 'Well, if this was commission, I dread to think what the property was like that you found. Must have been a palace, at least.'

He looked embarrassed, and his eyes slid away. 'It's not really like that. Doesn't work that way. Anyway –' with a burst of what seemed like self-justification – 'it's not all roses. I don't have the penthouse completely to myself.'

'Don't tell me Caroline lives here too!' Jenna said.

'God, no. But Dad and Uncle Ben have dibs on the place, if they have posh clients they want to put up, or do a favour for. I have to move out and sleep in my old room back home. It's a nuisance, but . . .' He shrugged.

'Poor little rich boy,' she teased. 'What about that coffee you promised me?'

'Oh, bother coffee,' he said, stepping close. 'Anyway, as I remember, it was a drink that was discussed.'

'Was it?' He was very close now, and her nerve endings were quivering.

'To the best of my recollection,' he said, putting his arms round her. And then they were kissing.

Delightful smell of warm, clean man, delightful feeling of strong arms and nice lean body. His lips were warm, his breath sweet, and he kissed really well, not mashing her lips against her teeth or jabbing a tongue like a poker into her tonsils like some. The kiss prolonged itself, and she felt herself melting into it, revelling in the taste of a man after weeks of famine (and it was a long time, anyway, since Patrick had kissed her like this). Their tongues arced against each other and she felt him growing hard against her, felt the automatic response in her body. Then he moved one hand upwards from her hip to cup her breast, and it was like a bucket of cold water. Gently, so as not to offend him, but firmly, she disengaged her mouth and pulled back from him.

'I'm sorry,' she said. 'I can't do this.'

He looked confused. 'Oi,' he protested.

She pushed his hands down and stepped back a pace. 'I'm sorry,' she said. 'I did say no hanky-panky,' she reminded him.

'I thought you were enjoying it. It felt as though you were,' he said in wounded tones.

'I'm sorry,' she said again. 'I didn't mean to lead you on. And it *was* nice. You're a good kisser. But it's too soon for me. I'm only just out of a long relationship. It was a bad bust-up and it still smarts.'

He smiled beguilingly. 'All the more reason. Let me soothe those smarts! I promise I won't ask for a relationship, just meaningless sex. Good for the health, mental and physical.'

She couldn't help smiling. 'When I want a therapist, I promise I'll come to you first. But at the moment, it would be a really, really bad idea. I'm just not ready. Forgive me?'

He shrugged. 'Forgive? Of course. I'm disappointed, but – hey, them's the breaks. So, what *can* I offer you? How about some champagne?'

'Do you know, it's dreadful, but I think I *would* like some,' she said. 'It's this place – makes me feel as if I'm on the set of *Dirty Sexy Money*.'

'Oh my God, I hope you're not casting me as Jeremy!' He led the way towards the kitchen end, and opened the brushed-steel door of the massive larder fridge.

'How come you've got champagne here all ready, anyway?' she asked idly, as he extracted a bottle. Vintage Bollinger, she noticed with a mental whistle. Nothing but the best!

'I told you, Dad puts his business contacts in here when he wants to sweeten them. There's always champagne, and—' He stopped, and reddened.

'And?' she prompted.

He slipped off the foil and metal cap with expert movements, opened a cupboard and took out two flutes, and then popped the cork soundlessly in the best style.

'Very impressive,' she said, watching the champagne slide into the glass. 'But what was the "and" you baulked at?'

He handed her a glass and looked at her seriously across the rim. 'I don't want you to think I'm like them,' he said. 'I know I behave flip, but underneath—'

'You're a choir boy,' she finished for him. 'I knew that from the first moment I saw you. So what's the "and"?'

'A collection of pornographic movies,' he admitted. She burst out laughing, and he looked surprised. 'I thought you'd be mad,' he said.

'Why should I? It's not your fault. But it's so – *hackneyed*!'

'Tacky,' he amended.

'That too. Tell me, is there also a supply of fruit-flavoured condoms? Or do they have to bring their own?' She tried to drink while still laughing and the bubbles went up her nose, choking her.

He took the glass away from her while she recovered, then gave it back and said, 'A toast, then – to nice, normal, innocent friendships.'

'I'll drink to that,' she agreed, and they touched glasses. 'To friendship.'

'You and me *contra mundum*,' he added.

'Well, if necessary,' she said.

'It's a big, bad world out there. It might well be,' he said solemnly. 'And now, if I can't entertain you any other way, how about a tour of the flat?'

'There's more?'

'Bedroom and bathroom, of course. And the second bedroom has been kitted out in a particular way.'

He said it with a sly emphasis, and she cocked her head and said, 'This I must see. Lead me to the second bedroom.'

It was on the other side of the flat, occupying about two thirds as much space as the huge canal-side room. And it wasn't set up as a bedroom, but as a gym and games room. Jenna looked round with interest. 'I thought you were going to show me rubber suits and hanging frames with furry shackles.'

'*Would* I? Please, how you malign me!' He set down his glass on a table just inside the room. 'Now let's have some fun,' he said with relish.

There was a large trampoline; rowing, cross-training and weights machines; a treadmill; and a mechanical horse that reproduced the movements of a bucking bronco. 'That one's a lot of fun,' he said. There was a snooker table at one end, a foosball machine, and along the adjacent wall was a selection of arcade pleasures, including pinball.

'Now that's what *I* call exercise,' Jenna said. 'I'm a demon at pinball.'

'No woman can be a demon at pinball,' he said provocatively.

'Right, that does it,' she said, pretending to roll up her sleeves. 'You are *so* busted!'

Seventeen

Jenna woke refreshed and energetic after her evening out with Harry, which she counted to his credit. She didn't mind that he had made a move on her – she'd have been surprised if he hadn't – but she respected the way he took the rejection. In fact they had had a lot of fun, playing with his boy's toys. It was almost like being with a brother. She thought he enjoyed it too – he must have had a lonely childhood, with his mother dying so young, and a string of 'housekeepers' to bring him up until he was old enough to be packed off to school. Then when he finally got a sister, it was the Ice Queen.

Harry had told her quite a lot about Caroline in the course of their pinball tournament (she won) and several games of foosball (played to salve his dignity, because he beat her zillions-to-nil every time). As a result she, too, was puzzled as to what Caroline saw in Xander, and was forced to conclude that perhaps she really loved him. Her previous amours had all been rich, powerful and influential men and generally quite a bit older than her (Harry referred to them as 'uncles'). Searching for a father figure, Jenna supposed. Maybe, then, Xander was a sign that she was growing out of it at last and was ready to engage with the real world.

However, when she aired this idea to Harry he laughed so much he nearly hurt himself.

'She couldn't go straight if she was on rails,' he said when he recovered. 'She's up to something. She was *born* up to something. Conspiracy is the oxygen of life to her. I just haven't figured out what it is yet. And I wouldn't care, either, if it weren't that I quite like old Xander. He's been pretty decent to me once or twice, and he'll be hurt when Caro blows him off. He took such a beating when old Stephanie dumped him, and I hate to see a man kicked when he's down.'

Jenna reflected on all this in an absent way during her morning's work, and felt it was an object lesson in not getting caught on the rebound. But that naturally made her think about Patrick, and what Oliver had said about his wanting to get back together with her. Part of her yearned to 'go home'. It would be so easy: back to the flat, which she had loved, and Patrick, whom she had adored, and the job he said he could get her, the life she had enjoyed, the habits, comforts, friends and assumptions that had been the furniture inside her head for the past four years. She missed him, and she had made such an investment in him that, if he really wanted her back, it would be crazy to give it all up, wouldn't it? Perhaps the debauch with the blonde had been a seven year itch thing, and now it was out of his system everything would be set fair.

They might get married, move into a house, have kids. She and Patrick, a couple for life, like Olly and Syb.

But that thought pulled her up sharply. It wouldn't really be like Olly and Syb, would it? Because Olly would never have done something like that. And even if it was a one-off, what sort of a man would betray his partner *in their own bed*? How could she ever trust him again? And indeed, why should she? She must resist the yearning to go home and concentrate on indignation. How dare he say he wanted her back, as if it was that easy, as if she was his for the summoning?

Having fumed for a while, she dragged her thoughts away from her situation and got stuck into her work. After lunch, she walked down to the village post office for Kitty. On the return leg she saw the tall shape of Xander inside his shop. Remembering that he had queried why she hadn't stopped the day before when he had waved, she decided to be neighbourly and pop in.

He was alone in the shop, going through a box of silver objects, apparently checking them against a sale list. He looked up, with a frown on his brows which she took to be absence in thought, and by way of advancing a reason for her visit she said brightly, 'Hello! I was passing, so I thought I'd check on the arrangements for Monday, in case I don't see you before then. You did say you had plans for the weekend.'

'Monday?' he said, the frown deepening.

'Our ride,' she reminded him.

The frown became a positive scowl. 'I'm surprised you even mention that. I'm surprised, in fact, you have the gall to come in here. Or perhaps I'm not,' he added, with a scornful curl of the lip. 'You made it clear from the beginning that you thought your London ways were superior to ours.'

She was bewildered. 'What are you talking about? What have I done?'

'You know very well. Did you think you could just do as you pleased and no one would know about it? Belminster may be five miles away but that's nothing in the country. I warned you that everyone knows everything about everybody here.'

The 'Belminster' gave her a clue. 'Are you talking about my going out for dinner with Harry?' she asked in astonishment.

'Except that it wasn't just dinner, was it? You spent the night at his place. My God, it didn't take you long to show your true colours, did it?'

She almost told him that she *hadn't* spent the night there, when sweet reason caught her up. 'What on *earth* has it got to do with you?' she said. 'Do you really think I'm going to clear everything I do with you?'

'No, obviously you think you can go around doing whatever you like without regard to anyone else at all. You seem to think you're the only person on the planet. As to what it has to do with me, you're living in my godmother's house: what you do reflects on her. And as you clearly have no concept of things like honour, loyalty and respect, it falls to me to point them out to you.'

She stared at him, more in astonishment than anger. 'Oh, this is medieval!' she exclaimed.

The word seemed to inflame him. 'Yes, I imagine anything to do with decency strikes you as medieval, with your background, but it's how we live down here.'

'Decency? Because I, a single woman, have a date with a single man?'

'A date, you call it? Are you trying to tell me you didn't sleep with him?'

Again she almost did, but indignation saved her. She smiled, thinking of the trampoline. 'Well, we did bounce some springs,' she began.

He boiled over. 'My God, any bed will do for your sort, won't it? So much for your broken heart: you haven't been here two weeks and you're already working your way through the men. You *are* like your mother. The morals of an alley cat – and you don't care who you hurt. I should have known you don't look like her for nothing.'

'What's my mother got to do with it?' she demanded, angry now. 'You mentioned her before. What have you got against her?'

'You know perfectly well. It's obvious she taught you everything you know.' He turned away, looking suddenly bleak, unhappy and tired, the energy of anger leaving him. 'I'd be obliged if you would leave now,' he said with cold politeness. 'I have a great deal of work to do.'

He looked so miserable that in spite of everything he had said, she hadn't the heart to kick him further. Besides, not really understanding what it had all been about left her short of ammunition. She was more mystified than anything – though there was a low swell of anger that she was going to enjoy revisiting later, when she had stopped trembling – but the injustice and suddenness of the attack had left her close to tears. Without speaking she turned on her heel and went out.

Walking fast relieved her feelings somewhat, and when she came in sight of the gate to Holtby House, she slowed and examined her feelings. She had stopped shaking, and she didn't want to cry any more, but she felt utterly miserable. To have him think so little of her was painful, even though it was wildly old-fashioned of him to object to a woman sleeping with a man on the first date. But there *must* be something more than that going on, she reasoned. He thought her a loose woman, OK, but why would that upset him so much? Not because of Kitty, surely? Or did he think that loose sexual morals inevitably led to criminal behaviour, like theft and embezzlement? In that case, he would probably try to get Kitty to throw her out. She hated the idea of Kitty's turning against her. Perhaps she ought to get her word in first.

But that would mean telling Kitty about the row in the shop, and she was loath to do that. Kitty loved Xander so much, and she was fond of Jenna, too – Jenna knew that. Why upset her, shake up her world, for no reason? No, unless Xander said anything, she would keep quiet about it. After all, she would only be here a couple more weeks, and then she'd be out of everyone's hair and Xander could find someone else to vent his weird anger on.

It seemed that he didn't say anything to Kitty, because she was her usual self, and made no reference to Xander, or Jenna's date with Harry.

Harry phoned Jenna in the afternoon. 'I had a nice time, Red.'

'So did I. Thank you.'

'No ill effects from the nasty foreign food?'

'None at all.'

'Fancy doing it again some time?'

'Yes, I'd like that. As long as it's understood—'

'I know – no hanky-panky.' He sighed. 'You don't take me seriously.'

'Oh, was I meant to?'

'Cruel! I really must look up "hanky-panky" in the dictionary, see what I *am* allowed.'

'Nothing but a friendly goodnight kiss.'

'On the lips?'

'Maybe.'

'With a bit of tongue?'

'No! Way over to the side, practically on the cheek. Very dry.'

'Spoilsport. How about this weekend?'

She hesitated. 'I'm going to have a lot on this weekend,' she said. She was thinking of doing her exposition to Kitty about the options, and there'd be lots to discuss, possibly plans to make. She wanted to be there, free and uncluttered.

'Next week some time, then?'

'Yes, why not.'

'Are you going to the planning meeting on Tuesday?'

'I don't know. Am I?'

'I expect you'll want to hold Kitty's hand. How about a drink afterwards?'

'*You're* going?'

'Wouldn't miss it. I'll see you there.'

When she was packing up for the evening, Xander called.

'I wanted to apologize for getting angry,' he said stiffly. 'It was bad form. I hope you'll agree to forget it – for Kitty's sake. I don't want to upset her.'

'Nor do I,' Jenna said. 'Whatever you might think.'

'I—' He stopped, and seemed unable to finish whatever he had been going to say.

'Look,' she said, 'we just have to be polite to each other when we meet, and I don't suppose we'll meet often. I'll be leaving soon—'

'Soon?' he interrupted, sounding surprised.

'When I've finished the job.'

'Oh yes. I'd forgotten.'

'It won't be more than a couple of weeks, and then we can forget we ever met each other.'

'Yes,' he said. He didn't sound happy.

'So can you be polite to a species of lowlife like me?' she said archly. 'Your usual icy correctness will do. I promise you I won't think it implies approval.'

There was a long silence, as if he was thinking of a number of things he couldn't say. 'I can be polite,' he said at last. He hesitated. 'Look, about the ride on Monday—'

'Oh, don't worry about that,' she said, briskly efficient. 'I'll tell Kitty I cancelled it. I'll think of a reason. Just forget about it.'

'Oh. All right then,' he said. And then he put the phone down.

And that's that, Jenna thought. It was a pity it didn't make her feel any happier.

For the evening meal, Mrs Phillips had left a panful of bolognese sauce, since Jenna had assured her she was perfectly capable of cooking some pasta to go with it. She and Kitty had that with a salad on the side (Bill's own lettuce, spring onions and fiery radishes, with local glass-grown tomatoes – his weren't ready yet). They followed it with Mrs Phillips's apricot almond tart, and clotted cream from Parker's Farm.

'So what's on this weekend?' Jenna asked, replete and waiting for the energy to go and switch on the coffee.

'Well,' Kitty said, 'I assume you'll be going out on Saturday evening?'

'I haven't any plans.'

Kitty looked troubled. 'Oh, but that's not natural. A young woman like you *ought* to go out on a Saturday night. I don't want to cramp your social life.'

'You're not. I just haven't any plans.'

Kitty looked relieved. 'So you might make some, then?'

Jenna smiled. 'White woman speak with forked tongue. What's going on? You want me out of the house for some reason.'

'Oh, it isn't that – of course not! But as it happens, *I* have plans for Saturday, and I didn't want just to abandon you.'

'I'm a big girl. I can be alone in a house once in a while. Can I know where you're going?'

'Oh, goodness, it isn't a secret – well, not from you. There's a big country show on at Taunton on Saturday, and Jim and I thought we'd go – we both love those things – and then have dinner and stay the night. There's a lovely country inn we know in the Quantocks.'

'Sounds wonderful.'

'But I'd feel so much better about it,' Kitty said doubtfully, 'if I knew you were out somewhere having fun at the same time.'

Jenna laughed. 'Well, if it's a matter of soothing your feelings, I'll try and rustle up some plans.'

'Oh, *do*,' said Kitty, looking relieved. 'You oughtn't to stay shut in at home night after night at your time of life. It will make me happy to think of you being out on the spree like other girls.'

The spree, even a moderate one, had already got her into trouble, Jenna thought. Perhaps she'd make a nice safe date with a girlfriend instead. She hadn't seen Izzy since the break-up with Patrick. Perhaps they could meet halfway somewhere – if Izzy wasn't engaged, waiting in by the telephone on the off chance that Toby might call.

It didn't take much to persuade Izzy to abandon her phone-watching duties in favour of a girls' night out. 'It'll serve Toby right if he does phone and I'm not there,' she said with more defiance than conviction, as they had a pre-dinner drink in the bar of the White Hart in Andover, their chosen halfway house. 'Anyway, it's good to have a change of horizon now and then.'

'I needed to get out. I was getting cabin fever,' Jenna said.

'Oh rubbish! How can you get cabin fever in a great, big, huge, mansion-y palace of a stately home?'

'Nevertheless, without a change of scene from time to time I could go completely mad and start murdering people with an axe.'

'You won't go mad,' Izzy said confidently.

'It's been known to happen,' Jenna said darkly. 'There are people around the village who don't seem one hundred per cent mentally stable, if you get my drift.'

'I'll lend you my Uzi,' she promised. 'So what's with this house, anyway? How can people living in a stately home be so poor they have to move?'

Jenna explained about the running costs and Kitty's fixed income.

'But there must be a million ways of making money out of a

house like that,' Izzy said when at last she was convinced. 'Weddings, for instance.'

'That's one of the things on my list. But it would involve huge organization and I'm not sure one little old lady would feel up to it.'

'She could get someone else in to run the thing. Or what about a country house hotel? All those bedrooms – perfect!'

Jenna burst out laughing. 'Can you imagine the investment needed to get the rooms up to standard, fit bathrooms and fire doors, rearrange the reception rooms, buy furniture and bedding and towels and cutlery and crockery, refit the kitchen to meet Health and Safety standards, not to mention all the staff you'd have to hire? You'd want to be a millionaire to begin with.'

'Oh phooey. You always see problems with everything. Never mind, I'll keep thinking.'

'You do that,' Jenna said.

'So tell me about the local wildlife,' Izzy said when they were settled at their table. 'Any exotic fauna?'

Jenna told her about her date with Harry.

'Oh, very cunning, throwing him a false scent by playing pinball and trampolining.'

'It wasn't a false scent. I don't fancy him.'

'Really?'

'Well, a bit. But not enough. And it's too soon.'

'Oh, this is a Patrick thing, is it? Don't let that lowlife stop you exercising your democratic right to bed anyone bedworthy who crosses your orbit.'

'You're a fine one to talk,' Jenna pointed out.

'I know.' Izzy sighed. 'And I see it all perfectly when I'm away from him, like now. Twenty-twenty vision. But as soon as I get home, that telephone starts staring at me like a little yellow one-eyed god – it's actually grey, but you know what I mean. It's sorcery, plain and simple. I mean, what's so special about Toby?'

'You'd have to tell me,' Jenna said. 'Obviously *I* can't see it.'

'He's not even really good-looking.' Izzy sighed again. 'And he's going thin on top, and I've a horrid feeling he's the sort that won't let go gracefully, and I'll be in the humiliating position of being in love with a man with a comb-over.'

'*Is* it love?'

'I suppose it must be. Or he mesmerizes me. One or the other. Oh, I wish I could just get free,' she said with a surge of passion. 'Cut loose, break it off, over, finished, just like that.' She made a chopping movement of her hand on the table that made the cutlery rattle. 'You were so brave getting out from Patrick the way you did.'

'It didn't *feel* brave. And I sometimes wonder if it was the right thing to do.'

Izzy looked alarmed. 'Oh no, don't *you* have second thoughts! He was a louse, a creep, a subhuman! You deserve so much better.'

'So do you.'

'Well, maybe. All right, promise me you won't go back to Patrick, and I'll give Toby the heave-ho.'

'Really?'

'Well, I'll think about it. I'll try.'

'I won't hold my breath.'

'Probably better not to. But come on, apart from the Toyman, there must be some other useful types down in deepest Zummerzet.'

'It isn't Somerset,' Jenna pointed out.

Izzy waved a hand. 'They're all the same to me, these rustic retreats. Anyway, there you are, living on the set of *Pride and Prejudice*, so don't tell me there's no Colin Firth striding around in breeches and riding boots. Aha! I can tell from your expression there is. You sly dog! Or dogette, I should say.'

'It's not like that,' Jenna said. 'I mean, he could probably play Darcy, with a bit of help, but there's nothing between us, and never will be.'

'Never say never, girl. Come on, give! All the details!'

So Jenna told her the sad history of relations between her and Xander. Izzy listened with rapt attention, and at the end said, 'It seems obvious to me that the man has feelings for you.'

'I knew you'd say that!' Jenna said, exasperated. 'Look, I know you're only being supportive and best-friendy, but not everyone falls instantly in love with me.'

'Think about it,' Izzy insisted. 'You said his behaviour when he got mad with you was irrational – well, jealousy *is* irrational. He was jealous when you went out with this Harry bloke. Think about that lovely evening you described to me, with him in front of the fire, when he was all gentle and relaxed and amusing and normal? "The person he ought to have been," you said to me. He let down his guard, let himself go with you, exposed the tender green shoots of his feelings – and then the very next day you heartlessly go out and bonk another bloke.'

'I didn't—'

'Yes, but he thinks you did. S'obvious. He was hurt, mad, jealous. And that proves he has feelings for you,' she concluded triumphantly.

'"Mad" is the only word in there that fits,' Jenna said. 'He is clearly nuts, mad as a badger, besides being a moral dinosaur. So don't try to cook up a romance there, because he regards me as pond slime. My only business is to avoid him for the next couple of weeks, and hope not to upset Kitty.'

'As you please,' Izzy said with a secret smile. 'He who lives longest shall see most, as the Bard says.'

'The *Bard*?'

'My boss said that the other day,' Izzy admitted. 'I've been waiting for a chance to use it. Hey, do you know who I saw coming out of Ottolenghi's last week?'

The talk went on to other subjects of common interest. It was wonderful to have a completely relaxed girly evening, with absolutely frank exchanges and no need to watch what you said in case of misunderstandings. It made her miss London, and made her life at Holtby House seem remote and bizarre and quite unreal.

It was while they were heads-together, looking over the bill, that a movement made Jenna glance up and she saw Caroline Russell coming into the restaurant on the arm of a man. She hunched down even further so as not to be seen. Fortunately they were being led to a different part of the restaurant, and neither was looking her way.

'What?' Izzy said.

'Don't look now, but that woman who's just come in is the Ice Queen.'

'*No!*' Izzy said with enormous gratification.

'I said don't look now! I don't want her to see me and come over.'

'Don't worry, she's got her back to me. Ooh, I *hate* that dress! Nasty, nasty. No one should wear that shade of blue outside of an institution. The waiter's seating them – she's still got her back to me. But don't tell me that's your Colin Firth she's with? It's all right, you can look now.'

Jenna straightened up cautiously. Caroline's companion was a tall, lean man who looked to be in his forties, with a perma-tan and carefully tended, prematurely silver hair – the Steve Martin look. The hair looked suspiciously full, as if it had been blow-dried by a hairdresser to disguise the fact that it was thinning. He had a very swish suit and an over-white smile that spoke of expensive dental work. The archetypal silver fox. Good-lookingish, but not as good looking as he probably thought he was. 'No, of course it isn't Xander,' she said. 'I've never seen him before.'

'Thank goodness for that,' Izzy said. 'Gak! Mister obvious or what? I bet he's wearing make-up. And look at the way he's looking round, as if he expects people to recognize him and ask for his autograph. I don't fancy your Ice Queen's taste, in dresses or men.'

'But who is he, and why are they meeting here?' Jenna said.

'Maybe the same reason we are – halfway to London. The White Hart's very well known, and it's right on the main road.'

'A business meeting?' Jenna suggested.

'Not entirely,' Izzy commented, as Mr Obvious put his hand across the table and laid it on Caroline's. 'And look at that leer.'

'It's not a leer, it's a smile,' Jenna said, but she felt a pang all the same and thought, *poor Xander*. Was Caroline reverting to type? The man was obviously rich and looked as though he was powerful. Much more what Harry said was her taste. And certainly he behaved as if he knew he was important. As she watched, he released Caroline's hand to take a call on his mobile phone. 'No manners,' she commented.

'D'you know, I'm sure I've seen him somewhere before,' Izzy said, frowning. 'On the news, maybe. I mean, he looks like a B-list celeb, doesn't he? Oh, look at him with that mobile! Swanketty swank.' She put on a voice. '"I'm so important my people have to be able to contact me twenty-four-seven."'

'Interface with me,' Jenna corrected, and copied the voice. '"Sorry, I have to take this – it's New York."'

'Wouldn't it be wonderful if the Ice Queen snatched it from him and hurled it across the room?'

'Or into the ice bucket,' Jenna said as the waiter arrived at their table with one.

'Champagne? Mr Obvious runs true to form. Pass the sick bag, Alice.'

'Sshhh! They'll hear you,' Jenna hissed. 'God, he's looking this way. Let's go, before she turns round and sees us.'

'All right. We can pay at the desk over there. You go first and I'll selflessly interpose my body between you and the enemy.'

'You'd throw yourself on the grenade for me?'

'In a minute!'

They crept out.

'But I wish I could remember where I've seen him before,' Izzy said when they were safe. 'It's on the tip of my brain.'

'As long as we never see him again, that's enough for me,' said Jenna.

Eighteen

Kitty and Jim arrived home around midday, looking relaxed and refreshed.

'Good show?' Jenna asked.

'Superb,' said Jim. 'Especially the heavy horses.'

'They had a decorated tradesmen's vehicle competition,' Kitty said. 'Won by an old-fashioned coal dray pulled by a pair of the most glorious shires, all ribbons and shining brasses. And the runner-up was a rag-and-bone cart and Fell pony, with a mane practically down to its knees. Put me in mind of Veronica Lake. Magnificent. First-rate show all round.'

She and Jim exchanged a glance, and he laughed. 'The evening and night weren't bad, either.'

'Don't put me to the blush, you dreadful man!'

He kissed her lightly. 'I'd better be off.'

'Oh, aren't you staying for lunch?' Jenna asked.

'No, I have to go and visit Rose,' he said without inflexion.

When Kitty came back from seeing him off, she looked sombre. Jenna said, 'Oh Kitty, I'm sorry for being clumsy just then. I should have thought—'

'No, no, don't trouble yourself,' Kitty said automatically. 'You didn't know. Sunday afternoon has always been his time for visiting the home. I should say, one of them. And he rings Erica when he gets back, and has a long chat with her. It's a sort of family day, really, and I try not to intrude on it.'

Jenna thought of Izzy, who had often told her that Sunday, when all the world was with its family, was the hardest day of all to be a mistress. Not that the cases were equivalent, but all the same . . .

'It must be painful for you,' she said.

Kitty sighed. 'When we're away – like yesterday and last night – we forget about the situation. It feels so normal, being together. But as soon as we come back here, it all comes down like a thick fog.' She met Jenna's eyes. 'I feel so guilty. I never set out to be an adulteress.'

Jenna was shocked by the word. 'I'm sure no one—' she began hotly, and then stopped, remembering what Bill had said to her.

'It's just a fact, my dear,' Kitty said. 'There's no escaping it. Whatever excuses we use to ourselves, it's quite simply wrong. That's the price we have to pay.' She tried a smile. 'What is it they say nowadays? If you can't do the time, don't do the crime.'

Jenna had nothing to offer by way of comfort, so instead she settled for distraction. 'I was wanting to talk to you about something,' she said as they walked towards the kitchen. 'I've jotted down some ideas for ways to make an income out of the house, so that you don't have to sell it, and I'd like to put them to you and go over some of the points, see what you think.'

Kitty brightened. 'Really? How exciting. You are sweet to do that for me! Is that what you've been working on?'

'Part of the time. I've got a folder with everything laid out that I'd like to show you.'

'You are efficient! But we must have Bill in on it – he has a first-rate brain. And anything to do with the house . . . Wait while I go and speak to him.'

Jenna turned into the kitchen to see what there was for lunch, while Kitty went on to the communicating door. She was back quickly. 'After lunch,' she said. 'He and Fatty are just sitting down; they'll come through when they've finished. He's as excited as me. I've promised him we won't discuss it until they get here, so we'll have to talk about other things. Tell me about your Saturday night out. Was it fun?'

It was a glorious afternoon, hot and sunny with a nice refreshing breeze. Because of the latter they didn't sit outside, where the papers would get blown about, but around the table in the conservatory. Both dogs were there too, spark out on the tiled floor for its cooling effect.

Jenna laid out her papers. 'I've been thinking about this ever since I first got here, and Kitty told me she might have to leave, but I've had a lot of help from the family, suggesting things and answering questions, so this is a bit of a joint Freemont effort.' She smiled around them. 'I didn't want you to think I was this much of a genius.'

'I promise I won't think that,' Bill said solemnly. 'Let's go.'

'All right. I'll start with a couple of ideas which I don't think are immediately viable, but which might be worth revisiting further along the road. The furthest out came from my friend Izzy, which was to turn Holtby House into a country house hotel.'

Bill rolled his eyes.

'Yes, I know,' Jenna went on. 'The house is ideal in many ways, but it would take big investment and involve a lot of staff and organization; and, most importantly, it would mean it wasn't Kitty's home any more.'

'That's what I was thinking,' Bill said. 'Might as well sell the place as do that.'

'I agree,' said Kitty.

'Fine. I wasn't really proposing it as a serious suggestion, but we might as well have everything on the table. Secondly, weddings. Now that could make a lot of money. People these days are spending twenty to thirty thousand on a wedding, even quite ordinary people – and you can multiply that by ten or twenty for celebrities. The thing they're all looking for – and are willing to spend a lot of money on – is a romantic venue, and country houses are top of the list, thanks to all those films like *Pride and Prejudice*. Holtby is perfect: pretty but grand enough, set in lovely grounds, and with good accessibility – not too far off the motorway, and there's a good railway connection from Belminster.'

'But wouldn't it involve an awful lot of work?' Kitty asked.

'Most of it would be done by the wedding planner. They'd arrange the caterers and transport and flowers and all that sort of thing, and see everyone was in the right place at the right time. You'd have to make sure the rooms were ready, and you might have to make bedrooms available, for the bridal party to get changed in. Plus there's the question of getting the kitchen passed by the Health and Safety people – the caterers would want to use it for final preparation.'

'It's quite a new kitchen,' Kitty said.

'Yes, and it's well fitted. I don't think there would be much to do to get it certified,' Jenna said. 'But it has to be considered. Also to take into account: people at weddings don't always behave very well. You'd have to put away anything valuable or fragile, and expect a certain amount of damage – drinks spilled on the carpets and marks on the walls and so on. You'd have to get a drinks licence – which is not difficult, but it's something to consider. And, of course, you'd have to get registered to hold the ceremony, which again shouldn't be a problem, but will take time.' She looked round at them. 'I think that is one definitely to consider further down the road, because apart from generating good money, it also generates publicity, gets the house more widely known about, which fits in to the other ideas I've come up with.' She waited for comments.

'I like very much weddings,' Fatty said. 'Pretty bride, pretty bridesmaids. Many flowers.'

'Drunken couples copulating in the shrubbery,' Bill added. 'Drunken women in tight satin dresses vomiting in the flower beds.'

Kitty looked alarmed. 'Oh, surely not?'

'The thing would be to charge enough to make it exclusive,' Jenna said. 'A high price keeps off bad company. But if you charge a high price you have to offer the facilities. That might mean letting them stay overnight, and while Lady Mary's room would be a wow as the nuptial chamber, you'd have to get the other bedrooms up to scratch, which means investment.'

'Let's put that aside for the moment,' Kitty said, looking a little daunted. 'I don't think I'm up to organization on that scale.'

Jenna smiled. 'Don't worry, I've got plenty more ideas yet.

Number three is the one I've already mentioned to you – registering the property as a location for film and TV, which also includes advertising, fashion and magazine shoots. I have some contacts in that world that could be useful. The beauty of this idea is that you don't have to do anything. They move everything they want moved and put it back afterwards. They even bring their own catering van.'

'There must be some downsides,' Bill said cautiously.

'Well, they might cut up the grass a bit, but they're supposed to leave everything as they found it, so theoretically they ought to put the turf right if they do.'

'Other downsides?'

'There's a lot of competition. But the same things that make Holtby suitable for weddings will count for it for film location: good access, fine grounds – and it has a very pretty exterior. It seems to me there isn't much to say against this idea. I've got the details of an agency that registers properties for this sort of thing, and it's just a matter of contacting them and getting them to come and inspect.'

Kitty said, 'I can't see any reason not to go that far, anyway. If they like it, and if they confirm what you've said about putting everything back – well, it seems to me like money for nothing, and any income for the house will help hold it together.'

'So I'll put a tick against that one, shall I?'

'I like very much movies, also,' Fatty said. 'Will film stars come here, in costumes? Horse and carriages?'

'That's the idea,' Jenna said.

'Colin Firth and Huge Grant,' she said firmly, as though she were putting in an order for them.

'Especially Huge Grant,' Jenna said solemnly.

'I thought I was your hero,' Bill said to his wife in wounded tones.

She lowered her eyelashes. 'A woman must have dreams also,' she said mysteriously.

'Moving on,' Jenna said, 'we come to my sister Harriet's idea, opening the garden to the public. With the walled gardens, the woodland walk, and particularly Centurion's Grave, I think there's enough there to make it attractive, and a lot of tourists holiday in this part of the world specifically to look at gardens, so if you can get on the route, people will come. There'd be a bit of work involved in preparation, but nothing we couldn't do ourselves, and a bit of investment – a load of bark to reinforce the woodland path, ditto gravel in the walled gardens, some signposts to mark out the route – nothing major.'

'We used to open the garden when the village had the annual fête,' Kitty said. 'I mentioned that to you, didn't I? I think that might be quite a viable idea.'

'I suppose I must do my usual growl,' Bill said, 'and ask: downsides?'

'Well, mainly that you are in hock to the weather. If it's cold and wet, people won't come, and we've had a couple of pretty dismal summers recently. And I don't think you could charge a huge amount for entrance to the garden alone, so you wouldn't make a lot of money. However,' she went on, 'taken in conjunction with idea number five—'

'What an orderly mind you have!' said Kitty. 'I'd already lost count.'

'Only when it comes to work. You should see inside my drawers. Anyway, idea number five is opening the house to the public.'

Kitty looked anxious. 'Oh dear, I should so hate having people running all over the house all the time.'

'Don't worry, it wouldn't be the whole house. I've looked into other properties, and I think it would work with just four rooms, plus the hall. You couldn't have people roaming about all over the place anyway – you have to control them.'

'You do?' Kitty said, looking alarmed.

'Most people who visit houses like this are nice people, but you have to take precautions against the odd rogue. They have to stick to a route. Your having the two staircases is a real plus: it makes a proper circuit, and you don't have to have people coming up and going down the same staircase at the same time.'

'Yes, I see that. And which four rooms were you thinking of?' Kitty asked.

'I'll come to that in a moment, if I may. I'd just like to go through the financial side first, because if it's not going to work for you that way, there's no point in doing it.'

'Good point,' said Bill. 'Fire away.'

'OK. Looking at other properties, it seems to me you could start off by charging seven fifty for a combined ticket for the house and garden. You have to pitch it right and not put people off until you get established, and that feels about right to me. And you could charge two fifty for the garden alone. On a nice day there'll always be some people who fancy a stroll in pleasant grounds, and they'll pay a small amount for the privilege, so you might as well take it from them.' She looked at her notes. 'I would recommend opening only on Saturdays and Sundays to begin with. Realistically, that's when most people would come anyway. Though if it worked, you always could look at opening for more days during the six weeks of school holiday – mid July to the end of August. But for now, opening Saturday and Sunday from ten until four would catch the main flow of visitors and still give you all the rest of the week to yourself. And on the experience of other houses, you could get a hundred people a day through the doors.'

'Really?' Kitty said, brightening. 'Do you think so?'

'That's only three people every ten minutes,' Jenna said. 'Of course I'm talking averages. On a wet day out of the main season it will be less, but on a fine day in high season you could easily double those figures. But taking it as an average of a hundred a day, two days a week, from the beginning of May to the end of September at seven fifty a head, that would give you an income of thirty thousand a year.'

There was a silence round the table, and she couldn't tell if it was disappointed or awestruck. 'Well?' she said. 'Is that the kind of figure that would make it viable for you?'

Kitty hugged her arms. 'Thirty thousand? It would make all the difference in the world! It would be enough to keep the house going and to do the repairs I've been putting off. It would be the saving of us!'

'I hadn't thought it would be that much. I was thinking more along the lines of ten thousand if we were lucky,' said Bill. 'Do you really think that's possible?'

Jenna was pleased. 'Certainly possible. I've tried to estimate on the conservative side so as not to raise false hopes. Of course, you wouldn't hit the ground running – it would take time to get known and build up the footfall. But you have added value

– wonderful artefacts, steeped in history, and loads of connections to famous people, which would give you the edge over other houses. I'm convinced word of mouth would quickly put Holtby on the tourist map.'

'Footfall? Added value?' Bill laughed. 'I like it when you talk management-speak. Makes what you say all the more convincing.'

Jenna grinned. 'Ah, but your thirty thousand is only the beginning. There are all sorts of ways you can add to that. Film locations we've dealt with. Booked, private tours on closed days is another – with all the history here, I'm pretty sure that would be attractive. Historical societies, Townswomen's Guilds, WI, Round Table, old people's homes – they're all looking for nice, safe, interesting outings. And the entrance fee doesn't have to be the only money you take. People on a day out love to spend money. The biggest thing, if you can manage it, is teas. Tea and cake – it doesn't have to be elaborate, but a sit down and a cuppa will really add to the attractiveness of the house. You'd catch the garden-only people that way, too. Tea on the terrace – put that in your advertisements. Or in the conservatory when it's wet.'

'Tea and cake – is that all? Not sandwiches?' Fatty asked.

'I'd keep it simple to start with. Nothing perishable. Sandwiches are labour-intensive to make, and if they don't sell on Saturday you can't keep them for Sunday, the way you can with cake.'

'What a clear-thinking girl you are,' Kitty said admiringly. 'But it seems mean only to give someone cake for their tea.'

Jenna laughed. 'You're not inviting them as guests,' she reminded her. 'These are strangers who are paying you money. I promise you, cake will pay, sandwiches won't – at this stage of the enter-prise, at least. The downside,' she added with a glance at Bill, 'is that you'd have to make some investment to begin with. Tables and chairs, crockery and so on.'

Kitty sat up straighter. 'But my dear, we have all that stuff in the cellar! Folding tables and chairs, and boxes and boxes of cups, plates and saucers. And the big teapots, and two huge urns. We used it when we had the garden party for the village fête, but it goes back further than that. These big houses all had their open days. I think Peter's grandfather probably bought the furniture, and his father the crockery.'

'Well, that's excellent,' Jenna said. 'That makes a big difference. So what do you think about teas?'

'I like the idea,' Kitty said. 'My only worry is who would do the baking? I can't cook to save my life, and I'm not sure if Mrs Phillips would have time to do it all.'

'I will bake,' Fatty said. 'I make good English cake. Cookies, too, and muffins.'

'You could ask around the village,' Bill said. 'I'm sure there are housewives stuck at home who wouldn't mind a bit of pin money – I can think of two just off the top of my head. They'd love a job, but taking the kids to school and picking them up doesn't leave enough time in between.'

'And you've the champagne fridge to keep the milk in,' Jenna said, 'and plenty of cold storage for cake tins. Shall we put a tick against teas?'

'Oh, I think so,' Kitty said, 'This is getting so exciting.'

'What other ideas did you have for increasing the take – is that the right phrase?' Bill asked.

'Well, there are plant sales – that's the other thing people love spending money on. It might not come off this year, because you haven't had enough notice, but if you have time to take cuttings and set seeds and whatever other things you gardeners do, a nice table with pots of healthy plants and herbs ought to do very well. And they aren't perishable,' she said, smiling.

'At least, not on the same timescale,' Bill said. 'I think I could manage that. What about you, Kitty?'

'I've always got seedlings and cuttings I need a home for. Would people really buy them?'

'Oh yes – Harriet never goes to a stately without coming back with something. But you must make sure you cost the pot and compost into the price. The other big add-on would be a little shop of some sort. National Trust properties make more on their shops than in entrance fees.'

'They *are* lovely,' Kitty said. 'I haven't been to a National Trust property for years, but I do remember loving the shop. I think I still have a tea towel I bought there.'

'But how could we do that sort of thing?' Bill objected. 'They have everything with their logo on it – soap, notepads, tins of toffee.'

'We couldn't copy them, of course. But what I thought was along similar lines to your housewives baking the cakes. If you ask around there are always lots of people who do craft things who would love an outlet – patchwork quilts, baby clothes, paintings, pottery, all sorts of things. You let them sell their stuff in your shop for a commission. They'll probably be willing to man it for you, too, on a rota. As long as you vet the quality, it will bring in extra money for little extra work. But the main importance of it is not how much the shop takes, but how much more attractive it makes Holtby as a place to visit.'

'Yes, I do see that,' Kitty said. 'House, gardens, plant sales, teas, shop – I do see.' She smiled. '*I'd* come on a day out, and I've seen it all before.'

Jenna said, 'There are really few limits on what you can do to add value, but I don't want to go into that too much, because I want to keep it as simple as possible so that you can get started. The rest of the stuff is for the future, when you see how it's going, how much you're making, how much time and work you're willing to put in. So I've come up with a sort of minimum plan that I think you could get under way quickly and without too much work or outlay.'

'All right,' Bill said, 'let's have it.' He looked at Kitty. 'You know Fatty and I are on board with this. We'll do everything we can to make it work.'

'Bless you, Bill. You're too good to me,' Kitty said. 'And Fatty – I don't know where I'd be without you.'

'Well, I know where Fatty and I would be without you – homeless. So no more of that. Jenna, the plan.'

'All right,' Jenna said. 'You remember I said four rooms would be enough? Well, the dining room and drawing room are obviously perfect. They need only a little rearranging, moving some things out, putting others in. You want your most interesting objets d'art and paintings in the visitors' rooms, the things with a backstory. My idea is that they should illustrate the history of the house, and I've got some ideas about that for later. So, visitors come in through the front door, into the magnificent hall, and they buy their ticket. They look at the drawing room and dining room, then up the fabulous main stairs – we ought to have some paintings on the staircase wall, by the way – and along the corridor to Lady Mary's room, which again needs only a bit of decluttering and rationalizing to make it perfect. Then down the backstairs to the housekeeper's room, and out through the hall again to look at the grounds and hopefully finish up at the terrace tea-room. You shut all other doors – lock them if possible – and put "Private, no entry" signs on them, and rope off the corridors to keep the punters from straying.'

'Very neat,' said Bill. 'But there's nothing in the housekeeper's room. It doesn't stack up to the rest of the tour.'

'I've thought of that,' said Jenna. 'I think the big round table should stay—'

'Good, because it weighs a ton. I'd hate to have to move it,' said Bill.

'We've nowhere else to put it,' Kitty added. 'That's really why it's still there.'

'I loved the story about the housekeeper and maids sewing round it,' Jenna said, 'so it should stay there, with the watercolour of the scene displayed somewhere, and an explanation in the room notes. If you've got any old photographs of Victorian maids or domestic scenes, you could get them framed and set them out on the table – people love that sort of thing.'

'I'm sure we must have, somewhere,' Kitty said.

'What else?' said Bill. 'One table isn't much to look at.'

'No. What I thought was that you have stacks of china and porcelain around the house that people would love to see. My visit to the museum made me realize how popular it is. How about emptying out those mineral cabinets on the top floor, sprucing them up a bit, and putting them in the housekeeper's room, filled with a choice selection of ceramic goodies? That would give people something to look at that would take up quite a bit of their time, and having it at the end of the tour would make them feel they'd got their money's worth. We could call it the China Room.'

'You've really thought this out, haven't you?' Bill said. 'It sounds like a doable plan, but there must be costs involved.'

'A few signs, which we can make ourselves and get laminated. Labels for the artefacts, ditto. A couple of those velvet ropes on stands. Mostly it's just a bit of hard work, rearranging things.'

'And cleaning things,' Fatty said happily. 'I do that.'

'And there will be the room notes to do – a description of what's in the room and the interesting bits of history surrounding it. And a general one about the house's history in the hall. A dozen of each should be plenty – people read them then leave them in the room when they move on. They'll need to be laminated for durability. There's a printers in Belminster that does laminating – I spotted it when I was there last. It would be good to have an official guide book, but I've put that on the backburner until the house is up and running, though you'll definitely need one if you're to keep going. People expect it. That means photographs and text and finding a printer willing to set it out.'

'Well, guidebook aside, that doesn't sound too daunting,' Kitty said.

'But—' Jenna began.

'Here it comes,' said Bill.

'You will need volunteers, even just to open the house, forgetting the add-ons like tea and shop.' She looked around them seriously. 'You need someone in the hall to take the money. Someone in each of the four rooms, to keep an eye on things and answer questions. And a floating someone to take over when they want to go to the loo or have a cup of tea. Probably someone outside to supervise car parking – and I'd recommend someone patrolling the walled gardens to stop too many people nipping off bits of your plants and sticking them in their handbags.'

'Staff,' Bill said. 'I thought there must be a catch. That's eight people. There are only four of us.'

'Jim would help,' Kitty said hopefully, unwilling to see the golden plan disappear.

Jenna passed over the fact that they were counting her in. 'Eight each day,' she amended. 'The same people might not want, or be able, to do both days. And they won't want to be doing it every weekend. You'll need a pool.'

'What do we do? We can't employ people, or there goes the profit,' said Bill. 'To say nothing of the complications of employment law.'

'That's why the National Trust does it with volunteers,' Jenna said. 'And I have been assuming, Kitty, that you will be able to rustle up enough support around the village and among your friends to get the thing started. Once it's up and running, you can cast the net wider. There are always retired people willing to do a few hours, for the sake of the company and getting out, and because they're interested in old houses and so on. But do you think you can find enough people to get started?'

Kitty was already deep in thought, mentally going through her acquaintance. 'I'm sure I can,' she said. She looked fierce. 'I'm determined I *will*. We *must* save Holtby, and my goodness, thirty thousand a year—!'

'Plus anything you might get from film locations,' Jenna put in.

'Ted Phillips – Mrs Phillips's husband – might do the car parking,' Kitty said, still thinking. 'On one of the days, anyway.'

'You might get a teenage boy to do it for pocket money,' Jenna suggested. 'They like anything to do with cars.'

'That Walton boy who's always hanging around Goomer's garage,' Jim suggested.

Fatty stood up. 'I go make tea,' she said. 'Much talking to do.'

While she was away, Bill and Kitty got their heads together and started to jot down the names of people who might help. The list, Jenna saw, was hearteningly long. When the tea arrived, she said, 'There's one more idea that I haven't mentioned yet, and it doesn't really have anything to do with opening the house, but if you are going for a multiple approach to making money, I should just put it on the table along with everything else. It's produce sales. Mad Enderby was asking about your asparagus, Bill, and saying that she could sell things like that and artichokes and strawberries in her shop.'

'I told her all the produce is Bill's,' Kitty said sharply. 'You shouldn't have brought that up, Jenna. I told Mad at the time it was not an option, Bill.'

'But why?' Bill said. 'It wouldn't take much rearranging to extend those things and cut back on others. I bet she'd take baby carrots, too. And other fruit in season – plums and apples and so on. Why didn't you tell me, Kitty?'

Kitty's cheeks were pink. 'Because they're yours, not mine. You grow them, and it was made plain from the beginning that you could do what you like with them.'

He nodded. 'All right, suppose what I want to do with them is sell them to Mad to help keep the house going?'

'But it's not *right*,' Kitty said.

'Oh Kitty, if you have to sell up, what will become of us? We'll lose more than a few vegetables – we'll lose everything. If you're going to let us help you open the house, there's no sense in stopping us helping this way as well.' He turned to Jenna. 'You were quite right to bring it up. Don't let the Dragon Lady tell you off.'

'Dragon Lady?' Kitty said indignantly, while Fatty began to laugh, putting her fingers over her mouth.

'I'll go and speak to Mad first thing tomorrow,' he said. 'It's a bit late to do anything about the early produce now, but I can get her views on my tomatoes, and the autumn fruit.'

'But you always gave the surplus away,' Kitty said. 'What about those people?'

'Charity begins at home,' Bill said simply. 'They'll survive.'

Nineteen

Kitty went straight out on Monday morning to talk to various friends and acquaintances and ask if they'd be volunteers. Bill made a start on emptying the cabinets, prior to refurbishing them, while Jenna studied the proposed 'open' rooms and made notes about what needed moving out and in.

Kitty came back enthused. 'Everyone I've spoken to seems to like the idea. The vicar thinks it can only be good for the village – the shops would benefit, and the people who have holiday lets and bed and breakfasts would gain from having Holtby become better known. It's such a relief to know I wouldn't be offending people! And I've already got three volunteers – Dorothy Markham, Peggy Hayes and Agnes Dexter all said they would do it, and Agnes says her sister Marjorie, who lives in Burford, would too. And Dorothy said I should ask Mad Enderby's mother, June, because she's always interested in anything that gets her out of the house. She lives with them, you know, and it's not that they don't get on, because they're all very fond of each other, but she hasn't enough to do, and there's only so much reading one can do in a day, isn't there?'

'That's a good start,' Jenna said cautiously. 'Of course, you'd need a larger pool than that even to get started.'

'Oh, I know that,' Kitty said. 'They're just the first three people I asked, because they're my closest friends here, and it's encouraging that they all said yes. That's all I had time for this morning, but there are lots more possibles, before even thinking about the other villages around, and Belminster and beyond. Jim's going to canvass in Burford – oh, and I called in at the shop and told Xander, and asked if he knew anyone in Chidding.'

With all there was to think about, Jenna had managed to forget about the row with Xander. Her heart sank a little at the mention of him. 'How did he take to the idea?' she asked.

'Well, you know Xander. I didn't expect him to jump up and down, because he's always cautious, and likes to think everything through before committing himself,' Kitty said.

'Did you tell him it was my idea?' Jenna asked. That would put the kybosh on it.

'Well, he'd know that anyway, wouldn't he?' Kitty said reasonably. 'But why should that make any difference?'

Jenna had to be careful. 'I think there's some feeling that I'm an outsider without a proper understanding of local matters,' she said.

'But that's exactly why you're so useful,' Kitty said indignantly. 'None of us came up with a single idea in all this time, but you brought a fresh perspective, and your London savvy, to the problem.'

'I think it's my "London savvy" that's suspect,' Jenna said, but smiled, to keep it light.

Kitty dismissed it. 'Oh, you shouldn't pay any attention to this country-versus-town nonsense. Anyway, Xander doesn't think like that. I've heard him say many times that the small-mindedness of county people drives him mad.'

'Um,' said Jenna, unconvinced. But at least it seemed he hadn't blown the gaff on his disgust and hatred for Jenna and her metropolitan morals. He had kept his word. 'So he thought it was a viable idea?'

'He didn't go that far. He said he'd think about it before giving his judgement.'

Good of him, Jenna thought. 'Would you not go ahead if he was against it?' she asked.

Kitty looked troubled. 'I shouldn't be happy not to have him onside. He's the nearest thing I have to a son. But I always make up my own mind in the end. I wouldn't give it up just because he didn't like it.'

Jenna was glad to hear that.

Bill came down on his way to lunch and said, 'I've put all those rocks and things into boxes and numbered them, and I've had a look at the cabinets. They're in pretty good condition really – I don't suppose they've seen much action, stuck away on the top floor like that. A bit of regluing here and there, touch up the scuffs, give them a good waxing. One's got a broken pane, but I've got a bit of glass in one of my sheds I can cut down for that. The satin inside is a bit marked and worn, but I imagine that'll be covered up by whatever you put in them. I'll work on them up there, and when you're ready I'll get young Kevin Walton to help me move them down. I'll pop up there this evening and have a word with him, sound him out about the parking job, too. And his mum, Jackie, might be good for helping with the teas. She cooks part-time at The Crown,' he explained to Jenna. 'I think she'd be willing to make some cakes, and she might even help serve. She's a nice, cheery person.'

Kitty told of her progress, and added, 'We seem to be getting on quite quickly. I'm beginning to think this really is possible.'

'Of course it's possible,' Bill said. 'Anything is, if you're willing to put in the effort.'

'I've had an idea about getting started,' Jenna said. 'We ought to have a grand opening day, by invitation, and invite all the local people who can help us. And by that I don't just mean people who might volunteer. We should mark a wide radius on the map and invite anyone inside who's in the tourist business. Anyone who does B and Bs or holiday lets, or who has another tourist attraction, whether it's a house or garden or riding stable or petting zoo.'

'Well, there are quite a few of those,' Bill said.

'Shop owners, pub and café owners. Petrol stations, hotels. Tourist information offices. Local newspapers. English Country Cottages. Other National Trust places in the district. Anyone who might be in a position to recommend us as a place to visit. Eventually we'll get leaflets done and give them to all these people to stock, but until then it'll have to be word of mouth, so we need to get them onside. Invite them to an opening gala, guided tour, impress them with the place, and give them a really terrific tea.' She smiled at Kitty. 'Just for this one time, sandwiches will be wanted, not to mentioned scones with jam and cream, cakes, and maybe even strawberries. What do you think?'

'I think it sounds wonderful,' Kitty said. 'It'll be just like the old days. I do love a party.'

'I think it sounds likes a good business plan,' Bill said more soberly. 'The local newspapers would cover a gala event, which would be free advertising for us, and having a launch party like that would give us something to aim for, and focus our efforts. Otherwise, given that we're none of us professionals in this business, we might just drift and put things off, and never get started.'

'My thoughts exactly,' Jenna said. 'But it does mean you have to be sure this is what you want to do, and commit yourself to it,' she added to Kitty, 'because there'll be some financial outlay and a lot of hard work involved.'

'And once everyone knows you're doing it,' Bill added with a smile, 'there's a certain loss of face involved if you fall flat on it.'

Kitty dismissed that with a wave of the hand. 'Oh, phooey, my face can stand a little falling on. My mind's already made up. I *want* to do this.'

'When do you think we should aim for?' Bill asked.

'Well,' Jenna said, looking at them speculatively, 'I think the sooner the better, otherwise you'll miss the whole of this season. It'll take a bit of effort, but I think it's doable: how about one month from now?'

'A month?' Kitty said.

'It can be done,' Bill said firmly. 'As long as we can get the pool of volunteers – that'll be your special task, Kitty. The rest, as Jenna said, is just hard work and organization.'

'You're right,' Kitty said, girding herself. 'We'll do it.' Then she seemed to remember something, and looked at Jenna doubtfully. 'Oh, but I was forgetting. You were only going to stay another couple of weeks, originally. You will stay on, won't you? I don't think we could do it without you.'

In the excitement of the moment, Jenna had forgotten all about the original timetable. She thought fleetingly of London, of taking up the threads of her old life and getting her career back on course, but that all seemed faint and shadowy compared with saving Holtby House. What was a few weeks, or even months, out of the mainstream? She couldn't leave them now. She didn't think either of them had the organizational and computer skills to pull it all together. 'If you want me to, of course I will,' she said warmly. 'I want to see how it comes out. And I wouldn't miss the gala tea for worlds.'

That afternoon, while Kitty went back out to canvass, Jenna completed her notes on the drawing room and dining room. She was about to go upstairs and make a start on Lady Mary's Room, when she received a surprise visitor. There was a skidding sound of gravel, a familiar black sports car pulled up on the turnaround, and Caroline came striding in through the front door. She was wearing beige slacks, a cream silk blouse, chocolate brown suede waistcoat, and a silk scarf knotted round her neck in a swirling pattern of the three shades. How coordinated of her, Jenna thought, noting also the dark brown courts and matching handbag. She had never had a matching handbag in her life. Hers were always long-serving, adored and singular, and had to fit in with whatever she was doing.

The Ice Queen's hair and make-up were also perfect, and as Jenna appeared from the dining room to greet her, she looked under her eyelids at the sweat pants, baggy T-shirt, bare feet, and hair scraped back in a scrunchie which Jenna had considered suitable for working attire.

'Hello, Caroline,' Jenna said, trying not to sound too unwelcoming. 'Kitty's out, I'm afraid.'

'It's all right, it was you I came to see,' Caroline said, surprisingly. Barney came from the conservatory to see what was what. 'Keep that dog away from me,' she commanded. 'I don't want his dirty footmarks on me.'

Jenna caught his collar as he reached her, and pressed his rump to make him sit. Barney looked up at her. *I wasn't going near the nasty old witch anyway*, he said. 'What can I do for you?' she asked.

'Oh, nothing. It's the other way round, really. I was quite upset to hear about this quarrel between you and Alexander.'

Jenna felt her mouth make a grim line. 'How did you hear about that?'

'He told me, of course.' Caroline smiled. 'He tells me *everything*.'

'How nice for you,' Jenna muttered.

'Well, one must have absolute trust in a relationship, and I must say, there are no secrets between Alexander and me. And I have *no doubts* about his feelings for me.' She gave a little laugh. 'He adores me. I can't deny it. It's touching, really.' The smile switched off. 'So when I heard about this silly tiff between you, I said straight away that he was wrong.'

'You did?' As well as being deeply ungrateful for the intervention, Jenna was surprised. She thought Caroline loathed her and would have sided with Xander against her.

'Of course,' said Caroline superbly. 'It's perfectly natural for two attractive young people like you and Harry to want to sleep together. Everyone does it these days.' *Did that mean she had slept with Xander*, Jenna was about to retort; and then thought that she didn't want to know. 'I can't see the harm in it,' Caroline went on. 'Neither of you has any interest anywhere else. I told Alexander that in no uncertain terms. You and Harry have every right to a sexual relationship.'

Jenna gritted her teeth. 'You really shouldn't concern yourself with my affairs,' she said.

'Not at all,' Caroline said graciously. 'I like to help where I can.'

'No, I mean you *really* shouldn't,' Jenna said. 'I can take care of myself. And it isn't your business, is it?'

Caroline stiffened with affront. 'I *beg* your pardon? I think when you're going out with my brother, it certainly is my business.'

Jenna left aside the weird world view this suggested, and said only, 'I'm not going out with your brother, not in the sense you mean.' Then she wished she hadn't. Why give Icy the satisfaction of telling her anything?

'Well, that's not what *I* heard,' Caroline said. 'But if my help and advice isn't wanted, I'm the last person to press it on you. I meant it kindly, and if this is the thanks I get, I'm sure I shall leave you to stew in your own juice in future.'

She was going off in a huff, when Jenna reflected that she couldn't afford to make any enemies in this village, with Kitty's big adventure about to be launched; and especially when it was Xander's beloved, known for her viciousness, and who could cause Kitty so much heartache with nothing more than a few words. So she gritted her teeth and said, 'Caroline, I'm sorry. It was – ungrateful of me. I do appreciate your kindness. I'm sorry if I offended you. Please forgive me.'

Caroline turned back, all graciousness again. 'That's quite all right. And I shall do my best to make Alexander understand that you and Harry are an item and he's not to mind.'

'Thank you, but it's not necessary. There's nothing between Harry and me. Really.'

Caroline looked taken aback. 'Oh. But you are seeing him again?'

'In a friendly way, that's all. And, please, don't let Kitty hear that Xander and I had words. He promised he wouldn't tell her, and I should hate her to be worried.'

'Oh, I won't say anything,' she said, looking thoughtful. 'I'm discretion itself. Anyone will tell you that.' She smiled suddenly. 'Anyway, you won't be here for much longer, so things will sort themselves out.'

Evidently she hadn't yet heard about the Holtby House gala and the extension to Jenna's stay. Jenna felt it best to leave her in ignorance. And for Kitty's sake, she waited until Caroline had got back into her car and was driving away before letting go of Barney's collar and saying, 'Kill, Barney! Bite her! Bite her!'

The planning meeting on Tuesday evening was held in the church hall, a stone-built, ecclesiastical-style Victorian building next door to the church which had once been the village primary school. The place was packed when Kitty and Jenna walked in. They were soon surrounded by Kitty's friends and acquaintances, and it was clear that the planning dispute was running only a short head in front of the Holtby House plan for conversational eminence. Jenna let Kitty do most of the talking, listening more to the tone of what people said than the substance, glad it was approving sounds she was hearing. Her attention was wandering about the room, and she realized she was looking for Xander – it would be the first time she had seen him since the quarrel and she wondered how he would behave. She couldn't see him anywhere. Perhaps he had gone home first, or was meeting with Caroline and coming on with her.

She had been wondering on and off all day about Caroline's visit of the day before. What had she been up to? She remembered what Harry said about his sister not being able to go straight even if she was on rails. She must have some agenda, Jenna concluded, but she couldn't think what it was. It was a pity, but she would have convinced Xander beyond doubting that Jenna had slept with Harry. She didn't know why she minded that – it was none of his business, as she told herself crossly. But all the same, she hated that he thought badly of her, for whatever reason. Oh, there he was now – without Caroline. She felt a rush of peculiar gladness at the sight of him, pushing his way slowly in from the back of the hall. It surprised her. She had expected to feel nothing but irritation, or perhaps apprehension. But instead, on seeing his tense, unhappy expression, she had a weird desire to cradle his head to her bosom and comfort him. She shook herself briskly, and seeing that he was aiming to join Kitty's group, she slid away in the opposite direction, and found herself shortly afterwards nose to nose with Harry.

'I didn't see you arrive,' she greeted him.

'I've been here a while. I can be pretty invisible when I want.'

'I believe you now. Why did you want?'

'I've been mingling and listening to what people are saying,' he said. 'It's quite entertaining when they don't realize you're paying attention. Your scheme for opening Holtby House is a big hit.'

'I'm really glad,' Jenna said gratefully. 'I was afraid, with this Benson business being so unpopular, that people wouldn't like it.'

'Oh, they're all National Trust members here,' Harry said. 'Only the nicer sorts are expected to turn up to look round the house: Volvo drivers, people with Labradors and children called Jemima and Tarquin. The Benson chalets are quite different. Common, you know. They'd be a blot on the landscape and bring undesirables to the hallowed precincts.'

'They'd spoil the view,' Jenna said. 'Will this planning application get through?'

'Hard to say. There's a lot of local opposition, but that doesn't usually count for anything when it gets to this stage.'

'That's a very cynical view,' Jenna said.

He looked surprised. 'Not cynical, just a fact,' he said.

'Oh, I was forgetting, this is sort of your turf, isn't it – development?'

'Sort of. I know a bit about it. And when it gets as far as the planning officer for the Department of the Environment, he's not worried about people's views being spoiled. It's traffic density and the pressure on water mains and sewerage that matter.' He grinned. 'And who's slipping what into whose hand in sealed brown envelopes.'

'Now that *is* cynical. By the way, I had a visit from your sister.'

'Bad luck!'

'No, she seemed to be saying she approved of me going out with you.'

'I told you that. She was all for it.'

'But why?'

'Keeps you occupied, stops you leading Xander astray maybe.'

'I hadn't thought of that,' Jenna said. She remembered. 'Oh, I saw her in Andover on Saturday.'

Harry wrinkled his brow. 'In Andover? She was supposed to be going to stay with an old school-friend in Shaftesbury. Made quite a thing about it – talked about a "sleepover" in a rather nauseatingly coy way. Are you sure it was her? You must have been mistaken.'

'No, I saw her quite clearly. She didn't see me, fortunately – I didn't want to have to talk to her.'

'Don't blame you.'

'She was with a man.' She described the Silver Fox. 'My friend Izzy said she felt sure she'd seen him somewhere – thought he might be famous in a small way – but she couldn't think who he was.'

Harry frowned. 'Sounds suspiciously like Derek Sullivan. You didn't see what car he came in?'

'No, sorry. Who's Derek Sullivan?'

'Local bigwig, and prospective Labour candidate for the north of the county, at the next election when Ron Farebrother retires. He's an old pal of Dad's, so he's been around our house a lot, one way and other. Drives a dark blue Aston Martin. Only nice thing about him. But why would Caro be meeting him? And why in Andover?'

'Izzy said maybe for the same reason we met there – convenient, halfway between here and London.'

'Yes, but I mean, why meet him anywhere?'

'I can't tell you that. But I'm sorry to say it looked a bit like a date.'

He stared, and then a slow smile spread across his face. '*No!* That would account for the secrecy. Sleepover, my arse! Oh, I shall have a lot of fun with her about this!'

'No,' Jenna said, alarmed. 'You mustn't say anything. I don't want her to think I was spying on her.'

'You weren't.'

'I know, but I don't want her to think I was.'

'No, you're right, anyway. Better she doesn't know I know, then I'll have more chance of finding out what she's up to. I say, fancy her two-timing poor old Xander!'

'Maybe she wasn't. I only said it *looked* like a date. I could be wrong. Most likely I am. Maybe it wasn't even her.'

He looked at her. 'What's going on? Why are you suddenly back-pedalling?'

She bit her lip. 'I don't want Xander to be hurt again.'

'Softy,' he said kindly. 'I didn't know you worried about him. But I'm afraid he's bound to get hurt one way or another, mixed up with my sister. She's a bad lot, and she'll do him no good in the end. But I won't say anything, don't worry. I shall just watch her with interest. She ought to be here – it'll be starting in a minute. She'll miss the fun.'

'People are sitting down,' Jenna said. 'Oh, Kitty's looking round for me.'

She was in the front row and had Bill on one side of her and Jim on the other, but Xander seemed to have left the group again. She caught a glimpse she thought was him, away to the side of the hall, standing up among the crowds for whom there weren't enough chairs.

'You don't want to be in the front row with the stuffy people. Stay with me and we'll stand at the side where we can see people's faces. Much more fun.'

Jenna wondered if that's why Xander had moved.

'Too late, anyway,' Harry went on. 'There's the bigwigs going up on the stage. You'll disrupt everyone, going down to the front now: they'll all look at you, you gorgeous, showy creature! You'll have to stay with me.'

They stood in the shadows at the side of the hall as the chairman thumped his gavel and called the meeting to order. Just as he started speaking, Harry dug her in the ribs and whispered, 'Caro's not here. Odd.'

Was it odd? With a glance around, Jenna thought she must be the only person in a ten mile radius who wasn't, so perhaps it was.

There was quite a festival mood as everyone spilled out on to the street afterwards. 'To The Crown!' Bill exclaimed. 'This demands a celebration.'

'I can't believe we've won,' Kitty said, beaming at Jim. 'I did hear correctly, didn't I? He did turn down the application?'

'You heard correctly,' Jim said, restraining himself from hugging her.

'One for the good guys!' Bill crowed. 'Come on, the first round's on me!'

Jenna was forcing her way through the crowds, with Harry at her heels, insisting that she had to congratulate Kitty, though he wanted to whisk her away. 'I only said I'd have a drink with you,' she told him.

'Yes, but I didn't expect a victory celebration. Everyone's going to be in The Crown. Let me take you somewhere else. I want you to myself.'

'Oh, stop pouting,' Jenna said, and broke through into Kitty's circle.

'Jenna, there you are!' Kitty cried, and they hugged each other.

'I'm so pleased for you. For everyone, really,' Jenna said.

It gave Kitty pause. 'Except poor old Benson, of course. He did look blue.'

Jenna laughed. 'You can't feel sorry for him now, just because he's the underdog. It's absurd. You called him unscrupulous before.'

'Oh, you're right. I'm very silly.' She turned to Xander, who was hovering uncomfortably behind her, avoiding Jenna's eye.

'You're coming for a drink, aren't you? What happened to Caroline? I thought she was coming.'

'So did I,' Xander said. 'I expect she was held up somewhere. I don't think I'll come for a drink, though.'

'Oh, nonsense, of course you must. It's a special occasion. And if Caroline does get here, she'll look for you in The Crown. Oh, there's the planning inspector talking to the vicar. What was his name? Purcell, wasn't it? Do you think we should get him to come for one?'

Jenna turned to speak sotto voce to Harry. 'You see we'll have to go, even if it's just for one. Kitty will insist.'

'All right,' he muttered, 'but I reserve the right to use all my powers to abduct you once your duty is done.'

'You can *try*,' Jenna said with a grin; and then, turning back, saw Xander's eyes on her, and felt a pang of – what? Guilt? Hardly. Regret then? Possible. She didn't want him to think there was anything between her and Harry. She didn't know why she didn't want that, but she didn't.

The talk went on. Why didn't they get on with going to the pub? Why did everyone have to stand around in the road?

'Oh, there's Caroline,' Kitty said suddenly. 'I didn't see you arrive. We're just going to The Crown for a celebration. Did you hear? We won!'

'Did you? How wonderful!' Caroline said, sidling up to Xander and kissing his cheek. 'Hello, darling. Sorry I'm late. Got caught up in some things.'

The vicar came over. 'I asked Purcell if he'd care to imbibe one with us, but he said he's being given a lift to the station, so he can't. He's just left.'

Slowly, by painful inches, the crowd made its way to the pub. Jenna discovered Harry was missing from behind her; but before she was actually at the door, he was back.

'Blimey, they should call you the Shadow,' she said. 'You really do become invisible. What were you doing?'

'Sleuthing.' He had a gleeful look. 'I've just had a bit of an "oho!" moment.'

'What's that when it's at home? Washing powder?'

'That's Omo. It means, "Oho, so that's how the milk got into the coconut!"'

'And how did it?'

'Are you ready for this? Caroline arrived—'

'I know, I saw her.'

'Wait! She arrived in a car, which stopped a bit further up the road to let her out, almost as if she didn't want anyone to see how she got here. And that car, ladies and gents, was a dark blue Aston Martin.'

'*No!*' Jenna said, gratified; and then, distressed: 'Oh no!'

'Yes, but that's not all. The planning officer from the Department of the Environment has just walked off up the road, and got into the same car.'

Jenna stared at him. 'Are you serious?'

'Absolutely.'

'The vicar said he said he was getting a lift to the station.'

'Maybe he is.'

'So – the planning officer secretly knows Derek Sullivan? Who secretly knows Caroline? What does it all mean?' She stared at Harry with buckled brow.

He looked portentous, approached his head close to hers, and spoke in a grave, hushed voice. 'I haven't the faintest idea,' he said.

Twenty

The Buckminsters' dinner, which Jenna had not been particularly looking forward to, actually came as a welcome break in what had rapidly become the routine of work on the house opening. There was so much to do, much more than Jenna had anticipated, and though she was sure she could get through it in time, it was no longer a dilettanti frolic but a hard grind.

She hadn't spoken much to the Buckminsters at Kitty's party, but had seen them as rather overpowering and very, very county. They were in their sixties like Kitty, but the heavyweight version, large people with well-kept clothes that had obviously been bought to last; leading lights of the various organizations that kept the countryside going, parish councils and WIs and police authorities and so on. In addition, Arthur Buckminster was a JP – Justice of the Peace – and Gloria was on the board of a big orphanage and care home in Wenchester. At Kitty's dinner they had spoken kindly to her, welcoming her to the village, but beyond discovering that she was a Londoner and that she didn't play bridge, they hadn't really engaged with her.

The Buckminsters lived in The Old Rectory, a large mid-Victorian house in ample grounds. Like Holtby House it had a spacious conservatory built on to the back, and that was where dinner was laid. 'Might as well enjoy this weather while we have it,' Gloria Buckminster said. She and her husband seemed different now they were hosts in their own house – no less overpowering, with their big voices and county solidness, but hearty and affable, sticking a vast gin and tonic into Jenna's hand as soon as she arrived and addressing her as if they were old friends.

'I won't bother introducing all these people,' Gloria said, waving a hand. 'Some you know and some you don't, but it's a bore trying to remember names on occasions like these. Now come out and let me show you the garden. Everyone else has seen it.'

Everyone else had settled into eagerly conversing groups, still standing up facing inwards, as if they had far too much to say to waste time finding seats. Arthur was already topping up the G and Ts – it looked like being a hard-drinking evening. Jenna followed Gloria out into the garden, but she before had time to exclaim over how lovely it looked – and it really did – the true reason for the segregation emerged.

'Now, tell me about this scheme of yours for Holtby House,' she commanded. 'Everyone is so excited. We've been worried about the situation for years. Simply must keep Kitty in residence. Can't have all the old families driven out. Besides, you never know who you're going to get in their place, and it's rarely a pleasant surprise. So, will it work?'

'I think so,' Jenna said, and told Gloria the plan.

Gloria listened attentively and her questions were sharp and intelligent. 'It sounds as though you've thought about it carefully,' she pronounced at the end. 'You must tell me if there's anything I can do to help.'

'Thank you, I'm sure there will be. Most important now is to get a pool of volunteers to man the rooms when the house is open.'

'As in the National Trust,' Gloria interrupted briskly. 'Yes, I know the drill. Done it myself in the past, before I got too busy. Don't worry, I'll start rallying the troops. I know Kitty's been asking, but she's too nice. People need chivvying, like hens, even to get them to do what they want to do anyway. There'll be no shortage, I promise you. There's tremendous goodwill for the scheme, and for Kitty, and I shall help her with the organization of the volunteers, otherwise we shall have a slacking off when the first excitement fades.'

'Thank you,' Jenna said. 'That's the biggest worry off my mind.'

'You can ask me for any help and advice you need, any time,' Gloria said. 'I was organizing things in my cradle, so it's no effort for me.'

'I'm good at organizing *things*, but I haven't had much practice with people,' Jenna admitted. 'And I was rather worried about the long term, how Kitty would keep it going, because of course I shan't be here for much longer.'

'Won't you?' Gloria said, looking surprised. 'I thought you were a fixture. Family, aren't you?'

'Distant cousin,' Jenna said. This staccato delivery was catching. 'Kitty asked me for a month, though we've extended that to cover the Gala Opening, but that's all.'

Gloria looked at her penetratingly, and then said, 'Oh, well, let's wait and see how things pan out. You might find you want to stay longer.' After a beat, she went off on another tack. 'I hear you're having a fling with young Harry Beale?'

Jenna blushed. 'Hardly that. We had a date.'

Gloria overrode her. 'I feel so sorry for that boy. He's virtually had to bring himself up, with his mother dying when he was so young, and his father – well, the less said about Roger Beale the better! The man's a disaster. And then when he does get Harry a stepmother, it's that ghastly Mona Russell woman. Caroline's mother.'

'Ghastly in what way?' Jenna felt emboldened to ask.

'Naked greed and ambition,' Gloria said succinctly. 'Mona Dillinger she was – I was at school with her, God help me! Boarding school in Queen's Camel. She was one of those showy

flowers that blooms early and only lasts a day. Not worth culti-
vating. Played on her looks to marry Phil Russell. Transferred
her ambition to Caroline. Push, push, push. Like one of those
frightful ballet mothers, you know?'

Jenna didn't, but she nodded as if she did.

'Hardly a wonder that Caroline turned out the way she did.
Mona and Roger Beale deserved each other, but Caroline was
quite a sweet girl when she was six or seven. I followed her
subsequent career with a sort of breathless horror. One bad hat
to another.'

'Alexander isn't a bad hat,' Jenna pointed out.

'No, quite the contrary. He's perhaps a bit too bland.'

Jenna was shocked. 'I never thought of him as bland.'

'The egg without the salt,' Gloria said. 'Men need a seasoning
of drive and ambition. I didn't like the way he went to pieces
when that girl Stephanie dumped him. Showed a lack of character.
Of course, he was a child of divorce, but still. And now he's been
caught by Caroline Russell.'

'Don't you think perhaps she really loves him?' Jenna said, more
in hope than belief.

'I suppose she must,' said Gloria, frowning over the problem,
'because he has nothing she could possibly want. But it won't
last. Marriage for love never does.'

'But don't you—?' Jenna stopped herself, but not quite in time.

Gloria's eyebrow went up. 'Goodness, we are being frank, aren't
we? Yes, of course Arthur and I love each other, but that sort of
love comes later. It grows out of liking each other and getting
on well and having the same interests. Remember that, when
you come to marry. The romantic stuff's all right, but it's much
more important to be friends. There's sex, of course – but your
generation has it much easier that way. Fortunately Arthur and I
clicked in that department, because our generation had no opportunity to find out beforehand. I wonder if Caroline and Alexander
have tried?' she mused. Jenna had wondered the same thing and
often wished she hadn't. 'I suppose they must have, but it's an
odd thing, somehow one can't imagine them doing it. Like a
dog riding a bicycle – it doesn't seem natural.'

Jenna was intrigued by this insight; but they had reached the
end of the garden and turned on to the path back and she thought

that, since her hostess was in such a frank mood, she ought to get in a few questions of her own while she had the chance. 'Do you know a man called Derek Sullivan?'

'Unfortunately, yes. One of Roger Beale's shady chums,' she said promptly. 'Why do you ask?'

'I thought I saw him after the planning meeting the other day,' she said, stretching the truth a little. 'I wondered what he had to do with it.'

'Nothing, one hopes,' Gloria said. 'Apart from Beale Cartwright, he has connections with another development company, English Country Homes – I wonder if that's who Benson was going to sell to if he got planning permission?' she added in parenthesis. She shook it away. 'But the permission's been denied, so that's all over anyway. Benson will have to sell it as agricultural land, and that won't be enough for his villa in Tenerife, or whatever it was he wanted. Serves him right, the grubby little man. I took him on as a gardener when he got laid off from the atomic plant at Corvington, though I didn't really need him. Everyone in the village has helped him out in one way or another over the years, and that's the loyalty we get.'

'When you say "connection" to English Country Homes . . .?' Jenna said.

'Sullivan was a local councillor for Wenchester,' Gloria said tersely. 'The government demanded every county build so many new houses. Once the land was designated, he made sure English Country Homes got the contract to build them.'

'And what did he get in return?'

'English Country Homes gave a large donation to the Labour Party, and now of course Sullivan's been adopted as their candidate for the next election. Not possible to prove any connection between the two, of course.' She looked thoughtful. 'If he's to run for MP, he'll need campaign funds. I wonder if he was hoping to repeat his coup with Benson's land? If so, he's fallen on his face.'

They had reached the house. The thoughtful look vanished and Gloria was straight back into social mode. 'Fascinating talking to you. We must find a way to keep you here, my dear, because you're a definite asset to our community. Find some suitable young man to bed and wed you. *Not* Harry Beale, though – too much of a lightweight, as I suspect you know if you're half as sharp as I think you are.' She smiled, like a light switching on. 'Come in and let Arthur top you up.' She looked around for someone to scrape Jenna off on to, and her eye alighted on Xander, who had arrived meanwhile and managed to get himself into a corner out of the way where he was scowling at the company as if he wished he were anywhere but here. 'Oh, there's Alexander. I'll leave you in his capable care because I *have* to speak to Dolly Cornwall about the retaining wall in Deeps Lane. If she doesn't do something about it we'll have it falling on someone's pushchair or pet dog, and then we'll be in the papers for all the wrong reasons. Alexander – delighted to see you, dear boy!'

Arthur arrived at the same time, filled both their glasses anew, and then both Buckminsters disappeared, with an effect like two vast liners departing: the backwash drove Jenna practically into Xander's arms.

'They displace a lot of water, don't they?' she said, in the hope of making him laugh. His gloom didn't lighten one whit. 'Look, we only have to be polite to each other. Shall we talk about the weather? Or I could move away,' she added when this elicited no response.

'This scheme of yours,' he began.

'Oh dear. What now?' she said wearily.

'Everyone's talking about it as a done deal. Why wasn't I consulted?'

She was surprised. 'If Kitty had wanted to consult you there was nothing stopping her.'

'It's put me in a very embarrassing position. Everyone thought I knew all about it. I suppose that was *your* doing, keeping me out of the discussion stages?'

'Of course not. It was nothing to do with me. Why would I want to keep you out of the discussions? I'd have assumed you'd be all for it.'

'It's a crackpot scheme,' he said. 'In the first place, it can't work. And in the second, have you even considered the strain it will put on Kitty? A frail, elderly woman, trying to shoulder a burden like that? The responsibility, the work, the endless worry – and when it fails, it will make leaving Holtby all the harder for her.

You've gone into this for your own glory – if you haven't got other, more sinister reasons – without giving a thought to the effect it will inevitably have on an old lady who's shown you nothing but kindness.'

'And that's Caroline's opinion, I take it?' she said shrewdly.

'Yes, and she—' He pulled himself up, realizing the trap she had set for him, and he coloured angrily. 'It's my opinion, with which she happens to agree.'

'I'll bet,' Jenna said. 'Look, if it's your opinion, go and express it to Kitty. Have it out with her. Why throw it at me, as if she hasn't a mind of her own? She isn't a frail old lady, and I think if you go and tell her to her face that she is, she might well deck you with a clout to the side of the head, which you will thoroughly deserve.' He opened his mouth to answer and she carried on quickly. 'Everything I have done, and everything I am doing, is entirely at her request. She can change her mind or pull out at any time. Why don't you try and talk her out of it if you feel so strongly? I'm sure your influence must be stronger than mine – and Bill's, because she's discussed everything with him, you know.'

'Oh, Bill,' he said witheringly. 'Who has a vested interest in keeping her at Holtby House.'

She eyed him curiously. 'I might well ask why you're so keen to get her *out* of there,' she said quietly.

'Because it—' he began hotly, and then stopped, with an arrested expression in his eyes. 'Get her out?'

'She wants to stay in her home. I'm trying to help her to do that. Why would you think it's such a bad idea, unless you wanted her out of there for some reason?'

'I don't,' he said, in a faint, distant voice. Evidently there was some hard thinking going on behind those dark brows. 'I'm – concerned for her welfare.'

Jenna shrugged. 'I don't know anyone who isn't. Do you?'

He turned abruptly and went away, pushing through the deafeningly chatting crowds like someone who was about to throw up and had to get to the bathroom before he did.

Jenna, left alone, stared at the space he had left. 'Nuts,' she addressed the wallpaper. 'Completely and utterly out to lunch.'

★   ★   ★

It was a couple of days after this that Fatty came in to the library, where Jenna was working on the computer, and said, 'Visitor for you.'

'Who is it?' Jenna asked without enthusiasm. There was so much to be done. She was working on the room notes for the drawing room, and it was not as easy as it sounded. Getting stuff in the right order, deciding what to put in and what to leave out, getting the balance between being interesting and overloading the reader with information, was tricky stuff. And hanging over her was the selection and cataloguing of the china for the cabinets – she was just realizing what a huge task that would be. She really didn't want to be disturbed. Registering the silence, she looked up and saw Fatty struggling with something mentally. 'Who is it?' she asked again.

'Mr Acorn,' Fatty said at last, with desperate certainty.

Jenna frowned. 'It can't be.'

Fatty looked defeated. 'Maybe Mr Harpoon.'

'Fatty, nobody's called Acorn or Harpoon.'

Fatty shrugged expressively. 'He say his name, but I don't understand him good. It sound like Haycorn.'

'Can't Kitty see him?'

'He ask for you,' Fatty said, and made a little gesture of her hands which implied that having gone thus far she was turning over all responsibility to Jenna.

'Oh, all right.' Jenna sighed, standing up. 'I'll go. Where is he?'

'I put him in drawing room,' Fatty said, and made herself scarce.

There was no one in the drawing room or the hall. She glanced into the sitting room, and then tried the dining room.

Patrick (whose surname was Á Court – all was now explained!) was standing opposite the fireplace with his hands clasped behind his back, examining the ceiling.

'You look like John Betjeman,' Jenna said, to cover the jittering and booming that was going on inside her. Shock, she told herself, that was all. Suddenly seeing him where she did not expect him.

'This is the original plasterwork,' he said. 'Unusual to see it in such good condition, not even touched up. Nice fireplace, too – not overdone. Georgian simplicity. When was the house built? Seventeen-seventies, seventeen-eighties?'

'Seventeen-ninety, they think. What are you *doing* here?'

'And that staircase is magnificent. Unusual to find a place like this that hasn't been vandalized. It's a gem.' He lowered his gaze to her at last. 'I came to see you, of course. To tell you to come home.'

'*Tell* me?'

'Ask you. Beg you, if you like.'

His presence, his handsomeness, old associations, were playing havoc with Jenna's willpower. Now, as he smiled and gazed into her eyes contritely, she was afraid she was a goner.

'I was an idiot,' he said. 'I was well out of order. You can tell me off as much as you like, but please come back. I need you.'

If he had said, 'I love you,' she might have cracked right then. As it was she found the strength to ask another question.

'How did you find me? I know for certain Sybil would never have told you.'

'She didn't. She was quite obdurate. I told her it was for your own benefit – I mean, this is no way to run your life. The longer you're off the career ladder the harder it will be to get back on, and I've got a delicious job waiting for you, right up your alley, and I'm pretty sure I can swing it for you. I'm not without influence in certain circles,' he said modestly. 'But Sybil wouldn't say a word, though I think she wanted to. I suppose you made her promise? I know you were mad at me, and I understand, but this nonsense has gone on long enough. Now be a sensible girl and come home.'

He smiled at her, and tilted his head slightly, giving her a beguiling look. Jenna's heart was slowing to normal speed, and this look left her cold. It was the look you might give a little girl of, say, ten or eleven. *Let's stop being silly and go and get an ice cream.*

'You didn't answer the question,' she said, marking time. 'How did you find me?'

'That's my business,' he said in his firm-but-fair voice. 'I'm here, that's all. *How* doesn't concern you.'

'I think it does,' she said equally firmly. 'My privacy has been invaded.'

He wrinkled his nose, laughing. '*Privacy*? You're not an actress being snapped by a pap with a telephoto lens. Come on, darling, get a sense of proportion.'

She continued to look at him steadily, her lips folded.

At last he shrugged, and said, 'Well, if you insist – and I didn't want to mention her name to you, so it's your own fault – but it was through Charlotte.'

'Charlotte, your new girlfriend, told you where I was so that you could come and get me back?' Jenna said with ripe disbelief.

'She's not my new girlfriend. It's all over with her. And, no, she didn't tell me. That would be—'

'Suicidal?'

He looked annoyed. 'All right, I see you won't let it go, so this is how it happened. An old school-friend of Charlotte's from Benenden rang her up, knowing she was in the business, to ask if she knew an architect called Patrick. She naturally said, "Oh, do you mean Patrick Á Court," and this friend asked did he recently break up with his partner, upon which Charlotte got upset and wouldn't talk about it any more. But the friend then didn't find it hard to trace me, of course, and she rang me direct. Established that I was who she was looking for, and told me you were living near her, heartbroken, moping around deep in misery and longing to go home. Said if I wanted you back I should come down and get you.'

'Strangely busy of her to take so much interest in your welfare when she didn't even know you,' Jenna said, with a grim idea of who this Samaritan might be.

'She said she was worried about you,' Patrick said. 'She wanted you to be happy, and she'd heard so much about me from you that she was convinced we belonged together. I thought it was pretty decent of her to take the trouble. Most people wouldn't.'

'I'm sure they wouldn't,' said Jenna.

'She knew you hadn't told me where you were but she believed you wanted me to know really. That you wanted me to come and beg you to come home. I said I wanted you back, that it was all over with Charlotte, and she gave me the address. Suggested I came without ringing first, because on the phone you might feel obliged to resist me, but if you saw me unexpectedly, in person – well, I thought that was sound advice. So here I am.' He smiled broadly. 'So all you have to do, my darling, is pack your things, and I'm ready to whisk you back to London, where you belong.'

'Where I belong,' she repeated blankly.

'Although,' he added, 'this is a beautiful house, and I can quite see why you came here. Shame to leave it, really. But these places may look good, but they're hell to live in, and double hell to maintain. You need a fortune just to keep the roof over your head. New build is so much more practical. Speaking of which, I've been asked to work on a new development in Kensington which is going to be pretty spectacular, and I'm sure I'll be offered one of the flats at a discount rate when it's finished. Kensington will be a definite step up for us from Fulham, and much more suited to our lifestyle, now I'm moving into the big time, and you're going to take this job I've got lined up for you. Don't you want to know what it is?' he asked her temptingly.

She shook her head. 'I just want to know one thing. This old school-chum of Charlotte's – did she give her name?'

He frowned. 'She did, but I've forgotten it. Chloe or Mary or something plain like that.'

'Caroline?'

'Could have been.'

'Caroline Russell?'

'She didn't give a surname. Just plunged straight in with "I went to school with Charlotte". Does it matter?'

'Not to you,' Jenna said. 'I'm sorry to say that you've been played for a fool. It was a hoax call. I'm not moping and I don't want to come back to you. I'm very happy – having a whale of a time, in fact – and I have a very important job here.'

'Here?' he said in rank disbelief. 'How can you have an important job in a one-horse place like this? My God, don't tell me you've gone native? You're working in a charity shop or something?' She laughed, and in annoyance that he couldn't move her, he looked her up and down critically. 'You have let yourself go somewhat, I can see. You'll have to smarten up if you want to get this job I've lined up for you.'

'Smarten up?'

'Some decent clothes and shoes. And do something about your hair.'

'Anything else?'

'Well, there's your habit of blurting out the first thing that comes into your mind. You might want to get some help with that, if you want to get on in the real world.'

'But suddenly I don't,' Jenna said. 'You're a perfect example of the people who inhabit the real world, and I'm beginning to wonder how I ever got involved with you. It must have been a sort of madness brought on by sniffing traffic fumes or something.'

'You really think you're going to have a better life down here?' he said in disbelief. 'My God, you *have* lost it! You'll be joining Friends of the Earth and voting for the Greens next. Weaving your own clothes and wearing sandals made from car tyres.' He stopped, perhaps thinking that insulting her was not the best way to win her back. 'Look, this is a temporary aberration of yours, and you'll get over it and want to come back. I don't want you to suddenly come to your senses when it's too late. Because I won't wait for ever, you know. This is your one window of opportunity.'

'Oh Patrick,' she said sadly. She looked at his lips, and the thought of kissing him made her shudder. Not shiver – shudder. It was gone, all of it, and completely. 'Four years we were together. What a waste.'

'That's what I'm saying,' he said eagerly. 'It would be a crime to waste it.'

'No, I'm saying it *was* a waste. What on earth was I doing with you? I bet you've never done up your trousers with a safety pin in your life.'

'Of course not,' he said, bewildered. 'What's that got to do with it?'

She waved it away. 'I'm not coming back,' she said. 'Not now, not ever.' She thought of what Gloria Buckminster had said. 'I couldn't marry you. I don't even like you very much.'

He was affronted. 'I don't remember *asking* you to marry me.'

'You didn't. Now, I'm afraid I'm going to have to shoo you away, because I've got a colossal amount of work to do.' She gestured him towards the door and in surprise he started walking.

'I think you're making a big mistake,' he said.

'Well, if I am, it's my mistake,' she said. 'I take full responsibility. You've done all you could. You can go home with a clear conscience.' Mischievously she added, 'And maybe it's not too late to make it up with Charlotte. She might take you back.'

'Of course she will,' he said.

'*Will?*' Jenna laughed. 'Oh Patrick! What a giveaway.' She patted his shoulder, speeding him towards the door. 'She'll suit your life much better than I did. Drive carefully, now.'

I'm free, she thought when he had gone. *Free of him.* It ought to have made her feel happy, but for the moment it only made her feel cold and alone. She really had no home now – she had burned her boats. The nice flat, good job, plenty of money, presentable man on her arm, agreeable social engagements – all that life was over, and she had to start again from scratch. It was a chilly prospect.

Oh, don't be wet, she told herself sharply. *You burned your boats long ago. And that life wasn't yours, it was his. You couldn't live for ever with a man with no sense of proportion.*

And then she thought, *Caroline*! Heat flooded her system at the thought that Caroline Russell – who else could it be? – would go to such lengths to get rid of her: fury at the cheek of the woman, indignation at being discussed behind her back, at having two people who thought they knew what was best for her and were willing to act on it. But when the rush of anger faded, she was left with a knotty puzzle to chew on. Caroline wanted Jenna to go back to London. Caroline was desperate to get her out of the way. But *why*?

Twenty-One

Kitty came in in high spirits. 'Gloria Buckminster is amazing! She's a force of nature. I don't know how she's done it, but everyone I've spoken to today had already heard from her, and they're ready to sign up. I shall have more volunteers than I know what to do with.'

'You'll need them all,' Jenna promised. 'A person I spoke to who runs a National Trust house says you need a pool of at least four times the number of stewards you use, and five times is better.'

'We'll soon be up to that level at this rate. It's such a weight off my mind!'

'Mine too. It was the bit I was most worried about – I suppose because it was the only bit we couldn't do ourselves. I get nervous about any part of a job that's not under my control.'

'How are you getting on?' Kitty asked, looking over her shoulder at the computer screen.

'Pretty well, but there's a lot to do. I was thinking: about the china for the cabinets? I could really do with some help on that. It occurred to me that I might ask that nice girl I spoke to at the museum in Wenchester, Nicola Pearson. If you have no objection. She was really knowledgeable – and enthusiastic, which might be more to the point. If she'd be willing to come and look at the stuff and pick out the most interesting bits, it would save me an awful lot of time.'

'What a good idea!' Kitty said. 'Of course I don't mind. I trust your judgement.'

'Oh, thanks! I'll pop over and see if I can catch her tomorrow.'

'And I'll go and see about a cup of tea. I expect you could do with one as well.' At the door she stopped and said hesitantly, 'I understand you had a visitor today?'

Jenna smiled to herself. 'Everyone really does know everything,' she murmured.

'I'm sorry. Bill told me, and I guessed who it was, but I don't mean to pry. I shan't say a word if you don't want me to, but I just wanted to be sure you weren't upset.'

'I was, a bit. But I'm not now,' Jenna said. She looked at Kitty. 'I'm amazed at myself, but I'm over him.'

'Really?' Kitty said doubtfully.

'I know. We were together four years, and you don't get over someone that quickly, but seeing him again only made me wonder what I'd ever seen in him.'

'Really?' Kitty said again, but hopefully this time.

'Yes, really! I think I must have been asleep and dreaming all that time.' She hesitated. 'I don't know if you'll understand, but dating is so difficult these days and there are so few decent men around – especially men willing to commit themselves to a relationship. When you find one, you tend to hang on to him, even if he isn't Mr Right.' She gave a short laugh. 'Generally you'll settle for Mr Just-about-do. In fact, a lot of the time you'll settle for

Mr-won't-do-at-all-but-at-least-he-rings-you- again-after-the-first-date.'

'Is it really that bad?'

Jenna nodded. 'All my friends said I was so lucky to have Patrick, and it seemed that's all that really mattered – I had a personable man, when so many of my friends, smarter and prettier than me, didn't have anyone. And the longer we were together, the harder it was to see beyond being lucky, especially when every year that passed was another year nearer thirty.'

Kitty laughed, and then shook her head. 'I'm sorry, I'm not making light of your feelings, but really, you know, from the vantage point of sixty-plus, thirty isn't a mountain. It isn't even a molehill!'

'Depends on where you're standing.'

'I know. I *do* know. But there are just as many men looking for women as vice versa, and you *will* find someone. I absolutely know it. Probably much sooner than you think. Just don't settle for second best – promise me? It's too important for that.'

Jenna gave a wry smile. 'But how do you know when you find the right one? That's the trouble. I didn't spend four years consciously thinking Patrick was second best.'

'You'll know when it happens,' Kitty said. 'We had a saying – *coup du foudre*. It'll hit you like a thunderbolt one day, and you'll know. And now,' she said resolutely, 'I'm definitely going to make some tea.'

After tea Jenna tried to work again but found herself going cross-eyed, and knew she needed some fresh air and exercise. She decided to take the dogs for a walk. Before she had finished taking the leads down from the hook in the kitchen, both dogs were there behind her, in that mysterious way they had of sensing from any distance up to half a mile that a w-a-l-k was in the offing. 'You guys!' she said in admiration.

'If you're going by the village, could you pop into the post office for me and get me some more stamps?' Kitty asked. 'And perhaps some chocolate to have with coffee after dinner? I feel a craving coming on.'

It was a lovely warm afternoon. Jenna shoved her purse down into her jeans' pocket, and went out in a cotton blouse, daring the weather. No doubt, she thought, as she clipped on the leads, Xander would take one glance at the sky and tell me it's going to turn cold and rain in exactly twenty-three minutes' time, but I'm risking it.

Xander! She remembered the last time she saw him, at the Buckminsters'. She had really upset him, suggesting he had no mind of his own and just repeated Caroline's opinions. But if the cap fits . . . Why on earth should he – or Caroline for that matter – not want to help Kitty stay on in her home? Well, if they had reasons, they probably weren't the same ones. She did him that much credit. Caroline's reason was probably devious and self-serving, but she couldn't quite believe Xander was like that. He was genuinely fond of Kitty. Maybe he really did think she was frail and might get hurt. Men could be very short-sighted when it came to the real properties of women. Like Patrick, thinking she'd come back for the asking!

No, Xander cared about Kitty, she was sure. She remembered the evening they'd had, the three of them, in front of the fire. They'd been so happy. It had been wonderful to hear Xander laugh. He'd even made silly jokes. Perhaps the stuffed shirt wasn't really him: perhaps it had been thrust on him by events. They were all governed by circumstance – the circumstance, for one thing, of just happening to meet the right person at the right time. It was all very well for Kitty to say there were men out there, but how did you actually get to meet them? That was the perennial problem. If you went to a pub, you met the sort of men who go to pubs. Ditto clubs, night classes, gyms – all the places the agony aunts told you to hang out. But what if you just wanted a . . . a . . . well, a Mr Right, to cut to the chase? A real human being, who just happened to fit into all your odd curves and angles? What then? You couldn't join a Real Human Being club.

She turned into the back lane down to the village, and the dogs at once dragged her, straining every fibre, to a large viburnum bush which was the equivalent, to them, of the students' union notice board in the university common room. Extensive sniffing ensued, and she waited, hands in pockets, staring at nothing, while they read all the notes and decided where to leave their own. And suddenly she realized she wasn't staring at nothing,

but at Xander, walking towards her. He wasn't in his business
suit, but in a very nice pair of chinos and a dark blue, short-
sleeved shirt, with a jumper tied round his neck. If Patrick had
ever appeared wearing a jumper that way she'd have laughed
herself sick, but it seemed perfectly all right when Xander did
it. And then she sighed and braced herself for the harangue of
the day.

'I was just coming to see you,' he said when he was a few
yards off.

'All right. What have I done this time?' she said. 'Have at me.
Spare the rod and spoil the child.'

He stopped and looked at her with a concerned expression.
'Is that how I seem to you? Like a stern parent?'

'Not the parent bit,' she said. Surprise – he didn't *sound* as if
he was going to lecture her! 'You're not that much older than
me. But I do seem to get a telling off every time you appear.'

'I'm sorry. I was in rather a bad mood at the Buckminsters'.'

'I noticed.'

'That wasn't meant for an excuse,' he said. 'In fact, the reason
I was coming to see you was to apologize.'

The dogs had finished with Central Exchange and looked
suggestively up the road. 'I'm bound for the post office for Kitty,'
Jenna said. 'Can we walk and talk?'

'I'd like that,' he said, and he sounded as if he meant it
literally.

But he said nothing for some time as they walked up the lane,
in the scent of damp grass and lilac, and with the sound of birdsong all around. Actually, it was quite nice walking with him
without talking, quite pleasant and chummy; but she felt at last
that she ought to help him get started, so she said, 'I'm really
getting to love this place.'

'Are you?' he said, sounding surprised, but pleased, too.

'What's not to love? Fresh air, green stuff everywhere, dogs to
walk – and I've never heard so many birds at one time. I wish I
knew more about them. What's that one over there, for instance
– the trilly, thrilly one? It's not a nightingale, is it?'

'Not likely,' he said. He listened and said, 'Over there? That's
a wren. Amazing volume of sound, isn't it, from such a tiny bird.
Have you never heard a nightingale?'

'I haven't spent much time in Berkeley Square.'

He smiled. 'I don't think they'd be singing there, either. They're woodland birds. In a few weeks they'll be singing night and day in Chiddingfold Woods, near where I live. Amazing sound. I'll take you one evening, if you like.'

She shook her head mentally, thinking when it came to mood swings, this man could out-menopause a fifty-year-old woman. But she said neutrally, 'I'd like that.'

He walked on a few paces, staring at his feet and giving off an aura of awkwardness. Then he said, 'I wanted to apologize for attacking you at the Buckminsters' party. I thought you'd deliberately kept me out of the loop about this scheme of yours.'

'Why on earth would you think that?' she said. *Because it was what Caroline told you,* she thought.

He didn't answer that question. Instead he put one of his own. 'But why *didn't* you tell me about it?' he said.

She glanced at him. 'I didn't tell anyone until I had it all worked out. Then I told Kitty, and she told you the next time she saw you, which was actually the next day, if I remember, so you weren't in ignorance for long.'

'But you could have called me in for the discussion, like Bill. I could have helped.'

'It was for Kitty to decide that, not me,' Jenna said. So that's what had hurt him – he had been *told*, not consulted. 'Bill was on the spot, that's all. And of course she wants your help – we all do. What puzzles me is why Caroline's so against the scheme, she managed to persuade you, too.'

He looked away from her and she saw the tips of his ears turn red. 'I don't want to discuss Caroline with you,' he said in a low voice. 'I don't think anyone would be doing themselves justice that way.'

'Suits me,' Jenna said cheerfully. 'As long as you don't discuss me with her.'

Another awkward silence.

'For the record,' Jenna said, breaking it, 'I think the scheme *will* work, and Kitty will make enough money to stay at Holtby, and I think she'll be very happy, and not stressed into a decline, or whatever it is that's supposed to happen to her.'

'I think so too,' he said, very low.

Well, for goodness' sake! Jenna thought. *Mr Consistent.* Aloud she said only, 'Good.'

'Look,' he said, although he didn't. 'I thought you were – well, you were a stranger, I didn't know anything about you, and suddenly you and Kitty were so thick, and I was—'

'Jealous,' she put in.

'What?' He was startled into looking at her. 'No, not jealous, of course not. I was wary, that's all. I wondered if you had some ulterior motive. I hoped – I hoped you were what you seemed.'

And someone else convinced you I wasn't. 'I like Kitty,' she said. 'I just want to help her.'

'I know. I believe that now, and I'm sorry. I hope you can forgive me.'

'Already done,' she said briskly. She smiled and stuck out her hand, and he looked surprised, but took it. His hand was large and firm and warm and dry, extremely male, a hand to trust, and a hand to enjoy touching. She looked into his eyes and imagined . . . she shivered. *No! Don't go there!*

He was still holding her hand. 'I wish—' He began. He didn't seem to be able to go on. She drew her hand back and he let it go. 'I wish we could have got off on the right foot from the beginning,' he said, but in such a different voice that it didn't sound as if that was what he had been going to stay.

'Better late than never,' she said. *God, why am I speaking in clichés?*

'It's nice of you to take it that way,' he said; and now he was just heartbreakingly polite. 'I'm going away tonight for a few days,' he went on. 'I don't know exactly how long I'll be away. But you won't be gone before I come back?'

'I'm staying until the grand opening,' she said. 'Mid-June.'

'Oh, I'll be back before then. It's – it's a buying trip. Just a few days. Up north. Lots of bargains still to be picked up in Lancashire and Northumberland. And I might stop off in London on my way back.'

'Well – have fun,' she said, not knowing what was the appropriate send-off.

'I wanted to see you before I left. I didn't want to leave it that way – I wanted to know if we could part as friends.'

'As friends? Yes, of course,' Jenna said. 'You do believe I'm not trying to rook Kitty or anything like that, then?'

'Of course. I'm sorry I ever suggested it.'

'Fine. Friends it is, then.'

They walked on in silence. He seemed depressed – or perhaps it was only thoughtful. When they turned into the village street, he stopped and said, 'Well, you're going to the post office? I'm going the other way, back to my car.'

'It must be fun, a buying trip,' she said. 'The thrill of the chase, spotting your prey, fighting off the opposition. A mixture of skill, cunning and aggression. Primordial stuff.'

He laughed in a puzzled way, as if he hadn't expected to be able to. 'Is that how you see it? Most people would think it would be dull.'

'I always look for the fun in a job.'

'It's a good attitude,' he said. 'I used to be like that, once.'

'So what changed?' she said, daringly.

His smile faded. 'Life, I suppose. People – letting you down.'

Back to Stephanie, she thought. *Or was it Caroline? Had he seen through her at last? Now there's a thought!* 'Change them,' she said. 'New life, new people. Whatever it takes.' She mimed a one-two in the air. 'Go down fighting. A right hook to the chin of circumstance, and a left cross to the jaw of bad luck.'

'That was a right cross and a left hook,' he informed her.

'He's down on the ground, whatever it was,' she said. 'You can't win if you don't take part – and I'm going to leave now, before I embarrass myself with any more clichés.'

'Every journey begins with a single step,' he said, so solemnly she didn't know if he was joking with her or had missed the whole point. She *so* hoped, as she headed with the dogs for the post office, that it was the former.

Jenna went into Wenchester on Saturday morning and was glad to find Ms Pearson – 'Oh, call me Nicky, please!' – on site. She invited Jenna into her office for a cup of coffee, and Jenna looked round with interest at the museum back rooms that the public never got to see. 'Apart from administration – and there's a lot of that, believe me! – we do preservation work and research. Ninety per cent of our time is spent out of sight. It was pure chance you caught me out there, really.'

'I'm glad I did,' said Jenna, and over a cup of coffee (the real thing, from a personal machine – these eggheady types did themselves all right) she explained her scheme and put her question. 'It's a bit cheeky of me, really,' she concluded, 'because I'm asking for your time on a voluntary basis. We can't afford to pay you, but I did just hope you might do it out of interest. There's such a lot of china in the house, of all sorts.'

'But of course I'll do it,' Nicky said at once. 'I'd love to see inside a house like that, *before* it's all tidied up for the public. Whenever I get to a National Trust place or whatever, it's always the closed rooms I want to see, and the backstairs, and the attics. Promise me I can look everywhere, and I'm your woman.'

'Absolutely everywhere,' Jenna promised with a laugh. 'We even have some cellars.'

'And the thought of all those ceramics is making my mouth water.' She grinned. 'You never know, I might find a really valuable piece nobody's noticed, worth so much you won't have to open to the public after all.'

Interestingly, Jenna felt a sharp pang of disappointment at the thought of not opening; but she said, 'I don't think that's likely, do you? Can china be that valuable?'

'Oh yes,' said Nicky. 'Some rare Chinese pieces can go into hundreds of thousands; and rare domestic pieces can easily be worth in the tens.'

'Well, we won't set our sights too high. If you can just pick out the best and most interesting for the cabinets and tell me what to put in the notes. It could be quite a long job, though.'

'And I have a full-time job here,' Nicky said. 'But I'm off next Saturday – I have one on and one off – and I could make a start then, if you like? And then there's Sunday and evenings, if I don't finish.'

'Next Saturday would be great,' said Jenna. 'We'll feed you coffee and cake and lunch and tea, and if you'd like to stay on for dinner, we'll break out the good wine.'

Nicky laughed. 'Let's see how we go. Too much of the good wine, and I won't be able to drive home.'

'We have nine bedrooms,' Jenna mentioned.

'But I have two little dogs at home.'

'Even better – bring them with you. They'll love it! Four acres to run around in, and two big new best friends.'

'That sounds like fun. I'll bring them, then, if you're sure it won't be a nuisance. I hate leaving them shut up all day. What sort are your big dogs? Are they friendly?'

'Heinz fifty-seven. Very friendly. They're supposed to be guard dogs, but they'd probably only lick a burglar into submission.'

Coming out into the sunny main street of Wenchester, Jenna was surprised – and yet, on reflection, was she, really? – to see Harry sitting on the stone balustrade at the bottom of the steps.

'What an amazing coincidence, finding you here,' she said drily.

He looked sheepish. 'As a matter of fact, it's not *quite* such a coincidence as it may at first appear.'

'You're spoiling my illusions. How did you know I was here?'

'I rang Holtby asking to speak to you, but Kitty said you were at the museum in Wenchester, and said it with an air of triumph that suggests she has you earmarked for some other man. Who is it, Red? You two-timin' me, sister?' He twirled an imaginary gun. ''Cos the Belminster Kid don't take that from any dame.'

She ignored all that. 'It's a long way to come just to tell me you knew where I was.'

'Long way? It's only five miles, if that. I thought you might like to come out and play, that's all. It's a lovely day, too nice to slave indoors over a hot computer.'

Jenna looked up at the blue sky, and a chestnut tree waving its leaves in the gentle breeze, and agreed with him. She was getting cabin fever again. 'What had you in mind? And I want the clean version.'

He looked hurt. 'How you misjudge me. I was going to suggest a picnic. What could be more wholesome and English than that?'

'Sounds good,' she said, and he blinked, evidently not having expected so easy a triumph. 'Have you got the basket already packed in your boot?'

'No, I thought we could pop into M and S and grab some stuff. But I do have the rug.' He beamed. 'Are you serious? You'll come?'

'Yes, why not? I deserve a break.'

'And I've got stuff to tell you.'

'About—?'

'I'll tell you later. First, the shopping.'

*　　*　　*

After a short drive, and a short walk through some woodland, they arrived at a very pretty spot on a grassy bank by a river, where Harry spread out his very handsome tartan rug. 'My lady – be seated,' he said, waving her to it.

Jenna dumped the M&S bags she was carrying and sat. 'This is nice,' she said. 'No, it's more than nice – it's close to gorgeous. That's a very handsome river.'

'The River Wend,' Harry said, starting to rummage in the bags. 'Hence Wenchester, saintly Wenhams, various, and even Wenderbridge, a no-horse town over thataway, which does however have a nice pub, The Land of Plenty, with a good line in home-made pies.'

'Is that the river your flat is on?'

He looked severe. 'My good woman, have you no sense of geography? Belminster has its very own river, the Bele, spelled B – E – L – E. Otherwise it would be called Wenminster, wouldn't it? Which could be a mite confusing for the BBC.'

'I'm sorry,' she said humbly. 'I didn't know.'

'Actually, the Bele joins the Wend further down, at Corvington, and they make one big river that runs into the sea, so I forgive you. My surname is supposed to come from the river, proving that I had ancestors here from time immemorial.'

'And that they couldn't spell,' Jenna offered.

'Well, who can?' he said lightly, laying things out on the rug. 'Ah, here's the bottle. Now where's the opener?'

'In this bag, with the glasses. Though I suppose we can't call them glasses, since they're plastic. Is it really done to drink wine from a plastic wine-glass?'

'Hole in the top, no hole in the bottom – looks perfect to me. Good old M and S.' He had bought everything they needed there, including the opener and an insulated wine bucket, a packet of paper napkins and a set of colourful plastic plates. 'Any fool can be uncomfortable,' he had said.

Jenna was laying out food. 'We've got too much,' she said. Four different packs of sandwiches, a pack of mini pork pies, ditto sausage rolls, a pot of hummus and a pack of pitta bread, bag of lettuce, tub of cherry tomatoes, grapes, strawberries, two slices of cheesecake and two of chocolate Swiss roll, a bottle of wine and a bottle of water.

'We've got all day,' he countered.

'You're very sure of yourself.'

'Ah, be nice to me, Red. I need comforting. I'm being turned out of my flat again tonight. I'm a poor homeless waif.'

'You'll be able to sleep in your car and finish off the picnic for dinner, then,' she said.

'You're heartless. I've got things to tell you,' he offered beguilingly.

'So you said.'

'Be nice and I'll tell you.'

'I am nice. Look, I'm smiling.'

'Fair enough. Have a glass of wine.'

'Thanks. Have a sandwich. Prawn, ham and salad, egg and cress, or – some dubious-looking red stuff. I've forgotten what it is.'

'Chinese-style chicken,' he said. 'I'll have one of those.'

Jenna took an egg and cress. 'So, what's the big news?'

'Caroline and Xander have had a big row,' he said, pleased with himself.

'Really? When? How do you know?'

'Thursday night, it happened, apparently. After he'd been to that dinner party – the Buckminsters, was it? He rang her up and one thing led to another.' He held up a hand to stop her asking another question. 'Wait, all will be revealed. I was over at Dad's on Friday morning, and Caro turned up, spitting tacks. Dad asked what was wrong, and she said Xander had rung her up and asked her "all sorts of impertinent questions" – I quote. Then she said, "This is getting ridiculous," and Dad gave her a sort of look that meant *not in front of the infants*, and took her into his study. They were talking in there for ages, but I couldn't hear what about.'

'Why would she tell your dad about quarrelling with Xander?' Jenna said, puzzled.

He shrugged. 'Search me. But I think there's something devious going on between her and Dad, something in the business line, because he wouldn't take her into his study to discuss affairs of the heart. To begin with, he hasn't got one, and to go on with, neither has she.'

'So you never found out what it was about?'

'Not entirely, but I'm pretty sure it was about Kitty and you and your scheme to save Holtby House. Because later on, when she was sitting out on the lawn, Xander rang her on her mobile, and I was up in my old bedroom and the window was open and I could hear bits of what she said. And at one point she said, "I think she's a lot more frail than she lets on. It would be a big mistake." Which has got to be Kitty, don't you think? And then later she got angry and said, "I resent that. Of course I don't. No one would be happier than me if she could stay." Which might be Kitty, or might be you. Then she looked up so I had to duck back, and I couldn't hear any more, except that she sounded angry, and then after that she seemed to be trying to make it up with him.' He looked at her hopefully. 'So, what do you think? Wasn't that worth coming for?'

'I met him on Friday afternoon,' Jenna said slowly, 'and he apologized for thinking I was a crook. He seemed depressed, a bit.'

'You'd be depressed if you'd suddenly woken up to what Caro's really like, but you were still stuck with her,' Harry said.

'He could get out of the engagement, surely?' Jenna said.

'He wouldn't do it. Not Xander,' Harry said. 'Very old-fashioned sort of bloke. He wouldn't let Caro down, if she still wanted to go through with it. Which she does. I asked her on her way out how things stood, and she gave me one of those manufactured smiles and said everything was fine between them and why wouldn't it be.'

'Xander's gone away on a buying trip for a few days,' Jenna said. 'I wonder if that's a last minute thing, to give him time to think?'

'No, it isn't, because even I knew about it. Caroline said last week he was going away this weekend. But he might be glad about it now – chance to get away from her for a bit. Poor geezer.' He topped up their glasses. 'And poor me, too, chucked out of my flat, and for a rat like that. I'll have to get the place fumigated afterwards.'

'A rat like who?'

'Oh, didn't I say? Dad told me yesterday when I was over there. Derek rotten Sullivan is using the place tonight. I have to

get it ready for him this afternoon – stock the fridge and change
the sheets and so on.'

'Using it for what?' Jenna asked.

Harry shrugged moodily. 'The usual, I suppose. Some girl, or
girls. I wouldn't be surprised if Dad was supplying them. He's
married, you know – Sullivan – so it has to be discreet.'

'Sullivan's using your flat for an illicit love-fest?' Jenna said.

'You're talking like a tabloid,' Harry noted with interest.

'Sorry, it comes from working in the magazine trade. But this
could be big.'

'Big? How?'

'Because he's standing in the next election, and that sort of
thing is frowned on in an MP.'

A slow smile spread over Harry's face. 'You're right. You're
absolutely right. Now, I wonder whether we can't make use of
that handy little fact.'

Twenty-Two

'What do you mean?' Jenna said.

'I mean, prepare a welcome for him. Electronically. Film what
he's doing. See who he meets.'

'Can you do that?'

'Me? I'm an electronics wizard. Besides,' he added, 'the whole
place is wired up already. Apart from all the home entertainments,
some of the people who borrow the place from Dad like to film
themselves having fun.' Jenna looked disgusted, and he shrugged.
'That's life. People get their jollies in different ways. But it makes
it easy, in the present case. I only have to alter some of the wiring
and feed it through to a recorder hidden somewhere he won't
look and – Bob's your uncle. I can track his every movement.'

'Don't these people ever wonder if your dad won't do the same
thing?'

He scowled. 'Are you suggesting my dad's a blackmailer?'

'God, no! I'm sorry – that's a terrible thing to say.'

Harry grinned. 'Just yankin' your chain. It wouldn't surprise me in the least, except that I reckon the people he lets use the flat must have as much on him as he has on them, otherwise they wouldn't trust him. So, shall we do it? Get a little something on old Derek Sullivan?'

'Absolutely not,' Jenna said. 'Apart from the idea of watching him have sex being nauseating in the extreme, it's wrong.'

'OK,' he said, suspiciously easily.

She looked at him narrowly. 'You're going to do it anyway, aren't you?'

'Well if I do, I won't tell you, so you'll never know. But I've found out some stuff about Sullivan, stuff you wanted to know. About this Benson business. Shall I tell you, or are you too virtuous?'

'Depends how you found out,' she said warily.

'Dad told me.'

'Oh, well, that's different. Tell away.'

'OK. First, it was Dad's firm that was going to buy Benson's land with the planning permission. It surprised me a bit, because Beale Cartwright doesn't usually go in for Mickey Mouse little developments like ten holiday chalets. But anyway, Dad was doing it under the name of BC International – that's the holding company – because it wouldn't have made him very popular locally.'

'You can say that again,' Jenna exclaimed. 'It would have finished Caroline's reign as county belle, too, given that she's his step-daughter. He was wise to keep it secret. And he *told* you that?'

'I found some papers in his desk when he was out. Well, that's a *kind* of telling me, isn't it?' he protested at her stern look. 'But he did tell me the rest. When he said Sullivan was getting my flat, I said, "What's that in aid of? Has he done you a favour over this Benson land?" Just guessing, you see, to make him think I knew. And he said, "ECH is buying it, if that's what you mean." That's English Country Homes, Sullivan's firm. Then he said, "But the favour's the other way round. He'll make plenty on it."'

'How will he, without the planning permission?' Jenna asked.

'Dunno. But I do know that ECH has been buying up all sorts of bits of land – banking them, it's called. Tesco do it, partly in case they can ever get planning permission, and partly to stop anyone else buying it. I was looking at Yew Tree Farm in Wenham

St James for Dad's firm just recently, because the Coopers are selling up, but the planning officer said there was no way we'd ever get permission to develop, so I left it alone. Then I heard that ECH had bought the land for a very low price, because obviously without planning permission it's just farmland.'

Jenna shook her head. 'I don't get it. Your dad said he did Sullivan a favour letting him buy Benson's land? But how was that a favour? And if he had done him a favour, why would he have to bribe him with use of your flat?'

'God knows. They're as crooked as a pig's tail, the pair of them. But I'll tell you another thing – Dad's firm's given Sullivan big money for campaign expenses.'

'I suppose he told you that, too?' she enquired ironically.

'His desk told me,' Harry said. 'I wish I could have a good poke round in his office one day, but he doesn't often leave it unlocked. I only managed to nip in that time because he was in the loo.'

'So we know there's some kind of connection between Sullivan, your dad and the Benson land,' Jenna said.

'And I did see the planning officer get into Sullivan's car after the meeting,' Harry said. 'But what it all means I haven't worked out. And I'm sure there's a connection as well with Holtby House, and that maybe Caro's in on it. Because she's been very suspicious of you from the moment you arrived. I thought at first it was because of Xander, but then she encouraged me to go out with you, which I'm sure was to find out what you were up to. And she seems to be against the rescue plan you've worked out. Enough against to make Xander quarrel with you over it.'

Jenna nodded. 'There's something else,' she said. 'Something you don't know.' And she told him about Patrick's visit. 'I can't prove it, of course, but it looks as though she tracked Patrick down to convince him that I was longing to go back to him, in the hope that he'd come and fetch me away.'

'Before you did any more damage,' Harry concluded. 'Phew. Lucky escape, Red! And poor old Caro, thwarted at every turn! But I didn't like seeing her go into my dad's office for a private chat. That girl's too ambitious to be let loose around a rogue like my dad.'

'You don't mind talking about him like that?'

He shrugged. 'I've got used to it. He's a bad hat. But he provides me with the necessary, and I'm not qualified to do anything else.'

'You could break away. Give up his money and make your own way in life.'

He looked sulky. 'You don't know what it's like. Once you've been rich it's hard to face not having things. I'm not cut out to be poor. Anyway, what else could I do?'

'Become an estate agent.' He made a face, and she said crossly, '*I* don't know. Work behind a bar. Anything, so long as it's respectable.'

'I could be a political researcher for an MP,' he said. 'That'd be an interesting job.'

'I *said* "respectable".'

He grinned. 'Never mind, Red. You can reform me another time. For now, there's our plot to film Sullivan and his shocking antics at my flat.'

'You're not to tell me about that,' she said. 'Have some cake.'

'All right, but I will say this. Watch out for Caroline. She was really mad yesterday, and since she definitely wants Xander for some reason, she might turn her anger on you.'

'What, you think she's going to attack me with a hatchet or something?'

'Don't laugh. She might do. If she's determined to stop you saving Kitty's house. But it would be more her sort of speed to find something out about you and ruin your life.'

'I've never done anything.'

'Everyone's done something. Or if not you, someone in your family. You asked if Dad was a blackmailer – well, I'd definitely not put it past old Caro. So just keep your wits about you, that's all I'm saying.'

'If she harms anyone in my family . . .' Jenna growled menacingly.

'Thattagirl. Keep that snarl handy.'

On Sunday Kitty went out for the day with Jim. Jenna did some more work in the morning, then took the afternoon off to sunbathe and read in a secluded part of the garden, the only fly in the idyll being Barney's desire to lie right next to her, and preferably with his great heavy head resting on her stomach. He was growing increasingly devoted to the only person who regularly took him out for walks, and no degree of heat could dissuade him from pressing his hot furry body up against hers, if she ever descended to his level.

Eventually she was too hot and sticky to enjoy it any more, so she went in and had a hot and then a cold shower, put on the lightest cottons she had, and went to see about fixing herself a salad. She ate it, accompanied by a chilly glass of Chablis, on the terrace. It was quite nice to be alone for once, and she was just contemplating a spot of telly on the sofa when the phone rang.

It was Harry. 'Are you alone?' he asked in a sepulchral voice.

Jenna snorted. 'You sound like an ad for a dating agency.'

'I'm serious. Are you alone in the house, or is Kitty there?'

'No, she's out for the day.'

'Or anyone else?'

'I'm alone, Mr Smiley,' Jenna said patiently.

'Good. I'm coming in.'

'Where are you?'

'Just outside.'

'Right. Will I recognize you, or will you have one of your devilish disguises on?'

'Ha-very-ha,' he said, and rang off.

In half a minute he was there, coming through the gate from the yard. He flung himself down on the seat next to her and said, 'I left the car down the road, just in case there were any visitors.'

'So what's all the cloak and daggery?' Jenna asked. 'Are you being followed?'

'I hope not,' he said seriously. 'Boy, have I got news for you!'

'Oh, is that programme on? I was just wondering what to watch tonight on TV. Glass of wine?'

'Oh, why not,' he said, frustrated. 'I can see I can't get you excited.'

'Never stop trying,' she told him solemnly, and went to fetch the bottle from the fridge and another glass.

'OK,' she said, when she had settled again, 'what have you got to tell me? Is it about Sullivan staying in your flat?'

'Yes, and I know who his visitor was. He left this morning so I was able to get in and retrieve the tapes this afternoon. I made you some stills – don't say I never give you anything. These are just from the security system.' He slapped a black-and-white print down in front of her. 'Ta-ra!' he trumpeted triumphantly. 'The camera never lies.'

Jenna picked it up and stared. It showed the back view and part profile of a silver-haired man holding open the front door to Harry's flat, but the person he was admitting was full-face. It was the usual grainy, poorly defined image you get from CCTV, but there was no mistaking that the man's female guest was Caroline Russell.

'Wow,' Jenna said. 'And yet, somehow I'm not surprised.' She looked up at Harry. 'But this isn't incriminating. She could have called on him for any reason – anything from taking a message from your dad to collecting for the Salvation Army.'

'There's more,' said Harry, slapping down number two. 'He kisses her.'

'That's just a social peck on the cheek. Everybody does that.'

'He gives her a drink.' In number three, they were sitting on the sofa, each with a glass in hand and a wine bottle on the coffee table in front of them.

'Just being polite,' she said.

'They canoodle.' Silver Fox's arm was round Caroline, and they were kissing properly, on the lips.

'Ah. That's a little harder to explain.'

'Why bother?' said Harry, and slapped down the fifth picture. 'Here they are going into the bedroom.'

Jenna was relieved to see it was the last. 'Maybe he had something he wanted to show her,' she managed feebly.

'Oh, he did,' said Harry.

'Don't tell me you filmed in the bedroom as well!' Jenna exclaimed.

'All right, I won't tell you,' said Harry, 'but the film in there is much better quality than this CCTV stuff, proper movie film. I told you some of Dad's pals like to film themselves and sometimes Dad makes them copies.'

'And did they – Sullivan and Caroline—?' Jenna didn't really want to ask, but she had to know.

Harry nodded. 'The lot. In colour.'

'Oh God. Poor Xander.'

'Lucky Xander, I should have thought,' said Harry. 'It's his perfect get-out. And if he doesn't want to get out – well, that girl's a bit of a goer. Amazing when you think how she presents herself to the world.'

'You haven't watched it?' she said reproachfully.

'Purely in the interests of research,' he assured her. 'I closed my eyes a lot of the time. But this film is dynamite, you do realize that?'

'I don't understand,' Jenna said. 'If it's so dangerous to Sullivan, why would he take it?'

'He didn't. There are two camera set-ups in the bedroom. One out in the open, for the punters, and another secret one for my dad's eyes only. I found it in the course of trying to set up exactly the same thing for myself. Obviously Dad likes to have a little something in reserve in case of necessity. I told you I was an electronics wiz, only I don't think you believed me.'

'I'm sorry. I do now. But what on earth are we going to do?'

'Oh, it's "we", is it? You're on board now?'

'Well, you've told me about it. I can't un-know it, can I?' She thought. 'Won't your dad expect to take the film away?'

'Of course. I told him I was going to be out tonight, so he'll be there now, retrieving it for his archive. But I've already made a copy.'

'Cunning devil. To do what with?' A thought came to her. 'You're not going to blackmail Derek Sullivan, are you? Because that's just a bit illegal, in case you didn't realize, and I couldn't have anything to do with it.'

He looked wounded. 'What do you take me for? Anyway, there'd be no point taking money from him because it's my dad's money anyway. Quicker to ask the old man for the dosh direct. No, my idea is to take a few nice stills, show them to Caroline, and threaten to blow the gaff unless she cuts me in on the deal, whatever it is. I think she'll come across much more freely if she thinks I'm as rotten as her and trying to feather my own nest, rather than if I pose as a self-righteous crusader. And we want to know what's at the bottom of all this, don't we?'

'We do. That's very cunning of you,' Jenna said. 'I'm sure you're right. Unless—' The thought occurred to her. 'Unless she's actually in love with this Sullivan guy, and doesn't know anything about the scheme, whatever it is.'

'Funnily enough,' Harry said thoughtfully, 'I think she *may* be in love with him. He's her usual uncle type, and she does seem – well – affectionate towards him in some parts of the film. Weird if she really was, eh? But you can't feel sorry for her,' he commanded, watching Jenna's face. 'Whether she loves Sullivan or not, she's not letting go of Xander, is she?'

'He's away. Maybe she'll break with him when he gets home.'

Harry shook his head at her naivety. 'Well, if she doesn't, you can show him one of your pretty pictures. The snogging one, I suggest. But not until I've had time to play my hand, please. And if you think she was just there for the action, you should have seen how long and hard they talked before the canoodling started. And the expressions on their faces while they were talking were purely businesslike, I promise you. No, my big sis is in this up to her earrings, and now I've got the perfect way to make her cough it up.' He stood up. 'I'd better go. Don't want to be here when Kitty gets back. Not a word about any of this to anyone, OK?'

'Of course not,' she said, but rather dolefully. She didn't like secrets, and everything about this one was horrible.

He surprised her by leaning down and kissing her full on the lips. 'Sorry,' he said as he straightened up. 'Couldn't resist. You looked so woebegone, like a half-drowned kitten.'

She burst out laughing. 'Your imagination! Anything less kitten-like than me . . .!'

'I know, you see yourself as an Amazon,' he said cheerily. 'But you forget I'm James Bond, licensed to thrill. Which makes you Pussy Galore.'

She laughed. 'Oh, get out of here, you fool.'

'I'll be in touch,' he said, and mimed pulling his collar up and his hat over his eyes as he slunk away down the terrace.

Unsurprisingly, Harry's visit and his revelations left Jenna feeling jumpy and unsettled. She watched television without being aware of anything on the screen, and then decided to go to bed early, because she didn't want to face Kitty like this and possibly give something away. She lay in bed unable to sleep, heard Kitty come home – there was a board outside her bedroom door that squeaked. She heard the owls calling back and forth across the gardens, and a terrible screeching bark which by now she knew was a fox. What a country girl you're becoming, she told herself ironically; and then thought that it was true, she was. She loved it here, loved Holtby House and the village and the people. It was like finding the serpent in Eden to discover that Caroline was two-timing Xander, and with a man who was himself married and two-timing his wife.

But was there more to it than that? She knew Harry was enjoying all the John le Carré stuff, but she hoped against hope that there was no plot, that he didn't find out anything more, that it was just a case of sexual attraction between people who were otherwise tied up. That was plain, everyday, understandable wrong – her own friend Izzy was engaged in it with Toby. And maybe, if that's all it was, Caroline was already planning to break it off with Xander when he came home from his buying trip. That would be bad enough: she imagined how shattered he would be to be betrayed and dumped again, after Stephanie. He might not get over that. He would probably pull back into his shell and never stick his head out again. But if there was a sinister plot involving her and Harry's dad and God knew who else in the neighbourhood . . .

She shivered, and got out of bed to go and shut the window. Outside, the gardens lay calm under the silvery light of the almost-full moon, the cedar tree still and cut out black against the sky, throwing an improbably sharp shadow across the grass. It looked unreal, like a theatre set; and when the owl called again a moment later, that sounded unreal, too. *Owls don't really say too-whit-too-woo except on bad radio plays*, she thought. Maybe nothing was real. Maybe she had dreamed it all. Or maybe she wasn't real either, and someone was dreaming her.

Suddenly her tension left her and she was desperately tired. She went back to bed, and fell heavily asleep as soon as her head hit the pillow.

She felt real enough when she woke up on Monday, still tired, and desperately hungry. That salad last night had had no staying power.

'Did you have a nice time?' she asked Kitty when they met at breakfast. Mrs Phillips had done mushroom omelettes with fried tomatoes, and she had to stop herself wolfing, and made herself eat politely.

'Lovely, thank you,' Kitty said. 'It was very comfortable, knowing you were here taking care of things.' She looked at Jenna more closely. 'You look tired. Your eyes especially. I think you've been on the computer too much lately. You ought to have a change of occupation.'

'Well, that works, as it happens,' Jenna said, 'because I think I ought to start rearranging the drawing room – taking stuff out and moving the furniture. A bit of physical work will make a nice change.'

'You've decided finally what's going on display, then?' Kitty asked.

'Decided? No, that's for you to do. But I've got my suggestions ready. I'll show it to you after breakfast and you can change anything you like. And then I'll start heaving things about.'

Kitty smiled. 'You can take things out if you like, but I know Fatty means to do a deep clean in there before any final rearranging. Polish the floor, wash the windows, clean the carpet, wax the furniture and so on. And that marble fireplace will take some cleaning – all those swags and bunches of grapes and cherubs' wings.'

'I'll help her,' Jenna said.

'She won't let you,' Kitty warned.

'She's going to have to learn not to be so possessive of her dirt,' Jenna decreed. 'Anyway, I'll tell her my broken heart is aching and I need to scrub. Cleaning things is wonderfully therapeutic.'

'I shall enjoy watching you take her on in her own territory,' Kitty said; and added: 'It isn't, is it?'

'What isn't what?'

'Your broken heart – aching?'

'Not a twinge.'

'Oh good. I should hate to think—'

'No, I told you I was over Patrick, and I am. I just feel a bit – empty, that's all.'

Kitty drank her coffee. 'I wonder when Xander will be back,' she said, as if it was apropos of nothing in particular.

Twenty-Three

'DARLING, HOW ARE YOU?'

'Hello, Mummy. There's no need to shout. Long-distance lines are very clear these days.'

'I just wanted to see how you're settling in.' Annabel modified the volume slightly. 'How are you getting on with Kitty?'

'Wonderfully! I love her.'

'Oh good. She always was a terrific girl. Full of bounce. Always up for everything.'

'She still is. We're opening her house to the public.'

'I know, darling, Sybil told me. I must say I think it's terrific of you, and just what's needed. Houses are such a *millstone*, even ordinary houses, and that great barracks of a place of Kitty's has, what, fifty bedrooms—?'

'Nine.'

'—and simply acres and *acres* of grounds. Must cost a fortune to keep up, but if you open it she can hire all the people she needs to keep it going, and go and live in a cottage somewhere.'

Jenna gathered that her mother had missed the point somewhere but it was too much effort to unravel it.

'House ownership is a fool's game these days,' Annabel went on blithely, from someone else's yacht on the way to someone else's villa. 'But I must come down and see you next time I'm in England, and visit darling Kitty.'

'I might not be here much longer,' Jenna mentioned. 'I'm supposed to be finishing mid-June.'

Annabel sounded alarmed. 'Darling, *we* can't have you. This wretched boat has to have something done to it – have its bottom scraped or something. It'll be out of commission for a month or something ghastly, so we have to move into a hotel until we can go to Cap. Clifford wants a Greek island, for the light – *just* the wrong time of year when the prices start to go up. And so inconvenient. I should see if Kitty can't keep you a bit longer, darling, really I should. Maybe until you're ready to go back to London.'

'Don't worry, Mummy, I shan't be bothering you.' Knowing how short her mother's calls generally were, Jenna hastened to get her question in. 'Mummy, do you remember the Lathams?'

'Kitty's friends? Of course I do, darling. We were all very inty at one time, the six of us, until Xenia Latham divorced Geoffrey and broke his heart. She was spectacularly beautiful. Only frightfully Russian and temperamental, you know? All smouldering passions and sultry seductiveness, interspersed with screaming rages. *Too* exhausting! It must have worn Geoffrey out, and the more she let everything out, the more he bottled it in. I always though they were a frightfully mismatched pair. Though he had hidden depths,' she mused.

Jenna was alarmed. 'Mummy, what do you mean?'

'Oh, nothing sinister, darling. He was typically English, that's all, frightfully buttoned up on the outside but very human inside if you could get past the shell, and with a nice sense of humour when it was allowed out, which Xenia never had, of course. These East Europeans are all so *serious*. I have to go, darling, Geoffrey's waiting to use the phone.'

'Wait, wait, Mummy, please!' Jenna said urgently. 'Do you remember Alexander?'

'Alexander who? Can't it wait until next time, darling?'

'No, it's important, I must know now. Alexander Latham, their son.'

'Oh, he was just a little boy. Yes, I remember him. Very dark, handsome, quite like Xenia to look at. Not that Geoffrey wasn't good-looking too in that very English way. Rupert Brooke-ish.'

'Alexander?'

'No, Geoffrey. Alexander was very quiet. Had a tendency to lurk, as I remember.'

'Lurk?'

'You'd turn around and there'd he'd be, watching you. You never saw him come or go, but you'd stumble over him in doorways and dark corners. Strange child.'

'Mummy, this is really, really important, so please tell me: has Alexander got any reason to disapprove of you?'

'Of *me*? Of course not. What *can* you mean?'

'When he wants to disapprove of me, he says, "You're just like your mother." What does that mean?' She had a horrid thought. 'Mummy, you didn't have an affair with Geoffrey, did you?'

'What a thing to suggest! Of course not. I was always faithful to your father,' Annabel said with convincing indignation. Then she added, 'But, wait, now. I wonder . . .'

'What?'

'Well, after the split-up, Geoffrey was frightfully cut up. The fling he had didn't last, of course, and he really adored Xenia, and wanted to get back together but she was implacable. He had no one to turn to – you know these silent-suffering men. But somehow he managed to unburden himself to me. Used to phone me up and talk for hours. And we'd meet sometimes for lunch in town so he could sob on the shoulder – metaphorically speaking, of course. But it was all absolutely innocent, darling, I promise you. I was insanely in love with your father. Totally madders.'

'I believe you,' Jenna said. 'But I wonder if Alexander got hold of the wrong end of the stick somehow?'

'It's possible, I suppose,' Annabel acknowledged, 'because of the lurking thing that I mentioned. And later, when Xenia died, I spent a lot of time talking to Geoffrey, because he was devastated, even though they'd been divorced for a long time by then. Alexander would have been about seventeen or eighteen, I suppose. A bad time for a boy in the best of circumstances, but to lose his mother – and he *had* adored her, quite beyond her merits in my opinion. He might have misconstrued, being emotionally upset already. In fact,' she added thoughtfully, 'I seem to remember an occasion when he arrived at the flat – Geoffrey's – and found me there. We were only talking, of course, but was there a bit of smouldering and stalking out and door slamming? I think there might have been. Of course, one pays no attention to that sort of thing in teenage boys. Catching them *not* smouldering and slamming is the trick, so naturally one wouldn't have made anything of it at the time. Oh dear,' she said suddenly. 'Has that poor boy gone his whole life thinking I seduced his father?'

'I don't know, but it's possible. I'll bet that's what it is.'

'Well, give him my love when you see him,' Annabel said blithely.

The inappropriateness of the reaction made Jenna laugh. Her

mother was incorrigible, so there was no sense in worrying about it. 'Mummy, do you absolutely promise there was nothing going on between you and Geoffrey?'

'Most excellent oath, darling. I was fond of the poor chump, but no bodily fluids were ever exchanged, I swear. Does that satisfy you?'

'Absolutely,' Jenna said. 'Thanks, Mummy. That's made a lot of things clearer.'

'Darling,' Annabel said, 'I'm so intrigued. Are you getting a *thing* for Alexander Latham?'

'No!' Jenna protested.

'Not even a teensy *thinglet*? If he's half as handsome now as he was as a boy – and it would be *such* a good match for you, because he's bound to come into Holtby House when Kitty dies. She hasn't any other relatives.'

'I thought you said house ownership was an intolerable burden?'

'Not if it pays its way. You don't have to live there. And, darling, you're not getting any younger. It's time you settled down. One's looks start to go off after thirty, no matter what cream one uses – though I do recommend you use a good one. It's false economy to go for the cheaper brands, when it's something as important as your skin.'

Jenna could only laugh. 'I'll do my best to get married, I promise, but Alexander Latham's already engaged, and in any case, he won't be inheriting Holtby House.'

'Oh. Well, that's no use then. In that case, you'd better keep looking. But don't take too long, darling. Must go now, Clifford's having a fit about the phone bill. Love to Kitty.'

And she was gone.

Jenna put the phone down thoughtfully. Yes, it did make a lot of things clearer. If he really believed Annabel had had an affair with his father – and given his feelings about women running off with other men, Stephanie-style, and his deep belief in faith-fulness and reliability – it was no wonder that seeing Jenna, who everyone said looked very like her mother, had aroused unhappy memories and suspicions. She would tell him the truth, and hope that it would draw a splinter that had been troubling him for a long time. It would be a case of choosing the right moment, of course, for a tricky revelation like that. But at their last parting he seemed to have been softening towards her, so perhaps when he came back – whenever that was – he would be more receptive. She ought to do it, for his sake and the sake of Truth, before she left Holtby House, because it was unlikely their paths would ever cross after that.

It was surprising how sad that thought made her feel.

Watch did not come when she rattled the dog leads in the kitchen, but Barney glued his head to her thigh and smiled up at her, so she went for her afternoon walk with only one dog. Afterwards she was very glad she had, for if Watch had been with her as well, the outcome might have been tragic. She was walking along one of the lanes, with Barney ambling somewhere near on a loose lead, and her mind was preoccupied with all the unanswered questions that had been put into it recently, so she wasn't much attending to externals. Afterwards she realized she had heard the car coming, but had paid no attention: after all, this was a road, so you expected traffic on it, and country people all seemed to drive too fast.

But the car, coming up behind her, actually accelerated at the point the driver must have seen her. Barney, just ahead of her, turned his head, and in the last second some instinct of self pres-ervation made her jump. There was hardly any grass verge at that point, just a narrow strip of grass between the road and a big, thick hawthorn hedge which at this time of year was in full growth. There was virtually nowhere *to* jump, but she flung herself sideways into the hedge as the car screamed past, still accelerating. She heard Barney give a high yelp of pain, at the same moment as the bushy hedge bounced her back and her thigh hit something hard which reeled her round and made her fall. She landed on her seat in the road, sprayed with a shower of grit and bits of dead leaf. Her momentum tossed her on to her back with her legs in the air, so she only got a brief glimpse of a low black car, and by the time she had sat up it had disappeared.

Her thigh was white-hot with pain, and she was afraid for a moment it had been broken. Her hands were trembling with shock as she tried, flinchingly, to examine it. Her jeans had not torn and there was no blood, which was a relief, and she could wiggle her toes, which was a good sign. She hitched herself out of the road on to the grass trip as a precaution, and after a few minutes when the pain had subsided to a throb, she undid her zip and eased the jeans down to look at the damage. A big red mark promised the mother and father of a bruise, but she was fairly sure now that's all it was. She must have just glanced the car as she rebounded out of the hedge.

Barney was licking at his flank, and she remembered his yelp of pain and pulled him to her. She felt where he was licking and found a piece of gypsum the size of her thumbnail – left in the road from the last resurfacing, presumably – embedded in his flesh. It must have been spat out from under the wheels, she supposed, and hit poor Barn. She whipped it out and it bled a little, but Barney made no fuss, and at once began licking at it again. When she dragged herself to her feet he got up too and seemed to be moving without difficulty. Cautiously she put her weight on the injured leg and there was no sharp pain. With Barney on a short leash on the safe side of her, and keeping as far on to the grass as the hedge would allow, she made her way home.

By the time she got back to Holtby House, she was sure her leg was all right, though she would have a pretty fine trophy in all the colours of the rainbow by the next day. Barney seemed all right, too, but she determined to clean the wound properly with antiseptic. She would have to tell Kitty, for that reason if no other, but she decided to make light of the incident, and not mention her bruise. She would say it was a car going too fast that had spat a stone out – a common enough phenomenon – and that she hadn't seen the make or number plate, which was true. Kitty knew, as they all did, that people drove too fast round these lanes, and there had been accidents enough over the years, some of them fatal.

But Jenna couldn't help remembering, when she replayed the tape in her mind, how the car had speeded up, and how close it had been when it passed her. If it had kept to the centre of the lane there would have been plenty of room. If she had not jumped . . . Could it possibly be that someone had tried to hit her, perhaps to kill her? No, surely not! Those things didn't happen in real life, only in books. And it was a terribly inefficient method of murder. Unless it had been just a spur of the moment thing, seeing her and driving at her on impulse . . . It would have had to be someone so overcome with rage and hate for the instant that they weren't thinking clearly of the consequences. She might not have been killed, only injured.

Hospitalized. Put out of the game.

By a hit-and-run driver who couldn't be identified.

Someone who hated her and wanted to get rid of her, at least as far as the County Hospital, if not all the way to a specialist unit or private hospital in London.

Someone who drove a low black car, possibly a sports car.

Kitty was concerned, but it was not in her nature to fuss. She made Jenna sit down in the kitchen for a strong cup of tea for the shock. 'Because you're quite white,' she said. 'I think it upset you more than you realized. Poor Barney. He seems all right, though. I've pressed his ribs and he doesn't wince, so I don't think any of them is broken. And the cut isn't big enough for stitches. I think he'll be all right, poor old boy. People drive like such maniacs around here. Did you see who it was?'

'No, it was all too quick. It went past like a bat out of hell, in a cloud of dust, and it was round the bend before I could take it in.'

'Thank heaven it wasn't worse,' Kitty said. 'If you knew the make of the car or the number, I'd report it to the police, because these people ought to be stopped, but without either I'm afraid it's a hopeless task.'

'I really didn't see it,' Jenna said, truthfully. She stood up and, the bruise having stiffened, her first step was a limp which she tried unsuccessfully to hide.

'Are you sure you're not hurt?' Kitty said with quick concern.

'I fell over when I jumped out of the way, and banged my leg. It's just a bruise.' She had to distract her. 'Are you sure we shouldn't take Barney to the vet?'

'I don't think so,' she said, looking at the dog, who was sloshing up vast quantities of water from the big bowl by the door. 'Look at him. He seems fine. But we'll keep an eye on him for the rest of the day. Should I have a look at your leg for you?'

'No, I'm fine. Were there any phone calls for me while I was out?'

'No. Were you expecting something?'

'I thought Harry might ring. Do you know when Alexander is coming back?'

'I'm not sure. He was doing sales on Saturday and Sunday so he should have come back today, but I think he said he was going to London on the way back, so it depends on how long he means to stay there. It won't be before tomorrow, anyway,' Kitty said, a little wistfully. 'I hope he's going to come back in a better frame of mind about our scheme. He was very cool about it when I told him – and he could be such a help if he would throw himself into it.'

Jenna said tentatively, 'I get the impression that Caroline's not keen on it, for some reason, so perhaps that's affecting him.'

She thought Kitty might pooh-pooh the idea, but she said, 'Caroline thinks I'm too old and incapable for something like this. Wait until she gets to sixty and has people suggesting she needs help crossing roads.'

So Kitty had picked up the negative vibes, Jenna thought. It was good that she didn't seem too upset by them.

Kitty had gone to bed, and Jenna was sitting at the little wrought-iron table on the terrace with the dogs, having a last whisky in the hope of drowning out her bruise, which hurt like toothache. Though the sun had long set there was still light in the sky, against which the trees were cut out like black paper, and she was enchanted to see bats flickering about in the dusk – she had never seen one in the flesh before.

Both the dogs were lying at her feet, enjoying the cooler air, when suddenly Watch lifted his head and give a little wuff of warning, and both dogs got up and turned towards the gate at the end of the terrace that led to the stable yard. Someone was coming. She hadn't heard a car, and wondered for a thrilling moment if it was the mystery hit-and-runner come to finish her off. But the dogs were wagging their tails and there was no growling, so Jenna was not worried: whoever it was, they knew and liked the smell – and she didn't think they particularly liked Caroline.

The gate opened – not in a stealthy way – and a tall, dark shape came through, resolving itself, as it shook off the shadows, into Alexander. Her heart leapt in an unruly way, surprising her, and she forced herself to take some slow, deep breaths. *He's not for you, simpleton!*

When he got close enough she could see that he was not smiling, and looked tired, even a little grim. The dogs ran up to greet him, looking up at his face for acknowledgement.

'Hello,' Jenna said. 'I didn't hear your car.'

'I left it in the road,' he said. 'I didn't want to wake Bill and Fatty.'

'Kitty's gone to bed,' she said. 'I was just enjoying the cool air and the bats.'

'It was you I wanted to talk to,' he said, but there was nothing in his face to make her heart flip. He sat down on the other metal chair with the heavy movement of a tired or disappointed man.

'I'm having a malt whisky,' Jenna said when he didn't go on. 'Can I get you one?'

He shook his head.

'Or anything?'

'I've got things to tell you,' he said, 'and it's difficult. I want to run them past you, because you're an independent mind, in a way. You're not affected, so you can be objective. I'd like your judgement – if you don't mind?'

'Shoot,' she said, and because he looked so unhappy, 'I'd be glad to help.'

He leaned forward, resting his arms on his thighs so that his hands dangled between his knees. Barney decided that what a man needed in this circumstance was a dog's cold wet nose in his palm, and provided one. Xander fondled the dog's ear absently as he spoke. 'I don't know how much you know about Benson's planning application,' he began.

Jenna's heart sank a little. So he was suspicious already? But he would have to know sooner or later. 'A little,' she said. 'Benson wanted to sell his land with planning permission because he'd get more money that way. But the village objected because they didn't want a lot of holiday chalets on the land.'

'In a nutshell,' Xander agreed. 'And the DoE sent a planning officer, John Purcell, who turned down the application at appeal and that was that.'

'Except that it wasn't?' she hazarded.

'On Wednesday morning,' Xander said, 'I was at Belminster to pick up a package, and as I went past the station I saw Purcell getting out of Derek Sullivan's car. Looked as if he was dropping him off for the train. You know who Sullivan is?'

She nodded. 'He must have stayed the night with Sullivan after the meeting,' she mused.

'It's possible. But obviously there's some kind of connection between them, and I've never liked or trusted Sullivan, so it made me suspicious about the whole planning thing. So that evening I got hold of old Benson and took him for a drink. He's never hard to persuade into a pint or two at The Castle, especially if someone else is buying. He's famously tight-fisted. We went into the snug and I plied him with Covington Best.'

'And it loosened his tongue?'

'He hardly needed encouraging,' Xander said. 'He told me that it was Beale Cartwright that had been going to buy his land, but only with the planning permission in place.'

'Why wouldn't they apply for the permission themselves?'

'Because – according to Benson – they'd had trouble over some unsympathetic developments in other parts of the county and didn't think they'd get it, whereas he might. Once outline permission is granted, it's much easier to get it expanded afterwards. If Benson got permission for ten chalets, they could work it up later into something bigger.'

'So what did they really want the land for?'

He shrugged. 'Who knows? But it didn't matter because it was turned down anyway. Benson was furious because now he was faced with selling the land as farmland. He'd already received an offer, he told me, and it was peanuts compared with what Beale Cartwright would have paid.'

'And the offer – did he tell you who it was from?'

'English Country Homes,' said Xander. 'But I couldn't think what they wanted it for. It's useless without planning permission. That's what I went to London for, to do a little research at Companies' House. It turns out that ECH's two main shareholders are Derek Sullivan and Roger Beale. Derek Sullivan is also a shareholder in a company called BC International, which turns out to be the parent company of Beale Cartwright.'

'So Sullivan and Mr Beale were in it together,' Jenna said, glad he had got there on his own steam. 'But what's it about?'

'That's what puzzled me. I couldn't see where the collusion got them. ECH was going to get the land Beale Cartwright was interested in for next to nothing, but neither could build on it. And then I started wondering about Purcell, the planning officer. So I did a bit more research, and I found out that Purcell has recently changed his address, from the cheap bit of Battersea to a nice part of Highgate. And Purcell's immediate boss is the junior minister in the DoE whose name is Culver, who just happens to be Derek Sullivan's brother-in-law.'

'No!' Jenna breathed.

'Sullivan's wife has a PR firm where she goes under her maiden name of Shirley Culver.'

'So Purcell was primed to reject the planning permission?' Jenna hazarded. 'And paid a lot of money, with which to buy a big new house in a nicer part of town?'

'It's a supposition. But that can't be all there is to it. Once you've got a tame planning officer, you don't just use him to turn down one application. Turning down's the easy bit.'

Jenna was there. 'Yes, and it's popular with the locals. Makes you look like a good guy.'

He looked at her and nodded to her grasp of the situation. 'And gives you a reputation for being impartial.'

'So that when you later give approval to another scheme on the same land . . .'

'Meanwhile the development company has been able to get the land for a fraction of the price,' Xander concluded. 'And I don't suppose Purcell's usefulness – or maybe we should call it Culver's usefulness – will end there.'

'Roger Beale has given Derek Sullivan money towards his campaign expenses,' Jenna said. 'If he gets into Parliament, he'll have a lot more influence in a lot of other ways.'

Xander looked at her sharply. 'How do you know that?'

'Harry told me. He – found out,' she said unwillingly.

An obscure expression of hurt crossed his face. 'Oh, Harry. Of course, I forgot you were so close to him.'

She had to distract him. 'He's had the same suspicions as you about the Benson business, triggered by the fact that he saw Purcell getting into Sullivan's car after the meeting.'

'Why didn't you tell me that?' Xander said sharply.

'Well, he only *thought* it was Sullivan's car – only had a glimpse and didn't see the number, so it wasn't police-grade evidence. But he's been hunting around for information since then. And he was turned out of his flat on Saturday – his father lets various business colleagues use it from time to time, as a sort of . . . sweetener, I suppose.'

'Yes, I know about that,' Xander said, as if he didn't approve.

Blimey, wait till you know the rest, Jenna thought in dismay.

'Don't tell me – it was Purcell,' Xander continued.

'No,' Jenna said, a little reluctantly. 'It was Sullivan.'

Xander frowned. 'What did he want to stay there for? He lives in Wenham St Olave, which is only about six or seven miles from Belminster. Why couldn't he go home?'

'Well, he was meeting someone,' Jenna said.

'Oh,' Xander said. 'I suppose it was an assignation of some sort, then. A woman. The usual sort of thing. Unless –' his expression sharpened – 'it was for a business meeting. It would be more private than a hotel.'

'No, it was a woman,' Jenna said sadly.

He shrugged. 'I'm not surprised. Sleazy in one respect often goes with sleazy in another. It's not his wife one minds about so much, but they have two children – and children always find out in the end.'

She wanted to fling her arms round him and ease the pain, but she could only sit still and watch him suffer. The moon, which had been edging up from the trees, finally cleared its lower rim and sailed out into the luminous sky like a great gold-white soap bubble.

'It's full tonight,' Xander said absently.

'It's beautiful,' she said quietly. Barney gave up on caresses, since Xander's hands had forgotten him for the last few minutes, and he lay down on his side on the warm terrace stone with a huge sigh which could have been content or disappointment.

Xander frowned. 'Just a minute,' he said. 'How did Harry know Sullivan was meeting a woman there, and not a business colleague or even his father?'

Best, she thought, to get it done now, in the quiet of this moonlit garden, where he didn't have to look at her face or reveal his own.

'There are security cameras in the sitting room – in case of burglary, I suppose. Harry's an electronics wiz. He was able to access the tapes, and he saw Sullivan opening the door to the visitor and sitting with them and – stuff.'

Xander was not looking at her. His eyes were fixed on the dark tree-line below the moon.

He knows, she thought. *He's guessed*.

'Did he recognize her?' he asked softly.

'Yes,' she said. She looked at his averted profile, and was puzzled. 'But . . . how did you guess? Have you suspected something?'

'Not really – not that. But it was obviously something you didn't want to tell me, and what else could it be?' Then he looked at her sharply. 'But Harry could be lying. I know he doesn't like her very much. Or he might be mistaken. Often with these security cameras you can't really identify the person clearly.'

'No, you can see it's Caroline all right. There's no mistake.'

His mouth turned down with pain, and he looked at her almost with dislike. 'You've seen the film?'

'He made me some stills. He thought I'd need convincing.'

'Show me,' Xander commanded.

Jenna shrugged. It was all going to come out now, anyway. He might as well see, or he'd think she was just trying to blacken Caroline's name. She got up to go and fetch them. When she came back, he said, 'Why are you limping?'

'A car came too close to me in the lane and I fell. Bruised my leg.' He seemed about to say something else, so she handed him the stills to distract him. 'Here,' she said.

He looked at them one by one, pausing over what she thought of as the snogging scene, but he did not allow his expression to alter one whit, not even when he saw the going-into-the-bedroom one. He might have been carved from stone.

'I'm sorry,' she said. 'Really sorry. I know it must hurt you—'

'We won't talk about that,' he said, and it was an order. He stared at the trees again. 'I need to know what her involvement is,' he said. 'Why is she doing this? What has she to gain? How much does she know? Or is it—?' He didn't finish that sentence, but she knew how it would have gone: *or is it just that she's in love with him?* 'I suppose,' he went on dully, 'the thing to do is to ask her. But how can I? How can I admit to having looked at these?' He flipped the pictures with a contemptuous hand.

She wanted to save him. 'I'm waiting to hear from Harry,' she said. 'He's going to ask Caroline what she's up to, make her tell him by using – using the pictures.'

'Why would she do that?' he asked grimly. 'There's nothing much to this, except – except between her and me.'

'He's got more,' Jenna said wretchedly. 'Much more. Not just to compromise her with you, but to compromise Sullivan with the world. He says it's dynamite. He'd never get to be an MP.'

'Blackmail,' said Xander. 'I must say, you and your chum Harry have some nice habits. You know that blackmail's illegal, I suppose?'

'I didn't agree with it,' Jenna said, desperate not to have him look at her like that. 'Not all of it. But Harry's doing it for himself anyway. He wants to know what's going on. I couldn't have stopped him.'

'You wouldn't have wanted to stop him, would you?' he said coldly. 'I know you've never liked Caroline.'

'Don't *you* want to know?' she cried. 'She's betrayed you with another man. Why are you making me the villain here?'

'I hate schemers and back-stabbers. I hate spying and every kind of subterfuge,' he said. 'And blackmail is the lowest vice of all. I was beginning to think better of you, but that you should stoop to this method to expose a woman who's never done you any harm—'

'She's done *you* harm!'

'That's between her and me. It's none of your damn business,' he said, and he was on his feet and walking away down the terrace even before the dogs could move.

She watched him go, miserably. She wanted to call out to him, but she couldn't think of a single thing to say.

Twenty-Four

At last she looked at her watch, and realized it wasn't actually that late. Not too late to phone Harry. He ought to be warned that Xander now knew most of the story, and might well be gunning for him as principle blackmailer. She rang his mobile number.

Harry answered at once, and from the background noise she guessed he was in a pub.

'Hey, it's you!' he said when she spoke. 'I was just going to ring you. I've got things to tell you.'

'I can't hear you properly. Too much noise there.'

'It's OK, I'm going outside. Listen, where are you? At home? Can you come and meet me?'

'Where?'

'I'm at the Blue Posts in Belminster.' His voice was jerky with his steps, but then the noise faded a little. 'That's better. I'm out in the street now. I've just had an interview with you-know-who. I got it all out of her. But then I thought I'd better go to a public place, in case she tried to murder me before I could pass it on.'

Jenna jumped at the words. 'You don't really think—?'

'Not really, but just in case she couldn't help herself. She's a ruthless girl. And I needed a drink anyway. I was a bit shaken up.'

'And you've only just spoken to her?'

'Hey, I couldn't find her earlier. I've been looking all day, and I only just ran her down—'

'Don't use that expression,' Jenna said. But the car incident had been this morning, before Harry had got to her. It must have just been a bad driver.

'But I have to talk to you about what we do next. And I don't want to come out there for obvious reasons. So can you come here?'

'All right. You'd better stay put, anyway. I've just seen Xander, and he might come looking for you, so don't go home yet.'

'Oh my God, what did you tell him?'

'It was what he told *me*. Look, I can't tell you over the phone. Where's this pub?'

'In Catton Street, just off Market Street.'

'I'll be there as soon as I can,' Jenna said.

Jenna sat with a lemonade and lime, thinking she had better not drink any more after the malt whisky, though her leg was hollering after the drive over. Harry, who was within walking distance of home, made inroads into his third pint.

'Well, she's in it up to her dainty eyeballs, my illustrious stepsister,' he said. 'She was so furious about my having the CCTV pictures, I thought I'd better tell her about the film right away, in case she strangled me there and then. I told her I'd lodged a copy with a solicitor. I don't know if she believed me – I hope so. But it slowed her down a bit – I could see her replaying the film in her mind and realizing what must be on it. That was food for thought all right! And of course she knew about my dad's pals filming themselves so it made sense to her that there was another, secret system, because she knows my dad and how he operates. Sullivan had made sure first thing that the obvious system wasn't running, so they'd thought they were safe. I told her enough about where it was hidden and what I'd seen to convince her there *was* a film, and then she called me a dirty little skunk and asked me what I wanted. I told her I'd no desire to blackmail anybody, but I wanted in. Convinced her I was a shady lowlife like her and my dad and just wanted my share of their ill-gotten gains.' He took another draught. 'What did Xander tell you?'

She told him in synopsis what Xander had found out in London.

Harry nodded. 'Yes, that's pretty much what I got from Caro, except for this Culver character. I don't know whether she knows about him. She knew about Purcell. Apparently my dad's already got the local planning officer, Puddephat, under his thumb, but Purcell was what Sullivan brought to the party. And Xander's not wrong about extending the planning permission once it's granted.' He looked at Jenna gravely. 'It's not just chalets they want to build on Benson's land, it's a whole holiday park – something like Center Parcs, I gathered, complete with artificial lake, woodland walks, petting zoo and fairground. The whole tombola.'

'Oh no!' Jenna said. 'In that lovely place? It would be ghastly! We can't let it happen.'

'Well, not everyone would hate it,' he said reasonably. 'It would create a lot of employment for locals, and generate a lot of taxes, and Sullivan would be able to claim all sorts of government spending for the area on the back of it, assuming he got elected.'

'But poor Holtby! And poor Kitty!'

'Yes, that's where the real tragedy lies. Because the scheme doesn't end with the holiday park. Once the building starts, they're sure that Kitty won't be able to bear staying on. She'll want to sell up and get out, and the value of the house will have gone through the floor, so they'll be able to snap it up as a bargain.' He grinned. 'You can see why you were such a thorn in Caroline's side. First of all you turn up and she doesn't know what your game is – thinks maybe you're getting ready to bleed Kitty yourself. Then this scheme to open the house to the public looks like stymieing them. No wonder she hated you. I did her an injustice thinking it was jealousy of Xander: it was pure business on her part.'

'But why do they want Holtby House?'

'To turn it into an expensive country-house hotel. With their own tame planning officer they can get round the listing – and it's only Grade Two.'

'But the view will be ruined.'

'Doesn't matter for a hotel. Anyway, they plan to put tennis courts down the bottom where it's noisiest. And a swimming pool inside the walls of Kitty's flower garden.'

'Oh no! That's horrible!'

'The worse it is for Kitty, the better for them.' He looked sombre. 'Caroline was quite cold about it. Not only would Kitty be driven out, but she thought the shock of it all might even kill her, which she liked the idea of even more.'

'Oh my God, what a bitch!'

'Yes, she is that.' Harry nodded thoughtfully. 'That's why she latched on to Xander. She assumed Kitty would have left the house to him in her will, so if she did die, Caro would be married to Xander and have all the bases covered. And if Kitty didn't die, she might give it to them as a wedding present, or at least she'd probably be happier selling to them rather than selling on the open market. That way Kitty would never get an unbiased view of what the place was really worth.'

'I don't think she realizes that (a) Kitty isn't frail and (b) she isn't daft,' said Jenna. 'And what if Xander didn't want to go along with it? What if he didn't want the place once it had a theme park on its doorstep?'

'She's quite confident she can manipulate him. You should hear her talk about him! You'd think he was a tailor's dummy. And besides, if Xander did object to buying the place, she could always say it was for Kitty's sake, because she'd get a better price from them than on the open market.'

'So she doesn't really love Xander at all?'

'I'm not sure. She obviously thinks he's handsome and a credit to be seen with. Except that he doesn't like being seen at the sort of things she hoping to be seen at. I think she definitely fancied him at one time, but it's plain to me that it's Derek Sullivan she wants now.'

'Even though he's already married?'

'She sees herself as a big business mogul, like my dad. Her, Dad and Sullivan working this big scam. Because of course a Purcell isn't just for Christmas, a Purcell is for life. There's no limit to how often they can work this wheeze – especially if, as you say, the Environment Minister is onside. A string of developments on land bought for peanuts. And once Sullivan's in Parliament, the sky's the limit. And who knows – maybe one day Mrs Sullivan will turn out to be surplus to requirements, and Caro can step in. I think she reckons he might be prime minister one day, and then she'll be the Cherie Blair *de nos jours*.' He shook his head in wonder. 'I wouldn't be surprised if she didn't ask my dad for a copy of the film, in case she wants to blackmail old Derek one day into divorcing the missus and marrying her. I wouldn't put it past her.'

Jenna shook her head. 'But what do we *do* with this?'

He looked glum. 'I don't know,' he said. 'That's what's been worrying me ever since. I reckon the first thing Caro'll do is go to my dad, and I don't think he'll like the idea that I've tried to beat him at his own game – out-videoed him for my own ends. He's going to be angry.' The prospect clearly alarmed him. 'And

I don't know whether he'll believe I'm just trying to get my share – or whether he'll want me in on his schemes if he does believe it.'

'So, what then?' Jenna asked. 'Tell Kitty? Go to the newspapers? What do we do?'

'*You* do nothing.'

The new voice startled Jenna so much she bit her tongue, and swung her head round so fast she ricked her neck. Xander was standing behind them.

'A fine pair of conspirators you make,' he said witheringly, 'sitting with your backs to the door.'

'How long have you been there?' Jenna asked, colouring at the thought of the awful things they had said about Caroline, the awful things she had done.

'How did you find me?' Harry asked at the same moment.

'When you weren't at home, I knew you'd be in a pub,' Xander said. 'It was just a matter of trying them.' He looked at Jenna. 'I've been here quite long enough. And I think I know everything. Except—' He pulled out a spare chair at the table and sat down facing them. 'Do you really have a film of – what went on in the bedroom?'

Harry nodded unhappily. Xander held out a hand, and Harry dug reluctantly into his pocket and brought out a DVD case.

'Thank God you had the sense not to leave it at home,' Xander said. 'You *should* have lodged it with a solicitor. I will do that myself, along with a notarized statement of what I know so far. Then I will go and see Derek Sullivan and make sure he understands that the game is up, and leave it to him to convince your father likewise. You've got your car here?' he said to Jenna.

She nodded.

'Go straight home, and take Harry with you, and both of you, don't leave Holtby House until you hear from me.'

Jenna paled. 'You don't think – they wouldn't—?'

Xander looked grim. 'This isn't a child's game you're playing. There are huge sums of money at stake. And this film is dynamite. Until I know they understand that it remains in a safe place as surety for their good behaviour, it's best not to take chances.'

Harry stared. 'You don't think they'd try and bump us off?'

'Accidents can be arranged if you're ruthless enough and have enough money. A fatal fall from your roof terrace – a hit and run driver—'

Jenna must have made some sound, though she was not aware of having done so, because Xander looked at her, and now he paled too, reading her face. 'You said – a car came too close?'

She shook her head frantically, still wanting to save him. 'It was before Harry talked to Caroline. It was just coincidence.'

His mouth set into a grim line. 'Go home,' he said. 'And don't say anything to Kitty.'

'How do I explain bringing Harry home?' Jenna asked.

Xander looked bitter. 'I dare say you'll think of something.'

Jenna slept like the dead, and woke late with a sense of doom hanging over her. It was a moment before she remembered the events of the day before, and remembering did nothing to lighten the gloom. She remembered the way Xander had looked at her before he swung on his heel and went out. He hated her. Or despised her, which was worse. She would be for ever besmirched in his mind with the taint of conspiracy, even if she had helped save Kitty's house, exposed villains and saved him from marrying an evil woman.

Oh my God, unless he still means to marry her? she thought, feeling sick. Maybe he loved her so much that, whatever she had done, he would stick by her. Try to save her from herself – a noble work. Maybe he didn't believe she was really in on it. But he had the DVD. He only had to watch it – another swooping of her stomach at the thought. Oh poor, poor Xander! Well, maybe he wouldn't watch it, just lodge it with a solicitor? But he had to know what was on it to make Sullivan and Beale do his bidding. And – excuse me, but wasn't that a form of blackmail, even if for the best of reasons? How come he was OK to do it, but not her and Harry?

Oh my God, Harry! How was she going to explain him away to Kitty?

She imagined Xander interviewing Derek Sullivan. She wasn't much afraid of the Silver Fox, whatever his connections, but the thought of Roger Beale made her shiver. She guessed he was the real brains behind the business, and the really ruthless one as well. Suppose he just decided to have Xander killed? She sat up in bed clutching her arms around her in dread. But no, that's what the DVD was for, to make sure nothing happened to him, as well as to apply leverage for the scheme to be dropped.

She hauled herself out of bed, stood under the shower for ten minutes, then dressed and limped downstairs. Her thigh looked like a Jackson Pollock, and ached like a broken heart, but that was nothing to the pain of her broken heart, which ached worse than a broken leg. She had done everything for the right reasons, and still Xander hated her. Maybe it was better if Roger Beale did get her. At least it would be quick.

She was too late for Mrs Phillips's breakfast, so she sneaked along to the kitchen to put the kettle on and rummage for a slice of bread. The pop of the gas lighting sounded too loud in the silence of the house, and as if she had been summoned by it like a genie, Kitty appeared in the kitchen door. Jenna smiled at her, and for the first time in their acquaintance Kitty didn't smile back. She folded her arms grimly and said, 'Awake at last? Now you are going to tell me what's going on.'

'Why should anything be going on?' Jenna said feebly.

'Xander came here late last night and talked to you for ages on the terrace.'

'How did you—?'

'I was awake. I'd finished reading and I remembered it was a full moon so I went to one of the back bedrooms to look at it. I always wish on a full moon.' She waved away any comment. 'Old habit, from childhood. Anyway, I saw you down there. Then he walked off, not looking happy. You phoned someone and then you went off. I heard your car start, so I know you drove some-where. You came back later, and now there's someone sleeping in one of my spare rooms. Not Xander, I suppose?'

She shook her head. 'Harry Beale.'

'Harry Beale. *He's* up to no good, if I know him! Now, are you going to tell me what's happening?'

'I can't. I'm not supposed to say anything,' Jenna said unhappily.

'Does it concern me?' Kitty said sharply.

'Well – yes, but—'

'Then you tell me, right now! When I want protection from the truth I'll let you know, but it won't be until I really *am* old, frail and senile. Until then, I won't be patronized. So out with it.'

So Jenna told her everything.

Kitty took it very well, better than Jenna would have thought. She seemed, in fact, almost braced by it. 'If they think they're getting Holtby that easily, they have another think coming,' she said. 'Why did you bring Harry here?'

'Xander thought he might be in danger.'

'In *danger?*' It was derisive rather than nervous.

'Just until he'd let them know the DVD was with a solicitor.'

Kitty snorted. 'I've known Roger Beale for years, and I can tell you he's not *that* big a man. He's a vulgar blowhard and a bully, but he'd never risk murder. Besides, Harry's his own son! Whatever he thinks of him, he'd never hurt him. What can Xander have been thinking?'

'I think he was upset. We all were, but—'

'Yes, it must have been hard for him to learn what Caroline is really like. Oh dear!' It came home to her. 'First Stephanie, and now Caroline. And he sets such store by loyalty and honour and so on. This will be a terrible blow to him.'

'I'm afraid he blames me,' Jenna said in a small voice.

'A case of shooting the messenger?'

'Partly that. And he doesn't like the underhand way Harry and I went about it.'

'Well, I don't see how else you could have found things out. And he went and found out about this Purcell chap, didn't he?'

'All the same—'

'Yes. But I expect he'll get over it, in time,' Kitty said. 'He'll see it wasn't your fault. He's a just man, and he'll treat you justly. But it's going to be hell for him, breaking his engagement with Caroline. It's bound to get out – some of it, at least – and whatever she's done, he'll want to defend her purely from chivalry.'

'Do you think he really will break his engagement?'

'My dear, he can't marry a girl who was trying to force me

from my home. And who was involved in bribing public officials for monetary gain.'

'I suppose not,' Jenna said. It ought to have made her happy to think that at least he wasn't going to be Caroline's dupe any more, but it didn't.

Harry appeared at last, bleary eyed, and Jenna made him coffee while Kitty sat with him on the terrace and questioned him some more about the whole sorry business. He seemed relieved that she knew, and babbled away to her for ages. They were all still sitting there when, in the middle of the afternoon, Alexander arrived, looking as if he hadn't slept for a week.

He took in the situation with a single glance, and Kitty jumped to their defence. 'I made them tell me,' she said. 'I suppose it was your ridiculous idea to keep it from me. I'm not a child, Xander – or a helpless old lady. I have every right to know when my home is threatened.'

'You're right,' he said, rather dazedly. Jenna jumped up and brought another chair out from the conservatory and he almost fell on to it without seeming to have noticed who brought it. 'Well, I've seen them both,' he said. 'I showed them a copy of my notarized statement – which included the fact that I had deposited a DVD with Hudson Carstairs. They both read it.'

'And?' said Kitty.

'There was a certain amount of bluster,' said Xander, 'but Roger Beale at least could see the game was up. Sullivan tried to threaten me, but he told him to shut up in the end. Then he asked me what I wanted. I told him there must be an end to any scheme surrounding this house or any land in or adjacent to Holtby. And no reprisals against anyone involved.' He stopped, and Kitty had to prompt him.

'He agreed?'

'Oh yes. But he couldn't believe that was all. He thought I must want something for myself – money, or to be part of some other scam he's running. Then Sullivan asked when he would get the DVD back. I told him never. It would be surety for his good behaviour, and Beale's. They didn't like that. I think they thought there would be some easy end to it all.'

Kitty frowned. 'They'll leave Holtby alone? But what about

their other schemes? Are you going to let them get away with it? Bribery and corruption?' she said indignantly. 'And Sullivan getting into Parliament so he can do more wicked things? They ought to go to prison, both of them.' She caught sight of Harry and said, 'I'm sorry, but you know it's true.'

'I know,' he said. 'My dad's a bad lot. I've always known it.'

Her pity was instantly aroused. 'Oh, my poor boy! I wasn't thinking how awful it must be for you – and having lost your mother, too. What will Roger Beale do about Harry, Xander?'

'He's promised no reprisals. But he may cut him off, of course. I can't really prevent that. And there's the question of the flat.'

'I don't care if he does cut me off,' Harry said, with as much conviction as he could manage. 'I'd sooner try and make my own way.'

Jenna smiled faintly, remembering their conversation on that point.

'Good for you,' Kitty said heartily. 'And you can come and stay here if you need to. Look on this as your home from now on.'

Jenna was watching Xander's face. 'But what about Caroline?'

He looked at her, and spread his hands slightly. 'That's why I can't go too far – why I have to let them "get away with it", Kitty, to a certain extent. Caroline's bound up in it, and I know it's her own fault, but she's a woman, and you can't destroy a woman's reputation the way you can a man's. I had a long talk with her after I'd left Beale and Sullivan.'

No wonder he looked exhausted, Jenna thought.

'She'll have to remake a life for herself,' he said quietly, 'if she gets away from her stepfather. I can't make it too hard for her.'

'If?' Kitty queried.

'She was defiant at first,' he admitted. 'Said it was none of my affair, and I didn't understand how business worked these days. Said she was putting our finances on a firm footing for our future together. I told her it was her finances, not mine, and that I wanted nothing to do with any money she made that way. Told her she was a beautiful woman and could do better for herself than that sort of grubby scheme.'

'But – you're not still going to marry her?' Kitty said doubtfully, hopefully.

'No, that's all over,' he said. He looked round vaguely, as if half waking from a dream. 'What time is it? Is it lunchtime?'

'Nearly teatime,' Kitty said. She looked round too. 'None of us has had any lunch.'

Jenna got up. 'Omelettes all round, I think.'

'I'll come and help,' said Harry.

'And let's have some champagne,' Kitty added. 'To celebrate the scotching of a wicked plan.' She looked at Xander. 'And because it's very good for shock,' she added.

Later, when Jenna had carried the empty plates back into the house, Xander followed her and caught her up in the kitchen.

'I owe you an apology,' he said.

'Oh no,' she said. 'It's all right. I understand.'

'I implied you were wrong to use the methods you did,' he went on, determined. 'I'm really very grateful that you went to so much trouble for Kitty's sake. Anything I said to you that – well, if I hurt you, I'm sorry. I wasn't thinking straight.'

'Hardly surprising,' she said.

'I see now that Caroline was suspicious of you from the start, and she coloured my view of you. It was when you asked me at the Buckminsters' party why I wanted Kitty out of here that it made me think about Caroline's attitudes – wonder whether in fact *she* wanted Kitty out, and why. I started to reassess a lot of things she'd said and done. It was painful to me to start doubting her, but once I started I couldn't stop. And it made me realize I'd been uneasy about her for a long time.'

'It must have been hard for you.'

'It was. I value loyalty, and the last thing I wanted was to be disloyal myself.' He frowned. 'I haven't come very well out of all this. I let Caroline influence me when I should have stepped back and used my own judgement. I think I behaved badly towards you on several occasions, when all the time you were Kitty's truest friend.'

She couldn't bear this. 'Well, it's all over now,' she said. 'Least said, soonest mended.' *God, there I go with the clichés again!* 'What will you do now?'

She didn't know why she asked that, except to try to move

on from the awkward apologies, but it seemed to release some-thing in him and words burst out of him.

'When I said to her she could do better, she said – she said she could certainly do better than me, and that she was going to marry a man with real power and drive who would go to the top, not a weakling content to sell second-hand furniture all his life.'

'Oh Xander, I'm sorry,' Jenna said, her throat tightening at the thought of the hurt to him.

'I suppose that's what I am, when it comes down to it,' he said bitterly, staring at the floor.

'People aren't their jobs. I mean, that's not how you measure the worth of someone.'

'Isn't it?'

'Well, look at me – I don't have a job at all. Does that make me nothing?'

He did look at her, with that odd, arrested look in his eyes she had seen once before. 'No, you're not nothing,' he said at last. And then, 'I'm very glad you came here to help Kitty. You might have been the saving of us all. I dread to think—'

'Well, now we can all concentrate on Kitty's opening,' she said, a little too heartily. When he looked at her like that she could only think that he had loved Caroline, and must now be heartbroken.

'Yes,' he said, and removed his too-intent gaze from her at last. 'I'd like to help with that, if I may?'

'Kitty would be delighted,' she said, and then, thinking it sounded unwelcoming: 'We'd all be delighted. There's an awful lot to do, and you have expertise that will be invaluable.'

'Yes,' he said thoughtfully, 'we must move on, and the opening will be a very good therapy for us all.'

She waited, but he didn't say any more, and seemed, in fact, lost in his own thoughts, so she went past him to go out and fetch in the rest of the dirty things.

As she reached the door, he said, 'Did Caroline really try to kill you? Hit and run?'

She froze. Surely Caroline hadn't said anything on the subject? Or was she so mad and so sure of herself she felt she could even boast of that to her infatuated lover? But how it would hurt him if he thought he had loved someone capable of that!

'I didn't see the car,' she said. 'It was all too quick. But I'm sure it wasn't intentional. Just bad driving, I guess.'

'Yes,' he said. 'That must be what it was.'

Twenty-Five

The following Saturday Nicky Pearson arrived promptly in her rather beat-up old Peugeot 205. Jenna and Kitty went out on to the turnaround to meet her. She stepped out of the car, and opened the back door to let out her dogs: two miniature dachshunds. 'Maisie and Molly,' she said.

Watch and Barney approached with interest. The dachs took one look at them and flopped to the ground, rolling on their backs and wriggling their bottoms in humble greeting.

'It's all right,' Kitty said, 'they're very dog-friendly.' In a matter of moments the dachs were up and frisking around, with Barney and Watch following them, intrigued, trying to get a nose to these fast-moving strangers. 'Why don't you just let them have fun while we go inside?'

'Is it safe?' Nicky asked, looking doubtfully around at the wide open spaces.

'There's chicken wire round the whole perimeter – more to keep the neighbourhood dogs out than my chaps in,' Kitty said, 'so they can't get lost. Barney will look after them. He always wanted to be a mother. I expect they'd enjoy a run.'

'I'm sure they will,' Nicky said. 'I don't think they've ever seen so much space in their whole lives.'

Kitty and Jenna conducted her round the house and she raved over the ceramics. 'I've never seen such a collection. And some pieces must be quite valuable.'

'I made a start cataloguing them,' Jenna said, when they retired to the conservatory for coffee, 'but I don't really know the subject. You're welcome to my notes, such as they are, as a starting point.'

'What we want,' Kitty said, 'is for you to choose enough items to fill the cabinets – we'll show you those when you've had your coffee. I leave the choice completely up to you, because I know less than Jenna about it. Just make an attractive display for the visitors.'

'And, of course, they'll need notes for the room sheets, and labels. I can do those, if you tell me what to put on them.'

Nicky said that it made more sense for her to do the notes than to have to tell Jenna what to write. 'And I can print the labels at work – we have the right card and printer for it there. I say, this shortbread is delicious.'

'Home-made,' Jenna said. 'Have another piece.'

'Oh, look at those dogs!' Kitty said with a smile in her voice, as they frisked up, panting, from their first long run around. Watch sloshed up water from the big bowl that stood just outside on the terrace, and Barney flopped on his back while the dachs jumped on him, in a fine reversal of roles. 'I think they're friends.'

They showed Nicky the cabinets, which Bill had finished restoring, and had moved into position in the housekeeper's room – soon to be the China Room. 'Oh, lots of space,' she said. 'I'm glad, because I'm going to want to choose a lot of things. And with several cabinets we can group things nicely.'

'It's very good of you to do this for us,' Kitty said.

'Not at all. I'm going to enjoy it. Really! I'm not just being polite.'

'Then, could I ask you another favour? Could you pick out a few pieces for the drawing room and dining room? Jenna will show you the spaces we'd like to fill.'

'I'd be happy to,' Nicky said. 'It's so exciting to be in on the start of something like this. I've so often gone round houses and wondered about who chose what to go where.' She smiled. 'And generally disagreed with the choice, I have to say!'

It was Nicky who, on seeing the dining room for the first time, suggested the table should be laid as if for a formal dinner. 'If you have some nice china for it. It looks rather bare as it is, and people do like seeing how other people lived.'

Jenna said, 'That's a good idea. Like "dressing" a house when you want to sell it?'

'Exactly. Let the visitors see it's not just a museum. It's nice to leave a book or two around in the drawing room, too, and perhaps some music open on the piano.'

'I can see you're going to be a great help,' Jenna said approvingly.

They had seen nothing of Xander in the week since the Great Revelation. He had been busy, Jenna supposed, with sorting out the detail of the agreement with Beale and Sullivan, policing its implementation – and finalizing matters with Caroline. A notice had appeared in the papers on Thursday.

> The marriage previously announced between Caroline Eleanor Russell and Alexander Latham will not now take place. The couple have parted by mutual consent and request that their privacy be respected.

So that's that, Jenna thought. She passed it silently to Kitty at the breakfast table.

'It doesn't look good for him,' Kitty said, 'after a similar announcement with Stephanie. It will make him look inconstant.'

'I don't know why people put engagements in the paper in the first place,' Jenna said.

'Usually it's the bride's mother who insists on that particular tradition,' Kitty said. Then she sighed. 'I wonder when we'll see him again. I do hope he doesn't go and hide himself away.'

'He did say he wanted to help us with the opening.'

'Did he? We must make a point of making him indispensable. Give him lots to do.'

'There *is* lots to do,' Jenna pointed out. 'We could even have done with Harry.'

But Harry, after half-heartedly helping Bill move things around on Monday, had gone home on Tuesday. 'It's *my* flat,' he said defiantly, even though it wasn't really. 'And I'll have to face Dad some time.' He hadn't reappeared, so Jenna assumed that Roger Beale hadn't turned him out on the street, at least.

Things were looking promising for the launch party. Acceptances were running at nearly a hundred per cent. The MP for the south of the county, Nick Easter, had rung Kitty personally to say he would be coming. Then he added, 'I believe you had something to do with the fact that Derek Sullivan will not be standing at the election after all.'

'Me? Not at all,' Kitty said, flustered. 'I knew nothing about it until it was over.'

He chuckled. 'Don't worry, I shan't spread any rumours. But everyone ought to be grateful to you: Sullivan's a worm, and he wouldn't have been a credit to the House.'

'Do you know who's replacing him?' she plucked up courage to ask.

'The constituency party's chosen Harriet Hale, I believe.'

'I don't know her. What's she like?'

'Mostly harmless,' he said. 'She's a bit of a party drone. But I don't think she'll get in anyway. It's not natural Labour country. Ronnie Farebrother only held the seat for all those years because he was a farmer and a leading light of the NFU. They were betting everything on Sullivan because he was a local celebrity, but now he's out of the frame, it's blown the election wide open, so you can imagine how grateful *we* are to you.'

'Not to me,' Kitty said firmly.

'Understood. But I wondered if your godson has ever thought of standing?'

'Alexander? I don't think it has ever crossed his mind,' Kitty said in surprise.

'Perhaps you might persuade him to let it,' he said. 'He's just the sort of man we need – local, personable, intelligent, and with a reputation for probity.'

'He's the most honest man I know,' Kitty said.

'That's what I mean. He might well crack the north of the county for us. Something to think about?'

'You must speak to him yourself,' Kitty said firmly. 'I couldn't possibly answer for him.'

'I will. Perhaps at the party. And thank you again for the opportunity.'

Jenna was intrigued when Kitty relayed this conversation. 'Xander in Parliament? He'd certainly look good in those interviews on the green outside. Most politicians aren't much to look at.'

Kitty looked shocked. 'That is not what people are elected for – their looks!'

'I know – I was teasing.' She thought that he would probably hate all the back-scratching – and stabbing – that went on in Parliament, if one believed the newspapers. On the other hand, it would mean he would be in London a lot more often, and she might therefore see him sometimes. The thought that in a couple of weeks' time she would be going away, never to see him again, was clouding the otherwise perfect pleasure she was getting from this job for Kitty.

All the arrangements were going well. Gloria Buckminster was proving invaluable. She had not only recruited a pool of room stewards and drawn up a rota for the first month, she had got extra volunteers for the opening gala and was well on the way to having the tea done and dusted.

'Mad Enderby's getting us strawberries from her supplier – free – and she's going to let us have her own cream. She says opening Holtby House will improve passing trade, and her supplier apparently agrees. I've got ten local ladies who will come in and make sandwiches early on the morning, and come back in the afternoon to serve. Paulson's in Wenchester are donating the sandwich loaves, and Tealson's Foods four dozen sausage rolls. Now, large cakes I've got organized, some from people in the village, and Paulson's are giving a dozen of their Swiss rolls, but I need promises for small cakes. I'm working on Betty's Tea Rooms in Belminster and the Copper Kettle in Wenchester, but that will probably only raise two dozen each – mustn't over-milk the cow you know. And scones to go with the strawberries and cream: commercial ones are *so* disappointing, so I'd like them home-made.'

'Nicky Pearson's mum wants to help in some way. And my sister is a superb cook,' Jenna said. 'I'm sure she'll do some scones.'

'See if you can get her to promise two dozen. We'll probably need six dozen at least. I'm going to work on Mrs Phillips – she used to make scones for the cricket tea and they were as light as a feather. If all else fails I can fall back on my sister, but it's a problem getting them here. Where does your sister live?'

'In London, but she won't mind delivering. She'll want to come to the opening: it was partly her idea.'

'Invite her, dear! Don't leave it to chance. And she can help serve the teas while she's here. Get the Pearson person too. Get them involved in the beginning and you can call on them down the line if you need them. Now, I want to talk to you about car parking – and what your arrangements will be if it rains.'

Gloria Buckminster could be exhausting, but Jenna was glad to know there was someone effective she could leave Kitty with when she went.

Harry phoned the following week. 'Hey, Red!' he said, but he sounded a little more subdued than previously.

'Hello, stranger.'

'Sorry I didn't phone before,' he said. 'It's been a bit hairy.'

'I imagine so.'

'I thought Dad was going to burst a blood vessel. He yelled at me for an hour solid, stamping around the room like a bull in a china shop.'

'I don't envy you.'

'Well, it wasn't nice. I thought I was going to cry at one point – when he asked what my mother would think if she was alive. But then I suppose he thought about the bedroom camera and decided she wouldn't have approved of that, so he sort of calmed down and went thoughtful. That's when I thought he was going to disown me – never darken my door again, sort of thing.'

'I assumed he would,' Jenna said. 'We half expected you back here with a suitcase.'

'Probably would have been if it weren't that I'm the only son. And to tell you the truth, I don't think he really *likes* Caroline much. I mean, he'll use her like he uses everyone, but he said something about how "that's the worst of women, always bring their emotions into it when it should be a matter of business", which I think was a reference to Caro falling for old Derek Sullivan, which wasn't part of the plan. Anyway, he suddenly decided I was a chip off the old block, and he even chuckled a bit that I'd managed to find the second camera loop.'

'So he didn't throw you out?'

'No, he said from now on I was working for him and him

only, and if I ever pulled another stunt like that he'd kill me,' Harry said, a little dolefully.

'But, look, you don't have to do what he says,' Jenna said. 'You're over eighteen, and he won't *actually* kill you. And you don't want to get mixed up in his shady schemes and end up in jail, do you?'

'I said that to him, but he told me he's learned his lesson, and he's going straight from now on. He promised Xander the same thing – said the shock had been therapeutic, and he realized how close to the wind he'd been sailing.'

'Do you believe him?' Jenna said doubtfully.

'Well,' Harry said simply, 'old Xander's got the film and the statement to hold over Dad's head if he does stray from the straight and narrow.'

'I don't think Xander was meaning to spend the rest of his life monitoring your father's actions.'

'I know. Look, Red, all you can do is hope, right? I hope Dad's going to go straight. And I'm going to watch my back, make sure I don't get pulled into anything dodgy. What else can I do?'

Break out and go your own way, she thought, but she didn't say it. 'So what job is he going to give you? The same as you've been doing?'

'No – this is the good news! – I'm going to America.'

'For a holiday?'

'No, to work, dimwit! He's got this business colleague who's developing holiday condos in Florida, and I'm going over there to learn the ropes. How 'bout that? Imagine me surfin', sailin', and barbecuing on the beach, babe!'

'Sounds wonderful.'

'Yes, and when I'm up to speed, he's going to set me up on my own. I get a salary and a share of the profits, and the chance to buy the business out in ten years and be my own man. So what do you think?'

Jenna thought that it sounded as if Roger Beale was getting his son out of the way; but if it was really a chance for him to become independent, she was glad for him. The 'business colleague in Florida' sounded a bit suspect, but probably she was being paranoid. Anyway, it was obvious Harry was glad about it so there was no point in trying to rain on his parade.

'It sounds like a wonderful opportunity. So you're going to make your life over there?'

'Looks like it. I won't complain about the sunshine, anyway – though I'll miss the old country,' he added wistfully.

'You can come back on holidays,' she said to comfort him.

'Yeah. And – hey, you could come out! Come and have a beach holiday – all expenses paid.'

She laughed. 'Don't start spending the money before you've earned it,' she said.

Xander finally surfaced in the middle of that week. He rang Kitty on the Wednesday evening and they talked for a long time. Then she came and found Jenna. 'He wants to talk to you.'

Jenna found her heart beating ridiculously fast as she picked up the receiver. She hadn't so much as heard his voice for ten days.

'Kitty tells me you're working too hard and getting pale,' he said without preamble.

'That woman has a fertile imagination,' she said. But she knew where it came from. She had been rather quiet lately. The more she worked on the plan, the more she loved the house and the place and the people, and the less she wanted to leave them all.

'Perhaps,' he said, 'but she *is* my godmother and I owe her the duty of obedience. She's ordered me to take you out riding tomorrow, so I can only appeal to your kindness and not make me disappoint her.'

The thought of riding with him was bliss, but the fact that he was making a joke about it was even better, suggesting that he was coping better with the whole disaster than she could have hoped.

'For Kitty's sake, I consent,' she said solemnly.

'I know it isn't for mine,' he said. 'I'll pick you up at five, if that's all right?'

He arrived, as before, in the back yard, on Victor and leading Tabitha. 'She's rather fresh, I'm afraid,' he called out in greeting. 'I hope you'll be able to manage her.'

'Don't start that again,' she said, remembering their first ride.

'Hello, baby, remember me?' She pushed a carrot chunk under Tabitha's velvet muzzle, which was enough to convince the mare she did. She took the bribe and then rubbed her face up and down Jenna's front. 'There, you see, she likes me,' Jenna said.

'She's just rubbing her eyes because they're itchy,' Xander said automatically.

'God, I know that! You have to learn to recognize irony when you hear it.'

'Sorry,' he said.

She looked up at him. He looked tired to death, his face drawn from the events of the past two weeks, but he was still shiverily gorgeous, his lean, muscular body so tempting in breeches, boots and a chambray shirt that brought out the blue of his eyes. *Not for you*, Jenna warned herself, but she couldn't help feeling a surge of pure, foolish happiness just at being with him.

'You look tired,' she said.

His eyes met hers for a burning second and she felt a thump in the pit of her stomach. Then he looked away. 'It's been tough,' he said offhandedly. 'Shall we go? Check your girth before you mount.'

In deference to his tiredness, she didn't rib him for daddying her. She mounted with a bit of a struggle – Tabitha didn't want to stand still – and found her stirrups. 'Ready,' she said.

They followed the same route as last time, along the road, on to the track, cantering as far as the first gate to settle the horses, then turning on to the track beside the open field. Here, however, Xander said, 'The reason I called for you a bit earlier is that I thought you might like to ride as far as the Monument. Up on the hills – you remember? There's a fine view.'

'Lovely,' Jenna said, touched he'd remembered.

In a short while they came to another gate on their left and he opened it and let her through, and then said, 'We can have a really good gallop along here, if you're up for it. I'll go first, if you don't mind, then I can control the pace.'

'OK,' she said, and thought, *you always want to control the pace. Maybe that's what's wrong with you.*

But he set a good one, and Victor had a long, ground-eating stride: fast though Tabitha was, she couldn't pass him, even galloping flat out. The speed was exhilarating, and as she crouched over the mare's neck and felt the air whip past her, all the tensions and anxieties of the past weeks slipped away in a wonderful release of pure physical delight. When Victor slowed at last, Tabitha made one mad effort of acceleration and caught up to him, and then Jenna pulled her back and they dropped into a trot and then a walk. Both horses were heaving and sweaty, proof they were grass-fed and unfit; and at once a cloud of tiny black flies descended on them and their riders to feast on the salt water.

'It'll be all right once we get up to the hills,' Xander said. 'The breeze there will blow them away.'

But that was all he did say. He didn't seem inclined to talk, and Jenna could think of nothing to say – or nothing, in reality, that she *could* say. So they rode in silence, with the hoof beats and the chorus of birds as their soundtrack. But it was companionable. She felt that he was unhappy as well as tired, but that none of it was directed towards her, and though he did not look at her, she believed he was glad she was there. It had not been *all* Kitty's idea, this ride, she concluded.

The horses had recovered by the time they reached the bottom of the hill, and climbed energetically on a loose rein up the tracks that wound back and forth across the steep slope. Xander was looking around at the view as they rode. *He's feeling better*, she thought. And he was right about the flies. The air up here felt less muggy, and a little breeze saw off the pests, giving relief to the horses. The track emerged at last on a flattish top, with the Monument small in the distance to the right. 'Ready for another canter?' he asked.

The track was wide enough to canter side by side. Jenna eased her weight out of the saddle to rest Tabitha's back, and they settled in for a long, delicious run over the hill top. He slowed and stopped when they reached the Monument, dismounted, and came round to take Tabitha's head. 'We'll give them a breather here, and look at the view,' he said. There was a sort of lookout point, with a stout wooden fence, presumably erected by a cautious County Council to stop visitors falling over, which made a useful tethering-rail for the horses. They loosened the girths and both horses settled down to tearing at the short downland turf.

Xander led the way past the fence to a spot where they could sit right on the edge of the scarp, and when they were settled, he said, 'What do you think of the view?'

'Magnificent,' she said. 'Worth the climb.'

He pointed. 'There's Holtby, over there; and you can just see Holtby House – that oblong roof, d'you see? And the shape of the walled gardens?'

'Oh yes, I see it. Hi, Kitty.' She waved. 'I don't think she saw me.' He didn't laugh, and she felt foolish. 'Show me some more.'

'Well, that's Burford, Chidding, Belminster, and Wenchester's just about visible through the haze, over there. And if we went round the hill in the other direction, you'd be able to see Corvington, and beyond that, the sea. It's higher than it looks, this hill.'

'I suppose that's why the Romans had a beacon here,' she tried.

'You remembered,' he said, and looked at her.

'Did you think I wouldn't?' It was a daring thing for her to say, too close to personal, and he looked away. She thought he sighed. She felt he needed to talk but couldn't begin, so she said, 'I read the notice in the paper about the engagement being cancelled. I'm sorry.'

'It was by mutual consent,' he said woodenly.

'I read that, too. I hoped it was true.'

'In what sense?' He was staring out at the view.

'I hoped that you felt it was over, not just that you knew it was.'

He didn't answer for a while. Then he said, 'She wasn't the person I thought she was. I suppose, on reflection, I must have known that for some time. The hints were there. But I didn't want to admit it.' A long pause. 'I've been horribly weak. I wanted it so much for her to be the right one, I let it cloud my judgement.'

'That's a very human trait,' she said. 'We all do that.'

He shook his head. 'I spoke to her yesterday. There were some things I had to return – I won't bore you with the details. She insisted I bring them, rather than post them. I didn't understand why, but it seems what she wanted was to boast about how she had never loved me, and how she already has someone else.'

'I'm sorry.'

'Don't be.' He threw one quick glance at her, one flash of blue. 'It's what she's like. She wanted to hurt me, but mostly, I think, she wanted to impress me.'

'That's just sad,' said Jenna.

'Yes, it is. It seems she's now hooked up with Barry Watson, the Labour peer. He's junior minister in the Department of Energy. She showed me an engagement ring.'

'Already?' Jenna was astonished. 'It's only a week since the notice in the paper.'

'Roger Beale works fast,' he said.

'You think it's his doing?'

'Sullivan's no use to him any more, and Watson presumably has procurement influence. I wouldn't be surprised if the new power station at Corvington comes Beale Cartwright's way.' He stared resolutely outwards. 'Beale made a point of telling me he'd made a large donation to charity – reparation for his past misdeeds, proof of his change of heart. I was almost impressed.'

'Almost?'

'I looked up the charity. It seems Lord Watson of Cheam is the President.'

Jenna didn't know what to say. After a bit she said tentatively, 'Do you think Caroline – I mean, is she a victim in this? I wouldn't like to think—'

Now he looked at her properly, his expression softening. 'You're a nice person,' he said. 'To be concerned about her after all that's happened. But she'll be *Lady* Watson.'

'I see.' A pause. 'Do you mind very much?'

'No,' he said. 'I've let it all go. You can't change people. I shall have to keep an eye on things, to make sure they don't hurt anyone I care about, or do anything too outrageous, but for the rest – I just have to say, *never mind*.'

They sat in silence for a bit, until he roused himself with an obvious effort to say, 'Beale told me about Harry going to the States. I'm sorry.'

'Sorry?' she said, surprised. 'I think it will be very good for him.'

'Oh, but – I mean—' He seemed confused, and there was a touch of colour in his face. 'Will you be going? Visiting? Or anything?'

'My sister keeps inviting me,' she said, 'but I've never been. And if I don't go for her, I'm not likely to go for Harry Beale, am I?' She hesitated. 'We weren't a couple, you know. That's just what Caroline wanted you to believe.'

He didn't say anything, but she felt him relax, and they sat for a long time, watching the cloud shadows chase over the eternally English countryside of patchwork fields, little woods and snug stone villages.

'Seeing all this,' he said at last, 'always improves my perspective. This is what really matters.'

'I know what you mean,' she said.

'Yes,' he said, 'I think you do.' He sounded different – not strained any more. Content.

'How do you feel?' she dared to ask eventually.

'Empty,' he said. It wasn't exactly what she wanted to hear, but it was a start. And he added, 'Clean.'

The gala opening was going so well Jenna was almost afraid of tempting the gods. The weather was perfect, one of those crystal clear June days, with a blameless blue sky and just a little refreshing breeze. She had conducted several tours of the parts of the house that would be open – as had Kitty, Xander and Nicky Pearson, dividing the invitees between them into small groups. She had to admit that the rooms looked fabulous – cleaned to within an inch of their lives by Fatty, arranged with selected furniture and artefacts, and decorated with some of Kitty's top floral efforts. The drawing room was replete with links to famous people who had stayed over the ages. The dining table was set for dinner for twenty, with full Crown Derby (Peter's mother's wedding present china) silver and crystal. Lady Mary's room had been thinned out and rationalized, with almost everything in period; and in the China Room, visitors pored over Nicky's selections with fascination.

Out in the grounds everyone wandered at will, visiting the walled gardens, the woodland walk – which was very popular on such a hot day – and Centurion's grave. When Jenna was outside, she was constantly approached by people to congratulate her, ask questions about future opening, or tell her how it would affect their own business and the area. The press came, and Nick Easter MP turned up at just the right moment to get his photograph taken with Kitty. Later he made a speech – very professional – and more or less declared tea open. The subsequent stampede towards the tea tables proved Harriet's contention that people always wanted tea and cakes on a day out.

She was there with her husband and Martha, as were Sybil and her children, and Michael and his lot had turned up as well, so it was pleasantly like a family day. The children raced around, enjoying the open spaces and the impromptu pack of dogs: Watch and Barney, the dachs, and Mad Enderby's terriers. They romped together and dashed perilously between the legs of the crowds; Sybil was resigned to a lot more pleas for a dog of their own when they got home.

'All we want to make it perfect is pony rides,' she said. 'You missed a trick there, Jen — I thought you'd have had that organized. This place must be lousy with ponies, given all the posh kids around.'

'I wish I had thought of it,' Jenna said. 'But this is just the beginning. I've already got plans for a children's room, if we can work out where to put it. There are antique toys and Victorian baby clothes I've found, plus the wonderful butterfly collection and dozens of stuffed birds. I thought I could combine it with all the stuff I've got together about Centurion, plus photos and portraits of various other horses and pet dogs.'

'Sounds marvellous. This place has really got to you, hasn't it?'

Jenna struck her chest. 'Right in through here. Hook, line and sinker.'

'Are you really over Patrick?'

'So much over him, I've sent back Charlotte's watch with my blessing,' said Jenna. 'I must say it made me feel like a better person.'

Kitty, passing just then, said, 'Darling, I do wish you'd go and rescue Xander. Nick Easter has got him cornered. I'm sure he's haranguing him about standing for the North County, and this isn't the time or place.'

'Improving the shining hour — I don't suppose politicians have a moment to waste.'

'That's why it won't do for Xander. Do go and save him.'

'OK,' Jenna said. But before she reached them, Easter had disengaged and walked off, and Xander disappeared into the house. Without really thinking, she followed, and discovered him in the kitchen, getting a glass of water from the tap.

'Thirsty work,' he said. 'Can I get you one?'

'Oh — no thanks.'

'Did you want me for something?' he asked.

She looked blank. 'Kitty wanted me to rescue you from Nick Easter, but you escaped.'

'He wants me to stand for Parliament.'

'And will you?'

'I don't know. There's a lot of good that needs to be done, but I'm not convinced one would be allowed to do it. It all sounds so – sewn up.'

'I imagine it is.' Being so close to him was making her feel faint, and also sad, because there wouldn't be many more times like this. He seemed relaxed, almost smiling. They had spent a lot more time together recently, working on the house, often alone, and he was no longer awkward with her. There had sometimes even been a little warmth, and she had caught a glimpse of the man who had sat by the fire that wet evening, the man he ought to have been. He was recovering from Caroline, she felt, better than expected, and she put that down to having something good and positive to do in saving Holtby House.

There was one thing she still had to clear up before she left, and it seemed to her that this was probably the best chance she was going to get, so she said, 'Xander, there's something I want to tell you. It's a bit delicate, because it makes assumptions, but – well, you have said on occasion that I'm like my mother. You've said it as if it wasn't a good thing.'

'I'm sorry,' he said. 'I didn't really know you before.'

She waved that away. 'I didn't mean you to apologize. But I did wonder if you had something against my mother, something that had upset you. I wanted you to know,' she hurried on, seeing he was going to speak, 'that if you've been thinking she had an affair with your father – well, she didn't. He was very upset about your mother, and she was someone to talk to, that's all. It was just talking.'

'She told you that?' he said neutrally.

'I know what you're thinking. But she swore to me there was nothing in it, and she never swears when something isn't true, so please, please accept it.'

'Why are you so anxious for me to believe that?' he asked, still neutrally.

She felt herself blushing. 'Because I don't want you to carry it round any more, if it's been hurting you all these years. Because I want you to be happy. And because I may never have another chance to set things straight.' Tears jumped into her eyes as she said the last bit, and she blinked them back furiously. She mustn't cry, not now.

'Why not?' he asked.

'Because my job here is finished, and I shall have to go,' she said.

'*Have* to?'

'I have to find a job. Kitty's paying me pocket money, but she can't go on doing that for ever, and I have to make a life for myself somewhere.'

'Wouldn't you like to stay?' he asked.

'Of course. I don't want to leave Holtby, and Kitty, and—'

'And?'

'Everything.'

He looked keenly into her face. She had to lower her eyes, or she might have flung herself at him incontinently. 'I thought – Kitty thought you were probably desperate to get back to London by now,' he said.

'How could she think that?' She looked up now, in sheer surprise. 'I *love* it here.'

Their eyes met, and without, it seemed, the slightest volition on either part, they were in each other's arms, and he was kissing her, kissing her as if he never meant to stop. They heard someone come to the door, make a surprised sound and go away, and even that didn't stop them. At least Jenna broke the surface to breathe, and said, weakly, 'You do believe me – about my mother?'

'I believe you,' he said. 'I don't care about it any more. *You* are the only thing that matters. I love you.'

'God, I love you too,' she said, amazed to hear herself saying it. Could this really be happening?

'I think I've been in love with you for weeks,' he said, 'but, my God, the situation was complicated.'

She couldn't help smiling. 'Understatement.'

He kissed her again, until she felt quite light-headed. *I could get used to this*, she thought. She adored the smell of his skin and the feeling of his lips and his strong, male body under her hands.

Her legs were trembling, and if he hadn't been holding her up she'd have sat down on the floor. For some bizarre reason she thought of Gloria Buckminster – her wise words. *It's all right, Gloria,* she thought. They were friends; they had the same interests.

But this was terribly important, too important for there to be any doubt about it. And the Caroline thing had ended so recently. When they next paused for breath, she looked up into his face searchingly and said, 'Are you *sure?*'

He drew a little, shuddering breath, and pulled her tightly against him. 'Completely sure. Caroline was an illusion. It was all part of a sort of madness. But I'm absolutely sane now.'

They held on to each other tightly. Jenna leaned her head against his chest and he rested his cheek against her hair. It felt so right to be here. It was like coming home.

Someone else came to the door, and this time coughed loudly. They broke apart. It was one of the tea helpers, carrying one of the massive teapots. 'Sorry,' she said brightly. 'Just come to empty out.'

'We'd better go outside,' Xander said. 'We'll be missed.' She fell in beside him, feeling dazed by the turn of events, but comforted to discover her hand had somehow remained in his.

In the hall they found Kitty, only too obviously waiting for them, her face in bloom with delight. 'It was me, I'm afraid,' she said. 'So sorry to have interrupted you. But I'm so pleased! It was what I wanted from the beginning – I could see how you were attracted to each other, and I *knew* you'd suit, but of course the situation was difficult.'

Jenna and Xander looked at each other, and there was mischief in his eyes.

'What situation?' he said blankly.

'*What* was what you wanted?' Jenna asked innocently.

Kitty's eyes widened. '*This,*' she said. 'But there was Caroline – and then that wretched Harry Beale complicated things. But I knew you would be so good together if it could all just be managed.'

'Really, Kitty, I've no idea what you're talking about,' Xander said in a wonderful imitation of his old, stiff self.

'Oh you joker! You and Jenna, of course,' she said indignantly. 'You're holding hands, so you can't pretend.'

They laughed and looked at each other.

'And it's especially wonderful, because it means she won't go away, and I was dreading that.'

Jenna was embarrassed for him. 'I think you're jumping the gun rather,' she said.

'Nonsense! If you're getting married, you have to stay.'

She didn't dare meet his eyes; but he hadn't dropped her hand. 'Nobody's asked anyone to marry anyone,' she said.

'I've hardly had a chance, yet, with all the interruptions,' Xander said. 'Jenna, will you marry me?'

'There, you see,' Kitty rushed in before she could answer. 'So that's settled! And it occurred to me that, as you obviously can't live in Xander's cottage, it would make much more sense for you both to live here. You can have the whole top floor and I *promise* I won't get in the way. It will be more convenient for the shop, Xander, and as I mean to leave the house to you anyway—'

'You want to leave me the house?' he said in astonishment. 'You never mentioned it before.'

'I've only just decided. You see, I always thought I was going to have to sell, but now it looks as if I won't – and I wouldn't be leaving a millstone, which I couldn't have done to *anyone*, but a going concern,' Kitty said. 'But actually, you aren't a blood relative, and Jenna is, so when I said "you", I meant both of you. But only if you marry each other. It makes things too awkward otherwise.'

Xander's eyes were positively dancing with amusement now. 'I can quite see that. Well –' to Jenna – 'it looks as though you'll have to marry me now.'

She narrowed her eyes at him. 'So that's why you want me?'

He looked down at her, with an expression that made her shiver. 'If you think that's why I want you, you haven't been paying attention for the past ten minutes. Do I have to show you all over again, and embarrass Kitty?'

'Oh, don't mind me,' Kitty said hastily departing. 'I'm going outside.'

So he showed her.